THE DADDY DANCE

BY

MINDY KLASKY

First published in Great Britain 2012
by Mills & Boon, an imprint of Harlequin (UK) Limited,
Eton House, 18-24 Paradise Road, Richmond, Surrey TW9 1SR

2in1 ISBN: 978 0 263 89422 6

23-0412

Harlequin (UK) policy is to use papers that are natural, renewable and recyclable products and made from wood grown in sustainable forests. The logging and manufacturing processes conform to the legal environmental regulations of the country of origin.

Printed and bound in Spain
by Blackprint CPI, Barcelona

Mindy Klasky learned to read when her parents shoved a book in her hands and told her that she could travel anywhere in the world through stories. She never forgot that advice. These days, Mindy works and plays in a suburb of Washington, DC, where she lives with her family. In her spare time, Mindy knits, quilts and tries to tame the endless to-be-read shelf in her home library. You can visit Mindy at her website—www.mindyklasky.com.

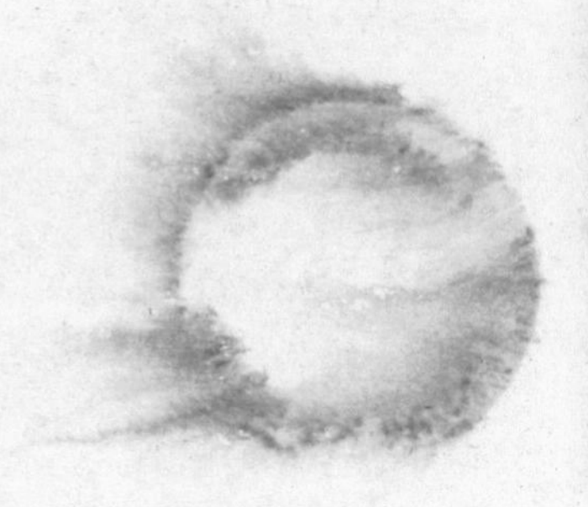

To my writers' retreat girlfriends, who gave Rye
his name—Nancy Hunter, Jeri Smith-Ready,
Maria V. Snyder, and Kristina Watson

Chapter One

Kat Morehouse pushed her sunglasses higher on her nose as the train chugged away from Eden Falls, leaving her behind on the platform. Heat rose in waves off the tiny station's cracked parking lot. Plucking at her silk T-shirt, Kat realized for the first time since she'd left New York that solid black might not be the most comfortable wardrobe for her trip home to Virginia. Not this year. Not during this unseasonably hot spring.

But that was ridiculous. She was a dancer from New York—black was what she wore every day of her life. She wasn't about to buy new clothes just because she was visiting Eden Falls.

Her foot already itched inside her walking boot cast. She resisted the urge to flex her toes, knowing that would only make her injury ache more. Dancer's Fracture, the doctors had grimly diagnosed, brought on by overuse. The only cure was a walking boot and complete rest from ballet for several weeks.

Looking down at her small roller suitcase, Kat grimaced and reminded herself that she wasn't going to be in Eden Falls for very long. Just time enough to help her family a bit—give her mother a little assistance as Susan nursed Kat's father, Mike, who was recovering from a nasty bout of pneumonia. Take care of her niece for a few days while Kat's irresponsible twin sister roamed somewhere off the beaten track. Look in on her mother's dance studio, the Morehouse Dance Academy, where Kat had gotten her start so many years ago. She'd be in Eden Falls for five days. Maybe six. A week at most.

Kat glanced at her watch. She might not live in Eden Falls anymore, but she knew the train schedule by heart, had known it ever since she'd first dreamed of making a life for herself in the big city. The southbound Crescent stopped at one-thirty in the afternoon. The northbound Clipper would churn through at two-fifteen.

Now, it was one forty-five, and Susan Morehouse was nowhere in sight. In fact, there was only one other person standing on the edge of the parking lot, a passenger who had disembarked with Kat. That woman was tall, with broad shoulders that looked like they were made for milking cows or kneading bread dough. Her oval face and regular features looked vaguely familiar, and Kat realized she must be one of the Harmons, the oldest family in Eden Falls.

Shrugging, Kat dug her cell phone out of her purse, resigned to calling home. She tapped the screen and waited for the phone to wake from its electronic slumber. A round icon spun for a few seconds. A minute.

More. The phone finally emitted a faint chirp, dutifully informing her that she was out of range of a recognized cell tower. Out of range of civilization.

Kat rolled her eyes. It was one thing to leave New York City for a week of playing Florence Nightingale in Eden Falls, Virginia. It was another to be cut off without the backbone of modern communications technology. Even *if* Kat was looking forward to helping her mother, a week was really going to stretch out if she didn't have a working smart phone.

Squinting in the bright sunlight, Kat read a message sent by Haley, her roommate back in New York. The text must have come in during the train ride, before Kat had slipped out of range. OMG, said the text. A + S r here. "A," Adam. The boyfriend of three years whom Kat had sent packing one week before, after discovering his side relationship with Selene Johnson. That would be "S," the corp's newest phenom dancer.

Haley had sent another message, five minutes later. 2 gross.

And a third one, five minutes after that. Hands all over.

All over. Right. Kat and Adam were all over. Adam hadn't had the decency to admit what was going on with Selene. Not even when Kat showed him the silk panties she'd found beneath his pillow—panties that *she* had definitely not left behind. Panties that Selene must have intended Kat to find.

Even now, Kat swallowed hard, trying to force her feelings past the raw, empty space in the middle of her chest. She had honestly believed she and Adam were meant for each other. She had thought that he alone *understood* her, believed in all the crazy sacrifices she had to make as a dancer. He was the first guy—the *only* guy—she had ever gotten involved with, the only one who had seemed worth sacrificing some of her carefully allocated time and energy.

How could Kat have been so wrong? In reality, Adam had just been waiting for the next younger, more fit, more flexible dancer to come along. Kat hated herself for every minute she had invested in their broken relationship, every second she had stolen from her true focus: her dancing career. She closed her eyes, and once again she could see that slinky thong in Adam's bed.

"2 gross" was right.

Kat dropped her useless cell phone into her purse and wiped her palms against her jet-black jeans, feeling the afternoon sun shimmer off the denim. At least her hair was up, off her neck in this heat. Small mercy. She started to rummage deep in her bag, digging for her wallet. A place like Eden Falls had to have pay phones somewhere. She could call her mother, figure out where their wires had crossed. Reach out to her cousin Amanda, if she needed to. Amanda was always good for a ride, whenever Kat made one of her rare weekend appearances.

Before she could find a couple of quarters, though, a huge silver pickup truck rolled to a stop in the parking lot. The Harmon woman smiled as she held out her thumb, pretending to hitch a ride. The driver—another Harmon, by the broad set of his shoulders, by his shock of chestnut hair—laughed as he walked around the front of his truck. He gave his sister a bear hug, swinging her around in a circle that swept her feet off the dusty asphalt. The woman whooped and punched at his shoulder, demanding to be set down. The guy obliged, opening the truck's passenger door before he hefted her huge suitcase into the vehicle's gleaming bed.

He was heading back to the driver's side when he noticed Kat. "Hey!" he called across the small lot, shielding his eyes from the sun. "Kat, right? Kat Morehouse?"

Startled by the easy note of recognition in the man's voice, Kat darted a glance to his face, really studying him for the first time. No. It couldn't be. There was no possible way Rye Harmon was the first guy she was seeing, here in Eden Falls. He started to walk toward her, and Kat started to forget the English language.

But those were definitely Rye Harmon's eyes, coal black and warm as a panther's flank. And that was Rye Harmon's smile, generous and kind amid a few days' worth of unshaved stubble. And that was Rye Harmon's hand, strong and sinewy, extended toward her in a common gesture of civil greeting.

Kat's belly completed a fouetté, flipping so rapidly that she could barely catch her breath.

Rye Harmon had played Curly in the high school production of *Oklahoma* the year Kat had left for New York. Kat had still been in middle school, too young to audition for the musical. Nevertheless, the high school drama teacher had actually recruited her to dance the part of Laurey in the show's famous dream sequence. The role had been ideal for a budding young ballerina, and Kat had loved her first true chance to perform. There had been costumes and makeup and lights—and there had been Rye Harmon.

Rye had been the star pitcher on the high school baseball team, with a reasonable baritone voice and an easy manner that translated well to the high school auditorium stage. Sure, he didn't know the first thing about dancing, but with careful choreography, the audience never discovered the truth. Week after week, Kat had nurtured a silly crush on her partner, even though she *knew* it could never amount to anything. Not when she was a precocious middle-school brat, and he was a high school hero. Not when she had her entire New York career ahead of herself, and he was Eden Falls incarnate—born, bred and content to stay in town forever.

In the intervening years, Kat had danced on stages around the world. She had kissed and been kissed a thousand times—in ballets and in real life, too. She was a grown, competent, mature woman, come back to town to help her family when they needed her most.

But she was also the child who had lived in Eden Falls, the shy girl who had craved attention from the unattainable senior.

And so she reacted the way a classically trained New York ballerina would act. She raised her chin. She narrowed her eyes. She tilted her head slightly to the right. And she said, "I'm sorry. Have we met?"

Rye stopped short as Kat Morehouse pinned him with her silver-gray eyes. He had no doubt that he was looking at Kat and not her twin, Rachel. Kat had always been the sister with the cool reserve, with the poised pride, even before she'd left Eden Falls. When was that? Ten years ago? Rye had just graduated from high school, but he'd still been impressed with all the gossip about one of Eden Falls's own heading up to New York City to make her fortune at some fancy ballet school.

Of course, Rye had seen plenty of Kat's sister, Rachel, around town over the past decade. Done more than see her, six years ago. He'd actually dated her for three of the most tempestuous weeks of his life. She'd been six months out of high school then, and she had flirted with him mercilessly, showing up at job sites, throwing pebbles at his window until he came down to see her in the middle of the night. It had taken him a while to figure out that she was just bent on getting revenge against one of Rye's fraternity brothers, Josh Barton. Barton had dumped her, saying she was nuts.

It had taken Rye just a few weeks to reach the same conclusion, then a few more to extricate himself from Rachel's crazy, melodramatic life. Just as well—a couple of months later, Rachel had turned up pregnant. Rye could still remember the frozen wave of disbelief that had washed over him when she told him the news, the shattering sound of all his dreams crashing to earth. And he could still remember stammering out a promise to be there for Rachel, to support his child. Most of all, though, he recalled the searing rush of relief when Rachel laughed, told him the baby was Josh's, entitled to its own share of the legendary Barton fortune.

Rye had dodged a bullet there.

If he had fathered Rachel's daughter—what was her name? Jessica? Jennifer?—he never could have left town. Never could have moved up to Richmond, set up his own contracting business. As it was, it had taken him six years after that wake-up call, and he still felt the constant demands of his family, had felt it with half a dozen girlfriends over the years. With a kid in the picture, he never could have fulfilled his vow to be a fully independent contractor by his thirtieth birthday.

He'd been well shed of Rachel, six years ago.

And he had no doubt he was looking at Kat now. Rachel and Kat were about as opposite as any two human beings could be—even if they were sisters. Even if they were twins. Kat's sharp eyes were the same as they'd been in middle school—but that was the only resemblance she bore to the freakishly good dancer he had once known.

That Kat Morehouse had been a kid.

This Kat Morehouse was a woman.

She was a full head taller than when he'd seen her last. Skinnier, too, all long legs and bare arms and a neck that looked like it was carved out of rare marble. Her jet-black hair was piled on top of her head in some sort of spiky ponytail, but he could see that it would be long and straight and thick, if she ever let it down. She was wearing a trim black T-shirt and matching jeans that looked like they'd been specially sewn in Paris or Italy or one of those fashion places.

And she had a bright blue walking boot on her left leg—the sort of boot that he'd worn through a few injuries over the years. The sort of boot that itched like hell in the heat. The sort of boot that made it a pain to stand on the edge of a ragged blacktop parking lot in front of the Eden Falls train station, waiting for a ride that was obviously late or, more likely, not coming at all.

Rye realized he was still standing there, his hand extended toward Kat like he was some idiot farm boy gawking at the state fair Dairy Princess. He squared his shoulders and wiped his palms across the worn denim thighs of his jeans. From the ice in Kat's platinum gaze, she clearly had no recollection of who he was. Well, at least he could fix that.

He stepped forward, finally closing the distance between them. "Rye," he said by way of introduction. "Rye Harmon. We met in high school. I mean, when I was in high school. You were in middle school. I was Curly, in *Oklahoma*. I mean, the play."

Yeah, genius, Rye thought to himself. *Like she really thought you meant Oklahoma, the state.*

Kat hadn't graduated from the National Ballet School without plenty of acting classes. She put those skills to good use, flashing a bright smile of supposedly sudden recognition. "Rye!" she said. "Of course!"

She sounded fake to herself, but she suspected no one else could tell. Well, maybe her mother. Her father. Rachel, if she bothered to pay attention. But certainly not a practical stranger like Rye Harmon. A practical stranger who said, "Going to your folks' house? I can drop you there." He reached for her overnight bag, as if his assistance was a forgone conclusion.

"Oh, no," she protested. "I couldn't ask you to do that!" She grabbed for the handle of the roller bag as well, flinching when her fingers settled on top of his. What was *wrong* with her? She wasn't usually this jumpy.

She wasn't usually in Eden Falls, Virginia.

"It's no problem," Rye said, and she remembered that easy smile from a decade before. "Your parents live three blocks from mine—from where I'm taking Lisa."

Kat wanted to say no. She had been solving her own problems for ten long years.

Not that she had such a great track record lately. Her walking boot was testament to that. And the box of things piled in the corner of her bedroom, waiting for cheating Adam to pick up while she was out of town.

But what was she going to do? Watch Rye drive out of the parking lot, and then discover she had no change at the bottom of her purse? Or that the pay phone—if there even *was* a pay phone—was out of order? Or that no one was at the Morehouse home, that Mike had some doctor's appointment Susan had forgotten when they made their plans?

"Okay," Kat said, only then realizing that her hand was still on Rye's, that they both still held her suitcase. "Um, thanks."

She let him take the bag, hobbling after him to the gleaming truck. Lisa shifted over on the bench seat, saying, "Hey," in a friendly voice.

"Hi," Kat answered, aware of the Northern inflection in her voice, of the clipped vowel sound that made her seem like she was in a hurry. She *was* in a hurry, though. She'd come all the way from New York City—almost five hundred miles.

It wasn't just the distance, though. It was the lifetime. It was the return to her awkward, unhappy childhood, where she'd always been the odd one out, the dancer, the kid who was destined to move away.

She'd left Eden Falls for a reason—to build her dream career. Now that she was back in the South, she felt like her life was seizing up in quicksand. She was being forced to move slower, trapped by convention and expectation and the life she had not led.

Determined to regain a bit of control, she turned back to the truck door, ready to tug it closed behind her. She was startled to find Rye standing there. "Oh!" she said, leaping away. The motion tumbled her purse from her lap to her feet. Silently cursing her uncharacteristic lack of grace, she leaned forward to scoop everything back inside her bag. Rye reached out to help, but she angled her shoulder, finishing the embarrassing task before he could join in.

"I didn't mean to startle you," he drawled. He reached inside the truck and passed her the seat belt, pulling it forward from its awkward position over her right shoulder.

"You didn't!" But, of course, he had. And if she made any more protest, he might take more time to apologize, time she did not want to waste. It was all well and good for him to take all day on a run to the train station. What else could he have to do in slow-paced Eden Falls? But she was there to help her family, and she might as well get started. She pulled the seat belt across her chest, settling it in its slot with the precision of a brain surgeon. "I'm fine. And if you don't mind, I'm sort of in a hurry."

She almost winced when she realized how brusque she sounded.

Recognizing dismissal when he heard it, Rye shut the door carefully. He shook his head as he walked around the front of his truck. Ten years had passed, but he still remembered Kat's precise attention to detail. Kat Morehouse had been a determined girl. And she had clearly grown into a formidable woman.

Formidable. Not exactly the type he was used to dating. Certainly not like Rachel had been, with her constant breaking of rules, pushing of boundaries. And not like the sweet, small-town girls he had dated here in Eden Falls.

His brothers teased him, saying he'd moved to Richmond because he needed a deeper dating pool. Needed to find a real woman—all the girls in Eden Falls knew him too well.

He hadn't actually had time for a date in the past year—not since he'd been burned by Marissa. Marissa Turner. He swallowed the bitter taste in his mouth as he thought of the woman who had been his girlfriend for two long years. Two long years, when he had torn apart his own life plans, forfeited his fledgling business, all to support her beauty salon.

Every time Rye mentioned making it big in Richmond, Marissa had thrown a fit. He had wanted her to be happy, and so he had circumscribed all of his dreams. It was easier, after all. Easier to stay in Eden Falls. Easier to keep doing the same handyman work he'd been doing all of his adult life. At least Marissa was happy.

Until she got some crazy-ass chance to work on a movie out in Hollywood, doing the hair for some leading-man hunk. Marissa had flown cross-country without a single look back, not even bothering to break up with Rye by phone. And he had been left utterly alone, feeling like a fool.

A fool who was two years behind on his business plan.

But not anymore. With Marissa gone, Rye had finally made the leap, moving up to Richmond, finding the perfect office, hunting down a tolerable apartment. He was finally moving on with his life, and it felt damn good to make choices for himself. Not for his family. Not for his girlfriend. For him.

At least, most of the time.

Lisa was chatting with Kat by the time he settled into the driver's seat. "It's no problem, really," his sister was saying. "Rye already came down from Richmond to get me. Things are crazy at home—Mama's out West visiting her sister, and Daddy's busy with the spring planting. Half my brothers and sisters sent up a distress call to get Rye home for the weekend. He's walking dogs for our sister Jordana—she's out of town for a wedding, so she can't take care of her usual clients. At least he could fit taxi service in before coaching T-ball practice this afternoon, filling in for Noah."

Listening to Lisa's friendly banter, Rye had to shake his head. It was no wonder he had moved all the way to Richmond to make his business work. Of course, he loved his family, loved the fact that they all looked to him to fix whatever was wrong. But here in Eden Falls, there was *always* a brother who needed a hand, a sister with one more errand, cousins, aunts, uncles, friends—*people* who pulled him away from his business.

He'd only been living in Richmond for a month, and he'd already come back to Eden Falls a half-dozen times. He promised himself he'd get more control over his calendar in the weeks to come.

Lisa nudged his ribs with a sharp elbow. "Right? Tell Kat that it's no big deal, or she's going to get out at the traffic light and walk home from there!"

Rye couldn't help but smile. He could grouse all he wanted about being called home, but he loved his family, loved the fact that they needed him. "It's no big deal," he said dutifully, and then he nodded to Kat. "And you shouldn't be walking anywhere on that boot. Broken foot?"

Kat fought against her automatic frown. "Stress fracture."

"Ow. Our brother Logan had one of those, a couple of years back. He plays baseball for the Eagles. It took about a month for his foot to heal. A month until he could get back to playing, anyway."

Kat started to ask if Logan pitched, like Rye had done, but then she remembered she wasn't supposed to have recognized Rye. She settled for shrugging instead and saying, "The doctors say I've got about a month to wait, myself. I figured it was a good time to come down here. Help out my parents."

Rye gave her a sympathetic glance. "I was at their house a few months ago, to install a handheld shower for your father. How's he doing?"

"Fine." Kat curved her lips into the smile she had mastered in her long-ago acting classes. Her father was fine. Susan was fine. Jenny was fine. Everyone was fine, and Kat would be on a northbound train in less than a week.

"Colon cancer can be rough." Rye's voice was filled with sympathy.

"They say they caught it in time." Kat was afraid to voice her fears—Mike's recovery had taken longer than anyone had expected. He'd been in and out of the hospital for six months, and now, with pneumonia…

At least Rye seemed to believe her. He didn't ask any more questions. Instead, he assured her, "Everyone's been real worried about them. Just last week, my mother had me bring by some of her chicken almond casserole. It'll get your father back on his feet in no time."

Kat couldn't remember the last time she'd cooked for a sick friend. Oh, well. Things were different down here. People had different ways to show they cared. She tried to recall the lessons in politeness that her mother had drilled into her, years before. "I'm sure it was delicious. It was kind of you to bring it by."

Rye wondered if he'd somehow made Kat angry—she sounded so stiff. Her hands were folded in her lap, her fingers wrapped around each other in perfect precision, like coils of rope, fresh from the factory. She sat upright like a soldier, keeping her spine from touching the back of her seat. Her eyes flashed as they drove past familiar streets, and each intersection tightened the cords in her throat.

And then it came to him: Kat wasn't angry. She was frightened.

One thing Rye had learned in almost thirty years of dealing with siblings and cousins was how to ease the mind of someone who was afraid. Just talk to them. It was easy enough to spin out a story or two about Eden Falls. He might have moved away, but he could always dredge up something entertaining about the only real home he'd ever known.

He nodded to the row of little shops they were passing. "Miss Emily just closed up her pet store."

Kat barely glanced at the brightly painted storefront, and for a second he thought she might not take the bait. Finally, though, she asked, "What happened?"

"She couldn't stand to see any of the animals in cages. She sold off all the mice and gerbils and fish, and then she took in a couple of litters of kittens. She gave them free rein over the whole shop. Problem was, she fell in love with the kittens too much to sell them. If she took money, she couldn't be sure the animals were going to a good home. So instead of selling them, she gave them away to the best owners she could find. In the end, she decided it didn't make much sense to pay rent. Anyone who wants a kitten now just goes up to her house and knocks on the front door."

There. That was better. He actually caught a hint of a smile on Kat's lips. Lisa, of course, was rolling her eyes, but at least his sister didn't call him a liar. As long as he was on a roll, he nodded toward the elementary school they were passing. "Remember classes there? They had to skip the Christmas pageant last December because the boa constrictor in the fourth-grade classroom got out. None of the parents would come see the show until the snake was found. The kids are going to sing 'Jingle Bells' for the Easter parade."

Kat couldn't help herself. She had to ask. "Did they ever find the snake?"

"He finally came out about a week ago. The janitor found him sunning himself on the parking lot, none the worse for wear. He was hungry, though. They used to feed him mice from Miss Emily's."

Kat wrinkled her nose, but she had to laugh. She had to admit—she couldn't imagine the National Ballet School having similar problems. And they would *never* have postponed a performance, snake or no snake, especially a holiday showcase like a Christmas pageant.

Rye eased up to the curb in front of her parents' house, shoving the gearshift into Park. He hopped out of the truck as Kat said goodbye to Lisa. She joined him by the deep bed. "Thank you," she said. And somehow, she meant to thank him for more than the ride. She meant to tell him that she appreciated the effort he had made, the way that he had tried to distract her from her worry.

"My pleasure," he said, tipping an imaginary hat. "Harmon Contracting is a full-service provider." He hefted her suitcase out of the truck, shrugging it into a more comfortable position as he nodded for Kat to precede him up the driveway.

"Oh, I can get that," she said, reaching for the bag.

"It's no problem."

"Please," she said, carving an edge onto the word. She'd learned long ago how to get her way in the bustling streets of New York. She knew the precise angle to hold her shoulders, the exact line to set her chin. No one would dare argue with her when she'd strapped on her big city armor.

Rye recognized that stance; he'd seen it often enough in his own sisters, in his mother. Kat Morehouse was not going to give in easily.

And there really wasn't any reason to push the matter. It wasn't as if he didn't have a thousand other things to do that afternoon—the dog walking Lisa had mentioned, and the T-ball practice, but also phone calls back to Richmond, trying to keep his fledgling business alive while he was on the road.

And yet, he really didn't want to leave Kat here, alone. If he turned his head just a little, he could still see the girl she'd been, the stubborn, studious child who had defied convention, who had done what *she* wanted to do, had carved out the life *she* wanted, never letting little Eden Falls stop her in her tracks.

But there would be time enough to see Kat again. She wasn't going to disappear overnight, and he was in town for the whole weekend. He could stop by the next day. Think of some excuse between now and then. He extended the handle on the roller bag, turning it around to make it easier for Kat to grasp. "Have it your way," he said, adding a smile.

"Thanks," Kat said, and she hustled up the driveway, relying on the roller bag to disguise the lurch of her booted foot. Only when she reached the door did she wonder if she should go back to Rye's truck, thank him properly for the ride. After all, he'd done her a real favor, bringing her home. And she wouldn't mind taking one last look at those slate-black eyes, at the smooth planes of his face, at his rugged jaw….

She shook her head, though, reminding herself to concentrate. She was through with men. Through with distractions that just consumed her time, that took her away from the things that were truly important, from the things that mattered. She might have been an idiot to get involved with Adam, but at least she could translate her disappointing experience into something useful.

Waving a calculatedly jaunty farewell toward Rye and Lisa, Kat threw back her shoulders, took a deep breath and turned the doorknob. Of course the front door was unlocked; it always was. In New York, Kat had to work three different locks on the door of the apartment she shared with Haley, every single time she went in or out. Things were simpler here in Eden Falls. Easier. Safer.

Boring.

Pushing down her automatic derogatory thoughts about the town that had kept her parents happy for their entire lives, Kat stepped over the threshold. And then she caught her breath at the scene inside the old brick rambler.

Chaos. Utter, complete chaos.

A radio blasted from the kitchen, some mournful weatherman announcing that the temperature was going to top ninety, a new record high for the last day in March. A teakettle shrieked on the stovetop, piercing the entire house with its urgent demand. In the living room, a television roared the jingle from a video game, the same four bars of music, over and over and over again. From the master bedroom, a man shouted, "Fine! Let me do it, then!" and a shrill child's voice repeated, "I'm helping! I'm helping!"

All of a sudden, it seemed pretty clear how Susan had forgotten to meet Kat at the train station.

Resisting the urge to hobble back to the curb and

beg Rye to take her to a motel out on the highway—or better yet, back to the train station so she could catch the two-fifteen northbound Clipper—Kat closed the front door behind her. She pushed her little suitcase into the corner of the foyer and dropped her purse beside it. She headed to the kitchen first, grabbing a pot holder from the side of the refrigerator where her mother had kept them forever. The kettle stopped screaming as soon as she lifted it from the heat. The blue flame died immediately when Kat turned the knob on the stove. She palmed off the radio before the local news break could end.

Next stop was the living room, where Kat cast the television into silence, resorting to pushing buttons on the actual set, rather than seeking out the missing remote control. A scramble of half-clothed Barbie dolls lay on the floor, pink dresses tangled with a rose-colored sports car that had plunged into a dry fuchsia swimming pool. A handful of board games was splattered across the entire mess—tiny cones from Sorry mixing with Jenga rods and piles of Monopoly money. Kat shook her head—there would be plenty of time to sort that mess later.

And that left the voices coming from the master bedroom, down the hallway. Kat could make out her father's gruff tones as he insisted someone hand him something immediately. The whining child—it had to be Jenny—was still saying "I'm helping," as if she had to prove her worthiness to someone. And Kat surprised herself by finding tears in her eyes when she heard a low murmur—her calm, unflappable mother, trying to soothe both her husband and her granddaughter.

Kat clumped down the hall, resenting the awkward

walking boot more than ever. When she reached the doorway, she was surprised by the tableau before her.

A hospital bed loomed between her parents' ancient double mattress and the far wall. Mike lay prone between the raised bars, but he craned his neck at a sharp angle. He held out a calloused hand, demanding that a tiny raven-haired child hand over the controls to the bed. The girl kept pressing buttons without any effect; she obviously did not understand how to make the bed work. Susan was framed in the doorway to the bathroom, her gray face cut deep with worry lines as she balanced a small tray, complete with a glass of water and a cup of pills.

"Kat!" Susan exclaimed. "What time—?"

"I caught a ride home with Rye Harmon," Kat said, wrestling to keep her gait as close to normal as possible. The last thing she wanted was for her mother to fuss over a stupid stress fracture. Not when Susan obviously had so much else to worry about.

Kat plucked the bed controls from her niece's hand and passed the bulky plastic block to her father. She settled firm fingers on the child's shoulder, turning her toward the doorway and the living room. "Thank you, Jenny," she said, pushing pretend warmth into the words. "You were a big help. Now there are some toys out there, just waiting for you to straighten up."

Jenny sighed, but she shuffled down the hallway. Kat leaned down to brush a kiss against her father's forehead, easing an arm beneath his shoulders as he started to manipulate the mechanical bed, fighting to raise himself into a seated position. When she was certain he was more comfortable, Kat said, "Come sit down, Mama." She heard the hard New York edge on her words, and she smiled to soften her voice. “Why don’t you rest, and let me take care of that for a while?”

Even as Susan settled on the edge of the double bed, Kat heard the distant whistle of the Clipper, the New York-bound train, leaving town for the day. The wild, lonesome sound immediately made her think about Rye Harmon, about how he had offered to come inside, to help. He’d scooped her up from the train station like a knight in shining armor—a friendly, easygoing knight whom she’d known all her life. Kat blinked and she could see his kind smile, his warm black eyes. She could picture the steady, sturdy way he had settled her into his truck.

She shook her head. She didn’t have time to think about Rye. Instead, she handed her father his medicine, taking care to balance her weight, keeping her spine in alignment despite her cursed walking boot. She had come to Eden Falls to help out her family, to be there for Susan and Mike. And as soon as humanly possible, she was heading back to New York, and the National Ballet Company and the life she had worked so hard to attain. She didn’t have time for Rye Harmon. Rye Harmon, or anything else that might delay her escape from Eden Falls.

Chapter Two

Three hours later, Kat wondered if she had made the greatest mistake of her life. She leaned against the headrest in her cousin Amanda's ancient sedan, resisting the urge to strangle her five-year-old niece.

"But *why* isn't Aunt Kat driving?" Jenny asked for the fourth time.

"I'm happy to drive you both home, Jenny," Amanda deflected, applying one of the tricks she'd learned as a schoolteacher.

"But *why*—"

Kat interrupted the whining question, spitting out an answer through gritted teeth. "Because I don't know how!"

Amanda laughed at Kat's frustration. The cousins had been quite close when they were children—certainly closer than Kat had been to her own sister. Nevertheless, Amanda always thought it was hysterical that

Kat had never gotten her driver's license. More than once, she had teased Kat about moving away to the magical kingdom of Oz, where she was carried around by flying monkeys.

Jenny, though, wasn't teasing Kat. The five-year-old child was simply astonished, her mouth stretched into an amazed O before she stammered, "B-but *all* grown-ups know how to drive!"

"Maybe your Aunt Kat isn't a grown-up," Amanda suggested helpfully.

Kat gave her a dirty look before saying, "I am a grown-up, Jenny, but I don't drive. The two things are totally separate."

"But how do you go to the grocery store?"

"I walk there," Kat said, exasperated. How could one little girl make her feel like such a sideshow freak?

"But what do you do with the bags of groceries?"

"I carry them!"

Kat's voice was rough enough that even the head-strong Jenny declined to ask another follow-up question. It wasn't so ridiculous, that Kat couldn't drive. She'd left Eden Falls when she was fourteen, long before she'd even thought of getting behind the wheel of a car. She'd spent the next ten years living in Manhattan, where subways, buses and the occasional taxi met her transportation needs. Anything heavy or bulky could be delivered.

But try explaining that to someone who had never even heard of the Mason-Dixon line, much less traveled above it.

Amanda's laugh smoothed over the awkward moment as she pulled into the driveway of a run-down brick Colonial. Weeds poked through the crumbling asphalt, and the lawn was long dead from lack of water—

just as well, since it had not been cut for months. One shutter hung at a defeated angle, and the screen on the front door was slashed and rusted. A collapsing carport signaled imminent danger to any vehicle unfortunate enough to be parked beneath it.

"I don't believe it!" Kat said. The last time she had seen this house, it had been neat and trim, kept in perfect shape. Years ago, it had belonged to her grandmother, to Susan's mother. The Morehouses had kept it in the family after Granny died; it was easy enough to keep up the little Colonial.

Easy enough, that was, until Rachel got her hands on the place. Susan and Mike had let Rachel move in after she'd graduated from high school, when the constant fights had become too difficult under their own roof. The arrangement had been intended to be temporary, but once Rachel gave birth to Jenny, it had somehow slipped into something permanent.

Now, though, looking at the wreck of Granny's neat little home, Kat could not help but begrudge that decision. Did Rachel destroy *everything* she touched?

Amanda's voice shone with forced brightness. "It always looks bad after winter. Once everything's freshened up for spring, it'll be better."

Sure it would. Because Rachel had such a green thumb, she had surely taken care of basic gardening over the past several years. Rachel always worked so hard to bring good things into her life. Not.

Kat swallowed hard and undid her seat belt. *One week,* she reminded herself. She only had to stay here one week. Then Jenny could return to Susan and Mike. Or, who knew? Rachel might even be back from wherever she had gone. "Well..." Kat tried to think of something positive to say about the house. Failing miserably, she fell back on something she *could* be grateful for. "Thanks for the ride."

Amanda's soft features settled into a frown. "Do you need any help with your bag? Are you sure—"

"We'll be fine."

"We could all go out to dinner—"

That was the last thing Kat wanted—drawing out the day, eating in some Eden Falls greasy spoon, where the food would send any thinking dancer to the work-out room for at least ten straight hours, just to break even. Besides, she really didn't want to impose on her cousin's good nature—and driver's license—any more than was strictly necessary. "We'll be *fine,* Amanda. I'm sure Aunt Sarah and Uncle Bill are already wondering what took you so long, just running Jenny and me across town. You don't want them to start worrying."

At least Kat's case was bolstered by her niece's behavior. Jenny had already hopped out of her seat and scuffed her way to the faded front door. Amanda sighed. "I don't know what sort of food you'll find in there, Kat."

"We can always—" What? She was going to say, they could always have D'Agostino deliver groceries. But there wasn't a D'Agostino in Eden Falls. There wasn't *any* grocery store that delivered. She swallowed hard and pushed her way through to the end of the sentence. "We can always order a pizza."

That was the right thing to say. Amanda relaxed, obviously eased by the sheer normalcy of Kat's suggestion.

As *if* Kat would eat a pizza. She'd given up mozzarella the year she'd first gone on pointe. "Thanks so much for the ride," Kat said. "Give my love to Aunt Sarah and Uncle Bill."

By the time Kat dragged her roller bag through the front door, Jenny was in the kitchen, kneeling on a chair in front of the open pantry. Her hand was shoved deep in a bag of cookies, and telltale chocolate crumbs ringed her lips. Kat's reproach was automatic. "Are you eating cookies for dinner?"

"No." Jenny eyed her defiantly.

"Don't lie to me, young lady." *Ach*, Kat thought. *Did I really just say that? I sound like everyone's stereotype of the strict maiden aunt.* Annoyed, Kat looked around the kitchen. Used paper plates cascaded out of an open trash can. A jar of peanut butter lay on its side, its lid teetering at a crazy angle. A dozen plastic cups were strewn across the counter, with varying amounts of sticky residue pooling inside.

On top of the toaster oven curled three bananas. Kat broke one off from the bunch and passed it to her niece. "Here", she said. "Eat this."

"I don't like them when they're brown."

"That's dinner."

"You said we were ordering a pizza."

"Pizza isn't good for you."

"Mommy likes pizza."

"Mommy would." Kat closed her eyes and took a deep breath. This wasn't the time or the place to get into a discussion about Rachel. Kat dug in the pantry, managing to excavate a sealed packet of lemon-pepper tuna. "Here. You can have tuna and a banana. I'll go to the grocery store tomorrow."

"How are you going to do that, when you don't drive? It's too far to walk."

Good question. "I'll manage."

Kat took a quick tour of the rest of the house while Jenny ate her dinner. Alas, the kitchen wasn't some terrible aberration. The living room was ankle-deep in pizza boxes and gossip magazines. The disgusting bathroom hadn't been cleaned in centuries. Jenny's bedroom was a sea of musty, tangled sheets and stuffed animals.

Back in the kitchen, Jenny's sullen silence was nearly enough to make Kat put cookies back on the menu. Almost. But Jenny didn't need cookies. She needed some rules. Some structure. A pattern or two in her life. Starting now.

"Okay, kiddo. We're going to get some cleaning done."

"Cleaning?" Jenny's whine stretched the word into four or five syllables at least.

Kat turned to the stove—ironically, the cleanest thing in the house, because Rachel had never cooked a meal in her life. Kat twisted the old-fashioned timer to give them fifteen minutes to work. "Let's go. Fifteen minutes, to make this kitchen look new."

Jenny stared at her as if she'd lost her mind. Squaring her shoulders, though, and ignoring the blooming ache in her foot, Kat started to tame the pile of paper plates. "Let's go," she said. "March! You're in charge of throwing away those paper cups!"

With the use of three supersize trash bags, they made surprising progress. When those fifteen minutes were done, Kat set the alarm again, targeting the mess in the living room. The bathroom was next, and finally Jenny's room. The little girl was yawning and rubbing her eyes by the time they finished.

"Mommy never makes me clean up."

"I'm not Mommy," Kat said. She was *so* not Mommy—not in a million different ways. But she knew what was good for Jenny. She knew what had been good for her, even when she was Jenny's age. Setting goals. Developing strategies. Following rules. When Kat had lived in her parents' home, Susan had built the foundation for orderly management of life's problems. Unlike her sister, Kat had absorbed those lessons with a vengeance. Her *rules* were the only thing that had gotten her through those first homesick months when she moved to New York. As Jenny started to collapse on the living-room couch, Kat said, "It's time for you to go to bed."

"I haven't watched TV yet!"

"No TV. It's a school night."

"Mommy lets me watch TV every night."

"I'm not Mommy," Kat repeated, wondering if she should record the sentence, so that she could play it back every time she needed it.

Over the next half hour, Kat found out that she was cruel and heartless and evil and mean, just like the worst villains of Jenny's favorite animated movies. But the child eventually got to bed wearing her pajamas, with her teeth brushed, her hair braided and her prayers said.

Exhausted, and unwilling to admit just how much her foot was aching, Kat collapsed onto the sagging living-room couch. Six more days. She could take six more days of anything. They couldn't all be this difficult. She glanced at her watch and was shocked to see it was only eight-thirty.

That left her plenty of time to call Haley. Plenty of time to catch up on the exploits of Adam and Selene, to remember why Kat was so much better off without that miserable excuse for a man in her life.

Kat summoned her willpower and stumped over to her purse, where she'd left it on the kitchen table.

She rooted for her cell phone. Nothing. She scrambled around, digging past her wallet. Still nothing. She dumped the contents out on the kitchen table, where it immediately became clear that she had no cell phone.

And then she remembered spilling everything in the cab of Rye's truck in her rush of surprise to see him standing beside her. She had been shocked by the elemental response to his body near hers. She'd acted like a silly schoolgirl, like a brainless child, jumping the way she had, dropping her purse.

But even as she berated herself, she remembered Rye's easy smile. He'd been truly gallant, rescuing her at the train station. It had been mean of her to pretend not to remember him. Uncomfortably, she thought of the confused flash in his eyes, the tiny flicker of hurt that was almost immediately smothered beneath the blanket of his good nature.

And then, her belly did that funny thing again, that flutter that was part nervous anticipation, part unreasoning dread. The closest thing she could compare it to was the thrill of opening night, the excitement of standing in the wings while a new audience hummed in the theater's red-velvet seats.

But she wasn't in the theater. She was in Eden Falls.

And whether she wanted to or not, Kat was going to have to track down Rye Harmon the following day. Track him down, and retrieve her phone, and hope she had a better signal at Rachel's house than she'd had at the station.

All things considered, though, she couldn't get too upset about the lack of signal that she'd encountered. If she'd been able to call Susan or Amanda, then Rye would never have given her a ride. And those few minutes of talking with Rye Harmon had been the high point of her very long, very stressful, very exhausting first afternoon and evening in Eden Falls.

By noon the next day, Kat had decided that retrieving her cell phone was the least of her concerns.

Susan had swung by that morning, just after Kat had hustled a reluctant Jenny onto her school bus. Looking around the straightened house, Susan said, "It looks like you and Jenny were busy last night."

"The place was a pigsty."

"I'm sorry, dear. I just wasn't able to get over here before you arrived, to clean things up."

Kat immediately felt terrible for her judgmental tone. "I wasn't criticizing *you,* Mama. I just can't believe Rachel lives like that."

Susan shook her head. Kat knew from long experience that her mother would never say anything directly critical about her other daughter. But sometimes Susan's silences echoed with a thousand shades of meaning.

Pushing aside a lifetime of criticism about her sister, Kat said, "Thank you so much for bringing by that casserole. Jenny and I will really enjoy it tonight."

Susan apologized again. "I can't believe I didn't think of giving you anything last night. The church ladies have been so helpful—they've kept our freezer stocked for months."

"I'm glad you've had that type of support," Kat said. And she was. She still couldn't imagine any of her friends in New York cooking for a colleague in need. Certainly no one would organize food week after week. "How was Daddy last night? Did either of you get any sleep?"

Susan's smile was brilliant, warming Kat from

across the room. "Oh, yes, sweetheart. I had to wake him up once for his meds, but he fell back to sleep right away. It was the best night he's had in months."

Glancing around the living room, Kat swallowed a proud grin. She had been right to come down here. If one night could help Susan so much, what would an entire week accomplish?

Susan went on. "And it was a godsend, not fixing breakfast for Jenny before the sun was up. That elementary school bus comes so early, it's a crime."

Kat was accustomed to being awake well before the sun rose. She usually fit in ninety minutes on the treadmill in the company gym before she even thought about attending her first dance rehearsal of the day. Of course, with the walking boot, she hadn't been able to indulge in the tension tamer of her typical exercise routine. She'd had to make due with a punishing regimen of crunches instead, alternating sets with modified planks and a series of leg lifts meant to keep her hamstrings as close to dancing strength as possible.

As for Jenny's breakfast? It had been some hideous purple-and-green cereal, eaten dry, because there wasn't any milk in the house. Kat had been willing to concede the point on cold cereal first thing in the morning, but she had silently vowed that the artificially dyed stuff would be out of the house by the time Jenny got home that afternoon. Whole-grain oats would be better for the little girl—and they wouldn't stain the milk in Jenny's bowl.

There'd be time enough to pick up some groceries that afternoon. For now, Kat knew her mother had another task in mind. "So, are you going to drop me off at the studio now?"

Susan looked worried. "It's really too much for me

to ask. I shouldn't even have mentioned it when I called you, dear. I'm sure I can take care of everything in the next couple of weeks."

"Don't be silly," Kat said. "I know Rachel was running things for you. She's been gone for a while, though, and someone has to pick up the slack. I came to Eden Falls to help."

Susan fussed some more, but she was already leading the way out to her car. It may have been ten years since Kat had lived in Eden Falls, but she knew the way to the Morehouse Dance Academy by heart. As a child, she had practically lived in her mother's dance studio, from the moment she could pull on her first leotard.

The building was smaller than she remembered, though. It seemed lost in the sea of its huge parking lot. A broken window was covered over with a cardboard box, and a handful of yellowed newspapers rested against the door, like kindling.

Kat glanced at her mother's pinched face, and she consciously coated her next words with a smile. "Don't worry, Mama. It'll just take a couple of hours to make sure everything is running smoothly. Go home and take care of Daddy. I'll call Amanda to bring me back to Rachel's."

"Let me just come in with you…."

Kat shook her head. Once her mother started in on straightening the studio, she'd stay all morning. Susan wasn't the sort of woman to walk away from a project half-done. Even *if* she had a recuperating husband who needed her back at the house.

"I'll be fine, Mama. I know this place like the back of my hand. And I'm sure Rachel left everything in good shape."

Good shape. Right.

The roof was leaking in the main classroom, a slow drip that had curled up the ceiling tiles and stained one wall. Kat shuddered to think about the state of the warped hardwood floor. Both toilets were running in the public restroom, and the sinks were stained from dripping faucets. Kat ran the hot water for five minutes before she gave up on getting more than an icy trickle.

The damage wasn't limited to the building. When Kat turned on the main computer, she heard a grinding sound, and the screen flashed blue before it died altogether. The telephone handset was sticky; a quick sniff confirmed that someone had handled it with maple syrup on their fingers.

In short, the dance studio was an absolute and complete mess.

Kat seethed. How could students be taking classes here? How could her parents' hard-earned investment be ruined so quickly? What had Rachel done?

Muttering to herself, Kat started to sift through the papers on the desk in the small, paneled office. She found a printout of an electronic spreadsheet—at least the computer had been functional back in January.

The news on the spreadsheet, though, told a depressing story. Class sizes for the winter term had dwindled from their robust fall enrollment. Many of those payments had never been collected. Digging deeper, Kat found worse news—a dozen checks, dating back to September—had never been cashed. Search as she might, she could find no checks at all for the spring term; she couldn't even find an enrollment list for the classes.

Susan had been absolutely clear, every time Kat talked to her: Rachel had shaped up. Rachel had run the dance studio for the past six months, ever since

Mike's diagnosis had thrown Susan's life into utter disarray. Rachel had lined up teachers, had taken care of the books, had kept everything functioning like clockwork.

Rachel had lied through her teeth.

Kat's fingers trembled with rage as she looked around the studio. Her heart pounded, and her breath came in short gasps. Tears pricked at the corners of her eyes, angry tears that made her chew on her lower lip.

And so Kat did the only thing she knew how to do. She tried to relieve her stress the only way she could. She walked across the floor of the classroom, her feet automatically turning out in a ballerina's stance, even though she wore her hated blue boot. Resenting that handicap, she planted her good foot, setting one hand on the barre with a lifetime of familiarity.

She closed her eyes and ran through the simplest of exercises. First position, second position, third position, fourth. She swept her free arm in a graceful arc, automatically tilting her head to an angle that maximized the long line of her neck. She repeated the motions again, three times, four. Each pass through, she felt a little of her tension drain, a little of her rage fade.

She was almost able to take a lung-filling breath when heavy footsteps dragged her back to messy, disorganized reality. "*There* you are!"

Rye stopped in the doorway, frozen into place by the vision of Kat at the barre. All of a sudden, he was catapulted back ten years in time, to the high school auditorium, to the rough stage where he had plodded through the role of Curly.

He had caught Kat stretching out for dancing there, too, backstage one spring afternoon. She'd had her heel firmly anchored on a table, bending her willowy limbs with a grace that had made his own hulking, teenage body awaken to desire. He could see her now, only a few feet away, close enough for him to touch.

But his interest had been instantly quenched when he'd glimpsed Kat's face, that day so long ago. Tears had tracked down her smooth cheeks, silvering the rosy skin that was completely bare of the blush and concealer and all the other makeup crap that high school girls used. Even as he took one step closer, he had seen her flinch, caught her eyes darting toward the dressing room. He'd heard the brassy laugh of one of the senior girls, one of the cheerleaders, and he'd immediately understood that the popular kids had been teasing the young middle-school dancer. Again.

Rye had done the only thing that made sense at the time, the one thing that he thought would make Kat forget that she was an outsider. He'd leaned forward to brush a quick fraternal kiss against her cheek.

But somehow—even now, he couldn't say how—he'd ended up touching his lips to hers. They'd been joined for just a heartbeat, a single, chaste connection that had jolted through him with the power of a thousand sunsets.

Rye could still remember the awkward blush that had flamed his face. He really had meant to kiss her on the cheek. He'd swear it—on his letter jacket and his game baseball, and everything else that had mattered to him back in high school. He had no idea if he had moved wrong, or if she had, but after the kiss she had leaped away as if he'd scorched her with a blowtorch.

Thinking back, Rye still wanted to wince. How had he screwed *that* up? He had three sisters. He had a lifetime of experience kissing cheeks, offering old-fashioned, brotherly support. He'd certainly never kissed one of his sisters on the lips by mistake.

Kat's embarrassment had only been heightened when a voice spoke up from the curtains that led to the stage. "What would Mom think, Kat? Should I go get her, so she can see what you're really like?" They'd both looked up to see Rachel watching them. Her eyes had been narrowed, those eyes that were so like Kat's but so very, very different. Even then, ten years ago, there hadn't been any confusing the sisters. Only an eighth grader, Rachel hadn't yet resorted to the dyed hair and tattoos that she sported as an adult. But she'd painted heavy black outlines around her eyes, and she wore clunky earrings and half a dozen rings on either hand. Rachel had laughed at her sister then, obviously relishing Kat's embarrassment over that awful mistake of a kiss.

Rachel must not have told, though. There hadn't been any repercussions. And Rye's fumbling obviously hadn't made any lasting impression—Kat hadn't even remembered his name, yesterday at the train station.

Kat stiffened as she heard Rye's voice. A jumble of emotions flashed through her head—guilt, because she shouldn't be caught at the barre, not when she was supposed to be resting her injured foot. Shame, because no one should see the studio in its current state of disarray. Anger, because Rachel should never have let things get so out of hand, should never have left so much mess for Kat to clean up. And a sudden swooping sense of something else, something that she couldn't name precisely. Something that she vaguely thought of as pleasure.

Shoving down that last thought—one that she didn't have time for, that she didn't deserve—she lowered her arm and turned to face Rye. "How did you get in here?"

"The front door was open. Maybe the latch didn't catch when you came in?"

Kat barked a harsh laugh. "That makes one more thing that's broken."

Rye glanced around the studio, his eyes immediately taking in the ceiling leak. "That looks bad," he said. "And the water damage isn't new."

Kat grimaced. "It's probably about six months old."

"Why do you say that?"

"It's been six months since my father got sick. My sister, Rachel, has been running this place and…she's not the best at keeping things together."

Rye fought the urge to scowl when he heard Rachel's name. Sure, the woman had her problems. But it was practically criminal to have let so much water get into a hardwood floor like this one. He barely managed not to shake his head. He'd dodged a bullet with Rachel, seeing through to her irresponsible self before he could be dragged down with her.

But it wasn't Rachel standing in front of him, looking so discouraged. It was Kat. Kat, who had come home to help out her family, giving up her own fame and success because her people needed her.

Rye couldn't claim to have found fame or success in Richmond. Not yet. But he certainly understood being called back home because of family. Before he was fully aware of the fact that he was speaking, he heard himself say, "I can help clean things up. Patch the roof, replace the drywall. The floor will take a bit more work, but I can probably get it all done in ten days or so."

Kat saw the earnestness in Rye's black eyes, and she found herself melting just a little. Rye Harmon was coming to her rescue. Again. Just as he had at the train station the day before.

That was silly, though. It wasn't like she was still the starry-eyed eighth grader who had been enchanted by the baseball star in the lead role of the musical. She hardened her voice, so that she could remind herself she had no use for Eden Falls. "That sounds like a huge job! You'll need help, and I'm obviously in no shape to get up on a ladder." She waved a frustrated hand toward her booted foot.

Rye scarcely acknowledged her injury. "There's no need for you to get involved. I have plenty of debts that I can call in."

"Debts?"

"Brothers. Sisters. Cousins. Half of Eden Falls calls me in from Richmond, day or night, to help them out of a bind. What's a little leak repair, in repayment?"

"Do any of those relatives know anything about plumbing?"

Rye looked concerned. "What's wrong with the plumbing?"

For answer, Kat turned on her heel and walked toward the small restroom. The running toilets sounded louder now that she was staring at them with an eye toward repair. She nodded toward the sink. "There isn't any hot water, either."

Rye whistled, long and low. "This place looks like it's been through a war."

"In a manner of speaking." Kat shrugged. "As I said, my sister's been in charge. She's not really a, um, detail person."

"How have they been holding classes here?" Rye asked. "Haven't the students complained?"

And that's when the penny dropped. Students would

have complained the first time they tried to wash their hands. Their parents would have been furious about the warped floor, the chance of injury.

Kat limped to the office and picked up the maple-coated telephone handset. She punched in the studio's number, relying on memories that had been set early in her childhood. The answering machine picked up immediately.

"We're sorry to inform you that, due to a family emergency, Morehouse Dance Academy will not be offering classes for the spring term. If you need help with any other matter, please leave a message, and one of our staff will contact you promptly."

Rachel's voice. The vowels cut short, as if she were trying to sound mature. Official. Kat's attention zeroed in on the nearby answering machine. "57" flashed in angry red numerals. So much for "our staff" returning messages—promptly or at all.

Kat's rage was like a physical thing, a towering wave that broke over her head and drenched her with an emotion so powerful that she was left shaking. If students hadn't been able to sign up for classes, then no money could possibly come into the studio. Rachel couldn't have made a deposit for months. But the water was still on, and the electricity. Susan must have set up the utilities for automatic payment. Even now, the studio's bank account might be overdrawn.

Susan was probably too stressed, too distracted, to have noticed any correspondence from the bank. Fiscal disaster might be only a pen stroke away. All because of Rachel.

Kat's voice shook with fury as she slammed her hand down on the desk. "I cannot be*lieve* her! How could

Rachel do this? How could she ruin everything that Mama worked so hard to achieve?"

Of course Rye didn't answer. He didn't even know Rachel. He couldn't have any idea how irresponsible she was.

Somehow, though, Rye's silence gave Kat permission to think out loud. "I have to get this all fixed up. I can't let my mother see the studio like this. It would break her heart. I have to get the floor fixed, and the plumbing. Get people enrolled in classes."

"I can do the plumbing myself," Rye said, as calmly as if he had planned on walking into this particular viper's nest when he strolled through the studio door. "I'll round up the troops to take care of the leak. You can get started on the paperwork here in the office, see if you find any more problems."

"You make it sound so simple!"

He laughed, the easy sound filling the little office. "I should. It's my job."

She gave him a confused look. "Job?"

"Believe it or not, I can't make a living picking up stranded passengers at the train station every day. I'm a building contractor—renovations, installations, all of that."

That's right. He'd said something as he handed her the roller bag yesterday, something about Harmon Contracting. Rye was a guy who made the world neater, one job at a time. A guy who made his living with projects like hers. "But didn't Lisa say you were living up in Richmond now?"

A quick frown darted across his face, gone before she was certain she had seen it. "I moved there a month ago. But I've been back in town every weekend. A few more days around here won't hurt me."

What was he saying? Why was he volunteering to spend *more* time in Eden Falls?

Kat wasn't even family. He didn't owe her a thing. What the hell was he thinking, taking on a job like this? More hours going back and forth on I-95. More time behind the wheel of his truck. More time away from the business that he really needed to nurture, from the promise he'd made to himself.

This was Marissa, all over again—a woman, tying him down, making him trade in his own dreams for hers. This was the same rotten truth he'd lived, over and over and over, the same reflexive way that he had set his dreams aside, just because he had the skills to help someone else. Just because he could.

But one look at the relief on Kat's face, and Rye knew he'd said the right thing.

And Harmon Contracting wasn't exactly taking Richmond by storm. He didn't need to be up the road, full-time, every day. And it sure looked like Kat needed him here, now.

She shook her head, and he wasn't sure if the disbelief in her next words was because of the generosity of his offer, or the scale of the disaster she was still taking in, in the studio. "I don't even know how I'll pay you. I can't let my mother find out about this."

"We'll work out something," Rye said. "Maybe some of my cousins can take a ballet class or two."

Kat just stared. Rye sounded like he rescued maidens in distress every day. Well, he had yesterday, hadn't he? "Just like that? Don't we need to write up a contract or something?"

Rye raised a mahogany eyebrow. "If you don't trust me to finish the job, we can definitely put something in writing."

"No!" She surprised herself by the vehemence she forced into the word. "I thought that *you* wouldn't trust *me*."

"That wouldn't be very neighborly of me, would it?" She fumbled for a reply, but he laughed. "Relax. You're back in Eden Falls. We pretty much do things on a handshake around here. If either one of us backs out of the deal, the entire town will know by sunset." He lowered his voice to a growl, putting on a hefty country twang. "If that happens, you'll never do business in this town again."

Kat surprised herself by laughing. "That's the voice you used when you played Curly!"

"Ha!" Rye barked. "You *did* recognize me!"

Rye watched embarrassment paint Kat's cheeks. She was beautiful when she blushed. The color took away all the hard lines of her face, relaxed the tension around her eyes.

"I —" she started to say, fumbling for words. He cocked an eyebrow, determined not to make things easier for her. "You —" she started again. She stared at her hands, at her fingers twisting around each other, as if she were weaving invisible cloth.

"You thought it would be cruel to remind me how clumsy I was on stage, in *Oklahoma*. That was mighty considerate of you."

"No!"

There. Her gaze shot up, as if she had something to prove. Another blush washed over her face. This time, the color spread across her collarbones, the tender pink heating the edges of that crisp black top she wore. He had a sudden image of the way her skin would feel against his lips, the heat that would shimmer off her as he tasted…

"No," she repeated, as if she could read his mind. Now it was his turn to feel the spark of embarrassment. He most definitely did not want Kat Morehouse reading his mind just then. "You weren't clumsy. That dance scene would have been a challenge for anyone."

"Except for you." He said the words softly, purposely pitching his voice so that she had to take a step closer to hear.

Her lips twisted into a frown. "Except for me," she agreed reluctantly. "But I wasn't a normal kid. I mean, I already knew I was going to be a dancer. I'd known since I was five. I was a freak."

Before he could think of how she would react, he raised a hand to her face, brushing back an escaped lock of her coal-black hair. "You weren't a freak. You were never a freak."

Her belly tightened as she felt the wiry hairs on the back of his fingers, rough against her cheek. She caught her breath, freezing like a doe startled on the edge of a clearing. *Stop it*, she told herself. *He doesn't mean anything by it. You're a mess after one morning spent in this disaster zone, and he's just trying to help you out. Like a neighbor should.*

Those were the words she forced herself to think, but that's not what she wanted to believe. Rye Harmon had been the first boy to kiss her. Sure, she had pretended not to know him the day before. And over the years, she'd told herself that it had never actually happened. Even if it had, it had been a total accident, a complete surprise to both of them. But his lips had touched hers when she was only fourteen—his lips, so soft and sweet and kind—and sometimes it had seemed that she'd been spoiled for any other boy after that.

She forced herself to laugh, and to take a step

away. "We all think we're freaks when we're teenagers," she said.

For just an instant, she thought that he was going to follow her. She thought that he was going to take the single step to close the distance between them, to gather up her hair again, to put those hands to even better use.

But then he matched her shaky laugh, tone for tone, and the moment was past. "Thank God no one judges us on the mistakes we make when we're young," he said.

Rye berated himself as Kat sought refuge behind the desk. What the hell was he doing, reacting like that, to a woman he hadn't seen since she was a kid? For a single, horrible second, he thought it was because of Rachel. Because of those few tumultuous weeks, almost six years before.

But that couldn't be. Despite the DNA that Kat and Rachel shared, they were nothing alike. Physically, emotionally—they might as well live on two different planets. He was certain of that—his body was every bit as sure as his mind.

It was Kat who drew him now. Kat who attracted him. Kat whom he did not want to scare away.

He squared his shoulders and shoved his left hand deep into the pocket of his jeans. "Here," he said, producing a small leather case. "You left your cell phone in my car. I found it this morning, and I called your parents' house, but your mother said you were over here."

Kat snatched the phone from his open palm, like a squirrel grabbing a peanut from a friendly hand. She retreated behind the desk, using the cell as an excuse to avoid Rye's eyes, to escape that warm black gaze. Staring at the phone's screen, she bit her lip when she realized she still had no reception. "Stupid carrier," she said.

"Pretty much all of them have lousy reception around here. It's better up on the bluffs."

The bluffs. Kat may have left town when she was fourteen, but she had already heard rumors about the bluffs. About the kids who drove up there, telling their parents they were going to the movies. About the kids who climbed into backseats, who got caught by flashlight-wielding policemen.

But that was stupid. She wasn't a kid. And it only made sense that she'd get better cell phone reception at the highest point in town. "I'll head up there, then, if I need to make a call."

Damn. She hadn't quite managed to keep her voice even. Well, in for an inch, in for a mile. She might as well apologize now, for having pretended not to know him.

She took a deep breath before she forced herself to meet his eyes. He seemed to be laughing at her, gently chiding her for her discomfort. She cleared her throat. "I'm sorry about yesterday. About acting like I didn't know who you were. I guess I just felt strange, coming back here. Coming back to a place that's like home, but isn't."

He could have made a joke. He could have tossed away her apology. He could have scolded her for being foolish. But instead, he said, "'Like home, but isn't.' I'm learning what you mean." At her questioning look, he went on. "Moving up to Richmond. It's what I've always wanted. When I'm here, I can't wait to get back there, can't wait to get back to work. But when I'm there…I worry about everyone here. I think about everything I'm missing."

It didn't help that everyone in Eden Falls thought he was nuts for moving away. Every single member of his family believed that the little town was the perfect place to raise kids, the perfect place to grow up, surrounded by generations. Marissa had said that to him, over and over again, and he'd believed her, because Eden Falls was the only place he'd ever known.

But now, having gotten away to Richmond, he knew that there was a whole wide world out there. He owed it to himself to explore further, to test himself, to see exactly how much he could achieve.

Like Kat had, daring to leave so long ago. If anyone was going to understand him, Kat would.

He met her gaze as if she'd challenged him out loud. "I have to do it. It's like I…I have to prove something. To my family and to myself—I can make this work, and not just because I'm a Harmon. Not just because I know everyone in town, and my daddy knows everyone, and his daddy before him. If I can make Harmon Contracting succeed, it'll be because of who *I* am. What *I* do."

Kat heard the earnestness in Rye's voice, the absolute certainty that he was going to make it. For just a second, she felt a flash of pain somewhere beneath her breastbone, as if her soul was crying out because she had lost something precious.

But that was absurd. Rye had moved to Richmond, the same way that she had moved to New York. They both had found their true paths, found their way out of Eden Falls. And she'd be back in her true home shortly, back with the National Ballet, back on stage, just as soon as she could get out of her stupid walking boot.

And as soon as she got the Morehouse Dance Academy back on its feet. She pasted on her very best smile and extended her hand, offering the handshake that would seal their deal. “I almost feel guilty,” she said. “Keeping you away from Richmond. But you’re the one who offered.”

His fingers folded around hers, and she suddenly had to fight against the sensation that she was falling, tumbling down a slope so steep that she could not begin to see the bottom. “I did,” he said. “And I always keep my word.”

His promise shivered down her spine, and she had to remind herself that they were talking about a business proposition. Nothing more. Rye Harmon would never be anything more to her. He couldn’t be. Their past and their future made anything else impossible.

Chapter Three

Three days later, Kat was back in the studio office, sorting through a stack of papers. Rye was working in the bathroom, replacing the insides of the running toilets. The occasional clank of metal against porcelain created an offbeat music for Kat's work.

She'd been productive all morning long. That was after seeing Jenny off to school, ignoring the child's demands for sugar on her corn flakes, an extra sparkling ribbon for her hair and a stuffed animal to keep her company throughout the day. Kat had a plan—to bring order to Jenny's life—and she was going to stick with it. If it took Jenny another day or week or month to get on board, it was just going to take that long.

Not that Kat had any intention of still being in Eden Falls in a month.

That morning, Susan had driven her to the studio. When her mother had put the car in Park and taken off her own seat belt, Kat had practically squawked. "You have to get back to Daddy!"

"I can stay away for an hour," Susan had said. "Let me help you here."

"I'm fine! Seriously. There's hardly anything left for me to do." Susan had looked doubtful, until Kat added, "I just want to have a quiet morning. Maybe do a few exercises. You know, I need to keep in shape." Kat was desperate to keep her mother from seeing the devastation inside the studio. "Please, Mama. The whole reason I'm here in Eden Falls is so that you can rest. Take advantage of me while you can. Relax a little. Go back home and make yourself a cup of that peach tea you like so much."

"I *did* want to get your father sitting up for the rest of the morning. He's feeling so much stronger now that he's getting his sleep."

"Perfect!" Kat had said, letting some of her real pleasure color the word. If her father was recovering, then it was worth all the little struggles to get Jenny in line. "Go home. I'll call Amanda to pick me up when I'm done here."

Susan had smiled then. "My little general," she said, patting Kat's hand fondly. "You've got a plan for everything, don't you?"

Planning. That was Kat's strong suit. Over the weekend, she had written up a list of everything that had to be done at the studio, from computer repair to roofing. She had placed her initials beside each item that she was taking charge of, and she'd dashed off Rye's initials next to his responsibilities. A few items—like the computer—needed to be outsourced, but she would take care of them one by one, doing her best to support the Eden Falls economy.

Goals. Strategies. Rules.

Those were the words that had brought her great success over the years. Sure, as a young girl, miles away from home in New York, she had wondered how she would ever succeed at National Ballet. But she had built her own structure, given her life solid bones—and she had succeeded beyond her wildest dreams.

Okay. Not her wildest dreams. Some of her dreams were pretty wild—she saw herself dancing the tortured maiden Giselle, the girl who died when her love was spurned by the handsome Prince Albrecht. Or the playful animation of the wooden-doll-come-to-life in *Coppelia*. Or the soul-wrenching dual roles of the black and white swans in *Swan Lake*.

All in due time, Kat told herself. As soon as she was out of her hated walking boot, she would exercise like a demon. She would get herself back in top dancing form in no time, transform her body into a more efficient tool than it had been before her injury. Goals. Strategies. Rules.

She could do it. She always had before.

Just thinking about her favorite roles made her long for the National Ballet Company. She hadn't spent more than a weekend away from her ballet friends since moving to New York ten years before. Sitting down at the desk in the office, Kat punched in Haley's phone number. Her roommate picked up on the third ring.

"Tell me that they're making you work like dogs, and I'm impossibly lucky to be trapped here in Small Town Hell," Kat said without preamble.

"I don't know what you're talking about," Haley responded with a mocking tone of wide-eyed wonder. "The company has been treating us to champagne and chocolate-covered strawberries. Free mani-pedis, and hot stone massages for all."

"I hate you," Kat said, laughing.

"How are things on the home front?"

"Well, the good news is that my father seems to be doing better."

"I know you well enough to read *that* tone of voice. What's the bad news?"

Where to start? Kat could say that her niece was a brat. That her sister was a lazy, irresponsible waste of an excuse for a grown woman. That the dance studio was falling down around her ears.

Or she could step back and make herself laugh at the mess she'd volunteered to put right. Squaring her shoulders, she chose the latter route. "There's not a single coffee cart on one corner in all of Eden Falls. And they've never heard of an all-night drugstore."

Haley laughed. "I'd send you a care package, but you'll probably be gone by the time it could get there. Any sign of the prodigal daughter?"

"Rachel? Not a hint. As near as I can tell, she actually took off about three months ago."

"Ouch. You guys really *don't* talk to each other, do you? But didn't your mother just tell you last week?"

"Exactly," Kat said grimly, not bothering to recite the hundreds of reasons she didn't keep in touch with her sister. "Mama didn't want to worry me, or so she says." Kat wouldn't have worried about Rachel. Not for one single, solitary second. Getting *enraged* with her, now that was something else entirely….

"Do they have any idea where she is?"

"She sends my niece postcards. The last one arrived two weeks ago, from New Orleans. A picture of a fan dancer on the front, and postage due."

Haley clicked her tongue. "She really is a piece of work, isn't she?"

Kat sighed. "The thing is, I don't even care what she does with her own life. I just hate seeing the effect it has on my parents. And Jenny, too. She's not a bad kid, but she hasn't had any structure in her life for so long that she doesn't even know *how* to be good."

"How much longer are you staying?"

That was the sixty-four-thousand-dollar question, wasn't it? "I'm not sure. At first, I thought that I could only stand a week here, at most."

"But now?"

"Now I'm realizing that there's more work to take care of than I thought there was. Mama's dance studio has been a bit…ignored since Daddy got sick."

"I thought your sister was taking care of all that."

"I'll give you a moment, to think about the logic of that statement." Over the years, Kat had vented to Haley plenty of times about Rachel. "I've got my goals in place, though. Rye should be able to get everything pulled together in another week or so. Ten days at most."

"Rye?" There were a hundred questions pumped into the single syllable and more than one blatantly indecent suggestion. Kat's heart pounded harder, and she glanced toward the hallway where Rye was working.

"Don't I wish," Kat said, doing her best to sound bored. Haley had been intent on making Kat forget about her disastrous relationship with Adam; her roommate had even threatened to set up an online dating profile for her. Haley would be head over heels with the *idea* of Rye Harmon, even though she'd never met the guy. Trying to seem breezy and dismissive, Kat said, "Just one of the locals. A handyman."

But that wasn't the truth. Not exactly. Rye had driven down from Richmond that morning, to take care of the studio's plumbing. And he wasn't just a handyman—he was a contractor. A contractor who was taking her project quite seriously…

"Mmm," Haley said. "Does he have any power tools?"

"Haley!" Kat squawked at the suggestive tone.

"Fine. If you're not going to share any intimate details, then I'm going to head out for Master Class."

A jolt of longing shot through Kat, and she glared at the paneled wall of the studio office. She had really been looking forward to the six-week Master Class session taught by one of Russia's most prominent ballerinas. She pushed down her disappointment, though. It didn't have anything to do with her being trapped here in Virginia. In fact, she would have felt even worse to be out of commission in New York, completely surrounded by an ideal that she couldn't achieve.

"I want to hear all about it!" she said, and she almost sounded enthusiastic for her friend.

"Every word," Haley vowed. They promised to talk later in the week, and Kat cradled the phone.

Her conversation with Haley had left her restless, painfully aware of everything she was missing back home. She wanted to dance. Or at least stretch out at the barre.

But there was other work to complete first. She sighed and sat at the desk, which was still overflowing with coffee-stained papers. Even if Rachel *had* maintained perfect records, they'd be impossible to locate in this blizzard. Tightening her core muscles, Kat got to work.

* * *

Two hours later, she could see clear physical evidence of her hard labor. Raising her chin, Kat clutched the last pile of sorted papers, tapping the edges against the glass surface of the newly cleaned desk. Pens stood at attention in a plastic cylinder. Paper clips were corralled in a circular dish. A stapler and a tape dispenser toed the line, ready to do service. The entire office smelled of lemon and ammonia—sharp, clean smells that spurred Kat toward accomplishing even more of her goals.

Next up: the computer. She had to find out if any of the files could be salvaged, if there was any way to access the hard drive and its list of classes, of students.

She frowned as she glanced at her watch. She could call Amanda and ask for a ride to the tiny computer shop on Main Street. But she was pretty sure Amanda was taking an accounting class over at the community college, taking advantage of her flexible teaching schedule. There was Susan, of course, but Kat wasn't certain that she could deflect her mother again. Susan would almost definitely insist on coming into the studio, and then she'd discover the water damage, the plumbing problems, the utter chaos that Rachel had left behind.

Not to mention the bank account. Kat still dreaded stopping by the bank on Water Street, finding out just how short the studio's account really was.

She sighed. She'd been cleaning up after her sister for twenty-four years. It never got any easier.

Well, there *was* another option for dealing with the computer. There was an able-bodied man working just down the hall. An able-bodied man with a shining silver pickup truck. Firming her resolve, Kat marched down to the bathroom.

She found Rye in the second stall, wedged into an awkward position between the toilet and the wall. He was shaking his head as she entered, and she was pretty sure that the words he was muttering would not be fit for little Jenny's ears—or the ears of any Morehouse Dance Academy students, either. He scowled down at the water cutoff with a ferocity that should have shocked the chrome into immediate obedience.

"Oh!" Kat said in surprise. "I'll come back later."

Rye pushed himself up into a sitting position. "Sorry," he said. "I don't usually sound like a sailor while I work."

"Some jobs require strong language," Kat said, quoting one of the stagehands at the National. "Seriously, I'll let you get back to that. It was nothing important. I'm sorry I interrupted."

"I'll always welcome an interruption from you."

There was that blush again. Rye could honestly say that he hadn't been trying to sweet-talk Kat; he had just spoken the truth, the first thing that came to mind.

That rosy tint on her cheeks, though, made her look like she was a kid. The ice princess ballerina melted away so quickly, leaving behind the girl who had been such an eager dancer, such an enthusiastic artist. He wondered what they had taught her at that fancy high school in New York City. How had they channeled her spirit, cutting off her sense of humor, her spirit of adventure? Because the Kat Morehouse he had known had been quiet, determined, focused. But she had known how to laugh.

This Kat Morehouse looked like she had all the cares of the world balanced on her elegant shoulders. He was pleased that he had made her blush again. Maybe he could even make her smile. A smile would make the whole day worthwhile, balance out the drive down from Richmond, the day spent away from Harmon Contracting business.

"What's up?" he asked, climbing to his feet. The flange was frozen shut. He was going to have to turn the water off at its source, then cut out the difficult piece.

She cleared her throat. It was obviously difficult for her to say whatever she was thinking. "I just wondered if you could drive me down to Main Street. I need to take in the computer, to see if they can salvage anything from the hard drive."

Huh. Why should it be so difficult for her to ask a favor? Didn't people help each other out, up in New York? He fished in his pocket and pulled out his key ring. "Here. Take the truck. That'll give me a chance to talk to this thing the way I really need to."

Kat backed away as if he were handing her a live snake. She knew he didn't mean anything by the casual offer of the keys. He wasn't trying to make her feel uncomfortable, abnormal. But as the fluorescent light glinted off the brass keys, all she could hear was Jenny's querulous voice asking, "But why *can't* Aunt Kat drive?"

She cleared her throat and reminded herself that she had a perfectly good excuse. It would have been a waste of her time to get behind the wheel in New York—time that she had spent perfecting her arabesque, mastering her pirouettes. "I can't drive," she said flatly. She saw a question flash in his eyes, and she immediately added, "It's not like I've lost my license or anything. I never had one."

"Never—" he started to say, but then he seemed to piece together the puzzle. "Okay. Give me a minute to wash up, and we can head there together."

"Thank you," she said, and a flood of gratitude tinted the words. She was grateful for more than his agreeing to run the errand with her. She appreciated the fact that he hadn't pushed the matter, that he hadn't forced her to go into any details.

It felt odd to watch as Rye lifted the computer tower from beneath the desk in the office. It was strange to follow him out to the truck. She was used to being the person who did things, the woman who executed the action plan. But she had to admit she would have had a hard time handling the heavy computer and the studio door, all while keeping her balance with her walking boot.

Rye settled the computer in the back of the truck, nestling it in a bed of convenient blankets. She started to hobble toward the passenger door, but he stopped her with a single word: "Nope."

She turned to face him, squinting a little in the brilliant spring sun. "What?"

"Why don't you get behind the wheel?"

So much for gratitude that he hadn't pressed the issue. She felt iron settle over her tone. "I told you. I don't know how to drive."

"No time like the present. I'm a good teacher. I've taught five siblings."

A stutter of panic rocketed through Kat's gut. She wasn't about to show Rye how incompetent she was, how unsuited to life in Eden Falls. She forced a semblance of calm into her words. "Maybe one of them will drive me, then."

Rye's voice was gentle. Kind. "It's not that difficult. I promise. You don't have to be afraid."

Kat did not get afraid. She leaped from the stage into a partner's arms. She let herself be tossed through the air, all limbs extended. She spun herself in tight, orchestrated circles until any ordinary woman would have collapsed from dizziness. "Fine," she snapped. But her spine was ice by the time she reached the driver's door.

With her long legs, she didn't need to move the seat up. She fastened her seat belt, tugging the cloth band firmly, and she glared at Rye until he did the same. She put her hands on the steering wheel, gripping tightly as she tried to slow her pounding heart. The muscles in her arms were rigid, and her legs felt like boards.

"Relax," Rye said beside her. "You're going to do fine."

"You say that now," she muttered. "But what are you going to say when I crash your truck?"

"I know that's not going to happen."

She wished that she had his confidence. She stared at the dashboard, as if she were going to control the vehicle solely through the power of her mind.

"Relax," he said again. "Seriously. Take a deep breath. And exhale…"

Well, that was one thing she could do. She'd always been able to control her body, to make it do her bidding. She breathed into the bottom of her lungs, holding the air for a full count of five, before letting it go. Alas, the tension failed to flow away.

Rye reached over and touched her right leg. Already on edge, Kat twitched as if he'd used a live electric wire. "Easy," he said, flattening his palm against her black trousers. She could feel the heat of his palm, the weight of each finger. Nervous as she was, she found his touch soothing. Relaxing. Compelling.

Leaving his hand in place, Rye said, "The pedal on the right is gas. The one on the left is the brake. You'll shift your foot between them. You want to be gentle—I told my brothers to pretend that there were eggs beneath the pedals."

He lifted his hand, and her leg was suddenly chilled. She wanted to protest, wanted him to touch her again, but she knew that she was being ridiculous. Any fool could see that she was just trying to delay the inevitable driving lesson.

"Put your foot on the brake," he said. "Go ahead. You can't hurt anything. I promise."

I promise. He was so sure of himself. He had so much faith in her. She wanted to tell him that he was wrong, that he was mistaken, that she didn't know the rules for driving a car. She didn't have a system. Tenuously, though, she complied with the instruction. He nodded, then said, "Good. Now, take this."

She watched him select a key, a long silver one with jagged teeth on either side. He dangled it in front of her until she collected it, willing her hand to stop shaking, to stop jangling all the other keys together. He nodded toward the ignition, and she inserted the key, completing the action after only two false starts.

"See?" he said. "I told you this was easy."

"Piece of cake," she muttered, sounding like a prisoner on the way to her own execution.

Rye chuckled and said, "Go ahead. Turn it. Start the truck."

"I—I don't know how."

"Exactly the same way you open the lock on a door.

You do that all the time, up in New York, don't you? It's the exact same motion."

Tightening her elbow against her side to still her trembling, she bit on her lower lip. Millions of people drove every single day. People younger than she was. People without her discipline. She was just being stupid—like the time that she'd been afraid to try the fish dives in *Sleeping Beauty.*

She turned the key.

The truck purred to life, shuddering slightly as the engine kicked in. Her hand flew off the key, but Rye only laughed, catching her fingers before she could plant them in her lap. He guided them to the gearshift, covering her hand with his own. His palm felt hot against her flesh, like sunshine pooling on black velvet. She thought about pulling her hand away, about blowing on her fingers so that they weren't quite icicles, but she was afraid to call even more attention to herself.

"The truck is in Park. You're going to shift it into Drive." His fingers tightened around hers, almost imperceptibly. The motion made her glance at his face. His black eyes were steady on hers, patient, waiting. "You can do this, Kat," he said, and the words vibrated through her. She didn't know if her sudden breathlessness was because of his touch, or because she was one step closer to driving the truck.

She shifted the gear.

"There you go." He crooned to her as if she were a frightened kitten. "Now, shift your foot to the gas. The truck will roll forward just a little—that's the power of the engine pulling it, without giving it any fuel. When you're ready, push down on the gas pedal to really make it move." He waited a moment, but she could not move. "Come on," he urged. "Let's go."

She looked out the windshield, her heart pounding wildly. “Here?” she managed to squeak.

“We’re in a parking lot. There’s not another vehicle around. No lights. Nothing for you to hit.” He turned the words into a soothing poem.

He was being so patient. So kind. She had to reward his calm expectation, had to show him that his confidence was not misplaced. She tensed the muscles in her calf and eased her foot off the brake. As he had predicted, the truck edged forward, crunching on gravel with enough volume that she slammed back onto the brake.

Rye laughed as he slid his thumb underneath his seat belt, loosening the band where it had seized tight against his shoulder. “That’s why they make seat belts,” he said. “Try it again.”

This time, it was easier to desert the brake. She let the truck roll forward several feet, getting used to the feel of the engine vibrating through the steering wheel, up her arms, into the center of her body. She knew that she had to try the gas pedal next, had to make the silver monster pick up speed. Steeling herself, she plunged her foot down on the gas pedal.

The truck jumped forward like a thoroughbred out of the gate. Panicked, she pounded on the brake, throwing herself forward with enough momentum that her teeth clicked shut.

“Easy, cowboy!” Rye ran a hand through his chestnut curls. “Remember—like an egg beneath the pedal.”

She set her jaw with grim determination. She could do this. It was a simple matter of controlling her body, of making her muscles meet her demands. She just needed to tense her foot, tighten her calf. She just needed to lower her toes, that much…that much…a little more….

The truck glided forward, like an ocean liner pulling away from a dock. She traveled about ten yards before she braked to a smooth stop. Again, she told herself, and she repeated the maneuver three times.

"Very good," Rye said, and she realized that she'd been concentrating so hard she had almost forgotten the man beside her. "Now you just have to add in steering."

She saw that they were nearing the end of the parking lot. It was time to turn, or to learn how to drive in Reverse. She rapidly chose the lesser of the two evils. Controlling the steering wheel was just another matter of muscle coordination. Just another matter of using her body, of adapting her dance training. Concentrating with every strand of her awareness, she eased onto the gas and turned the truck in a sweeping circle.

Rye watched Kat gain control over the truck, becoming more comfortable with each pass around the parking lot. He couldn't remember ever seeing a woman who held herself in check so rigidly. Maybe it was her dancer's training, or maybe it was true terror about managing two tons of metal. He longed to reach out, to smooth the tension from her arms, from the thigh that had trembled beneath his palm.

Mentally, he snorted at himself. He hadn't lied when he told her that he'd taught each of his siblings. They'd been easy to guide, though—each had been eager to fly the nest, to gain the freedom of wheels in a small Virginia town.

Suddenly, he flashed on a memory of his own youthful days. He'd been driving his first truck, the one that he had bought with his own money, saved from long summers working as a carpenter's apprentice. He'd just graduated from college, just started dating Rachel Morehouse.

She hadn't been afraid, the way that Kat was. Rachel had tricked him with a demon's kiss, digging into his pockets when he was most distracted. She had taken his keys and run to his truck, barely giving him time to haul himself into the passenger side before she had raced the engine. She had laughed as she sped toward the county road, flooring the old Ford until it shuddered in surrender. Rachel had laughed at Rye's shouted protest, jerking the wheel back and forth, crossing the center line on the deserted nighttime stretch of asphalt. When a truck crested a distant rise, Rachel had taken the headlights as a challenge; she had pulled back into their own lane only at the last possible instant.

He had sworn every curse he knew, hollering until Rachel finally pulled onto the crumbling dirt shoulder. He'd stomped around the truck, glaring as she slid across the bench seat with mock meekness. He'd dropped her back at her house, pointedly ignoring her pursed lips, her expectation of a good-night kiss.

And he'd broken up with her the next morning.

He would never have believed that Rachel and Kat were related, if their faces hadn't betrayed them. Their personalities were opposites—a tornado and an ice storm.

He cleared his throat, certain that his next words would lock another sheet of Kat's iron control into place. "All right. Let's go out on the road." He wasn't disappointed; she clenched her jaw tight like a spring-bound door slamming shut.

"I can't do that," Kat said. It was one thing to drive in an abandoned parking lot. It was another to take the truck out onto the open road. There would be other drivers there. Innocent pedestrians. Maybe even a dog or two, running off leash. She could cause immeasurable damage out on the road.

"The computer store isn't going to come to you." Rye's laugh made it sound as if he didn't have a care in the world. "Come on, Kat," he cajoled when she stopped in the middle of the parking lot. "What's the worst that can happen?"

"A fifteen-car pileup on Main Street," she said immediately, voicing the least bloody of the images that tormented her.

"There aren't even fifteen cars on the road at this time of day. You're making excuses. Let's go."

There. He'd set their goal—she would drive them to the store. She knew the strategies—she needed to put the truck in gear, to turn out onto Elm Street, to navigate the several blocks down to Main. She was familiar with the rules, had observed them all her life: stay on the right side of the road, keep to the speed limit, observe all the stop signs.

At least there weren't any traffic lights, dangerous things that could change from green to red in a heartbeat, with scarcely a stop at yellow.

She took a deep breath and pulled onto Elm.

For the first couple of blocks, she felt like a computer, processing a million different facts, arriving at specific conclusions. She had never realized how many details there were in the world around her, how many things moved. But she completed her first turn without incident. She even followed Rye's instruction when he suggested that she take a roundabout path, that she experiment with more right turns, and a single, terrifying left.

She wasn't thinking when Rye told her to take one

more left turn; she didn't realize that they were on the county road until after the steering wheel had spun back to center. There was oncoming traffic here—a half-dozen cars whooshed by at speeds that made her cringe.

"Give it a bit more gas," Rye said. "You need to get up to forty."

She wanted to yell at him, to complain that he had tricked her onto this dangerous stretch of road, but she knew that she should not divert her attention. She wanted to tell him that forty was impossibly fast, but she knew that he was right. She could see the black-and-white speed limit sign—she presented more of a danger to them, creeping along, than she would if she accelerated. She hunched a little closer to the steering wheel, as if that motion would give her precious seconds to respond to any disasters.

Maybe it was her concentration that kept her from being aware of the eighteen-wheeler that roared by, passing her on the left. One moment, she could dart a glance out at freshly tilled fields, at rich earth awaiting new crops. The next, a wall of metal screamed beside her, looming over her like a mountain. She thought that she was pounding on the brake, but she hadn't shifted her foot enough; the pickup leaped forward as she poured on more fuel, looking for all the world like she was trying to race the semi.

The surge terrified her, and she shifted her foot solidly onto the brake. At the same time, the truck cut back into her lane, close enough that the wind of its passing buffeted her vehicle. Kat overcorrected, and for one terrible moment, the pickup slid sideways across the asphalt road. She turned the wheel again, catching the rough edge of the shoulder, and one more twist sent her careening out of control.

The pickup bucked as it caught on the grass at the roadside, and she could do nothing as the vehicle slid into the ditch at the edge of the road. Finally, the brake did its job, and the truck shuddered to a stop. Kat was frozen, unable to lift her hands from the wheel.

Rye reached across and turned the key, killing the idling motor. “Are you okay?” he asked, his voice thick with concern.

“I’m fine,” Kat said automatically. *I’m mortified. I nearly got us killed. I’m a danger to myself and others.* “I’m fine,” she repeated. “How about you?”

Rye eased a hand beneath his seat belt once more. “I’m okay.”

“I’m so sorry,” Kat said, and her voice shook suspiciously. “I don’t know how that happened. One minute everything was fine, and then—” She cut herself off. “I could have killed us.”

“No blood, no foul,” Rye said.

Kat burst into tears.

“Hey,” he said. “Come on. You can drive out of this ditch. We don’t even need to get the truck towed.”

She nodded, as if she agreed with everything he said. At the same time, though, she was thinking that she was never going to drive again. She was never going to put herself in danger—herself or any innocent passenger. What if Susan had been with her? Or Mike, in his weakened state? What if, God forbid, Jenny had been sitting there?

She fumbled for the door handle and flung herself out of the truck. Rye met her by the hood, settling his firm hands on her biceps. “What’s wrong?” he asked.

"I can't do this!" Her words came out more a shout than a statement.

"You've just been shaken up. You know the drill—back up on the horse that threw you."

"I'm not a rodeo rider."

"No, but you're a dancer. And I have to believe that you stick with adversity on the stage better than this."

She shook her head. This wasn't dance. This wasn't her career. This was—literally—life or death. She couldn't think of working anymore for the day. "Please, Rye. Will you just drive me back to Rachel's?"

He looked at her for a long time, but she refused to meet his eyes. Instead, she hugged herself, trying to get her breathing back under control, trying to get her body to believe that it wasn't in imminent danger.

At last, Rye shrugged and walked around the cab of the truck, sliding into the driver's seat with a disgruntled sigh. Kat took her place meekly, refusing to look at him as he turned the key in the ignition. The truck started up easily enough, and it only took a little manhandling to get it up the side of the ditch, back onto the road.

Rye knew that he should press the matter. He should make Kat get back behind the wheel. She had to get over her fear. If she walked away from driving now, she'd probably never return.

But who was he to force her to do anything? He was just a guy she'd met ten years before, a guy who lived in Richmond, who kept coming home to a little town in the middle of nowhere, because he couldn't remember how to say no.

Kat was the one who'd had the guts to leave for real. She was the one who'd gone all the way to New York, far enough that it had taken a real disaster to bring her back to Eden Falls. Not the piddling demands that his family made on him day after day.

He tightened his grip on the steering wheel. It had been a mistake to agree to renovate the dance studio. He was building his own life away from Eden Falls. He couldn't let the first woman who'd caught his attention in months destroy his determination to make Harmon Contracting a success.

But he'd already done that, hadn't he? He'd already roped himself into finishing that damned plumbing job. And repairing the ceiling leak wasn't going to be easy, either. And he had a really bad feeling about what he'd find when he really looked at the hardwood floor.

He glanced over at Kat. What did Gran always say? "In for a penny, in for a pound." He'd started teaching Kat how to drive, and he'd let her scare herself half to death. She was his responsibility now. It was up to him to convince her to change her mind. To find the nerve to get back in the truck—if not today, then tomorrow. Wednesday at the latest.

He barely realized that he was committing himself to spending half a week away from Richmond.

Kat hopped out as soon as Rye pulled into the driveway. She didn't want to look at the weeds, at the lawn that was impossibly exhausted, even though it was only spring. "Thanks," she said as she slammed her door, and she tried to ignore the hitch in her stride as her boot slipped on the gritty walkway.

Rye didn't take the hint. He followed her to the front door, like a boy walking her home from a date.

Now, why did she think of that image? Rye wasn't her boyfriend. And they most definitely had not been out on a date. Besides, it was broad daylight, the middle of the afternoon.

She opened the unlocked door with an easy twist of her wrist. Not daring to meet his eyes, she pasted a cheery smile on her face. "Thanks for all your help at the studio this morning. Everything's coming along much faster than I thought it would." She stepped back and started to close the door.

Rye caught the swinging oak with the flat of his palm. "Kat," he said, but before he could continue, she saw him wince. He tried to hide the motion, but she was a dancer. She was an expert on all the ways that a body can mask pain.

"You *are* hurt!"

"It's nothing major," he said. "My shoulder's just a little sore from the seat belt."

"Come in here!" She opened the door wide, leaving him no opportunity to demur.

"I'm fine," he said.

She marched him into the kitchen, switching on the overhead light. "Go ahead," she said, nodding. "Take off your shirt. I need to see how bad this is."

Rye shook his head. He was used to his mother clucking over him like a nervous hen. His sisters bossed him around. And now Kat was giving him orders like a drill sergeant. From long experience, he knew he'd be better off to comply now, while he still had some dignity intact. He undid the top two buttons of his work shirt before tugging the garment over his head.

That motion *did* twinge his shoulder, and he was surprised to see the darkening bruise that striped his chest. The seat belt had done its job admirably, keeping him safe from true harm, but he'd have a mark for a few days.

Kat's lips tightened into a frown. "Ice," she said. She turned toward the pantry with military precision, collecting a heavy-duty plastic bag. The freezer yielded enough ice cubes to satisfy her, and then she twisted a cotton dishrag around the makeshift cold pack.

"I don't think—"

"I do." She cut him off. "Believe me, I've had enough bruises that I know how to treat them."

He didn't want to think about that. He didn't want to think about her body being hurt, her creamy skin mottled with evidence of her harsh profession. As if he were accepting some form of punishment, he let her place the ice pack over his chest.

"That's cold," he said ruefully.

"That's the idea." There wasn't any venom in her retort, though. Instead, her hands were gentle as she moved the ice, as she stepped closer, maneuvering the bag until it lay right along his collarbone. The action shifted the midnight curtain of her hair, and he caught a whiff of apricots and honey. Without thinking, he tangled his fingers in the smooth strands, brushing against her nape as he pulled her close. He heard her breath catch in her throat, but she didn't try to edge away. He found her lips and claimed them with his own, a sweet kiss, chaste as schoolkids on a playground.

"There," he whispered against her cheek. "That's a little warmer."

The rasp of his afternoon scruff against her face made Kat catch her breath. Her entire body was suddenly aware of the man before her, aware of him as a *man,* not just a collection of parts that could be manipulated into an entire encyclopedia of ballet poses. Her lips tingled where he had kissed her, ignited as if she had eaten an unexpected jalapeno.

Without making a conscious decision, she shifted her arms, settling into the long lines of his body. She felt his ribs against hers, measured the steady beat of his heart. She matched his legs to her own, shifting her thighs so that she could feel the solid strength of him. He chuckled as he found her lips again, and this time when he kissed her, she yielded to the gentle touch of his tongue.

Velvet against velvet, then, the soft pressure of eager exploration. She heard a sound, an urgent mew, and she realized with surprise that it rose from her own throat. His fingers, tangled in her hair, spread wide and cradled her head. She leaned back against the pressure, glorying in the sensation of strength and power and solid, firm control.

He lowered his lips to the arch of her neck, finding the solid drumbeat of her pulse. One flick of his tongue, another, and her knees grew weak, as if she had danced for an entire Master Class.

Danced. That was what she did. That was what she lived for.

She couldn't get involved with a man in Eden Falls—or Richmond, either, for that matter. She was only visiting; she was heading north as soon as she straightened things out in her parents' home, as soon as Rachel came back to keep an eye on Jenny.

Kat steeled herself and took a step away.

"I think heat might be better than ice for my shoulder," Rye said, a teasing smile on his lips. He laced his fingers between hers.

Those fingers!

Kat remonstrated with herself to focus on what was important. She freed her hand and took another step back. "Ice is better for bruises." She couldn't avoid the confusion that melted into Rye's gaze. "I—I'm sorry," she stammered. "I…" She wasn't sure what to say, didn't know how to explain. "I shouldn't have let myself get carried away."

Carried away. He hadn't begun to carry her away yet.

"I'm sorry," she said again, and this time he heard something that sounded suspiciously like tears, laced beneath her words. "I shouldn't have done that. I'm only here for a few… I can't… I belong in New York."

You belong here, he wanted to say. *Right beside me.* And then he wanted to prove that to her, in no uncertain terms.

But he had no doubt that those words would terrify her. She'd be right back to where she'd been in the ditch—rigid with fear. Rye forced himself to take a steadying breath. To let her go.

"Go ahead," she said after her own shaky breath. "Take the ice pack. You can give me back the towel at the studio, tomorrow."

Rye shrugged, resigning himself to her decision. "Yes ma'am," he said. "But aren't you forgetting something?"

She'd forgotten a lot. She'd forgotten that she was here to help out her parents. Her sister. Her niece. She'd forgotten that she lived in New York, that she had a life—a *career*—far away from Virginia. "What?" she croaked.

"You have a broken computer in the back of my pickup truck."

"Oh!" She hesitated, uncertain of what to do.

"Don't worry," he said, and she sensed that he was laughing at her. "I'll take it down to the shop."

She frowned, and her fingers moved involuntarily toward his shoulder. "But get someone else to lift it out of the truck."

"Yes, ma'am," he said again, but the glint in his eyes said that he was anything but a respectful schoolboy. She showed him to the door before she lost her resolve.

As she heard the truck come to life in the driveway, she shook her head in disbelief. Obviously, she'd been traumatized by her disaster of a driving lesson. She'd been terrified by the thought of dying in a ditch, and the adrenaline had overflowed here in the kitchen. She'd been overtaken by the basest of all her animal instincts.

Well, there was nothing to be done but to rein in those physical responses. Goals. Strategies. Rules. She grabbed a notepad from the drawer beneath the phone and started to revise her schedule for finishing up the studio renovation, for getting all the class records in order for the new term. If she pushed herself hard, she could be out of Eden Falls in one more week.

When she'd finished her schedule, though, she leaned against the counter. Her fingers rose to her lips, starting them tingling all over again. Maybe she'd been too optimistic when she wrote up that list. Seven days wasn't a lot, not to complete everything that needed to be done, and to keep an eye on Jenny, too. Maybe she should plan on staying in Eden Falls a little longer. Ten days. Two weeks. There was no telling *what* might happen in two full weeks.

She laughed at herself as she tore up her list. The renovation would take as long as it took.

And she had to admit—that wasn't a terrible thing. No, it most definitely was not a terrible thing to spend some more time with Rye Harmon. She shook her head and thought about how Haley would tease her when Kat explained why she was staying in Eden Falls a little longer than she had planned at first.

Chapter Four

Kat ushered Susan to the kitchen table, telling her mother to sit down and relax. "You don't need to wait on me like I'm a houseguest," Kat insisted. "I can put the teakettle on to boil."

Still, Susan fussed. "I just want you to rest that foot. You need it to heal, if you're going to get back to New York. Does it still hurt a lot?"

Kat shrugged. She didn't pay a lot of attention to pain. It was all part of her job. She took down two teacups and matching saucers, enjoying the look of the old-fashioned china that had once belonged to her grandmother. "Don't worry about me," she chided Susan. "You have enough on your plate."

"Your father looks so much better. I cannot tell you how much it means, that he's finally able to get a full night's sleep. Jenny is a sweetheart—she's so excited to be reading a book to her Pop-pop right now. But she is a *busy* child."

Busy was one word for her. Spoiled rotten was another. Kat was tired of playing policewoman, constantly telling her niece what to do and what not to do. Just the night before, Kat had caught herself complaining to Haley, saying that Jenny had been raised by wolves. Okay, that was an exaggeration. But not much of one.

But then, just when Kat thought that she had exhausted her last dram of patience with her niece, she was forced to realize that Jenny was just a little girl—a very little girl, who was working through one of the greatest challenges of her short life. Only that morning, after finishing her bowl of corn flakes, Jenny had looked up with such transparent sorrow in her eyes that Kat's heart had almost broken. "When is my mommy coming home?" Jenny had asked.

For once, her lower lip wasn't trembling because she wanted sugary cereal for breakfast, or a plate full of syrupy carbs, or some other disaster for her growing body. Instead, she was trying very hard to be stoic.

Kat had pushed down her own emotions, all of her anger and frustration with Rachel. "Soon," she'd said. "I hope she'll be home soon." She'd given Jenny a brisk hug and then sent her toward the toy chest, telling the child that she needed to collect all the scattered crayons at the bottom of the container, returning them to a plastic bucket neatly labeled for the purpose.

Hard work. That was what had carried Kat through the loneliness and confusion of being on her own in New York. That was the only prescription that she could offer Jenny now.

Standing in Susan's kitchen, Kat rescued the teakettle just before it shrieked. She filled the pot and ferried it over to the table before turning to snatch up a plate of gingersnaps. Somehow, though, her booted foot slipped on the worn linoleum. She caught her balance at the last possible second, but the china plate shattered on the floor.

"Oh, no!" she cried. "I am so sorry! I don't know how I could be so clumsy."

Susan rose from her chair.

"No," Kat cried. "You're only wearing your house shoes! I don't want you to cut your feet. Just sit down." She limped over to the laundry room, quickly procuring a dustpan and broom. Berating herself the entire time, she brushed up the debris, consigning shattered china and dirty cookies to the trash. "Mama, I am so sorry. I can't believe I did that. Here I am, trying to help, and I just make everything worse!"

"Nonsense," Susan said. "It was an accident. Nothing to get so flustered about. Now, sit down, dear, and pour yourself a cup of tea."

Kat complied, strangely soothed by her mother's calm. Susan pushed forward the sugar bowl, but Kat merely shook her head. She hadn't added sugar to her tea since she was younger than Jenny was now.

"Mama, I'll go online. I can find a plate to replace that one—there are websites to help people locate old china patterns."

"Don't worry about it."

"But it belonged to your mother!"

"And she'd be very upset to see you so concerned about breaking it. Please, Kat. Not another word."

Still not satisfied that she'd made appropriate amends, Kat fiddled with her teacup. She avoided her mother's eagle eye as she turned the saucer so that the floral pattern matched the cup precisely.

"I worry about you," Susan said, after Kat had finally taken a sip.

"That's the last thing I want, Mama! I'm here so that you don't have to worry. That's the whole idea!"

"And you're doing wonders, keeping an eye on Jenny and getting everything ready for the first summer classes at the studio."

Kat felt guilty about that. She still hadn't told her mother about the condition of the studio, about the utter lack of students for the spring session. Four times in the past week, she'd started to broach the matter of the bank account, of the money that Rachel had not accounted for during the winter term. Each time, though, Kat had chickened out, dreading the moment when she destroyed her mother's fragile peace of mind. Kat's cowardice was certain to catch up with her. There couldn't be much more time before Susan's life got back to normal, before she found the wherewithal to check her financial statements. Who knew? She might even stop by the columned bank building on Water Street, learn about the disaster firsthand. In public.

And that disaster would be made much worse, because Kat was involved. Kat, whom Susan expected to run things smoothly. Kat, who had never been irresponsible like Rachel. Every day that Kat remained silent was a horrible, festering lie.

She steeled herself to make the admission. After all, if she said something today, then she might still be able to help Susan to recover. Kat could stay on another week or so, help sort out the finances with the help of a sympathetic—or, at the very least, a professional—banker.

She took a deep breath, but Susan spoke before Kat could confess. "Sweetheart, it's *you* that I worry about.

I wish that you could learn to relax a little. To sit back and enjoy life." Susan shook her head, running her finger along the edge of her saucer. "You've always been such a grown-up, even when you were a very little girl. I could leave a slice of pie on the kitchen table, right between you and Rachel, and I always knew that *you* would have the self-restraint to eat your vegetables first." Susan smiled fondly, as if she could still see her twins sitting at her dining room table. "Sometimes, I wish that you still played Magic Zoo."

"Magic Zoo?"

"Don't you remember? It was a game that you invented, to entertain Rachel when she was recovering from that broken arm, the summer when you were six years old. The two of you and your cousin Amanda played it every single day!"

"I have no idea what you're talking about."

"Of course you do! You had all sorts of elaborate rules. Each of you girls chose an animal, and then you drew crayons out of a bucket. Each color crayon corresponded to a different magical food. The foods gave you special powers—you could be a flying horse, or a talking elephant, things like that. The three of you played it for hours on end."

Kat blinked. She had absolutely no recollection of such make-believe games. She couldn't imagine spending "hours on end" with Rachel—not without descending into screaming matches. Maybe Amanda had been a full-time referee?

Susan sighed. "I guess I'm just saying that sometimes you need to be more of a kid. Don't worry as much. Take whatever happens and just roll with it. Forget that you're an adult, for just a little while."

"Like Rachel does, every day." Kat said the words before she could stop herself, but even she was surprised by how bitter they sounded.

Susan's face grew even more serious. "Yes. If I were queen of the universe, I would give Rachel some of your maturity. And I would give you a little of her... what's that phrase? The French one? Joie de vivre?"

"I don't think it's joie de vivre to stay away from home when your own parents, your own *daughter,* need you. When was the last time you heard from Rachel? Do you have any idea when she's planning on coming home?"

"A postcard arrived just yesterday. It had a picture of the Eiffel Tower, but not the real one. She was in Las Vegas. At least that's where the postmark was from."

A postcard, sent what? Three or four days ago? Rachel had to know the phone number here at the house, the one that hadn't changed since they were children. She could have managed to call home, at least once. Responded to the text messages that Kat had sent. She obviously didn't want to be found. She wasn't ready to face up to her adult responsibilities.

Kat fought to keep her voice even. "I'm sure she's very happy there."

"Don't judge your sister," Susan said. "She's never had a skill like yours. She's never known what it means to succeed."

Kat bit back an acid response. Rachel had been given every opportunity Kat had; she had enjoyed the exact same chances in life. Even now, she could come back to Eden Falls, raise her daughter, do the right thing. She could help her parents and prove she was a responsible adult. But she'd rather play in Vegas, drawing out her childhood for countless more years.

Susan sighed. "I sometimes think being twins messed everything up for you girls. Each of you was supposed to get a mixture of responsibility and fun. Of adulthood and childhood. Instead, all the grown-up qualities ended up with you and all the rest…" She let her words drift for a moment, and when she continued she softened her words with a smile. "I want you to have fun, Kat. Go stomping in mud puddles for a change. Somersault down a hill. Don't always think about what something means for your future, for your career."

"Mama, I *need* to worry about my career. I'm a dancer. I don't have much longer to prove myself to the company director."

Susan shook her head. "Sometimes I wonder if we did the right thing, sending you to New York."

"How can you say that?" Kat's voice was etched with horror. She couldn't imagine what her life would have been like without New York. Without dancing.

"Don't look so shocked," Susan murmured. "Your father and I are very proud of you. But sometimes I worry that we took too much away from you by pushing you so hard. You had to grow up so young. You never got a chance to play, to make mistakes. You never even went to your senior prom. We just wanted you to be happy."

"I *was* happy," Kat said. As if to convince herself of the truth behind her words, she went on. "I *am* happy, Mama. The day I stop being happy dancing is the day I'll leave the company. I promise." Susan still looked doubtful. As if to finish the conversation, once and for all, Kat leaned over and gave her mother a hug. "I love you, Mama. You and Daddy, too. And I love everything that you've let me become. Now, can I freshen up your cup of tea?"

She pretended not to see the proud tears glinting in Susan's eyes.

A couple of hours later, after a lunch of tomato soup and grilled cheese sandwiches, Kat could see that her father was tiring. "Come on," she said to Jenny. "Let's go down to the park. Run off some of your energy."

Susan smiled gratefully as she saw them out the door. "Are you sure you're all right walking there?"

"It's only two blocks," Kat assured her. "That's why they call this a walking boot." She made a point of keeping her gait even as they made their way down the street.

When they arrived at the park, it seemed as if half of Eden Falls was taking advantage of yet another unseasonably warm April day. Children screamed with delight on the swings, and a pileup of toddlers blocked the bottom of the slide. A group of teenagers sat beneath a cluster of cherry trees, staring up into the cotton candy blossoms, carrying on a passionate discussion about something.

"What's that?" Jenny said, pointing toward a baseball diamond.

Kat narrowed her eyes against the brilliant sunshine. "A T-ball game."

"I love T-ball!" Jenny bounced on her toes, showing more enthusiasm than she had since Kat had come to town. "Can I play? Please? Please?"

"Let's go see." Kat started across the park, watching Jenny as the child raced ahead. Halfway to the playing field, Kat heard the coach call out, "Good job, Jake! Run! Run to first base!"

Kat knew that voice. She'd listened to it at the dance studio, smiled as it interrupted her organizing class records. She'd imagined it, in her dreams, ever since it had teased her in Rachel's kitchen. She met Rye's gaze as Jenny circled back to clutch at her hand.

"Hey," he said, nodding to include both of them. "Kat. Jenny."

"Hello, Mr. Harmon."

Kat smiled at her niece's polite greeting, and she remembered to model her own good behavior. "Mr. Harmon, Jenny was wondering if she could play T-ball with you."

"Absolutely." Rye gestured toward the outfield. "Go out there, between first and second base. You can play right field for us." Jenny trotted out, beaming as if her most secret wish had been granted.

"Thanks," Kat said, less formal now that none of the kids was paying attention. Her heart was skittering in her chest. It had been, what? Two days since she'd seen Rye? Two days since he had completed fixing the plumbing at the studio, and torn out all the rotten ceiling tiles and the damaged flooring. Two days since he had driven off, with the pair of silent cousins he had brought along to help. Or to serve as chaperones.

As if by agreement, Rye and Kat had made sure they did not spend a minute alone together. Not after that searing kiss they'd shared. Not after Kat had reminded herself that she had no time for an Eden Falls relationship.

She had to clear her throat before she could ask, "What are you doing down here? I thought you went back to Richmond Wednesday night!"

Of course he'd gone back to Richmond. He'd gone back to his rented office, to two beige rooms that had somehow shrunk while he'd been in Eden Falls. He'd gone back to his studio apartment, to a bachelor pad that should have been more than adequate for his needs.

He hadn't slept at all that night.

Every time he rolled over, he imagined having another conversation with Kat. Every time he punched his pillow into a more comfortable lump, he remembered another detail of the studio renovation. Every time he threw off his blankets, he thought about how he had let Kat down with the driving lesson, how she had panicked. And how she had warmed to him, afterward.

No.

It had taken him years to fight his way free, to sever enough family ties, enough social obligations, to give himself permission to live and work in Richmond. That whole mess with Marissa—the way he had pinned his hopes on her, on the life he thought they would have together… A white picket fence, two perfect kids and a dog. Until she decided that Hollywood was more glamorous, and she dropped him like a hot potato.

He might have taken too long to come to his senses, but he had finally carved out a life for himself. He could not—*would* not—let a woman drag him back to Eden Falls. Not now. Not when everything was about to break big for him.

Even a woman as intriguing as Kat. *Especially* a woman as intriguing as Kat. Part of her mystique was the fact that she didn't belong in his hometown. After ten years of living on her own, she had become a New Yorker, through and through. She'd be leaving, as soon as her father had recovered.

He'd be an idiot to forfeit his own life plans—again—for a woman who wasn't going to stick around.

But damn, Kat managed to distract him. Over and over again, even when she was a hundred miles away. And now? Standing beside her at the T-ball bleachers? It was all he could do not to cup a hand around her jean-clad hip. All he could do not to twist a strand of her mesmerizing hair around his finger and make a joke or two, draw out a smile on her lips. All he could do not to forget that a couple dozen kids were clamoring on the baseball diamond behind him, waiting for him to step up to the plate as their dedicated coach.

He cleared his throat and answered Kat's question, even though it seemed like a century had passed since she spoke. "I *was* up in Richmond. But something came up, and my brother Noah had to bail on T-ball practice."

"That seems to happen a lot," Kat said, remembering that Rye had filled in for Noah on her first day back in Eden Falls. "Nothing serious, I hope?"

"Her name is Britney."

Kat laughed. "You're a good brother."

"I'm keeping a log. So far he owes me 327 hours of favors. I get gas money and double credit for Saturdays."

"Oh, what else would you be doing today?"

"I'd find something to occupy my time," he said, giving her an appraising glance. There was no mistaking the rumble beneath his words, and her memory flashed back to the feel of him holding her, to the scratch of his jaw as he kissed her. She felt her cheeks grow warm.

"Mr. Harmon!" one of the kids called. "When do we start to play?"

Rye sighed in fake exasperation, careful to keep the

team from hearing him. "Duty calls. And you're going to have to help out, if we let Jenny play."

She gestured to her boot. "I don't think I'm really up to umpire work."

"I've got that covered. Your place is on the bench, behind home plate. Behind me. You get to be head cheerleader."

Kat caught a flicker of Rye's eyebrows, a comic leer as if he were envisioning her in a short skirt, carrying pom-poms. The expression was wiped away before she could even be certain he was teasing her. Laughing, she headed over to her seat, grateful to give her foot a rest.

Enjoying the fresh air outside the studio and—truth be told—the view of Rye's denim-clad backside behind home plate, Kat put her elbows on the bench above her. Stretching out like a long black cat in the heat of the spring sun, she closed her eyes and leaned her head back. She filled her lungs with the aroma of fresh-cut grass, focusing on what Rye was saying to his young players.

He helped one little girl choke up on the bat, instructing her on how to spread her legs for a more balanced stance. The child was not a natural athlete, but he talked her through two wildly missed swings. On the third, she toppled the ball from its plastic stand. "Run, Kaylee!" he shouted. "Run to first! You can make it!"

His enthusiasm for his charges was obvious. Each child improved under his tutelage. Everyone eventually connected the bat to the ball, and some even got a shot past the infield. Soon enough, the teams switched sides, and Kat watched as Jenny came to the plate.

"Okay, Jenny," Rye said. "Oh, you're left-handed? No, don't be embarrassed, I'm left-handed, too. Here, move to the other side of the plate. Now, Jenny—"

"I'm not Jenny."

Kat sat up, wondering what devilment her niece was working now.

"Really?" Rye said. "I was certain that your Aunt Kat told me your name was Jenny."

"I hate that name." Kat started to climb to her feet, ready to tell Jenny to adjust her tone or they'd be heading back home immediately. Before she could speak, though, the little girl whined pitiably, "There are two other Jennys in my class."

Rye nodded. "I guess that would be pretty annoying. I never had anyone else with my name in school. Should I call you Jennifer instead?"

The little girl shook her head. "I'm only Jennifer when I'm in trouble."

Kat started to laugh—her niece was only telling the truth. Rye, though, screwed up his face into a pensive frown. "What should we do, then? How about another nickname?"

"Like what?"

"Jen?"

"There's a Jen at Sunday School."

"Then how about Niffer?"

"Niffer?" She repeated the name like she'd never heard the last two syllables of her own name.

"Do you know anyone else called Niffer?" The child shook her head. "Then what do you say? Should we try it?" Rye was granted a grudging nod. "Okay, then, Niffer. Step up to the plate. Nope, the other side, for lefties. Now focus on the ball. Bring the bat back. And *swing!*"

The bat cracked against the ball, clearly the best shot of the afternoon. The tiny center fielder scrambled to catch the soaring ball, fighting the sunshine in his eyes. Rye shouted, "Go Niffer! Run around the bases!"

Fulfilling her role as head cheerleader, Kat was shouting by the time her niece completed her home run. The kids exploded with excitement, too, both the batting and the fielding teams chanting, "Nif-fer! Nif-fer!"

Obviously recognizing a climactic ending for the game when he saw one, Rye declared the practice over five minutes early, sending the kids off with their appreciative parents. Kat sat up straighter on the bench, watching Rye talk to the other adults. Several ribbed him about filling in for Noah, one telling him that he was taking his best man's duties too far. So, things must be really serious between Noah and…what was her name? Britney.

Rye was absolutely at home with every person he talked to. He shook hands with all the men; he accepted kisses on the cheek from most of the women. Kat supposed that he'd known these people all his life—he had gone to school with them, grown up with them.

She'd gone to school with them, too. Well, four years behind. She should have been every bit as comfortable in Eden Falls as Rye was. After all, how many places were left on earth where someone could leave her front door unlocked to go play T-ball in the park? How many places would band together to fill Susan and Mike's freezer with countless nourishing, home-cooked meals?

Kat was beginning to understand what had kept her parents here all these years. She even caught herself smiling as Rye crossed the diamond, Jenny at his heels.

"Aunt Kat!"

"You looked great out there, Jenny."

"I'm Niffer, now!"

"Niffer," Kat agreed, sternly reminding herself to use the new nickname.

"Can I go climb on the castle?"

"*May* I?" Kat reminded. Grammar rules were just as important as the other rules that Niffer needed to maintain while they lived together.

"*May* I go climb on the castle?"

"Go ahead," Kat said. "But we need to go back to Gram and Pop-pop's house in ten minutes."

Niffer was halfway to the jungle gym before all of the words were out of Kat's mouth. Rye settled on the bench beside her, grunting with mock exhaustion. "They'll wear a man out."

"You're great with them," Kat said. "I never know how to talk to kids."

"Most people think about it too much. It's better to just say what you're thinking."

"Easy for you! I've been living with…Niffer for a week and a half, and that's the first I heard that she didn't like her name. It's like you two share some special bond."

Special bond. Rye tensed at the words and the responsibility that they conjured up. Years ago, he'd worried about just such a "special bond," worried that the then-unborn Niffer was his daughter. Rachel had set him straight in no uncertain terms. If any guy shared a "special bond" with Niffer, with Rachel, it was Josh Barton.

And just as well. Rye could never have taken off for Richmond if he had a daughter here in Eden Falls. The games that Marissa had played, tying him to the town, would have been nothing compared to the bonds of fatherhood.

"She's a good kid," he finally said.

His lingering tension was telling him something, though. His lingering tension, and a couple of sleepless nights. Even if he had no hope for anything long-term with Kat, it was time to man up. Past time, actually. He flashed on the feel of her body pressed close to his in Rachel's kitchen, and he cleared his throat before saying gruffly, "I should tell you. Your sister and I went out a couple of times. It was a long time ago. Five, six years. We were only together for a few weeks."

Kat's face shuttered closed. "Rachel never mentioned anything. We, um, we haven't been close for a very long time."

Rye wanted to kick himself for making Kat pull away like that, for bringing out that guarded look in her eyes. Over the past few days, he'd relived that kitchen kiss so many times. He'd remembered the swift surge of passion that had boiled his blood as Kat settled her body against him, as her lips parted beneath his. Back in Richmond, he'd picked up the phone a half-dozen times, just wanting to hear her voice. Hell, he'd even grabbed his keys once, thinking about making the drive south in record time.

And he had to admit that he'd wondered—more than once—if she would bring that same sudden passion to his bed. He'd imagined her shifting above him, concentrating on their bodies joined together, fulfilling at last the promise that he'd made with a blushing kiss ten years before.

He was being an idiot, of course. He wasn't going to see Kat in his bed. He was going to honor her clearly stated desire, keep his distance, and finish up his work at the studio. Get the hell out of Eden Falls, and back to Richmond, where he belonged. That was the professional thing to do. The gentlemanly thing to do.

Damn. Sometimes, he hated being the good guy.

Still, his family had dragged him down here for the weekend, and he'd be an idiot not to take advantage of the fact that Kat was sitting right beside him. He just had to reassure her. "It was nothing serious, Kat. Rachel and me."

"With Rachel, it never is."

"She was really interested in another guy, a fraternity brother of mine. After about a month, we both realized the truth, and that was it."

"Of course."

Kat heard the stiffness in her tone. She knew that she had pulled away from Rye as soon as he mentioned Rachel. She was holding her back straight, as if she were about to spin away in a flawless pirouette.

She hated talking about her sister. She hated going over the poor choices Rachel had made, the easy ways out that she'd taken, over and over and over again. Just thinking about the old battles made Kat freeze up, clutching at her old formula—goals, strategies, rules. That's what she needed, here in Eden Falls. That's what she needed throughout her life.

But what had Susan told her, just that morning? *Go stomping in mud puddles for a change. Somersault down a hill.*

Impossible. Mud and hills were both in short supply, here in the public park. But Kat *could* let herself go. Just a bit.

"I'm sorry," she said, forcing herself to relax. "I really do appreciate your telling me about Rachel."

He continued to look grave, though. Her natural reaction had driven a wedge between them. But she could change that—even with stomping and somersaults off the menu for the day. Consciously setting aside her anger with Rachel, Kat dug her elbow into Rye's side. "Come on! I'd race you to the far end of the park, but I'm pretty sure you'd win."

He looked at her walking boot. "Yeah. I wouldn't want to take unfair advantage. What do you think, though? Could you manage the swings?"

"That's about my top speed, these days."

She took the hand that he offered, letting him pull her to her feet. They fell into step easily as they crossed to the swing set. She actually laughed as he gestured toward the center leather strap, waving his hand as if he were presenting her with a royal gift. "Mademoiselle," he said, holding the iron chains steady so that she could sit.

She settled herself gracefully, pretending that the playground equipment was some elegant carriage. Her fingers curled around the chains, and he sat next to her. Neither of them pushed off the scraped dirt, though. Instead, they braced their feet against the ground and continued talking.

"I feel terrible," she said, throwing her head back to look up at the clear blue sky. "Keeping you working in the studio when you should be up in Richmond."

"You shouldn't. A job's a job."

"But this job is taking so much of your time. What do you need, up in Richmond? What am I keeping you from doing?"

Sleeping, he wanted to say. *Concentrating on my work. Focusing on running a business instead of imagining what would have happened if I hadn't let you chicken out the other night.*

"I need to build a website," he said, somehow keeping his voice absolutely even. "Order business cards.

Envelopes. Stationery for bids. I'm lousy at that sort of stuff."

She nodded, as if she were writing down every word. "What else?"

"I've joined the Chamber of Commerce, but I haven't made it to a meeting yet. I've got to get the ball rolling with a little in-person networking. Start building that all-valuable word of mouth."

"That all sounds manageable."

"I've got some paperwork that I have to file with the state. Copies of my license, that sort of thing."

"I've got to say, Mr. Harmon. It sounds like you've got everything pretty much under control. Even *if* I keep dragging you back to Eden Falls."

"I'm glad one of us thinks so." He smiled, to make sure that she didn't take offense. It was his own damn fault that he couldn't stay away from here. His own damn fault that he put thousands of miles on the truck, wearing the tires thin on constant trips up and down the interstate. Old habits died hard.

Time to change the topic of conversation. Time to get away from the way he had screwed up his business plans, over and over and over again, ever since he'd graduated from college.

"So," he said, purposely tilting his voice into a light-hearted challenge. "What do you think? Who can pump higher, here on the swings?"

For answer, Kat laughed and pushed off, bending her knees and throwing back her head. Before he could match her, though, the bells on the courthouse started to toll, counting out five o'clock.

"Wait!" Kat said, stopping short. "Niffer and I have to get home. Mama will start to worry."

He bit his tongue to keep from cursing the bells.

Kat looked around the park, surprised to see that nearly everyone else had left. Of course, it was a Saturday in Eden Falls. Everyone had an early-bird dinner waiting at home. She glanced toward the castle jungle gym, ready to call Niffer and leave.

Except Niffer was nowhere to be seen.

Kat shook her head, forcing herself to swallow the immediate bile of panic. Of course her niece was on the playground equipment. She'd headed over there just a few minutes before.

Kat scrambled to her feet, taking off at a lopsided jog toward the castle. "Niffer!" she called. And then, "Jenny! Jenny!" The bright pink climbing bars mocked her as she reached the base of the toy. Up close, it looked impossibly tall, far too dangerous to be sitting in a public park. "Jenny!"

She looked around wildly. This couldn't be happening. She couldn't have lost her niece. She couldn't have let anything happen to Niffer, to Jenny, to Rachel's daughter.

"Kat! What's wrong?"

Rye skidded to a stop beside her, his ebony eyes flashing. She tried to pull up words past the horror that closed her throat, over the massive wave of guilt. He put a hand on her back, spread his fingers wide, as if to give her a web of support. She started to pull away—she didn't deserve to be touched. She was too irresponsible for anyone to stand near her. She had been given one single goal—watch Jenny—and she had broken all the rules by letting the child wander off unsupervised. Broken all the rules, just so that she could sit on the swings and flirt with Rye Harmon.

Broken all the rules, like Rachel.

"I can't find her," she sobbed. "I told her that she

could go to the castle, and I only looked away for a couple of minutes, but she's gone!"

Without thinking, Rye moved his hand from Kat's back, twining his fingers around hers. He felt her trembling beside him, understood that she was terrified as she darted her gaze around the park. She wasn't seeing anything, though. She was too frightened. No, beyond frightened. Panicked. Not thinking clearly.

He narrowed his eyes, staring into the deep shadows by the oak trees on the edge of the park. There! In the piles of leaves, left over from last autumn. Niffer was plowing through the dusty debris, obviously pretending that she was a tractor, or a dinosaur, or some imaginary creature.

"Look," he said to Kat, turning her so that she could see the child. "She's fine."

Kat stiffened the instant that she saw her niece. Instinctively, Rye tightened his grip on her hand, letting himself be dragged along as Kat stumbled across the uneven grass to the oak tree border.

"Jennifer Allison Morehouse, just what do you think you're doing?"

The little girl froze in midswoop, guilt painting her face. Instead of answering her aunt, though, she turned to Rye. "See? I told you that Jennifer is a bad name."

Incredibly, Kat felt Rye start to laugh beside her. He managed to wipe his face clear after only a moment, but he was standing close enough that she could feel his scarcely bridled amusement. For some reason, his good humor only stoked her anger. "I asked what you are doing over here, young lady! Didn't I give you permission to play on the castle? Not under the trees?"

The child's lower lip began to tremble. "I *was* playing on the castle. I was a princess. But the unicorn mermaids told me that I had to find their diamond ring over here."

Unicorn mermaids. Like Kat was going to buy that. She filled her lungs, ready to let her niece know exactly what she thought of unicorns and mermaids and diamond rings.

Before she could let loose, though, Rye squeezed her hand. Just a little. Barely enough that she was certain she felt it. Certainly not enough that Niffer could see.

Kat remembered her mother, sitting in the drab kitchen, sipping her cooling tea and saying that Kat should be more playful. She remembered Rye coaching the children, encouraging each of them in whatever they did best. She remembered the relaxed camaraderie of the T-ball parents, picking up their kids.

She took a deep breath and held it for a count of five. She exhaled slowly, just as she had when Rye taught her how to drive. No. Not like that. That had ended in disaster.

This was a new venture. A new effort to achieve a different goal. "You'll have to teach me about the unicorn mermaids," she said. "But that will be another day. Right now, we have to get home to Gram and Pop-pop."

Niffer looked as if she thought a magician might have somehow enchanted her Aunt Kat, turned her into a newt, or something worse—a bewitched, unreliable adult. "Okay," she said uncertainly.

"Come on, then," Kat said. "Let's go."

As Niffer started scuffling through the leaves, Kat caught a harsh reprimand at the back of her throat. Instead, she whispered to Rye under the cover of the rustling, "She scared me."

"I know," he whispered back, and he squeezed her hand again.

"She really, really scared me."

"But she's fine," he said. "And you will be, too."

Kat had to remind herself to breathe as they walked out of the park and down the block to her parents' house. Somehow, she forgot to reclaim her hand from Rye's.

Chapter Five

Kat raised her voice over the band, practically shouting so that Amanda could hear her. The crowd was raucous at Andy's Bar and Grill that night, and the musicians were making the most of having a full house. "Okay," she shouted. "You win! You said the music was great and I didn't believe you!"

Amanda laughed and clinked her mug of beer against Kat's. "Drink up!"

Kat obliged. After all, a bet was a bet. This mug tasted even better than the first had.

Kat couldn't remember the last time she'd had so much fun on a Friday night. Amanda had called her around noon, reporting that she'd already arranged for Susan and Mike to keep an eye on Niffer for the evening. Her cousin had picked her up at Rachel's house, only to frown when Kat answered the door in her skinny black jeans and a silk T-shirt. They'd made an emergency stop back at Amanda's house—Kat still wore black, but Amanda had rounded out the outfit with a flame-red scarf, lashed around Kat's hips like a belt. That, and a ruby-drop necklace that had belonged to their grandmother made Kat feel like she was someone new. Someone daring. Someone who wasn't afraid of being a little bit sexy, on a Friday night out on the town.

In fact, when Kat was hanging out with Amanda at the crowded bar, listening to her cousin's running commentary about the cute blond bartender, she felt like she was discovering a whole new world of fun. What had Susan said, the week before? That Kat had been cheated out of going to prom? Maybe Kat *had* lost out on a thing or two in New York, if this was what it felt like to hang out with her cousin, to cut loose, without a care in the world.

Kat certainly couldn't remember the last time she had indulged in drinking alcohol, anything more than a sip or two of champagne at an opening-night gala. Her entire body thrummed in time to the crashing music, and the roof of her mouth had started to tingle. Amanda, on the other hand, seemed entirely unaffected by the single glass of beer that she had sipped.

Before Kat could challenge Amanda to keep pace properly, a man shuffled over to the table. "Hey, Amanda," he said, mumbling a little and looking down at his boots.

"Hey," came Amanda's cool reply. "Brandon Harmon, don't be rude. You remember my cousin Kat, don't you?"

"Hey, Kat," the man said, still intent on studying the floor.

Brandon Harmon. Kat blinked hard and looked at

him as closely as she dared. Nope. She didn't remember him. This being Eden Falls, though, they had probably sat next to each other in fourth-grade social studies. From his name, he had to be one of Rye's countless siblings. Or cousins. Or whatever. It seemed like they comprised half the town.

As if he could read Kat's mind, Brandon looked over his shoulder. There was a cluster of men standing at the bar, their broad shoulders, chestnut curls and midnight eyes all proclaiming them part of the same clan.

Rye stood in the center of the bunch. He lifted his mug toward Kat in a wry salute. She was surprised by the sudden rush of warmth she felt at his attention. Unconsciously, she flexed her fingers, thinking about how strong his hand had felt in hers the Saturday before, after she had panicked about losing Niffer in the park. She'd spent the better part of the past week thinking about Rye's touch. His touch, and the patient humor in his voice… And that truly spectacular kiss that they had shared in Rachel's kitchen…

Kat's belly swooped in a way that had absolutely nothing to do with the beer that she had drunk. She'd felt the same sensation a hundred times in the past week. The past week, while Rye had been working up in Richmond. In between taking care of Niffer and running some errands for Susan, Kat had put in a lot of hours at the studio, but Rye had been nowhere in sight. The hardwood for the new floor had been delivered, though. It needed to spend a week acclimating to the temperature and humidity in the studio. A week when Rye had tended to other business. A week that Kat had been left alone with her memories, with her dreams.

But she was being ridiculous, mooning around, missing Rye. She knew perfectly well that he lived in Richmond now, that he was never moving back to Eden Falls.

And what did it matter? *She* had already spent two weeks in Eden Falls—seven days longer than she'd planned. It was time to turn her attention back to New York. Back to her career. She couldn't daydream about the way Rye's lips quirked just so when he smiled….

In front of her, Brandon shifted his weight from one foot to the other. "Amanda," he said, apparently summoning the nerve to bellow over the music. "Do you want to dance?"

Amanda laughed. "I'm sorry, Brandon. I can't leave my cousin here alone."

The poor man looked so crushed that Kat immediately took pity on him. She feared that he might never screw up his courage to ask out another woman again if she didn't free Amanda now. "Go ahead," she shouted to her cousin. "I'll be fine."

"Really?"

"Go! It's not like I can join you!" Kat gestured at her walking boot.

Amanda laughed and cast a quick glance toward Kat's mug, as if questioning her cousin's judgment. Kat shook her head. She wasn't drunk—not exactly. But she was definitely feeling…relaxed. Loose. Free, in a way that she hadn't felt since coming to Eden Falls. That she hadn't felt in *years*.

As Amanda mouthed a quick "Thank you" from the dance floor, Kat realized just how much her cousin had hoped Kat would let her go. Curious, Kat studied the cowboy, surprised to see how quickly he gained the confidence to place his hands on Amanda's trim waist, to guide her into a smooth Texas Two-Step.

There was something about those Harmon men….

Something about a Southern gentleman with the determination to go after something that he wanted… She swallowed hard, thinking once again of a very different Harmon. She wished that she and Amanda had been drinking soda, or sweet tea, or anything that came in a tall glass with ice, so that she could cool the pulse points in her wrists.

"You're a kind woman," Kat heard, close to her ear. She whirled to find herself face-to-face with Rye.

"What do you mean?" He was close enough that she barely needed to raise her voice. Thank heavens the band was playing, though. Otherwise, he would have heard her heart leap into high gear.

"It took Brandon two whiskey shots to get up the courage to ask Amanda to dance. If you hadn't let her go, all that booze would have gone to waste."

Kat laughed and said, "False courage for a silver-tongued devil like that?" As if to emphasize her words, she set the flat of her palm against Rye's broad chest. The action seemed to surprise him almost as much as it did her—he stiffened at the touch for just a moment. She tossed her hair, though, and thought, *What have I got to lose?* She continued in her best imitation of a carefree flirt. "Why, I bet that Brandon could have any woman in this place."

"Really?" Rye lowered his voice and stepped closer to Kat. He practically nuzzled her neck as he said, "*Any* woman?" She shivered, a delicious trembling that made him think truly evil thoughts. "Come on," he said. "Let's get some fresh air."

"I can't leave Amanda!"

He cupped his hands around his mouth and bellowed, "Hey, Amanda!" When the woman looked up from the dance floor, he pointed once to Kat, once to himself, and once to the door. Amanda laughed and nodded, waving goodbye to both of them. Rye settled one hand on the small of Kat's back as he guided her through the crowd.

A cool evening breeze hit them like an Arctic blast. "Come here," he said, pulling her around the corner of the building. They were sheltered from the wind there, and from the prying eyes of new arrivals to the bar. A bench was pushed up against the rough wooden wall. He gestured toward it and waited for Kat to take a seat. Before she had fully settled, he sat beside her, closer than was strictly necessary.

She wore some sort of sleek black top, one that revealed every bit as much of her figure as it covered, even with its long sleeves. The neckline swooped down, way down, reminding him of the sensitive hollow at the base of her throat. That patch of vulnerable flesh was now marked by a sparkling ruby pendant—as if he could forget it. His fingers twitched, and he resisted the urge to pull at the matching crimson scarf around her waist.

Shivering in the twilight air, Kat rubbed her hands against her arms. "I bet this is where you take all your women." She surprised him for the second time that night, squirming closer to his side, as if she wanted to soak up every ounce of his body heat.

"Just the ones I want to hear talk," he said, yawning a little in a useless attempt to clear the dullness from his ears. Andy's joint was always fun on Friday nights, but the band was far too loud.

"Talk," Kat purred, placing a hand on his thigh. "Is that why you asked me outside?"

This was a Kat he hadn't seen before. Sure, she'd let him kiss her in Rachel's kitchen. And it had seemed second nature to take her hand when she was so worried about Niffer. He'd enjoyed that feeling, that closeness, that sense of protecting her, and he hadn't let go as he walked her back to Susan and Mike's house.

He'd spent the week up in Richmond, though. A week of business. Of remembering his priorities. With his contractor's license properly filed and a dozen business meetings completed, he was newly charged with determination to make Harmon Contracting a success.

Except… Now that he was away from the office? Back in Eden Falls? And breathing in Kat's intoxicating scent…?

Her fingers started to move in distracting patterns, tracing the double-stitched seam on his jeans as if she'd glimpsed his dreams all week long. His body leaped to immediate attention, and he barely swallowed a groan. He leaned forward and found her face already tilted toward him, her lips eagerly parted for his kiss. Heat rolled through him as he breathed in the honey apricot of her hair. He tangled one hand in the lush strands, using the other to trace the shape of that incredible, clinging black top.

He outlined her lower lip with the tip of his tongue, grinning as he heard a needy moan gather at the back of her throat. Her hands were working their own magic, one fiddling with the top button of his shirt, the other continuing its exploration of his increasingly tented jeans. "Kat," he breathed, and then he sealed their kiss.

Heat, and slick velvet, and a pounding, urgent need. But behind that, under her sweet cry, he tasted the sharp bite of hops. Beer. He was shocked to realize that she'd been drinking. Sure, she was an adult; she was allowed to drink alcohol. But his mind refused to reconcile the notion of Kat, the ice princess, cutting loose. Kat, the tightly bound queen of control, tossing back a couple.

All of a sudden he understood the boldness in her hands, the brazen teasing in her words.

He shifted his hand from the back of her head, stopped crushing her close. Instead, he brought his palm around to cup the line of her jaw, using the motion to soften the end of his plunging kiss. She pulled back, just enough for him to look into her platinum eyes. He asked, "How much have you had to drink?"

She looked confused. "Just a couple of beers."

A couple of beers. With her frame? And he was willing to bet that she didn't have any tolerance at all—she couldn't possibly make a practice of hanging out at bars, pounding down a few brewskis on a Friday night.

He leaned in for another kiss, this one quick. Chaste.

"What?" she protested. "I'm an adult. I'm allowed to have a couple of beers."

"Of course you are. But I'm not going to take advantage of you like this."

"It's not taking advantage if I want it, too."

Her blustering response made him certain he was making the right decision. The Kat he knew would never throw herself at him like that. What had she told him, one of those days when he was hanging out at the dance studio? She had *goals* and *strategies* and *rules*.

He clenched his jaw and pulled away from her. "Come on," he said, keeping his voice as light as possible. "Let's get something to eat."

Kat shivered, freezing now that Rye had pulled away from her. She plucked at the scarf around her waist, suddenly ashamed. Two lousy beers. How much could that have impaired her judgment?

But the world was just starting to swirl around the

edges—not enough to make her dizzy, but more than enough to tell her she was over her limit. She thought about what she had done, about where her hands had just been, and she was overwhelmed with a scarlet wash of embarrassment.

"Kat?" Rye's voice was gentle. "Let's go get some dinner at the Garden Diner."

"I don't want dinner," she whispered.

"What? You're going to tell me that dinner goes against your dancer rules?"

More than fooling around on a bench outside a backroads bar? he meant. Her eyes shot up at the amusement in his voice, and her shame started to morph into anger. "What about you?" she challenged him. "Did it take you a couple of shots to come over and talk to me, just like Brandon? I bet you shouldn't be driving around Eden Falls right now."

"I don't need liquor to help me do what I want to do," Rye said. She heard the passion behind his words, the absolute certainty that he *had* wanted to talk to her, to be with her. Even if he'd been gone for the entire week. Even if he'd been the one to pull back just now. His voice was only marginally less fierce as he said, "I stuck to soda water tonight. I have an early day tomorrow, back up in Richmond. A site visit for a prospective client."

Ashamed of her actions all over again, she shook her head and hugged herself, trying to ignore the incipient spinning of the world around her.

"Come on, Kat. You're the one who said you're an adult. Let's be adults together." She flashed him a mortified glance. "Let's go get something to eat," he clarified.

She sighed and let him pull her to her feet. One

single step, though, on the gravel footpath, and she found that her balance was compromised by the damn walking boot. What had she been thinking, betting Amanda about the band, drinking that second beer?

She let Rye slip an arm around her waist, helping her to his truck. At least there was no question of his demanding that she drive tonight. That was one reason that she could actually thank Amanda. She closed her eyes in mortification as Rye reached across her to work her seat belt.

He made small talk as he drove to the diner. She couldn't be sure what he was saying, something about his father finding a new seed-line of heirloom carrots to plant on the family's organic farm, and Rye's sister Jordana developing a series of recipes based on the vegetables, something for a restaurant she was planning to start.

The more Rye talked, the hungrier Kat realized she was. By the time they got to the diner, she was fantasizing about home-cooked food—turkey dinner with mashed potatoes and gravy, meat loaf with peas and carrots. Rye helped her out of the truck, and he kept a protective hand beneath her elbow as he guided her into the diner, but she was already feeling much steadier on her feet.

She studied the entire menu, front to back, but ultimately, she followed Rye's lead. A bacon cheeseburger, slathered with blue cheese, thick with lettuce and juicy tomato. Fries on the side, with a single sizzling onion ring to top it all off.

Rye watched Kat tackle her meal with the single-minded determination that she devoted to everything. He'd half expected her to chicken out at the last moment, to order a side salad with a slice of lemon or some other girlie excuse for a meal.

But he had to hand it to her—she matched him bite for bite, washing down burger and fries with generous amounts of sweet tea. Maybe it was the beers that Amanda had conned her into drinking, maybe it was simple craving for a single ridiculous splurge of a meal, but Kat dug in with a gusto that astonished him.

Okay. Maybe not "astonished." He'd felt the illicit energy coiled inside her on the bench outside of Andy's. He'd felt a little of the wicked damage she could do when she let herself go unleashed.

But he'd never imagined that she would wreak so much havoc on a Smoky Blue Burger Platter. And he was damned pleased to see that she could.

"So," he said when they both finally came up for air. "The floorboards should be ready for installation next week. It'll take two days to get them down. Another day to set the ceiling tiles, and then a couple of days for painting. We'll be done in a week."

Seven days, Kat thought. Seven days, and then all the damage would be repaired. Rye would be finished at the studio, free to stay up in Richmond forever.

"Wonderful!" she said, forcing every ounce of fake cheerfulness that she could summon into the word. Oops. She must have poured it on a little *too* thick. Rye was looking at her funny. She cleared her throat. "I worked with Niffer's teacher, and I've sent home flyers with all the kids in the elementary school. We've already got two summer sessions of Beginning Ballet filled, and one of Intermediate."

"That's great! But I thought that you didn't have anyone to teach."

"Oh, I didn't tell you. I found an old recital program

in the back room on Tuesday. It was from last summer's performance, so I could still track down most of the teachers listed there. Three of them agreed to come back."

"I knew you could do it." There. That was the way enthusiasm really sounded.

Kat took another long swig of sweet tea. It was impossible to find the stuff in New York—not that she would have indulged at any point in the past ten years. Stirring artificial sweetener into iced tea didn't come anywhere close to savoring the supersaturated syrup of her childhood.

Feeling a little rebellious, she tried to imagine what her dance colleagues would say about her Eden Falls night out on the town—beer, burgers and enough sweet tea to float a luxury yacht. What did it matter, though? She couldn't remember the last time she had laughed as hard as she'd laughed with Amanda. And there were a lot worse ways to spend an evening than sitting across from a man as gorgeous as Rye Harmon.

Even if her fellow dancers would vow to eat nothing but lemon juice on iceberg lettuce for an entire week, if they had indulged like Kat.

"Hey," Rye prompted. "Are you okay?"

"I'm fine." She smiled. And she was. She was more than fine. She was relaxed and happy. "I was just thinking about what everyone is doing in New York. It's Friday night, so there's a lot of scrambling. The company does matinees on Saturday and Sunday, so everyone is probably a bit crazy."

He heard the fondness in her voice, the easy familiarity with routine. Sure, she might call them "crazy", but it was a craziness she knew and loved. "You must really miss it," he said.

"I do," she answered, but he caught the pause before she went on. As if she were looking for words. Searching for a memory. "I miss the feeling of testing myself, of pushing myself to do the most my body can do. I miss the feeling of becoming another person, someone totally different from me." She sighed. "I miss…" She trailed off, swirling an orphaned fry in ketchup.

"What, Kat?"

"Sometimes I'm not sure that I can do it." The admission seemed to unlock something in her, to free her to rush on with more words, more confessions. "The big parts, the principal dancer roles…I need to impress the company director, to prove I have what it takes. That's why I pushed myself so hard before I got hurt—extra rehearsals, extra sessions at the barre. And all I ended up with was this stupid boot and a forced month off."

He knew what she wanted him to say. He knew that she wanted to hear that she would succeed, that she would conquer her injury, that she would come back stronger than ever.

But he couldn't be certain of that. He didn't know enough about her world, about the demands of ballet life in distant New York City. No matter what *he* thought of her, how great he thought she was, he couldn't say that she had the pure strength, the unalloyed physical power to master her chosen profession's greatest challenges.

"You'll do the best that you can," he said. "And if the people who make the decisions are too foolish to take every last drop of devotion that you can give them, then you'll figure out the next step. And you'll master that. Goals, strategies and rules, right? That's what someone told me once."

She rolled her eyes. "Whoever said anything that stupid?"

"Not stupid." He shook his head. "Not stupid at all."

She flinched under the intensity of his gaze. Now that she had finished eating, the last tendrils of her tipsiness had floated away. She was sober, but her body still remembered the way that she had used it. She felt tired, raw. And with Rye staring at her that way, she felt totally exposed.

"I don't know," she said. "That stupid formula helped me when I was fourteen years old. It's probably not good for anything anymore. Not ten years later."

"It's good enough for me," Rye affirmed. "Up in Richmond this week, I applied your 'stupid formula.' I got more done in five days than I had in five weeks before that." Of course, that was the first time that he'd spent five consecutive days in his new office. The first time that he hadn't let a so-called emergency drag him back to Eden Falls.

"I'm glad I was able to help you," Kat said, trying to ignore the fact that her smile was a little wobbly around the edges.

It was funny, really. It was almost like there was a limited amount of "get up and go" to go around. Rye had listened to her, and he was moving forward with his career plan, full steam ahead. Kat, meanwhile, caught herself repeatedly musing on what life would be like if she stayed in Eden Falls.

How would it feel to teach at Morehouse Dance Academy? To stand in the center of the room, clapping out a rhythm for aspiring ballerinas, for good girls who wanted to be graceful and pretty and never, ever dance professionally on any stage, anywhere? How would it feel to stop by Susan and Mike's home every day, to watch her father continue to gain back his strength, to sit at her mother's kitchen table and drink tea using her grandmother's china? How would it feel to greet Niffer every afternoon as she got off her school bus, chattering about art projects, and reading class, and learning the capitals of all the states?

Wonderful, Kat realized, even as she was astonished to recognize that truth. Absolutely, unqualifiedly *wonderful.* In two weeks of living in Eden Falls, Kat had already had more fun than she had in the past two *years* in New York.

And what did that say about her chosen home? Her chosen career?

"Hey," Rye said, interrupting her thoughts. "Ready to get out of here?"

She nodded, sliding out of the fake leather booth. Rye paid at the cash register, waving away her attempt to reach her wallet. He held the door for her, and he ushered her into the truck, but this time she fastened her own seat belt. He smiled and stroked a single finger across her cheek before he closed the door. She shivered at the unspoken promise of that touch.

It took less time than she expected to drive to Rachel's house. Rye put the truck in Park and killed the engine. "Where's Niffer tonight?"

"Sleeping over at Mama and Daddy's. She has them wrapped around her little finger."

"Kids have a way of doing that."

She knew that it was her turn to say something, to make a joke about Niffer, about family, about something light and easy and funny. For the life of her, she couldn't imagine what she could possibly say. "Want to come in for a drink?" she finally settled on. "Of tea," she hastened to add. "Or, er, water. That's all we have inside."

"That'll be enough." Kat watched as he took the keys from the ignition, carelessly tossing them by his feet. That was yet another aspect of life in Eden Falls that she'd never see in New York. If anyone were foolish enough to own a pickup in New York, they'd keep it secured under lock and key—maybe with a mad Doberman in the cab to deter potential thieves. Somehow, it made Kat's heart sing to think of a place that was safe enough to leave car keys on the floor mat.

Inside Rachel's home, Kat headed toward the kitchen. "Let me get you a drink."

Rye caught her before she could cross the foyer, folding his hand across her flame-red scarf. "I have a confession. I'm not really thirsty."

A frisson of excitement raced across her scalp as she registered the rumble of his words. She let him turn her around, felt his other hand settle on her waist.

She was a dancer. She was used to being held by men. She was accustomed to the feeling of strong fingers on her flesh, gripping her tightly, holding her upright.

But all those sensations were her job. They were as routine, as mundane, as utterly bloodless as sitting down at a computer, typing an email, ordering supplies over the telephone.

This was something different. This was something more.

Rye felt the hitch in Kat's breath, and a lazy smile spread across his lips. He'd watched her through the evening; he knew how quickly she had sobered as she ate dinner. He had no qualms about kissing her now. Kissing. Or more.

"You know," he whispered, purposely keeping his voice so low that she had to pull closer to hear him, "we left Andy's too early tonight. We never got a chance to dance."

Her laughter was as soft as her silken hair. "In case you haven't noticed, I'm not exactly in dancing shape." She waved a hand toward her walking boot.

"I wasn't thinking of anything too strenuous. Not your pliés or arabesques or that sort of thing."

"Mmm," she whispered. "You've been doing your homework."

"All part of renovating the studio. I have to know how the space is going to be used, don't I?" That was a lie, though. He had whiled away hours in Richmond, thinking about Kat, thinking about what she did for a living. He had gone online, looking for pictures of her, and he'd picked up a bit about dance along the way.

He should have been working, of course, instead of spending his time online. Should have been focusing on Harmon Contracting. But all work and no play… He'd almost succeeded in convincing himself that his…research was good for business. That there was nothing personal in it. Nothing at all.

"Ready to sign up for a class?" she asked, obviously amused.

"I don't think either of us needs any training." He pulled her close, relishing her surprised gasp even as she yielded to his pressure. She felt marvelous in his arms, pliant but hard, melting into him even as she maintained her dancer's balance. He leaned down and found her mouth, sinking into her sweet silken heat.

Deepening the kiss, teasing her with his tongue, he raised his hand to the marble column of her throat. He could feel her pulse flutter beneath his thumb, a butterfly dancing against his flesh. His fingers wrapped around her nape, urging her closer, then skimming down the length of her spine, molding her fine-boned body to his.

He shifted his weight to match the angle of her hips, signaling his intention by an almost imperceptible tightening of his fingers against her waist. She followed his lead flawlessly, as if this were one of her fancy ballets, as if they'd practiced these moves hour after hour, night after night.

With choreography far more intimate than any Texas Two-Step, he guided her toward the couch. He half expected her to hesitate, to freeze, to refuse to follow his lead. But she sank down before he did, raising her arms above her head like some sort of exotic goddess, summoning him, asking him to join her.

Not that he required much urging.

Kat caught her breath as she lay back on the pillows of the overstuffed couch. Rye looked huge in the dim light from the foyer—sturdy and confident and *present* in a way that made her heart race. Sure, she had kissed other men. She had even fooled around on a couch or two. And practically lived with a jerk. But she had never felt this inner drive, this absolute certainty that she was doing the thing that she was meant to do, that she was with the man she was meant to be with.

For a fleeting moment, she thought of her mantra—goals, strategies, rules. There weren't any rules for the sort of passion she felt now. There wasn't any wrong or right. There was just being. Being in her own physical body. Being with Rye.

She needed to feel him, needed to know the weight of him against her.

She twined her hands around his forearm, tracing

the ropes of hard muscle, the scatter of chestnut hair. She tugged with a decisiveness that left no doubt of her intentions. “Rye,” she said. “Please…”

She didn’t have to ask a second time. He sank beside her, pulling her onto his lap as he sprawled against the back of the couch. She felt the rigid length of him against her thigh, the absolute confirmation that she wasn’t imagining his interest, wasn’t fooling herself about his need for her. Knowingly, she traced her fingernail along the denim ridge, barely restraining a grin as he groaned.

But there was more for her to explore, more of his body to know. Even as she yielded to another of his soul-rocking kisses, her fingers found the buttons of his shirt. Summoning all of her concentration, all of her determination, she undid one, and then another, and another. She tugged the tails of his shirt from his waistband and then did away with the garment altogether, tossing it onto the floor with reckless abandon.

All the while, he was doing incredible things to her neck, laving the tender spot beneath her earlobe, tangling his fingers in her hair. A crimson glow ignited in her belly as he stripped away the scarf around her hips. When he trailed the silk across her throat, drifting it over her ruby charm, the throbbing heat that rose inside her nearly made her lose her concentration, almost forced her to yield to his ministrations, to fall back against the soft couch and let him do whatever he wanted to her.

Almost.

Instead, she remembered that groan that she had incited as she traced the outline of his need. She wanted to draw that sound from him again. Relying on her taut dancer’s muscles, she pulled herself upright on his lap.

She placed her hands on his shoulders, straddling his waist so that she knelt above him. For one instant, she lost her balance, pulled askew by the unaccustomed weight of her walking boot, but his hands settled beneath her rib cage, holding her, steadying her.

Before she could continue with the exploration she was determined to complete, he stripped his hands up her body, skimming off the clinging black of her top. She gasped at the sensation of cool air bathing her skin, but she was immediately warmed by the satisfaction in his gaze. While one hand spread against the small of her back, giving her the support she needed, the other flirted with the lace edge of her bra, delivering the attention she craved.

His thumb brushed against one nipple, then the other, and the sensitive buds tightened so fast that she cried out. He repeated the motion, adding a caress to the smooth plane of her belly. The red-hot fire inside her turned incandescent. She arched her back, begging him for more attention, and he lost no time complying. One hand sprang the hook on her bra, the other bared her white and willing flesh. His mouth was hot against the underside of her breasts; his tongue traced arcane patterns that left her writhing. When his lips closed over one solid pearl, she thought that she would scream. When his teeth snagged the other, she did.

Panting, eager, she forced herself to concentrate, to return to her original plan. With ragged breath, she pushed against his shoulders, making his head loll back against the couch. She left a trail of kisses along the line of his jaw, featherlight and barely hinting at all that she could do to him, for him. Her lips tingling from his rough stubble, she traced the line that had been bruised the week before, the now-invisible ache that she had given him when she had driven his pickup off the road.

She followed the logical line of that diagonal, adding her tongue to the attention of her lips. She found the dark trail of hair that marched down his tight abs, and she traced its promise, first with her lips, then with all the soft heat of her mouth, ending with the knife-edged promise of a single fingernail.

"Kat," Rye groaned when the pressure became more than he could bear. He had to feel more of her, had to find the liquid heat that spoke to his arousal. He let his palms course over her sides, felt her eager body rise to meet his. He made short work of ripping open the walking boot's straps. She sighed as he eased her foot free of the device, as he tossed the contraption to the floor. His fingers found the hidden side zipper of her crazy New York pants, and he caught his breath at the unexpected gift of lace that he revealed.

She scrambled for his waist, for the familiar bronze button of his jeans, but he caught her wrists, holding them still, bringing the fluttering birds of her fingers to rest beside her hips. There was time enough for his pleasure, time enough to find the complete release that she promised him.

He walked his fingers along the delicate top of her panties, measuring the taut tremble of her belly. She followed his silent command, raising her hips to meet him, to beg him, to invite him to share in the glory that she promised. With the lightest of touches, he traced the hollow behind her right knee, the sensitive cave carved by her tendons. She bucked against the sensation, and he caught a laugh in the back of his throat.

Kat moaned his name, reaching up to pull him down on top of her. She needed to feel his weight against her, needed him to anchor her. Something about the gesture, though, brought full realization crashing down upon her. She'd had no intention of bringing a man back to Rachel's home. She'd had no plan to make love that night.

She had no protection.

"Rye," she whispered, hating every word she had to say. "I don't have…anything. We can't…"

"Hush," he said, and the fingers that he traced along her inner thigh nearly sent her over some crazed edge. "We won't."

Before she could flounder in the sea of disappointment that his words released upon her, his fingers went back to the lace edge of her panties, to the damp panel of silk beneath. "Rye —" she protested.

"Hush," he whispered again, but now he breathed the word against the most secret part of her, turning it into a promise. She closed her eyes as his fingers slipped beneath the lace; she caught her breath as his thumb found the pearl between her legs. One gentle flick, two and she was writhing for release.

He laughed again, ripping away the last of the lacy barrier. She felt his stubble against her thighs, gently raking one leg and then the other. Forgetting her dancer's control, she tilted her hips, longing for the ultimate pleasure that she knew he was prepared to give her.

A single velvet stroke of his tongue. Another. One last, savoring caress, and then she was crashing over a precipice, clutching at his hair, tumbling down an endless slope of clenching, throbbing pleasure.

Rye watched the storm pass over her body, the beautiful twist of her lips as she breathed his name, over and over and over again. When it was past, when he knew that she was drifting on a formless, shapeless sea of comfort, he eased himself up her body. She was utterly relaxed as he pulled her languid form to lie on top of him. Her hair spread across his chest, and the warmth of her flushed cheek soothed his own pounding heart.

"Mmm," she murmured, and her fingers drifted down his torso.

"Rest," he said, smoothing one hand down the plane of her back, while the other cupped the curve of her neck.

"I want…" she whispered, but she drifted into silence before she finished the sentence.

He eased himself to a more comfortable position, telling himself that his body's demands would quiet in a few minutes, that the ache below his belt would ease. He underestimated, though, the force of the woman whom he cradled. He had not considered the power of her honey-apricot scent, teasing him with every breath he drew. He had not taken into account her soft pressure against his chest, his thighs, his entire excruciatingly primed body.

But he managed to take comfort in Kat's utter peacefulness as her breathing slowed. He waited, and he watched, and he held her until she slipped into the deepest of sleeps.

Only then did he look around the living room, seeing the home that Rachel had let fall into disrepair. He could fix things up in short order. Rip out the awful carpet, put down a new floor. Replace the fogged storm windows with something that would insulate the house better. Renovate the entire kitchen, with its creaky old appliances.

It wouldn't take long. A couple of weeks. A month. He could stay in Eden Falls while he worked, keep an eye on every step of the process.

No.

He wasn't going to stay in Eden Falls. He lived in Richmond now. He had a life for himself, a business that he had fought hard for. For the first time in his adult life, he was free to do what he wanted to do, free from family and clinging girlfriends.

Kat shifted in her sleep, spreading her hand across his chest.

What the hell was he doing here? Maybe he had come home with Kat precisely because he knew that *she* wasn't sticking around Eden Falls. She had been absolutely clear—she was heading back to New York, just as soon as he could finish work on the studio. She was safe. She wasn't going to take over his life. She wasn't going to be another Marissa, teasing him, shaping his life to hers, then leaving him in her dust.

Kat had already built a life for herself, a life outside of Eden Falls. She had remained true to herself, true to the promises she'd made when she was just a kid.

Was he really such a wimp that he couldn't do the same? He had *vowed* that he would make a go of things in Richmond. Moving away was what he'd always wanted, what he needed, to prove that he was a real man.

He couldn't give all that away. Not for an impossible future. Not for an unknown, unmeasured relationship with Kat, who had already found her own path to independence.

A chill settled over the room as the final heat of their exertion faded. Rye fought against a shudder, forcing himself to stay perfectly still, lest he ruin Kat's sleep. The night grew long, and he watched and waited and thought about all the futures that might be, and one that he would never, ever have.

Chapter Six

Rye stood in the dance studio, surveying the stack of hardwood flooring. Brandon was the cousin he'd enlisted for assistance that day. He was pretty sure the guy had only agreed to come over because he hoped Amanda Morehouse would be visiting Kat. Rye had probably implied as much, now that he thought about it. He didn't feel too guilty, though. In the past, Brandon had roped Rye into worse duty on the family's huge organic farm.

"The staple guns are out in the truck," Rye said. "The saw is there, too, along with the rolls of waterproofing to lay out beneath the wood."

"I'm pretty sure that I'm the one who taught *you* how to install a hardwood floor," Brandon retorted.

"Just trying to be helpful," Rye said. He didn't mind his cousin's gruff reply. Instead, he took advantage of

Brandon's expertise to head toward the office, to the private refuge where he knew Kat was hard at work.

Kat. Even now, he could feel her weight on his chest, her body melted and cooling after the pleasure he had given her. The memory, though, made a corner of his heart curl in reflexive avoidance.

He hadn't thought this through. He hadn't realized quite how hard he was falling for Kat, how much she had come to mean to him. There was no way that their lives could ever come together—she was determined to get back to New York the second she was shed of that walking boot, if not before. It had been what? Three weeks already? She'd said that she was only going to wear it for a month. One more week—at most—and then she'd be gone forever.

And he certainly couldn't put all the blame on her for his current discomfort. He hadn't been lying when he'd told her he had an early Saturday meeting in Richmond. Late Friday night, actually early Saturday morning, he had finally carried her to her bed, tucked her in beneath her comforter and stroked her hair until she fell back to sleep. But then he'd left, hitting the road, letting the freeway roll out beneath his headlights as he drove home in the dark of night.

He hadn't called on Saturday. Sunday either. He'd needed to put some distance between them—emotional space to match the physical one.

This whole thing shouldn't be as difficult as it was turning out to be. So what if Kat was heading back to New York soon? Rye could always come down to Eden Falls, stay here until she left. Who knew what would grow between them in the time that they had?

No.

He wasn't going to do that again. Wasn't going to

cash in his dreams. If he walked away from Richmond now, he knew that he would never again find the nerve to build his own business. He would stay here in Eden Falls until he was old and withered and gray, until he couldn't even remember what to do with a woman as intoxicating as Kat.

Damn.

He knocked lightly on the door frame. "Mornin'," he said as Kat looked up from behind the desk.

God, she was beautiful. Her hair was back in one of those twists off her neck, making her look like every schoolboy's fantasy librarian. Her silvery eyes brightened when she saw him, and her smile made his heart ache.

"I missed you," she said. "It was a long weekend without you."

He was supposed to apologize for living in his new hometown. He couldn't. No. He *wouldn't*. Instead, he asked, "What did you do?"

"Niffer had a T-ball game. You didn't tell me that you're a million times better coach than Noah is."

He shrugged, fighting against the pang that told him he should have been there for the game. "Britney was out of town, so Noah didn't have an excuse not to be there."

Kat laughed. "Daddy was feeling so much better that Mama let him walk down to the park with us. We had to take it slow, but he made it. It was great to see him out of the house, soaking up the sunshine."

"That's good news." He felt stiff as he said the words. Awkward. This was terrible—he felt like he was lying to Kat with every word he said. Every word he didn't.

"How was Richmond?" she asked, the faintest hint of worry etching a thin line between her brows.

He forced himself to answer with a hearty smile. "Everything is going great. That Saturday morning meeting was with a new client—a massive kitchen renovation. Yesterday, I met with a computer guy—he's set up all my client files."

Kat wasn't an idiot. She could tell that something was wrong.

Something. There wasn't a lot of mystery about that, was there? What was the one thing that had changed since she and Rye had last talked, had been easy and comfortable and happy in each other's company? Her cheeks grew hot, and she wasn't sure whether the leap in her pulse was because of the memories of what they had done, or her regrets about what they hadn't.

But that wasn't all. She understood the warning behind Rye's stilted conversation. She *knew* that he lived in Richmond now, that he was only here in Eden Falls as a favor to her. He didn't even *want* to be working on the studio. That was just as well. She was going back to New York, after all, leaving all of this behind in just a matter of days.

And that thought left her strangely numb, as it had every time she thought it over the weekend.

But that was ridiculous. New York was her home, had been for ten years. New York was the place where she had her friends, her job, her life.

She thought of the gray concrete canyons, the buildings so tall that sunshine never touched the streets. Before she could be depressed by the memory of such a bleak landscape, though, she forced herself to confront the hard facts of living in Eden Falls. A big night out was stopping by the cinema to watch a first-release film. There wasn't a single twenty-four-hour business in town. The only restaurants that made deliveries were the pizza parlor on Elm Street and the Chinese place on Baker.

But she and Amanda had had a lot of fun at the movies, just last night. She'd left Niffer with her parents, and she and her cousin had shared a huge tub of popcorn, watched some silly chick-flick. After all, who needed to work twenty-four hours a day? And why would she ever need to order in anything other than pizza or Chinese?

No. She could never live in Eden Falls long-term. No matter how much fun she was having on this spring break. Vacation wasn't the real world, even a vacation rooted in caring for her healing father, for her wayward niece.

Bottom line—it was absolutely, positively 100% necessary to drive around a town like Eden Falls. Kat had been imposing on her mother and Amanda for the entire time she'd been here. Sooner or later, her family was going to refuse to ferry her from one place to another. And she had no intention of making another disastrous attempt at getting behind the wheel.

Eden Falls had nothing on New York. She just had to remember that.

In fact, there was one more dangerous thing about Eden Falls: Rye Harmon. She had a sudden vision of his lips on the inside of her thigh. Her cheeks flushed at the memory of the pleasure he had given her. At the thought of the fulfillment he'd denied himself. She had to say something, had to let him know that she had stopped by Doherty's Drugstore the day before. He needed to know that she had purchased a packet of silver-wrapped condoms, to use in the future.

Whatever future they had. She cleared her throat. "Rye, about Friday night," she began, even though she had no earthly idea what she was going to say after that.

He answered her quickly, too quickly. "I shouldn't have… I'm sorry. I live in Richmond now. I—"

"Rye!" She cut him off, touched by how flustered he'd become. "I know that. I understand."

"It's just that in the past… There was someone who…" He ran his fingers through his hair, leaving his chestnut curls in disarray. "I'm making a total mess out of this."

She caught his hands and pulled them close to her chest. "No," she said, meeting his eyes. "You're not. I'm not expecting you to drop everything and move back here to Eden Falls. I'd be crazy to ask that, when I'm only here for a while myself. Friday night was amazing—and I hope we'll spend more time together before I go back to New York. But I'm not expecting you to walk in here with an engagement ring and the keys to your family's Eden Falls house."

Right then, for just that moment, when her smile got a little crooked and she squeezed his fingers between her own, he would have left Richmond. He would have dropped Harmon Contracting, abandoned all his hopes and dreams.

But then he heard Brandon shift equipment out in the studio. It was like his cousin was trying to remind him of his business, of his future, of all the reasons he'd fought to get out of Eden Falls.

Rye was an independent businessman now. And Kat wasn't part of his past. She wasn't Marissa Turner. She was a woman who had found her way clear of Eden Falls years before. That was part of what made her so damned alluring.

He slipped his fingers free from her gentle grip, but he stepped even closer. His palm cupped the back of her neck, and he leaned down to steal a quick kiss. She was more hesitant than he'd expected, though, almost as if she were afraid of the spark that might ignite between them.

Well, spark be damned. His free hand settled on the small of her back, tugging her closer, so that he could feel the whole long line of her body. He traced her closed lips with his tongue, and his blood leaped high when she yielded to him. Before he could follow through, though, before he could think about easing up the rumpled cloth of her blouse, there was another clatter from the outer room.

"That's Brandon," he breathed, settling his forehead on Kat's shoulder and drawing a steadying breath. "He's ready to install the floorboards."

Kat's own breath hitched as she took a step back. What was she thinking, anyway? She wasn't exactly the type of girl to revel in a little afternoon delight—not with countless business details left to take care of.

"Great," she said, trying not to sound too rueful. Then, she repeated the word, broadcasting it for Brandon's hearing. "Great! Let me show you this website that I found. I can use it to design stationery for the studio—letterhead and flyers and business cards."

He edged around the desk, coming to stand behind her as she pulled her chair closer to the computer. She sat like a classical statue, straight and tall. Her hands flew over her computer keyboard, smoothly competent as she called up something on the screen. He didn't care about any stupid website. He was just pleased for the excuse to be standing so close to her.

"Look at this," she enthused. "They have hundreds

of templates—you can choose one that's right for you. Here, I'll show you. Let's make a flyer for Harmon Contracting. Didn't you say that you needed to do that?"

She looked at him expectantly, and he nodded, eager to see her smile. He wasn't disappointed.

"They have themes, like Medicine and Legal." She let the computer mouse hover over those choices for a moment to illustrate the possibilities, and then she swept it toward the top of the screen. "But we probably want Carpentry."

She clicked once, and the screen was filled with the image of a creamy white page. Silvery scrolls curled around the edges, folding into twined hearts in the corners. Ornate writing spelled out the formal words of an invitation: Mr. and Mrs. Robert Smith request the pleasure of your presence at the wedding of their daughter…

"Oops!" Kat slammed her palm down on the mouse, as if it were a living creature that might actually scurry away. "I clicked on Celebrations by mistake."

He couldn't help himself. He grinned at her obvious discomfort. She was acting like that one false click was a much bigger deal than it was. From her level of embarrassment, it was almost like she'd unveiled some deep dark secret, as if he had walked in on her while she was showering.

He felt the first stirring of his body responding to that delightful image, and he shifted his weight from one foot to the other. *Business, Harmon*, he remonstrated with himself. This was a business website that she was showing him.

By the time he had schooled his mind back to professionalism, she had brought up a different page. Hearts had been replaced with tiny images of a hammer and saw in one corner, a toolbox in another. Bold lettering stated John Smith Handyman Services, with a mock address at 123 Main Street.

"See?" Kat said, and she was studying the computer screen just a little too intensely, staring at the page as if it might turn into a bird and take flight. "I can click here, and we can change the name." He watched as her fingers picked out "Harmon Contracting." "We can add your Richmond address. There's room for an email address, a landline, and your cell phone. You can keep the dark brown, or you can make it any other color. Navy, maybe. Or maroon."

"What if I want the silver, from the other screen?"

He couldn't say what made him ask the question. It wasn't fair, really. He just wanted to see emotion skip across her features, flash across her platinum eyes. She darted a glance toward the office door, toward the studio where Brandon served as unwitting chaperone.

Kat cleared her throat, consciously deciding not to take the bait. Instead, she dashed her fingers across the keyboard, pulling up the draft files she had created for her own business, for the dance studio. Toe shoes filled the corners, and the lettering was a professional burgundy. Morehouse Dance Academy. The street address. Eden Falls, Virginia.

She had completed the flyer with information about all of the classes that they offered, from Introductory Ballet to Advanced Showcase. Instructors' names were listed inside parentheses—Miss Sarah, Miss Emma, Miss Virginia. The only blank class was the Advanced Showcase; the former teacher had not responded to the dozen messages Kat had left.

That made sense, actually. Miss Courtney Thomson had been the most accomplished of the studio's instructors. She was likely to take her career the most seriously, to have been the most turned off by Rachel's haphazard management. Kat suspected that she'd already taken on work in a neighboring town, moved on with her life. Kat really couldn't blame her.

"That's great," Rye said, and she realized that he'd been reading the full text on the page.

"It's nothing," she said, but she was pleased by the compliment. She'd spent a lot of time on Saturday writing the brochure. "I need to take it to my mother this afternoon."

"She'll love it. It reads like something from a professional advertising company."

"We can do something similar for you. Specific to plumbing and electricity and stuff."

"Stuff," he teased. "You make it sound so complicated."

"You know what I mean!"

"Yeah, I do," he admitted. Without fully intending to, he placed his hands on the back of her chair, spinning her around to face him. He heard her breath catch in her throat as he edged forward. She looked up at him, an uncertain smile quirking her lips. He leaned down and planted his palms on the arms of her chair, the motion bringing his lips close to hers. "I know exactly what you mean," he growled, and suddenly neither of them was talking about stationery or computers or… stuff.

Before he could follow through on the promise of the suddenly charged air between them, a clatter came from the studio. Something metal hit the floor, followed by a sharp curse.

"Brandon?" Rye called, already turning to the door.

"I'm all right," came the quick reply. "But I could use a hand out here."

Rye set his hand against Kat's cheek. "I—" he said, so softly that Brandon could never hear him. He wasn't sure what he was going to say. *I want to finish what we started Friday night. I don't care about stationery, not when we could be talking about something else.* Doing *something else. I don't give a damn about Richmond, or New York, or Eden Falls, or anyplace, so long as I'm with you.*

"Go," Kat said, and she watched him swallow hard. "I'll be here. Brandon needs you."

She slumped into her chair as he hurried out the door. She should have Rye check the air-conditioning in the office. It was about twenty degrees too hot in the small room. She pretended not to hear the muffled curses as the men negotiated over some spilled hardware.

Before Kat could pull herself together enough to go back to the stationery website, the computer chimed. She had new email. She clicked on the icon, opening up a message entitled Coppelia. The sender was Haley, writing from New York.

The first paragraph was a breathless apology for failing to write more often. Haley's on-again, off-again boyfriend was back in her life; he'd given her red roses for her birthday—*two dozen!!!* The apartment was fine. Slimeball Adam had finally come and picked up his junk. Skanky Selene had already dumped him and moved on to another dancer in the company. Kat's eyes skimmed over the words, as if she were reading some boring nineteenth-century novel about people she'd never met.

But then she saw the real reason for Haley's message.

Sign up for *Coppelia* auditions closes at midnight, May 1. You have to do it in person; they won't let me add your name to the list. Are you coming back in time?

Kat stared at the screen, at the Xes and Os that closed out Haley's message. *Are you coming back in time?*

Coppelia. Kat had always dreamed of dancing the lead role of Swanilda. The ballet had been her absolute favorite, ever since she was a little girl. It told the story of a lonely toymaker in a mountain village, a mad scientist who created a life-size doll who only needed the sacrifice of a human being to come to life. Swanilda was the wise village girl who figured out the madness of the toymaker's work—she saved her betrothed from being sacrificed. Swanilda defeated the mad woodcarver and married her beloved.

The role was physically demanding. In addition to classical ballet moves, the part required executing a number of country dances and one extended section where Swanilda pretended to be the jerky windup doll, Coppelia.

Kat flexed her toes inside her walking boot. Even when she arched them to their full reach, she felt nothing, no twinge of pain. Her foot was almost healed.

She looked around the office. Despite her still-elevated heart rate as she listened for Rye, out in the studio, her work here was nearly done. She could place her order for stationery right now. That would leave one last thing to clean up: the bank accounts. Kat couldn't believe that she'd let the problem linger for nearly three full weeks. But it wasn't really a surprise. The lost money was the one thing she couldn't fix. That was Rachel's one failing that Kat couldn't tidy up, couldn't erase away. Her parents would be devastated, and there was nothing Kat could do—and so she'd let herself shrug off the responsibility, ever since she'd identified the problem.

But for the past week or so, there had been another reason that she'd failed to handle the financial crisis. Once she told her mother about the lost money, there'd be no reason left to stay in Eden Falls. And Kat had to admit that part of her did not want to leave.

That was only natural, she tried to assure herself. Her father had looked so healthy as he walked to the park on Sunday. He was sitting up in his recliner at home, even heading to the kitchen to get his own snacks. Susan would be able to run the studio on her own soon enough; Amanda could probably juggle her own teaching schedule to help out for the first rough weeks of transition.

Even Niffer had calmed down. Sure, the child still whined when she didn't get her way. And she would choose candy over a healthy meal, given half a chance. But she'd taken to the new structure in her life like the duck to water. Just that morning, she had returned her crayons to her toy box without being asked to straighten up the kitchen table.

For all intents and purposes, Kat's work here was done. Except for the accounting ledger.

Out in the studio, Rye laughed at something Brandon said. No. Rye was not a reason to stay in Eden Falls. He lived in Richmond. He was on the threshold of his own successful career.

She flashed again on a memory of how incredible it had felt to lie within the shelter of his arms. His heartbeat had pounded against her own. His warmth had enfolded her as she drifted off to sleep.

She had braved the embarrassment of shopping at the drugstore, of securing the protection they needed, so that they could complete what they'd started Friday night.

No. Rye was a spring fling. A light touch of relief as she juggled all the responsibilities of family. An enjoyable confirmation that her demanding life in New York hadn't ruined her, that she could still be a desirable woman.

She didn't have any right to turn their fun and games into anything more. It wouldn't be fair to Rye. It wouldn't be fair to herself.

Squaring her shoulders, Kat clicked on the button to reply to Haley's email. She typed:

Glad to hear all is well. I'm wrapping things up here and should be home in time to sign up. Thanks a million times over! XOXO. Kat

She read the message four times before she clicked Send. And then she dug out the studio's oversize checkbook, determined to calculate all of Rachel's red ink, down to the last penny. Then, she'd be free to leave Eden Falls. To return to her home. To New York.

Out in the studio, Rye was pleased to find that a drop cloth had caught the spilled staples and oversize staple gun that Brandon had dropped. Nevertheless, he said to his cousin, "Let's take this thing outside. I don't want anything to scratch the new floorboards."

"You're the boss," Brandon said. He hitched up his Levi's before he helped Rye maneuver the heavy cloth out the door.

It was only when they stood in the parking lot that

Rye said, "Wait a second. There's just a handful of staples." He looked over at Brandon. "What the hell made so much noise?"

"You mean this?" Brandon reached into the bed of the truck, fishing out a clean metal tray for painting. He shoved it beneath the tarp and then emptied a box of staples onto it. The clatter was suitably dramatic.

"What the—"

"I had to get you out of that office, buddy."

"What are you talking about?"

"I heard the two of you talking. Don't you realize that girl thinks you're picking out wedding invitations?"

Rye laughed. "You don't know what you're talking about. She accidentally pulled up that screen. She was showing me how to put together flyers for the new business."

Brandon snorted. "You've got it bad, don't you? You'll believe just about anything."

"You couldn't see the computer screen, Bran. I'm telling you, it was filled with ballet shoes."

"*What if I want the silver, from the other screen?*" Brandon quoted.

Rye sighed. "I was just teasing her. There isn't anything serious between us. There can't be. She's heading back to New York in a week or two."

Brandon bent to retrieve the paint tray and staples, taking his time to stow them in the bed of the pickup. He was still facing the truck when he muttered, "That shouldn't be the only reason there isn't anything serious."

Of course, Rye heard him. Rye was pretty sure he was *supposed* to hear him. "What are you talking about?"

"Hey, I've got eyes. And I know you. I knew you a

couple of years ago, when that crazy Marissa chick was jerking you around, and you were practically living on my couch."

"I wasn't living on your couch."

Brandon pinned him with glittering eyes. "No, you just stopped by every other night because I'm such a wonderful cook. Come on, man. That was Johnnie Walker *Gold* that we killed the night your Marissa said she was heading out to California."

"She wasn't 'my' Marissa," Rye said automatically.

"Of course not. She was just the reason you forfeited the lease on your first place up in Richmond. And put off getting your contractor's license, for two years running. And didn't bid on that antebellum mansion gig. Or that showcase house. Or—"

"Okay!" Rye clenched his fists, his stomach churning at the memory of all the opportunities he'd let go because of Marissa.

"No," Brandon said. "It's not okay. Because I see you doing the same thing, all over again. You're throwing away your life, because of a woman. You're staying in Eden Falls, even after you promised to get the hell out of Dodge."

"I have an office up in Richmond, Bran." Rye barely held his temper in check.

"And just look at how much time you're spending up there." Brandon reached into the back of the truck, pulling a soda out of the cooler that was lashed to the bed. He popped the top and passed it to Rye before salvaging another for himself. He downed half the drink in a few noisy swallows before gesturing with the can. "Don't do this, buddy. I'm telling you. She isn't worth it."

She's worth a lot more than you know, Rye thought.

You haven't seen her, the way she can laugh. The way she cares about—really loves—her niece. The way she's set aside her own life, helping out her family when they need her. You haven't seen the way she looks with her hair down, and her lips swollen from a good kiss, and....

But of course he didn't say anything out loud. Instead, he sipped from his own soft drink can and stared across the parking lot, as if the billboard on the far side held the answer to all the secrets of the universe.

He wasn't going to fight his cousin over this. Especially when he knew that Brandon was right about one thing. Kat was going to leave Eden Falls, and then all the fun and games would be over. Kat was heading back to the National Ballet and New York, to the life that she'd built for herself.

And nothing Rye could say would change that. Marissa Turner had taught him that, for sure. He could never control a woman. Only himself. Only his own decisions.

Brandon finished his soda in another long swig, belching before he crushed the can and tossed it into the back of the truck. "I pity you, buddy. You've sure got it bad."

Rye punched him on the shoulder. "Shut up, Bran, okay? Let's get back in there. It's time to get this job done."

"You're the boss. Just remember, you can hang out on my couch, anytime you need to."

As Brandon headed back into the studio, Rye pretended to remember that he had to make a phone call. He was only standing there, though, with his mobile beside his ear. Standing there and realizing that Brandon was right. Rye did have it bad.

Because no matter how this ended, no matter how broken up he would be when Kat went back to New York, he wasn't ready to stop yet. No, this wasn't the same as it had been with Marissa. He wasn't going to throw his own life away, just because of a woman.

But he was going to enjoy himself while he could. He was going to follow through on the unspoken offer that Kat had made when she invited him in for a drink. He was going to enjoy whatever time they had together—a week, two weeks, whatever.

He just had to make sure things didn't get messy. He just had to make sure that neither of them expected more than the other was offering. He just had to make sure that there were no strings attached.

Picking out wedding invitations. Brandon didn't know what the hell he was talking about. Kat wasn't some flighty girl, living her entire life with the single goal of getting a wedding band on her finger. She'd be just as happy as Rye was to enjoy whatever they had, for however long they had it. And when it came time to put her on the Yankee Clipper and send her back north, that was exactly what he would do.

After a few minutes, Rye realized that he must look like an idiot, standing in a parking lot, holding a cell phone to his ear, not saying a word. As he slid his phone back into his pocket, he realized that he felt like an idiot, too. He could bluster and boast all he wanted, but there was a truth he had to admit—at least to himself.

He had fallen for Kat Morehouse. Fallen hard. And no amount of saying otherwise would change the shape of the hole she was going to leave in his heart when she headed back to New York City.

Chapter Seven

Kat watched proudly as Niffer ate the last bite of broccoli on her plate. “Thank you for dinner, Gram,” the little girl said. “It was almost as good as dinner last night.”

Well, so much for perfect manners, Kat thought. At least Susan was smiling at Niffer indulgently. “And what did you girls do for dinner last night?”

Niffer answered before Kat could. “Mr. Harmon took us out for tacos!”

“Oh, really?” Susan arched a smile toward Kat before darting a look at Mike. Kat’s father made a show of chewing his meat loaf.

“We just grabbed something quick, Mama. Sort of a celebration for getting the painting done at the studio.” Kat heard the way her voice rose in pitch, even though she tried to sound casual. There was just a shadow of a hint of a possibility of a chance that Susan would accept the fact that Rye had treated them to a casual Mexican dinner for no reason whatsoever.

The questions would never stop coming, though, if Kat gave any hint of the midday break she had taken Wednesday afternoon….

It had all started innocently enough. Rye had said that she should leave the office for the rest of the day, that the paint fumes would get too strong. He had driven her home, confirming that Niffer was well-occupied with her after-school program. And then, he had ushered Kat into her bedroom, barely taking time to close the door behind him. They had both laughed as they produced identical silver-wrapped packets from behind the counter at Doherty's.

No. Susan didn't need to know anything at all about that. If Kat had had *her* way, her mother wouldn't have known anything about the taco dinner the night before, either.

Completely innocent, Niffer wiped her mouth with her napkin before folding the cloth and putting it beside her plate. "May I be excused, Gram?"

Susan looked astonished by the polite request, but she nodded at the little girl. "Certainly, Jen—um, Niffer. Thank you for asking so nicely."

Kat helped her niece wriggle down from the dining room chair. When she turned back to the table, Susan was shaking her head in amazement. "You have worked wonders with her, sweetheart."

Kat lifted her chin and smiled. "I really think she wanted some structure in her life. You always said that you and Daddy set your rules so that Rachel and I would know how much you love us."

Mike looked up from his armchair at the head of the

table. "I didn't think you listened to a word your mother and I said while you were growing up."

"Daddy!" Kat laughed. "Of course I did. I can recite all your lessons by heart." She closed her eyes and raised up a finger, as if she were recounting the Ten Commandments. "A fool and his money are soon parted." She added a second finger. "If you don't have anything nice to say, don't say anything at all." One more finger. "Never assume malice, when stupidity is an explanation."

Susan laughed. "She has you there, love. I think the only thing she learned from me is 'stop making that face, or it might freeze that way.'"

Kat shook her head. "No, Mama. You taught us a lot more than that." Before she could elaborate, though, the phone rang.

Susan bustled into the kitchen, only to return with the handset. "What? I can't hear you! There's too much noise in the background!" Susan took the phone away from her ear and squinted at the buttons. She punched the one for volume five times in rapid succession. "Who is this?" she shouted back into the phone.

"Mom!" Now the sound was loud enough that Kat could make out her sister's voice.

"Rachel?" Susan looked as if she might drop the phone. Kat heard a skitter of footsteps, and Niffer was back in the room, hugging her grandmother and reaching for the handset as if it were a lifeline. Susan pulled back a little before she shouted, "Where are you?"

"I'm in D.C., Mom! Staying with friends! We're having a party!"

Mike muttered at the far end of the table, "Tell me something I don't know."

Niffer started whining, "Mommy! Let me talk to Mommy!"

Susan shushed her granddaughter. "Rachel, when are you coming home?"

"That's why I called, Mom!"

Niffer was still whimpering, trying to get her little hands on the phone. "Hush," Kat said. "Come here, Niffer. You can sit on my lap, and we'll talk to Mommy after Gram is done." She measured out the moment when the little girl thought about refusing, but then Niffer let herself be held.

Rachel was still shouting over the line. "I'm catching a ride tomorrow! I'll be there by noon!"

"Wonderful, dear," Susan said. "Niffer has a T-ball game tomorrow afternoon. You can see her play."

"Who?"

"Niffer. Jenny."

There was a commotion on the other end of the line, some sort of shouting match that resolved into a cluster of voices shouting "Ten! Nine! Eight!"

Rachel added her own treble above the countdown. "Gotta go, Mom! See you tomorrow!"

The silence in the room echoed after the connection was broken. Susan stared at the handset as if it might come back to life. Mike scowled, his thoughts about his wayward daughter patently clear on his face. Kat shook her head. Rachel hadn't mentioned her at all, hadn't even asked about their father's health.

Niffer, though, bounced off Kat's lap and ran across the room to hug Susan. "Mommy's coming home! I get to see Mommy tomorrow!"

Susan smoothed her granddaughter's hair. "Yes, dear," she said automatically.

Kat sat back in her chair. Looking at her parents'

faces, she realized that Susan and Mike thought the same thing she did. Rachel was about as likely to show up at Niffer's T-ball game as she was to win a Nobel Prize. The interstate to D.C. might as well have been the Trans-Continental Railroad. And there was no real way to cushion the blow for an excited little girl.

Kat had to do something, though. "Niffer, honey. Go pick up your toys in the other room. Gram is going to drive us home in five minutes."

When Niffer looked up, a spark of her old rebellion glinted deep in her coal-black eyes. "When Mommy's back, Gram won't have to drive us everywhere. Mommy's smart enough to drive a car."

"Niffer!" Susan warned.

Kat, though, waved off the confrontation. "Clean up your toys, Niffer. Now."

The little girl dragged her feet as she harrumphed across the room.

Mike glared after her. "I thought that child was through with all her back-talking."

Kat shrugged. "She's just excited. And I don't have the heart to get angry with her, because I know she's going to end up disappointed tomorrow."

"You don't *know* that," Susan tsked.

Kat sighed. "I hope you're right, Mama."

No one said another word on the topic. But Kat couldn't help but realize her father didn't correct her. He was as mistrustful of Rachel as she was. It was a long ride home, listening to Niffer ramble on about all the presents she hoped her mother would bring.

Rye glanced in the mirror of the hotel lobby, making sure that his tie was straight before he went into the conference room. He could already hear the murmur of conversation inside, the movers and shakers of the Richmond business world conducting their most important deals at the monthly Chamber of Commerce dinner. He was willing to bet that the salads had already been served, that the bone-dry breasts of chicken were on their way.

He'd rather be in Eden Falls. He'd rather be sitting in Susan and Mike Morehouse's dining room, watching Niffer wrinkle up her nose at the broccoli that she had already denounced when he took her out for tacos the night before. He'd made Niffer promise to eat every last bite, saying that her grandmother would be disappointed if she left any vegetables on her plate.

Kat's smile had been blinding. Or maybe he'd just been blinded by memories of Wednesday afternoon. Everything had seemed so simple when he had taken her home from the studio, using the paint fumes as an excuse for playing hooky. So easy. So *right*. Even now, he could hear her laughing as she told him some story about Niffer. He could hardly believe that he had ever thought of Kat as icy. As cold. As utterly, completely controlled in everything she did. He couldn't wait to see her lose that firm control again. As soon as he could get back down to Eden Falls.

"Hey, Rye!"

"Josh!" Rye extended his hand toward his fraternity brother. "I wasn't expecting to see you here."

"This is where the big deals get done, right?" Josh Barton flashed his old winning smile. "I heard a rumor you had set up shop here in Richmond."

"I figured it was finally time to get out of Eden Falls."

"Past time, I'd imagine." Josh had always been restless, even back in college. Rye supposed that was part of his charm with the ladies—the man dreamed big, and he wasn't afraid to have company on his journey. "What sort of work are you doing these days?"

Rye felt himself relax in the face of Josh's easy confidence. "A couple of kitchens, lately. Last winter, I did a complete restore on the old Wilson place. And just this week I finished renovating the Morehouse Dance Studio."

"*That* must have been a pain. Is that crazy Rachel still running the place for her mother?"

"Not for a while. She took off to visit friends out west." Rye shrugged. His explanation sounded better than, *she left town, ditching your daughter with her parents.* "Her sister came down from New York to help out. Kat."

"She's the one who went to that fancy ballet school?"

Rye nodded. He didn't want to talk to Josh about Kat. In fact, now that he thought about it, it was strange that Josh hadn't been around to help with Niffer. Take her for a weekend, at least. Especially since the guy still seemed to be pretty tied in to Eden Falls life. He'd asked about Rachel running the studio. He had to know about Mike Morehouse's illness, about the way the community was rallying to help out the family.

"At least one of those girls turned out sane." Josh gave Rye a knowing wink.

"What do you mean?"

"Come on! You know as well as I do—Rachel is *nuts!*"

No matter how much Rye might have agreed, the blatant criticism raised his chivalrous hackles. "She was always a little wild, yeah, but I wouldn't call her 'nuts.'"

Josh grinned. "Are we talking about the same woman? Played the field after she got out of high school? Spent half her time at the frat house, then tried to frame me for eighteen years of child support?"

A sliver of warning slipped into Josh's tone. "Frame?"

Josh shook his head. "That crazy bitch sued me for paternity. She had to withdraw the case, though, after all the tests came back. I dodged a bullet with that one!"

Rye laughed, because that's what he was supposed to do. Even as he responded on automatic pilot, though, his jaw was tightening into a stony line.

Josh shot his cuffs and nodded toward the conference room. "But enough about Eden Falls. You're in Richmond now. Ready to meet your new business partners?"

"You go ahead," Rye said. "I'm going to make a pit stop."

Rye watched in dismay as Josh disappeared down the hall. His ears were ringing, as if the lobby echoed. A metallic taste coated the back of his throat. *Dodged a bullet.*

Rachel Morehouse had told Rye, in no uncertain terms, that Josh Barton was the father of her baby. Rachel had said that her baby would never have a handyman for a father; no one but a lawyer was good enough for Rachel. Rachel had said that Rye was off the hook. Rachel had said…

Rye clutched at the marble counter in front of the mirror. Closing his eyes, he could see Niffer's jet-black hair, a perfect match for her mother's. But he could see the line of her jaw, as well, a line echoed in a dozen of Rye's nieces and nephews. And he could picture the girl standing at the plate in T-ball, getting ready to swing the bat left-handed. Rye looked down at his own left hand, staring at his palm as if he'd never seen it before.

For whatever twisted reason that passed as logic in

Rachel's rebellious mind, she had lied to him five years ago. Jennifer Morehouse was Rye's daughter.

Kat made sure that her father was comfortably settled on one of the benches behind home plate, and then she nodded toward a vendor who had set up his cart on the edge of the park. "Can I get you a hot dog, Daddy?"

"No, thanks. I'm fine."

"A Coke, then?"

"I don't need anything."

Susan had been worried about the late-afternoon start of the game; she hadn't wanted anyone to go hungry. As a result, she'd spent the afternoon setting out "nibbles"—cheese and crackers and fruit and cookies—three times as much food as any normal meal. Kat didn't think she'd ever be hungry again.

As much as she was inclined to fuss over her father, she had to admit that he *did* look strong. Sure, his shirt hung loose at his throat. And his tight-belted trousers rode a little high on his hips. But the fresh air had brought color to his cheeks. He'd made the walk from the house without getting winded, in his best time yet since his surgery. Kat sat down beside him, but barely a minute passed before she jumped up and looked over her shoulder.

Mike's mouth pursed into a frown. "Don't waste your time looking for her, Kat. You know as well as I do that she's not going to make it."

Kat wanted to berate him. She wanted to say that he was tired, that he was depressed because of his long illness, that he wasn't being fair. But deep in her heart, she knew that she agreed with him. Rachel had said that she'd be home by noon, and it was already almost four. For the hundredth time, Kat wondered what her sister's friends had been counting down. How many more drinks had they downed to celebrate whatever it was? What else had they consumed, substances stronger than alcohol?

Before Kat could figure out an appropriate reply to her father, Susan left a cluster of her friends and came to join them on the bench. "Kat! Lauren says she saw your flyer in every store on Main Street. I can't tell you how many people told me how professional it looks."

Kat smiled automatically, but there was a chill beneath her reaction. Sure, the paperwork looked good. The class rosters were filling up. But she *still* hadn't broached the subject of the bank account with her mother. Every day that passed made Kat more worried, but no matter how many times she promised herself, she just couldn't find the words to deliver the bad news. She felt like she was living a lie, every time she talked about the studio but stayed silent about the money.

Before Kat could respond to Susan's compliment, Niffer came skidding to a stop in front of them. "The game's about to start! Is Mommy here yet?" The child craned her neck, peering around at the benches as if a full-grown woman might somehow be hiding nearby.

Susan answered for all of them. "Not yet, dear. Oh, look! Coach Noah is looking for you."

Niffer, though, directed her eyes over Kat's shoulder. "Mr. Harmon! Guess what! My mommy is coming to see me play today!"

Rye felt like someone had kicked him in his gut as he watched Niffer run back to the T-ball diamond. Rachel? Here?

His hands instinctively flexed into fists, as if he needed to defend himself in some battle. He wasn't ready to see Rachel. Not yet.

After walking out of the Chamber of Commerce dinner the night before, he had spent the entire night thinking about Josh's revelation. He'd tossed and turned on his mattress, tangling himself in his sheets until he swore and got up to splash cold water on his face.

How had he not seen the truth before? Why had he let Rachel's lies derail him? Why hadn't Rachel come after him for child support? And how was he going to tell Kat the truth? How could he tell Niffer?

Over and over, he asked himself what Rachel had possibly hoped to gain, keeping him in the dark.

But it all made sense, in a twisted way. Rachel thrived on drama. In her heart of hearts, she had to know that Rye would have stepped up, faced his responsibility. Rye would have done everything he could to help Rachel, to ease Niffer's strange, unbalanced life.

But Rachel could get far more mileage out of Josh being Niffer's father. She could sulk about being rejected by the guy who'd made it big. She could complain about the vast wealth that should have been hers. She could lash out against a system that had cheated her, denied her rights, cast her loose. And Josh wasn't around Eden Falls often enough to bother setting the record straight.

Rye had to figure out what was right, how he could take responsibility for Niffer now, at this relatively late date. But to do that, he needed to talk to Rachel. Rachel, who Niffer had just sunnily proclaimed was coming to the park.

Shoving down the feeling that his world was rapidly spinning out of control, Rye forced himself to smile at an unsuspecting Kat, to shake hands with Mike. Susan made a big show of coming over to kiss him on his cheek, to tell him how pleased she was about the renovations he'd completed at the dance studio. A quick glance from Kat reminded him of the cover story they'd concocted. According to the lies, Rye had just come in to freshen up the paint, to update the appearance of the Morehouse Dance Academy. Susan was never to know how badly Rachel had managed the business.

He forced himself to smile and make small talk with Kat's mother.

Rachel's mother, too.

What the hell was he going to do when she showed up? For all he knew, she might be in one of her crazy moods. If she saw that Kat and Rye were together, she might announce their past relationship to the entire world, trumpet it to the heavens for all to hear, just to see how everyone reacted.

He could only imagine the look that Kat would turn on him then. He could picture the hurt in her eyes, almost as clearly as if he already saw it. Sure, he had already told Kat that he'd dated her sister for a few weeks. But he'd purposely kept the extent of that "dating" vague. He certainly hadn't given a hint that a child could have resulted from that brief time together.

He needed a break to think this through. "Excuse me," he said. "I'm going to grab a hot dog before the game."

"I'll come with you," Kat chimed in, smiling. His heart sank, but he gave her a hand as she stepped down from the benches. He regretted how easily she twined her fingers between his, how comfortably she fell into step beside him as they made their way to the edge of the park.

Kat deserved better than this. She deserved more from him than being mortally embarrassed when her sister walked into the middle of this supposedly perfect spring afternoon.

"It's going to be okay," Kat said, as soon as they were out of earshot from her parents.

Rye started when she spoke, almost as if he were a child caught stealing cookies from the cooling rack. "What will?" he choked out.

"This whole thing with Rachel. We've tried to let Niffer know that she can't rely on her mother, that just because Rachel *said* she'd be here today, doesn't mean it's going to happen. It's so hard, though. Niffer hears what she wants to hear. I guess all kids do. The whole time we were walking over here, Niffer kept telling us that she's going to hit three home runs, just for Rachel. As if Noah could have coached her on how to do *that*." They walked another few steps in silence before she said, "That was sort of like a joke, Rye."

He shook his head, looking at her as if he were truly seeing her for the first time that day. "I'm sorry. I guess I'm a little preoccupied."

"We all have been. It's one thing for us adults to know we can't depend on Rachel. It's another for Niffer to learn the truth." She squeezed his hand gently. "I'm really touched that you're taking this so hard. It means a lot to me that you care so much about Niffer."

There, Rye thought. That was the opening he was looking for. That was the introduction he needed to tell Kat what was really on his mind.

But could he do that to her? Before he'd had a chance to talk to Rachel himself, to confirm the facts one last time? And could he break the news to Kat here, in full view of half the town, with an innocent T-ball game starting up behind them? He could already hear the children's shouts, the good-natured cheering for the kids at bat, for the ones in the field. And Kat was already wound so tight, worried about how Niffer would cope when Rachel didn't show.

When Rachel didn't show. Despite Niffer's heart-stopping announcement, Kat didn't think that Rachel was going to make it to the game. In fact, from the look on Mike's face, the man had been pretty certain his other daughter was a no-show. Come to think of it, even Susan had looked unsure.

Well, if Rachel didn't come to the park today, then Rye's secret was safe for a while longer. He could still track her down, get absolute confirmation. Then he could choose his time and his place. He could break things to Kat gently.

Hunching his shoulders, he folded his misery deeper into the nauseating sea of his emotions. He *would* clean this up. He had to. But this was neither the time, nor the place.

"Want a hot dog?" he asked, pulling out his wallet.

"You have got to be kidding." Kat laughed. "Do you know how bad those things are for you?"

"Worse than a burger and fries?" he retorted.

That did the trick. He knew that she was immediately thinking of the booth they had shared at the Garden Diner, of the meal that she had enjoyed with so much primal enthusiasm. Of the passion that had followed, on her couch. And, if her memory worked anything like his, of the follow-through in her bedroom, just a few days before.

"You should be careful," he said, lathering mock concern over his words. "It looks like you're getting a sunburn."

He supposed that he really did deserve the punch that she delivered to his shoulder. It was worth it, to get another look at the blush on her cheeks. He leaned closer, whispered in her ear, “Do you blush all over? Head to toe?”

He loved the little squealing noise she made in protest. He relished the thought that she would make him pay for his impertinence. Later. In private.

As much as Kat enjoyed sitting next to Rye on the bench, basking in the sun and watching the kids play ball, she felt her stomach twist into knots as the innings crept by. She caught herself glancing at her watch for the third time in as many minutes.

It was nearly five o'clock.

Kat caught Niffer looking worriedly at the stands as she came up to bat for the last time. Rye made a point of waving spiritedly to the little girl, starting up a chant. "Niff-er! Niff-er!" The child seemed to perk up at his attention, lifting her chin in a show of athletic determination. Kat almost laughed—her niece seemed to have learned the gesture from her sometime coach.

The bat cracked against the ball, and Niffer took off around the bases. When she stopped at second, she dusted off her hands, looking every bit a pro. Kat's heart almost broke, though, when the child shielded her eyes, gazing plaintively back at the stands.

Another three batters, and the game was over; Niffer’s team had won by two runs. Each child trotted out toward the pitcher’s mound, shaking hands with the opposition, as if they'd competed in the Olympics. Niffer joined in the group cheer that rounded out the game, and then she raced back to the benches.

“Where’s Mommy?” she asked, craning her neck for a better view. “Did Mommy see me bat?”

Mike’s face was creased with a mixture of anger and

fatigue. Susan sighed deeply. Kat held out her arms, ready to gather in her disappointed niece. But it was Rye who said, "Sorry, Niffer, your mother didn't come." His tone was matter-of-fact.

"But she said she would be here!"

"She must have made a mistake." Kat was grateful that Rye was being so reasonable, that he was speaking to Niffer as if she were an intelligent person, capable of handling an emotional blow. Anything else, and Kat was afraid that *she* would lose her own firm resolve to stay cheerful.

"Grown-ups don't make mistakes!" Niffer whined.

Grown-ups make mistakes all the time, Rye wanted to say. He felt as if his heart was breaking as he faced the result of his own biggest mistake.

Because Niffer's disappointment was yet another consequence of what he'd done with Rachel. If he had insisted on proof, way back when, if he had forced Rachel to share the results of the paternity test, then Niffer would not be so bereft today. She would have known all along that she had one loving parent to watch her accomplishments, to cheer her on.

Unable to say the words that would make everything right, he tried to do the next best thing. Pulling Niffer close to his side, he rubbed her narrow back with a sympathetic hand. "I'm sorry, kiddo. I wish your mommy had made it." He didn't. Not at all. Not yet. But he could fake the words well enough to fool a child. "I can think of one thing that might make everything better."

Niffer dug the toe of her sneaker into the ground, obviously reluctant to accept any comfort. "What?"

"How about an ice-cream cone?" That got her attention. "You can get yours with sprinkles."

"And a cherry on top?"

"Yeah. I think we can manage that." He looked up at the semicircle of adults. "Who's up for ice cream?"

Mike cleared his throat. "I think it's about time for me to head home. It's been a long day."

Susan chimed in immediately. "That makes two of us. That was such an exciting game, Niffer! Thank you for inviting us."

Mike took his time managing the two short steps from the bleachers to the ground. Rye offered him a steady forearm to balance against as he dropped the final few inches. The older man leaned close, clapping Rye on the back. "Thank you, son." The grim look in Mike's watery blue eyes let Rye know that the thanks were for more than a helping hand. "Thank you for taking care of my girls."

Kat's father wouldn't be so grateful if he knew the full story.

For that matter, neither would Kat. Rye's belly tightened as he caught her appreciative smile.

Kat waited until her parents were well on their way across the park before she turned back to her niece. "Okay, Niffer. Go get your glove, and thank Coach Noah." The little girl ran off. Kat looked at Rye. "You don't have to do this, you know."

"I want to."

"I've had a lifetime of being disappointed by my sister. Niffer had better get used to it. And I can assure you, you don't want to get wrapped up in this particular drama. It just repeats itself, over and over and over. Steer as far away as you can get."

"I'm already involved," Rye said, his voice deadly earnest.

Kat half expected him to make a joke as he said the

words. Well, not a joke exactly, but some friendly gesture of comfort, a sly side comment that would make her blush, something that would make her wish that there were a lot more days left in the spring, that New York and Richmond were not so very far apart.

But there was no secret message behind Rye's statement. There was no hidden tweak. He was stating a fact as bare as the red earth of the pitcher's mound behind him—he *was* already involved. He'd become involved the instant that she'd let him drive her home from the train station, the moment that he'd offered to renovate the studio. The second that she had leaned against him in the kitchen, pulling him close for that deeper kiss, for that soul-shocking meld that had echoed through the past couple of weeks, culminating in the afternoon they'd spent in bed—was it already four days before?

He looked like he was thinking of saying something else, but Niffer came bouncing back, glove in hand. "Can I get mint chocolate chip?"

Rye said, "If they have it."

"What flavor are you getting, Aunt Kat?"

Kat smiled and ruffled her niece's hair. "I don't eat ice cream, sweetheart."

"Never?" Niffer's eyes got very big.

"Never."

Niffer scrunched up her nose. "Do you eat ice cream, Mr. Harmon?"

"Every chance I get," he said, making the little girl laugh. "My favorite is coffee mint mango crunch."

"That's not a real flavor!"

"Hmm," Rye said, as if he were considering the matter for the very first time. "Maybe I'll just get butter pecan, then."

As they drew close to the truck, Niffer said, "Mr. Harmon, why don't you let Aunt Kat drive?"

Rye's laugh was short. "That's a great idea. What do you think, Aunt Kat? Want to get behind the wheel?"

Kat shot daggers at him with her eyes. "No, thank you," she said, making her voice as cold as the ice cream the others were about to enjoy. She couldn't resist adding a sarcastic edge. "But I really appreciate your asking."

"My pleasure," Rye said mildly.

He should know better than that, trying to egg her on in front of her niece. There was absolutely no way she was going to get behind the wheel of the silver truck. She was no idiot. She'd learned her lesson, in no uncertain terms. Only after she and Niffer were strapped into their seat belts did she think to ask, "Why do you care so much about whether I know how to drive, Niffer?"

"That's what grown-ups *do,*" the child said, as if the concept were as simple as one plus one. "I'm just a kid, so I need to have a grown-up take care of me. Gram and Pop-pop and Mommy don't love me anymore, but I thought that *you* could be my grown-up. You know. Forever." Niffer had spoken matter-of-factly, but her lower lip started to tremble as she looked out the window. "But you can't do it, Aunt Kat, because you don't know how to drive."

"Oh, sweetheart!" Kat folded her niece into a hug, looking hopelessly at Rye as he pulled out of the parking lot. He seemed to be concerned about the traffic on the road; all of his attention was riveted on the cars that streamed by. She had no idea where to start unpacking all the misunderstandings in what the child had said. "Gram and Pop-pop love you very much, but they need their house to be quiet right now, so that Pop-pop can keep getting better. Your mommy loves you, too, but she just can't be with you now. And grown-ups can take care of you, even if they don't know how to drive. *I* can take care of you."

"Will you be my forever grown-up?"

Kat's throat swelled closed with the sudden threat of tears. "Forever is a very long time, Niffer. I can promise you this. You'll never be left alone. You'll have a grown-up to help you for as long as you need someone. Okay?"

Niffer's dark eyes were very serious, as if she were weighing every syllable of Kat's vow. "Okay," she said at last.

As soon as they arrived at the ice-cream parlor, Niffer saw a friend, and she ran across the room, squealing with delight, their serious conversation completely forgotten. "Yikes," Kat said to Rye as they took their place in line. "I had no idea how to respond to that!"

Yikes, indeed, Rye thought. It had been everything he could do not to stop the truck right there in the parking lot. Not to turn to Kat and Niffer and make his confession. Not to tell them the whole truth, get the horrible weight off his chest, shed it from around his heart.

Of course, he didn't say anything. Niffer would only be confused by what he had to say. The child was fragile enough, without witnessing her aunt's justified, unbridled rage. And Kat would—rightfully—be furious when she learned what had happened. And there was still a chance—a tiny one, but a chance nonetheless—that Rachel would tell him something different when he finally tracked her down, that she would have some other explanation, some proof.

But there was something else. Something he had only just started to work out for himself.

He didn't want to lose Kat, didn't want to miss out on her gorgeous smile, her easy companionship, the unrivaled excitement that she brought to their shared bed. Sure, they seemed great together. But she *was* heading back to New York soon, with or without Rye's big confession. He was going to lose her to the big city, to her life with the ballet—there had never been any other possible ending for their story together. This reckless spring was going to be a memory, probably in a week, maybe less.

Was it really so terrible to let Kat go without knowing the truth about him and Rachel? Was it the end of the world if she went back to her real life thinking fondly of Rye, of the time they had shared in Eden Falls?

Everything would be different, of course, if he had any chance of keeping her with him. But Kat was never going to come live with him in Richmond. She'd never trim her wings and settle for a second-rate city. Not when she could have it all in New York. And he had absolutely no basis for building a business in Manhattan.

It was only fair to Kat that he keep quiet—just for another week or two. Once she was safely in her real life, Rye would face the music. He'd step up and accept his responsibility, treat Niffer like his daughter, make sure that she was safe forever, that all her needs were met. There was just no need to make a formal acknowledgment now. No reason to ruin the short time that Kat had left in Eden Falls. This was a kindness to her. Really.

Rye resolved to ignore the headache that started

pounding behind his eyes as he ran through his justifications one more time.

Niffer came skipping to the counter when they neared the front of the line. Kat was pleased to see that Rye had finally relaxed after the tension of Rachel's no-show. He laughed as he ordered up Niffer's mint chocolate chip, complete with the mandatory sprinkles and cherry. Rye's own butter-pecan cone followed. He passed the ice cream to her so that he could pull his wallet out of his pocket.

Maybe it was the fragrance of the butter-rich ice cream. Maybe it was the freshly made waffle cone. Maybe it was the bright sunshine outside, or the emotional dam she had just built for Niffer. But suddenly Kat found herself saying to the woman behind the counter, "And I'll have a scoop of chocolate, please."

"Cone or cup?"

Cup was safest. No more calories. No greater threat to her dancer fitness.

But this was the first time she'd had ice cream in years. "Waffle cone, please." Rye laughed and paid the total.

"Aunt Kat!" Niffer said as they sat down at a tiny metal table. "You got ice cream!"

"I couldn't let you have all the fun, could I?" She licked her cone, and the ice cream melted across her tongue, cold and rich and satisfying. She laughed in pure enjoyment, marveling at the simple pleasure she had denied herself for so long. Niffer joined in, and Rye wasn't far behind. Before long, Kat couldn't even have said what was so funny. What was so perfect. All she knew was that *this* was living, *this* was embracing the world in a way that she had almost forgotten how to do.

They finished their treats and walked back to the

truck. Before Rye could open the door, a siren began to wail in the distance. Kat automatically looked around for the source, and she spotted a huge fire engine, barreling down the road. The deep horn boomed as the truck approached the intersection, making Niffer huddle against her hip. "It's okay," Kat said automatically. Nevertheless, she held her niece close until the truck had disappeared.

"Hmm," Kat mused, as Rye turned the key in the ignition. "That's the first siren I've heard since I came to Eden Falls. Back in New York, I hear a dozen before breakfast."

"A dozen fire trucks?" Niffer asked.

"Some fire trucks. And police cars and ambulances, too. You can hear the noise all day long. All night, too." Even as Kat thought about it, she realized that her nights had been peaceful in Eden Falls. In fact, she routinely fell asleep as soon as her head hit the pillow, and she slept so soundly that she couldn't remember her dreams in the morning.

Not like New York, at all. Back in the noisy apartment that she shared with Haley, she woke up nearly once an hour. If it wasn't sirens, it was barking dogs, or screeching garbage trucks, or noisy people on the street, six floors below. Even when Kat *did* sleep in New York, she was disturbed by vivid dreams, by nightmares that jolted her awake as she imagined tumbling off a stage, or breaking her leg when her partner failed to catch her after some dramatic leap.

Maybe that was why her foot had healed so fast here in Eden Falls. She was sleeping well for the first time in years.

Speaking of which… "Okay, Niffer. As soon as we

get home, I want you changing into your nightgown and brushing your teeth. Got it?"

"Got it!" The little girl was already yawning as Rye pulled into the driveway.

Kat took extra care tucking Niffer into bed. She smoothed the sheets carefully, folding them so that they weren't too high on the child's chest. She kissed Niffer on her forehead, switched on the night-light, told her to "Sleep tight!" She sat beside Niffer's bed, watching as the little girl's frown smoothed out, as her breathing evened, as she slipped deep into sleep.

Will you be my forever grown-up? Kat's heart seized at the earnestness behind Niffer's question.

Rye was waiting in the living room.

"I am going to murder my sister," she said, whispering so that Niffer couldn't hear.

For answer, Rye held out his arms. She let him fold her close to his chest. His shirt smelled of sunlight and spring air and something that was indefinably, unmistakably *Rye.* His arms tightened around her, carving out a refuge, making her feel safe. She felt his lips brush against the crown of her head.

"I'm sorry," he murmured.

She wanted to tell him that it wasn't his fault. She wanted to tell him that Rachel had always been a flake, that Kat truly could not remember a time when she had been able to trust her sister to keep a promise. She wanted to tell him that she was grateful for all that he had done, for coming to the game, for treating them to ice cream. For coming inside now, and for holding her close.

She pulled back enough that she could look up at his face, and all the need for words disappeared. Instead, he touched his lips to hers, sudden urgency overtaking his initial chaste sweetness. Kat laced her fingers between his and led him toward her bed.

Chapter Eight

Kat flexed her left ankle and walked across the dance studio floor. "I can't believe it," she said to her mother. "My foot feels so light!" She glared at the bright blue boot she had just removed.

"Are you sure you should be walking on it?" Susan fussed.

"The X-rays came back fine. Daddy's surgeon said that he could barely see where the original fracture was." That morning, Kat had insisted on visiting her father's doctor. Her foot felt entirely healed; she could not remember the last time she'd felt a twinge of pain. It was time to be shed of the boot.

Still, Susan shook her head. "I worry about you, Kat."

"Mama, I'm fine."

"You push yourself too hard. You always have. At least you've taken a bit of time off while you've been here. It seems like you and that Harmon boy are getting along quite well."

Kat laughed at her mother's not-so-subtle hint, even as she felt her cheeks flush crimson. "No, Mama," she said, meeting Susan's eyes in the mirror. "I *don't* have anything to tell you about Rye and me."

"I wasn't asking!"

"Of course not."

"It's just that I like seeing you happy. I understand that you actually had an ice-cream cone, when he took you and Niffer out after the game?"

"Who told you that?"

"Teresa Rodriguez saw the three of you sitting at a table."

"Does every single detail of everybody's life get broadcast in this town?" Kat tried to sound annoyed, but she was actually quite amused. Susan looked as pleased as a well-fed cat that she had gleaned information about Kat's not-date.

"Not every detail, dear. Teresa couldn't remember if you ordered chocolate or coffee crunch."

Kat's mock frown twisted into a laugh. "You know me. Chocolate was always my favorite. It's Rachel who likes coffee crunch."

"That's right," Susan agreed. "Besides, Teresa wasn't really reporting on ice-cream flavors. She was much more interested in telling me about your boyfriend."

"Rye isn't my boyfriend," Kat said, but she spat out the words a trifle too quickly. She wouldn't have believed herself, if she'd been on the receiving end of that denial. She tried to change the topic. "He *has* done a great job here, hasn't he?"

Susan looked around her studio, her fond smile testifying that she knew exactly what her daughter was doing. "I don't remember the last time the place looked so fine. We should be able to earn back all the lost income by autumn."

Kat's heart stuttered over a few beats. "Lost income?" she asked, as if she'd never heard the words before.

"Those checks from the fall session that Rachel never deposited? The money from spring and all those classes she let fall by the wayside?"

Susan sounded perfectly complacent as she enumerated her other daughter's shortcomings. Kat had rehearsed those words, over and over in her own mind. She'd tried to figure out how to say them simply, without affect, without any hint of the outrage that churned inside her whenever she thought of Rachel's failings. All that time Kat had rehearsed, but Susan had already known the lines. "Mama! When did you find out?"

Susan shrugged. "I've known all along. I kept hoping Rachel would pull herself together, that she'd get the money deposited for autumn term. Every day, I meant to ask her about the checks, to tell her that she wasn't being fair, failing to get the money to the bank. I never got around to it, though, with everything getting so crazy after your father got sick."

"She had an obligation to you, Mama! To the studio!"

Susan's smile reflected a lifetime of quiet hope, decades of constantly readjusting her expectations. "I knew what was going on. Fairness to me wasn't an issue. I never should have counted on Rachel to pull together an entire set of classes for spring. She's never had any interest in dance."

"She didn't have to be interested in dance! She had to be interested in *you!* In you and Daddy! She had to be interested in our family and do whatever she could to help out."

Susan shook her head sadly. "We both know that's not Rachel's strong suit, is it?"

"I don't think Rachel *has* a strong suit," Kat countered. Even as she said the spiteful words, though, she held up a hand. She didn't want to fight with her mother, to force a conversation about difficult things. "Forget I said that," she apologized. "But I still can't believe she just did nothing. That she let the studio fall apart like that."

"It wasn't all her fault, dear. I looked the other way. I knew the classes weren't going forward, and I let that happen. Sure, there were some disappointed little dancers…I know that. But I spoke to as many of the parents as I could, explained what was going on. Most of them already knew, of course. They were stopping by to bring meals, keeping me company at the hospital."

"But it didn't have to come to this! You should have called me back in December, when you first realized that things weren't on track for the spring term. I could have straightened things out before they ever got this bad!"

"And missed *Nutcracker?*"

The question cut like a knife. Of course Kat wouldn't have wanted to miss *The Nutcracker Suite*. She had been featured as the Sugar Plum Fairy. But now that she realized Susan had known what was happening, that Susan had been fully aware of how her lifetime's investment in the studio was fading away to nothing under Rachel's lazy management… "Mama, I would have come here in an instant. You know that."

"I know, dear. And honestly, that's why I didn't call

you. It's not fair that you should always be dragged in to clean up the messes that your sister leaves behind."

Susan sounded so sad, so utterly bereft, that Kat didn't know how to respond. She tried: "Mama, I've been so worried. I couldn't figure out how to tell you that the account was going to be low. I kept picturing you writing out a check and only then finding out that you had nothing left in the bank. The more I imagined it, the worse it became!"

"I keep a better eye on my checkbook than that, dear!"

"I know—or, at least, I always thought you did. I just figured that with Daddy so sick, and you so distracted, you hadn't even realized what was happening. I think I started to write you a hundred different letters, outlining everything and offering to help in any way that I could."

Susan shook her head. "I'm sorry this was all so stressful for you, dear. You should know by now—honesty is the best policy."

"Well I *do* know that, in general. But because Rachel was involved, I just felt like…" She trailed off, unsure of how she wanted to finish that statement.

"You just felt like you had to protect your sister."

Hearing those words brought tears to Kat's eyes. She *did* feel like she had to protect Rachel. Or, rather, she *had* felt that way. Now she was tired of covering for her twin, tired of spinning out reassurances and lies. It had taken twenty-four years, but Kat was finally ready to accept that she and Rachel were completely separate people. She wasn't responsible for the bad decisions that Rachel made. She couldn't change them, couldn't make them right.

"I'm sorry, Mama," she said, and it was an apology for all the things she'd said, and all the things she hadn't.

"Your father and I will always love both you girls. But we aren't blind. We see what Rachel has done with her life. It's taken us both a number of years, but we accept that we can't do anything to change that. To change her. The most we can do is to make sure that her daughter is taken care of, that an innocent child has the comfort and stability to grow into the person she is meant to be."

Kat thought of Niffer's matter-of-fact statement on the way to get ice cream, the child's certainty that she wasn't loved. "Niffer's a good girl, but she doesn't understand what's going on here. She's afraid she's going to be abandoned."

A shadow ghosted over Susan's face. "Your father and I worried about that when we asked you to come down here. We knew that Niffer would think we were pushing her away. But we hoped that she would find new strength with you, that she would realize there was yet another person who loves her, who wants to see her succeed. And in our wildest dreams, we never imagined that your father would recover so quickly, once the house settled down a little."

"I think I was too tough on Niffer when I first got here. I made her follow too many rules."

"Nonsense," Susan said. "The proof is in the pudding. That child is better than she's been in months."

Kat nodded. She'd seen Niffer's improvement. She'd seen the difference that her presence had made. And that was why Kat had reached a decision.

When she'd arrived in Eden Falls, Kat had planned on staying seven days, maybe ten. Those days, though, had stretched into weeks. And somewhere along the way, Kat had told herself a secret—she had decided to stay for even longer. She was going to stay in Eden Falls forever.

What had she told her mother, way back when she first came to town? She would leave the National Ballet Company the instant that dancing stopped being fun.

Sure, she had planned on dancing in New York for the rest of her life. She *knew* the company, understood the way it worked, knew its system in her very bones. She had set her goals, developed her strategies, lived by her very detailed rules. But somewhere along the way, it had stopped being fun. It had taken its toll on her sleep, on her physical health, on her mental stability.

When was the last time she'd even thought of the company? When had she spoken with Haley? It had been at least a week. No, almost two. Somehow, ballet gossip had become less compelling while she worked on finalizing things here at the studio. The hundred and one backstage dramas that she and Haley usually shared had lost a little—no, a *lot*—of their appeal. Life had come to seem so much richer, here in Eden Falls.

Besides, Kat could never get in shape in time for the *Coppelia* auditions. Of course she had always wanted to dance Swanilda. She was perfect for the role. But she could not deny that she had lost some muscle mass, with her foot confined to a cast. And she'd put on a couple of pounds, indulging in real meals, like a real woman, spending time with a real family.

Before, that weight would have sent her to the workout room, driven her to exercise as if she were harried by a thousand demons. But not anymore. Not now that Kat had made up her mind.

Not now that she was going to be Niffer's forever grown-up.

Amanda and Susan would just have to get used to driving her around town. They wouldn't mind, really. Shared drives would be a chance for all of them to spend time together.

Once Kat made up her mind, she felt as light as air, as certain as she'd been of anything since she'd been fourteen years old, since she'd headed up to New York to seek her fortune. She turned to face her mother. "Mama, I have something to tell you. I think I've known it for a while. Since I realized that we needed someone to teach the Advanced Showcase for the spring term."

"Darling, I can—"

"No, Mama. You can't. But I can. And I want to. I want to stay in Eden Falls." She saw that Susan didn't believe her, didn't truly understand, but she laughed all the same. "This feels right to me, Mama."

"But New York… Everything you've worked for. Everything you've spent your entire life—"

"Not my entire life, Mama. I spent more years here, with you and Daddy, than I've spent in New York. And it's time for me to come home now." Kat surprised herself, realizing how wonderful those words sounded. "It's time. Come on, Mama. Let me show you the calendar I set up on your computer."

She couldn't say whether she laughed because of Susan's expression of pleased surprise, or because her body felt so light and balanced as she crossed the studio floor without the hated walking cast.

By Sunday, Kat's foot felt as strong as it had before her fracture. She had tried hard to limit her time at the barre, conscientiously keeping from stretching her practices into hours-long torture sessions. Nevertheless, she was overjoyed to find that her strength had rebounded so quickly.

The absence of the boot made it easier to carry food to the sprawling picnic tables in the park. It was Sunday—May Day and Eden Falls's traditional Family Day celebration. In honor of the spring festivities, Kat had worn a green blouse. She'd actually bought it for the occasion, dragooning Amanda into driving her to one of the tiny shops on Main Street. Her cousin had been only too happy to help her pick out something more appropriate than New York black. Eventually, she'd have to choose a whole new wardrobe.

For now, though, Kat wasn't worried about clothes. Instead, she was worried about balancing the pair of desserts she had made with Susan. The lemon chess pie was a family favorite, and Niffer had begged for blackberry cobbler. Kat suspected that the child really just wanted to eat spoonfuls of the traditional whipped-cream topping.

"Go ahead, Niffer," Kat said, as they arrived at the park. "Go play with the other kids."

"I don't know anyone."

"Of course you do. I can see three different kids on your T-ball team."

"Will you come with me?"

Kat started to sigh in exasperation, but she thought better of herself. If Niffer wanted an adult's company, that was a small enough gift that Kat could provide. "You go over there, and I'll come see you in a moment. I just need to set these things down."

Kat added the desserts to a picnic table that looked like it might break under the combined weight of all the baked goods. The city of Eden Falls certainly knew how to throw a party. Kat could already smell hot dogs and hamburgers cooking on five or six grills. Another table was laden with salads, and there had to be a half-dozen coolers scattered under the trees, full of soft drinks and sweet tea.

After snagging a diet soda for herself and making sure that Susan and Mike were similarly cared for, Kat went to uphold her promise to her niece. Niffer came running up as Kat approached the gravel-covered playground.

"We're bored!" the child announced.

"How can you be bored?" Kat shaded her eyes, gesturing at all of the playground equipment. "You have a castle, and swings and a slide!"

"We *always* play on those. We need a new game."

A new game. Niffer had no idea just how foolish she was, coming to *Kat* for a new game. Ballet was the only game Kat had known for years. Somehow, she didn't think the kids would be excited about completing a hundred pliés. Then again, they might really get into the grand battements—those were basically an invitation to kick anyone who got within striking distance.

Somewhere between thinking about leg warm-ups and arm stretches, though, Kat remembered something Susan had said, weeks before. She smiled mischievously at Niffer and said, "How about Magic Zoo?"

"What's that?" Niffer sounded suspicious. Nevertheless, a half-dozen kids drew closer. Kat was going to have to make this good.

"First of all, everyone has to choose an animal, something you can find at the zoo. Think of it, but don't tell anyone yet!" She waited while the children selected their guises for the game. Several closed their eyes, as if they were imagining an entire menagerie. What had Susan said? That Kat had played the game by selecting crayons out of a bucket? The colors were supposed to mean something.... Well, there weren't any crayons around, so Kat was just going to have to improvise.

"Okay. Everyone choose a number between one and five. Got it?" Every child nodded, as serious as if they were completing a military exercise. "Now, listen carefully. Each number is a different magical ability. I'm going to tell you the magical abilities, and then you'll have to figure out how your animal uses its special skill. Everyone is going to close their eyes while you do that, and I'm going to hide this..." Kat hadn't thought that far ahead. What was she going to hide? What could the kids hunt for in their imaginary game?

"This bandanna." Rye made the announcement from directly behind her. She spun around to face him, astonished that she hadn't heard him approach. He'd been up in Richmond for the past week, tied up in business meetings, cementing the details on half a dozen new projects that had grown out of his attending that Chamber of Commerce dinner.

She had phoned him a week ago, after talking to her mother.

She had told him about her decision, about her choice to stay in Eden Falls.

He'd been shocked into silence at first, and then he'd started to apologize, started to explain that he had to stay in Richmond, that his business was there. She had laughed and told him that she knew. She understood. It was horrible, rotten luck that she hadn't returned home before he had left, but there were only a couple of hours of freeway between them. Somehow, some way, they would make it work.

She'd even said: "Rye, I know how it's been before. I know there were women who tied you to Eden Falls. Who made you feel like you had to stay here. I'm not those women. It's never going to be that way between us."

His voice had thickened then, as if he were overwhelmed with some emotion. He'd cleared his throat, said her name, almost as if he were bracing himself to make some grand confession. But that was silly. There wasn't anything for him to confess.

She'd missed him fiercely for the past week—more than she could have imagined, just a month before. But now he was back in Eden Falls, for Family Day. He was standing beside her, lowering his voice as if he were telling the children ghost stories at a campfire. He brandished his crimson bandanna before the children's fascinated faces. "This bandanna can work magic spells," he said. "It belongs to a princess who is being held captive in a tower, locked in by an evil magician. The princess can only be rescued by someone smart enough and brave enough to find the bandanna and wear it."

Kat watched the children's eyes grow wide at the fairy tale that Rye spun. "Okay," she said. "Remember your numbers now. One means you can fly. Two lets you be invisible. Three lets you walk through walls. Four gives you the ability to change into another animal. And five..." She trailed off. What was a fifth magical ability? What else could she factor into the kids' game?

Rye picked up the instructions, as if he'd known them all along. "And five lets you read minds."

Perfect. Kat flashed him a smile before she said, "Okay. Everyone cover your eyes, while the evil magician hides the bandanna!" The kids took the responsibility seriously—they buried their faces in the crooks of their arms. Kat waited until Rye had crossed the playground, planted the bandanna in the shadows at the base of the slide and sidled back to her. "All right, animals!" she shouted. "I'm going to count to five. And when I finish, you'll all be in the Magic Zoo!"

She drew out the count dramatically, stretching out the numbers until she shouted, "Five!" The kids flew off, lumbering like invisible elephants, roaring like flying lions.

Rye laughed as they tumbled across the playground. "That should keep them busy for a while."

"That was the idea," Kat said smugly.

Rye was suddenly nervous, standing alone with Kat. Every night for the past week, he'd tried to reach Rachel, calling her cell phone, sending text messages. While waiting for a response, he'd worked on how to tell Kat the truth about Niffer. He'd started to phone Kat a dozen times, mapping out the words in his mind, figuring out every single thing he had to say, so that it would be proper, so that she would understand.

And every time, he found he just couldn't tell her over the phone. And now, in the park, surrounded by the Eden Falls Family Day celebration, he had to wait yet again.

The breeze carried a whiff of her honey-apricot scent toward him, and he couldn't help but take a step closer. "So," he said, after swallowing hard. "You're wearing green to celebrate your jailbreak?"

"Jailbreak?" She looked confused.

He nodded toward her foot. "The boot?"

"Finally!" She spun in a circle, laughing. "I can move again. I didn't realize how confining that thing was until I had it off. But I'm wearing green for my new life, here in Eden Falls. For spring."

"It looks great on you," he said. "It sets off the color of your eyes." He couldn't resist trailing his hand along the garment's sleeve, touching the fold on the inside of her elbow. The fabric was nearly as soft as the tender flesh it covered. He felt the shiver that rocketed through Kat's body, and he almost laughed out loud.

Before he could lower his voice, though, before he could think of something that would make her move one step closer, a tumble of kids frothed around them, like puppies overturning a basket.

"That was too easy!"

"We found the bandanna!"

"Hide it again!"

Rye laughed and nodded toward Niffer, who brandished the bandanna as if it were a carnival prize. "You go ahead and hide it now. Find a better place. You can use the whole park."

The kids shrieked with excitement, barely managing to cover their eyes. Niffer flew off toward the castle, intent on securing her treasure. Soon enough, the entire herd had thundered away again.

"So," Rye said, stepping closer to Kat. "Where were we?"

"I think I was about to tell you my foot is as good as new." She flexed one of her long legs, extending her toes in a graceful arch that defied the strappy sandals she wore.

Laughing, he closed his hands around her waist. "Wasn't this where we started, ten years ago? With you stretching that leg?" He pulled her close and slanted his lips over hers. He might need to keep this kiss clean enough for a public park, but there was no reason it had to be the fraternal gesture he had tried—and failed—to deliver years before.

"I guess it was," Kat whispered against his throat. "Even though I didn't realize we were starting *anything* that day." She settled her arms around his neck, relishing the feeling that he was claiming her, announcing that she was his, at least for today, for as long as they were both in Eden Falls. She caught her breath against a sudden pang at the thought of being separated from Rye, of losing him forever.

No. She had already told him this. It was best that he continue with his business in Richmond. He had planned so long, worked so hard. He would hate her forever, if she asked him to give up his dreams. That was why she'd been patient for the past week. Why she'd managed not to phone him every single night. She had to be content with everything she had—and do her best to lure him to Eden Falls, early and often. "I have an idea," she whispered against the corner of his mouth. "For how we might *end* this. At least for today."

He chuckled and pulled her closer.

Even as she started to remind him—remind them both—that they were standing in a public park, in broad daylight, there was the sound of one person clapping. The noise was sharp, irregular, and Kat whirled around, barely noticing that Rye's hand on her waist helped her keep her balance on the soft grass.

"What would Mom think, Kat? Should I go get her, so she can see what you're really like?"

Kat recognized the voice, even before her mind processed the old words. "Rachel," Kat said, the two syllables clattering between them like hail.

"Kat," her sister replied evenly. "Rye."

Kat stared into eyes that matched her own silver-gray. But those other eyes were rimmed with heavy eyeliner and multiple coats of mascara. And framed by hair that had been dyed a brilliant, unnatural magenta. Rachel had put on weight since the last time Kat had seen her; the line of her jaw was soft, and there were bags beneath her eyes. But there was no mistaking her twin. And no mistaking the oath that Rye muttered, barely under his breath.

"What are you doing here?" Kat asked, scarcely aware that her fingers were curling into fists.

"You were in the room when I called Mom and Dad. I said I'd visit my baby."

"You were supposed to be here a week ago. Niffer expected you at her T-ball game."

"Niffer?" Rachel's laugh was as harsh as fingernails on a chalkboard. "Who came up with that idiotic name?"

"I did." Rye stepped forward.

Rachel's eyes narrowed. "There was nothing wrong with Jenny."

Rye answered evenly, as if he were measuring out each word with the level in his tool kit. "Except for the fact that she hated it."

Rachel's old look of cunning crept across her face. A block of ice settled in Kat's belly, and she realized that there was another conversation going on in front of her, a whole set of words that she could not understand, dared not predict. "Rye?" she asked, her fingers clutching at his forearm. "What's going on here?"

"Yes," Rachel said. "Why don't you tell her what's going on, Rye?"

There it was again, that complicated flash of meaning between Kat's boyfriend and her twin. Rye's face was ironed into lean planes; she heard him swallow hard. When he spoke, the words were taut, pulled thin as wire. "I don't want to do this here, Rachel. Let's get out of the park, at least. We can talk at your parents' house."

"But Rye! It's Family Day!" Rachel's response was cold, mocking.

Of course Rachel was doing this. Rachel had caught Kat kissing Rye. She was jealous of something she could never, ever have. Rachel had always been that way, whenever she saw Kat succeeding. Kat started to make excuses to Rye, started to explain away her sister's bad behavior. The jagged look in Rye's eyes, though, froze her to the spot. There was more to Rachel's riposte than the sibling rivalry Kat had lived with all her life.

Before Kat could tease out the meaning of what was going on in front of her, a brightly colored bullet shot across the clearing. "Mommy!" Niffer screamed. "Mommy, you're here!"

"Of course, baby. How could your mother be anywhere else?" Rachel put a curious emphasis on the word *mother,* as if she were staking claim to the title for the very first time. Nevertheless, Kat watched Rachel pull away from her daughter's clutching fingers, saw Rachel glare at Rye as if *he* were responsible for Niffer's clinginess.

Rachel's gaze was momentarily obscured by a cloud of Niffer's jet-black hair. Jet-black hair, like Kat's own. Like Rachel's, when it wasn't dyed.

But Niffer had eyes to match that hair. Eyes far darker than Kat's, than Rachel's. Eyes as dark as Rye's.

And as Kat looked more closely, she saw other resemblances, as well. The line of Niffer's jaw. The tilt of her nose. The way that she clutched a red bandanna, tight in her left hand.

Left.

Like Rye.

Suddenly, everything was bright around the four of them, as if they were illuminated from within. There was a buzz in Kat's ears, a humming sound. The roof of her mouth had gone numb, and she realized that her fingertips were tingling. She felt isolated from the world. Cut off. Alone.

"You're her father," Kat said.

Those three words jolted through Rye like a bolt cutter.

His first response was relief. At last, his secret was out. He was through with the lies, done with the stupid disclosure he'd been struggling to make since Josh had told him the truth.

His second response, though, was sickening fear. The color had drained from Kat's cheeks; she looked like she had seen a ghost.

He should have found a way to tell Kat sooner. He should have owned the situation instead of waiting for her to uncover it this way. If he'd stepped up to the plate, he could have broken the news more gently, explained everything more completely. Even over the phone—he could have protected her, guided her, made her see how this had happened.

Well, he hadn't chosen the time or the place, but he could still make Kat understand. Tenderly, he reached out to take her arm, to guide her toward the nearest bench.

She pulled away from him as if his hands were acid. "Don't touch me!" she snapped. Her voice was high.

Broken. She sounded as if she were fracturing into a million jagged pieces.

"Kat, it was a long time ago." He pitched his voice low, unconsciously slipping into the comforting register that he would use for an injured animal, for a sick child.

"Rachel is my *sister*." Kat's eyes were wide, unfocused. "You slept with my *sister!*"

Of course, what she said was true, the bare words. But there were a dozen things wrong with that sentence, a hundred ways that the facts failed to capture the reality. Starting with: "It was six years ago. We only dated for a few weeks."

"You told me that! But you never said you *slept* with her!"

Rye glared at Rachel, at the pink-haired harpy that was laughing at him over the head of her distraught daughter. "Tell her, Rachel. Tell her that it never meant anything."

Impossibly, Rachel was throwing back her head to laugh. But no. That wasn't *impossible*. Rachel had been manipulating Kat for years. Manipulating him, as well, even when he hadn't realized they were enmeshed in a game.

Now Rachel settled a hand over her daughter's—*their* daughter's—head. "I don't know, Rye," she said. "I wouldn't say that it never meant *anything*."

A strangled sound caught at the back of Kat's throat. Instinctively, Rye glanced around to see who was watching them. The kids were all playing at the far end of the park, shouting and running around in circles. A couple of the adults had glanced their way, but no one was close enough to hear. Kat whispered, "Were you planning on telling me anytime soon, Rye?"

"I didn't know… I only found out last week."

Rachel laughed—a harsh bark. "Not very observant, then, were you?"

"You stay out of this!" He would have said more, would have lashed out with the anger that flashed through his chest, but he saw Niffer cringe against her mother's side. He forced himself to lower his voice, and he bit out the words, "Rachel, you are not helping here."

"It's not my job to help you, is it?"

"Mommy?" Niffer whispered, but her question was perfectly clear. "Why is Mr. Harmon angry?"

"I don't know, baby," Rachel said, her voice as sweet as molasses dregs. "I think because he was caught lying to Aunt Kat."

"Gram says it's bad to tell a lie."

Rachel's laugh was loud, like the call of a raucous jay. "Yes, baby. Telling a lie is definitely bad."

Rye thought his heart would break as Niffer turned toward him, her jet-black eyes enormous in her pale face. "You shouldn't tell lies, Mr. Harmon."

"It wasn't a lie," he said, before he'd thought out a way to explain all of this to a child. "It was more of a… secret." As Rachel laughed again, Rye turned to Kat. The color had come back to her face with a vengeance; her cheeks were spotted with two hectic patches. He could hear her breath coming in short pants, and she hugged herself like a wounded creature. "Kat," he said. "Let me explain."

Kat heard his plea, and her belly twisted into a pulsing knot. Even so, she felt disconnected from her body, cut loose from the arms and legs and heart that she was so used to working, every minute of every day. Her hurt and fury cut her off from herself, like a shimmering electric curtain. She wasn't certain where her words came from, where she found the strength to ask, "What could you possibly have to say? How could you possibly have forgotten to mention something so important?"

It wasn't fair. It had never been fair. Rachel had always gotten her own way, done whatever she wanted to do, and damn the consequences. Rachel had never bothered with goals, with strategies. Rachel had always broken the rules. Rachel had lied to Susan and Mike all her life, lied to Kat, lied to her own daughter, Niffer.

Why *Rye?* Of all the men that Rachel could have had, why did it have to be Rye?

Kat's thoughts collapsed in on themselves, sending up embers of memories. She was back in the high school auditorium, her cheeks wet with tears of adolescent frustration, with shame at being laughed at by the high school kids. She was staring at Rye, confused by his kiss, even as she was delighted by the tenderness he had shown her.

She'd been mortified to find her sister waiting for her, embarrassed to hear that Susan was waiting outside, ready to drive them both home. Rachel had eyed Kat with a knowing expression. Rachel had bided her time, never telling Susan and Mike what she'd seen backstage in the high school auditorium. Rachel had known even then, even when they were in eighth grade, that she was going to set her hat for Rye Harmon.

But Rachel couldn't have done it alone. She couldn't have broken Kat's heart without an accomplice. She couldn't have turned Kat's life upside down without Rye playing along.

"Rye," Kat said, and her heart was breaking. "How could you?"

He sighed, unsure of the answer, even as he knew he

had to find one. "I swear I didn't know, Kat. Not until last week."

"Last *week?* You admitted that you dated her, but it went a bit beyond that, didn't it? A *lot* beyond that."

"I should have told you everything. I didn't think it mattered." He hadn't wanted it to matter.

Kat shook her head vehemently, clearly rejecting his excuses. "Where?" she demanded. "Where did you sleep with her?"

There wasn't any good answer, nothing that would help Kat to understand. "It doesn't matter."

"Was it in her house? Rye, were you on her couch? In her bedroom?" Kat twisted her mouth around the ugly questions.

Rye knew that she had to be picturing the room where they had embraced, where he had first realized the fragility of the soul inside her steel. Even now, he could picture Kat's mouth open in a perfect O of ecstasy as she shuddered beneath him, as she rode the waves of pleasure that he had given to her—*her*—because she was the woman he wanted to be with. She was the woman he loved.

The woman he loved. The realization tore through him, dragging him away from the perfection of memories, pushing him back to the terrible, horrible *now.* He loved Kat, and he had somehow managed to hurt her more than he had ever hurt anyone before. He shrugged helplessly, unable to imagine words that would reassure her.

Tears streamed down her cheeks, and her breath came in short gasps. "I thought we were working together, Rye."

"We were!"

Rachel chortled at his protest, even as Niffer asked her mother what was going on.

Kat could not believe Rye. Not when his secrets involved Rachel. Not when they involved the sister who had let her down—let her entire family down—so many times in the past. Kat laughed herself, but there was no humor behind her words. "I fell for everything, didn't I? Hook, line and sinker. Oh my God, I am so stupid!"

"Kat, you know that isn't true. Listen to me. This doesn't have to change anything between us. This doesn't have to be the end."

"Really? Rye Harmon, why should I believe anything you say, ever again?" Her words chased after each other, tumbling from her lips as if they had a life of their own. She was hurt. She was embarrassed. She was utterly terrified that Rye was telling her the truth now, and she feared that he was not. She didn't know what to believe, not anymore. Not after she'd been so blind.

The only way she could protect herself, the only way she could defend the wounded perimeter of her heart, was to lash out—fast, and furious, and with the sharpest weapon she had in her arsenal. "You don't know how to have a real relationship, do you, Rye? That's why you moved to Richmond in the first place. So that you wouldn't have to deal with *feelings,* with responsibility. Everything was fine between us, as long as we were both just having fun. But when things got serious, you shut down. When you learned the truth about Niffer, you stayed away—avoided me for an entire week! You chose Rachel and Richmond over Niffer, Rye. Over me."

How could she have let this happen?

Her mother had told her to be happy. Her mother had

told her to relax her rigid rules. Her mother had told her to take each day as it came, to enjoy herself.

And this was the result.

Kat had set her rules, years ago, for one simple reason. Rules protected her. Rules kept her safe. Rules preserved her from the jagged pain that was shattering her even now. She never should have relaxed her standards, never should have given in. She never should have let Rye take the fortress of her heart, of her solitude, of all the protective isolation she had built when she was a teenager.

"Kat, I never chose Rachel over you. I stayed in Richmond because I've spent the past week trying to figure out how to tell you the truth. You have to understand. I never meant to hurt you."

"But you did," she sobbed. "You really did, Rye. I thought we had something special. I thought there was a real connection between us. I thought you understood who I am, and what I want, what I *need*."

He had one last chance here. One final opportunity to use words to make it right. "I do, Kat. I promise you, I do."

She shook her head hard enough that her easy chignon fell loose about her face. "No! If you truly understood me, you would know that this is one thing that I can never, ever forgive."

He reached out for her, desperate to change her mind.

"Don't touch me!" That shout was loud enough to get attention. Out of the corner of his eye, Rye could see faces turn. He could measure the moment when everyone recognized Rachel, when they discovered the drama unfolding in their midst.

"Kat," he said again, stepping closer, trying to keep

this horrible, awkward conversation between the two of them.

"Leave me alone!" Kat jerked her arm up, pushing his away. The contact hurt, but not nearly as much as the desolate look in her eyes.

"Hey, buddy." Brandon's voice floated across the playground as his cousin jogged up to his side. "What's going on?"

"Nothing," Rye said tersely. Kat turned away, trying to hide her tear-streaked face. He took a step to close the new distance between them. Before he could say anything, though, Brandon's fingers closed on his biceps.

"Rye," Brandon said. "Buddy—"

"Leave me alone, *buddy.*" He jerked his arm away, letting some of his frustration curl his fingers into fists. "Kat and I are just talking."

"It doesn't look like Kat wants to talk right now." Brandon pitched his voice low.

"Kat—" Rye appealed.

"Please," she said through her tears. "Just leave me alone. I don't want to hear anymore. I can't think about this right now."

"Kat—" he tried one more time.

Brandon shouldered between them. "Come on, buddy—"

Hopeless, helpless anger flashed crimson across Rye's vision. Anger with Brandon, for acting like the town sheriff. Anger with himself, for hurting Kat so deeply. Anger with Rachel, for dragging him into this entire ridiculous mess so long ago, for avoiding his calls until she could inflict maximum damage here, today.

Rye turned on his heel and strode across the park, making his way past the laughing children and their naive game of rescuing the princess. He barely resisted the urge to shout at them, to tell them that the princess was never going to be rescued. The princess was lost forever.

Chapter Nine

Kat felt everyone's eyes turn toward her as Rye stalked off. Brandon took a step closer, asking, "Are you all right?"

"I'm fine," she said, knowing she was lying. How much did he know? How much had he overheard of her fight with Rye?

Her cousin Amanda appeared out of nowhere. "Kat!" Amanda's eyes slid over to Rachel, to the still-cowering Niffer. "What's going on? Are you okay?"

"I'm fine," she repeated, looking around for an escape, knowing that she had to get away from everyone. Amanda seemed to be the Pied Piper; half of Eden Falls followed behind her. A couple of people called out to Rachel, welcoming her home. A few more hollered for Susan and Mike to join the crowd. Kat looked at the sea of faces, and she felt like she was going to faint.

Susan took one glance at her daughters and set her

lips in a grim line. "Rachel," she said, and then she reached out for Kat. "Come sit down, baby. You look like you've seen a ghost! We're all worried about you."

Baby. That was what Rachel called her daughter. Called *Rye's* daughter. One more time, Kat said, "I'm fine." When it was obvious that no one believed her, she looked her mother right in the eye. "Did you know?"

"Know what?" Susan honestly looked perplexed.

"About Rye and Rachel. About Niffer." Kat watched the crowd jostle closer. She imagined the whispers that were even now skating away to those out of earshot. The scandal would be front-page news in seconds.

Susan said, "Dear, I don't know what you're talking about." Even as her kindly face registered concern, though, Kat read sudden comprehension in her eyes. There. Every single person in Eden Falls would add one and one together. They would all know how Kat had been deceived.

Kat pushed away her mother's fluttering hands. "I have to go, Mama."

"Where?"

"I don't know. I just have to get out of here."

Susan looked around helplessly. "Let me get your father—"

"No, you stay with Daddy. And Niffer, too. And Rachel." She practically spat her sister's name.

Susan sounded panicked as she said, "I don't want you going off on your own, dear. You've had a terrible shock. Amanda can—"

"No!" Kat heard the anguish in her voice, and she knew she shouldn't be shouting at her mother, shouldn't take her anger and pain out on an innocent victim. There had been enough innocent victims this spring—herself and Niffer heading up the list. But Kat couldn't hand herself over to Amanda's solicitous care. She couldn't face her cousin's concerned look, her certain questions. Not when Amanda knew so much already. Not when Amanda had been there, the night that Kat and Rye first… She forbade herself to think about that night, to think about the couch, to think about the white-hot heat that had… Forcing her voice to a quieter register, Kat said, "I'm fine, Mama. I just need to get away from here."

And then, because she knew she could not hold back the fresh tears, because she knew she could not bear the pitying looks of the crowd, because she knew she did not have the first idea of what she could ever say or do to make everything—anything—right again, Kat turned on her heel and strode across the park.

She surprised herself by arriving at the parking lot. Rye's truck hulked in a nearby spot, gleaming silver in the bright afternoon sunlight. And all of a sudden, Kat knew what she had to do.

She glanced at her watch. Half an hour. Plenty of time.

Ignoring the people who must still be staring at her, Kat pulled open the truck's door. His keys were exactly where she expected to find them—on the floor mat, just where he had dropped them the night he took her out to the diner. The night he brought her home. The night he fooled her into thinking she was special to him, that they had shared something beautiful and meaningful and unique.

Her mind was filled with memories of Rye. The weight of him, settling over her. The heat of his mouth on hers. The wild passion that he had stroked to life between her thighs. The crashing release that he had given her, the bonds that had pulled them closer to each other.

Or so she had thought.

Her fingers trembled as she picked up the keys. Even as she wanted to block Rye's voice from her memory forever, she heard him instructing her. Foot on the brake. Key in the ignition. Turn the key. Shift into Drive.

Before, when she had driven the truck, she had been haunted by all the things that could go wrong. She had cringed at every sound, shied away from every fast motion.

This time, she did not care. She did not worry about damaging the vehicle, about embarrassing herself in front of the patient man who had sat in the passenger's seat. She did not think about what it meant to conquer a simple summit, the sort of responsibility that nearly every person she knew had accomplished when they were mere teenagers, when they only *thought* they were burdened by all the cares in the world.

Remembering Rye's instruction, Kat looked left, then right, then left again. She shifted her foot off the brake, fully ready when the truck's massive engine began to pull it forward. She gripped the wheel and drove the pickup out of the parking lot.

Afterward, she could not have said how many stop signs she confronted. She could not have told whether the single traffic light was red or green. She could not recount how many trucks she passed, or how many passed her. She only knew that she drove the pickup to the train station, to the empty asphalt patch where her homecoming had begun, a month before.

Was it only a month? Kat felt as if she'd changed so much. When she had arrived in Eden Falls, she had been bound by her lifelong mantra—goals, strategies, rules. The *rules* especially—she'd had one for every situation. She'd known what to expect of herself, of others.

But in one short month, she'd discovered a new way of living. A way that included Magic Zoo and ice cream and late-night bacon blue cheeseburgers and glasses of beer swilled at an actual roadside bar. What had Susan said? That she wanted to see Kat embrace her impulsive side. Well, here was impulse, all right. Let Susan and Mike and Rye and Rachel settle everything, after Kat was back in New York. They'd work it out between them.

Kat shifted the truck into Park and dropped the keys on the floor mat. Entering the tiny station building, she immediately realized she was alone—no one to sell her a ticket. That was fine. She could buy one on the train.

Kat patted the tiny purse that swung from her shoulder. She had bought it when she splurged on her green blouse—was it only the day before? She'd somehow thought she'd been changing herself, remaking herself so that she could live in Eden Falls for the rest of her life.

Ironic, wasn't it? Kat had finally realized she could stay in Eden Falls, work beside her mother at the Morehouse Dance Academy, teach the Advanced Showcase class, and *be happy,* maybe for the first time in years.

But that was before the *Family* Day picnic. That was before she'd learned the truth about her family. About her sister and the man that Kat had come to love.

No. She couldn't say that. Couldn't believe it. She could not love Rye. Not after what he'd done. Not after the secret he had kept from her. Sure, he might only have known that he was Niffer's father for a week. But he had known that he'd slept with Rachel long before that. Slept with her, and kept the truth from Kat. Slept with her, and minimized the connection, made it sound casual, like nothing more than a meaningless fling.

No. She could not love Rye.

She had only *thought* she loved him. She'd been deceived. Rye had presented himself under false pretenses. Whatever emotions Kat thought she had felt were lies. Lies, like his silence had been.

She couldn't sit still on the station's hard wooden bench. She needed to pace, needed to shed some of the physical energy that still sparked through her. She wrapped her arms around her belly and measured out her steps, planting her heels as firmly as if she'd never been hampered by a walking boot.

She should call Haley. Let her roommate know she was coming back to their apartment. Kat was going to make the midnight deadline for the *Coppelia* sign-up after all. She was returning to her life as a dancer.

Forget about *fun*. Dance was her career.

And all that justifying she had done before, all the ways she had convinced herself that Eden Falls was right for her? That was just Kat's tactic for grappling with fear, just like she'd suffered from homesickness, years before, when she'd first moved to New York. She had been *afraid* to reach out for the role she really wanted. She had abandoned her goals, slashed through her strategies, trampled every one of her rules. All because she was afraid she might not have what it took to dance Swanilda.

What had Rye said to her, the day she ran his truck into the ditch? She had to get back on the horse that had thrown her? She had refused then, but she was never going to back down again. Ballet had thrown her, when she developed her stress fracture. Well, it was high time for her to head back to New York. To get back to her real life.

Of course, she didn't have a way to reach Haley. Her cell phone was useless here. And she didn't have any change with her; she couldn't place a call from the ancient pay phone in the corner.

What did it matter, though? She had a credit card; she could buy her train ticket north. And once she got back to the city, she had an apartment full of belongings.

Kat paced some more. This was what Susan had hoped for, wasn't it? That Kat would cast off all bonds, all limits. Susan just hadn't realized that her daughter would use her hard-won freedom to return to New York, without planning, without luggage, without restraint.

She crossed to the wall of windows and pushed her cheek against the glass to peer down the long line of tracks. No train in sight yet. She glanced at her watch. Five minutes.

A strong breeze gusted through the station as the far door opened and someone stepped inside.

When had she learned to recognize the sound of Rye's footsteps? She knew he was standing behind her. She could hear him breathing. She knew that he swallowed hard. She could imagine him reaching toward her, flexing his hands, letting his empty fists fall to his sides.

"Kat," he said. "Please."

She breathed in deeply, as if the gesture could pour steel down her spine, could give her the strength to withstand the next five minutes, until the Clipper chugged into the station. Setting her jaw so that she couldn't possibly say the wrong thing, she turned to face him.

Rye marveled at the change that had come over Kat in the four weeks since they had last been at the train station. Then, she had been a frigid woman, desperate to control the world around her, iced over with frozen fury at the dancer's body that had failed her. Now, he saw a passionate creature, someone who embraced challenge and battled it on her own ground. He had seen her consumed by passion, not just beneath his fingers, not just in response to his lips, but in the very way she tackled living every day.

He had tested a hundred conversational openings on the way from the park, so intent on finding the words to keep Kat in Eden Falls that he nearly crashed his brother Noah's sports car a dozen times. He thought he had worked out the perfect plea, but now all those eloquent words fled him. He was reduced to repeating the only thing that mattered: "Kat, please. Don't leave me."

She glanced at her watch.

He was afraid to check his own, afraid to discover how little time was left for him to plead his case. Instead, he took advantage of her silence, spinning out all the things he'd meant to tell her, all the confessions he'd longed to make. "I know it seems like I deceived you. Hell, I *did* deceive you. And I can't imagine how I've made you feel. But you have to understand—I didn't know. Not until I saw Josh Barton in Richmond. I've spent the past week trying to find Rachel and ask her if it was true. Trying to figure out the right way to tell you. Trying to figure out all the right words."

"But you didn't tell me. Rachel did."

She spoke so quietly that he almost missed her

words. She directed her speech to the knot of her fingers, white-knuckled across her flat belly.

Nevertheless, he took heart that she had said *something.* If she was willing to spare him any words at all, that meant they were having a conversation. They were still communicating. The door between them was still open, even if he could barely make out a glimmer of light on her side.

Even though he knew he was fighting against time, even though he was certain the hourglass was draining away, he chose his words carefully. "I wish it hadn't happened that way. I wish I had told you the second that Josh walked away, in Richmond. I wish I had taken out my phone, dialed your number and told you everything, all at once."

She did not seem to hear him. Instead, she looked around the train station, like a woman in a trance. "Did you know it was me that first day? Did you think I was Rachel?"

This time, she met his eyes. Her silver gaze was cloudy, shrouded in misery. He heard the tremble behind her words, knew she was questioning the very foundation of everything they'd had together.

He held her gaze and answered slowly, setting every syllable between them like an offering on an altar. "I could never confuse the two of you. Ever. You are so much more than the color of your hair and eyes, the shape of your face. Kat, think back to that day. *I* was the one who called out to you, across the parking lot. I knew who you were, even when you pretended not to recognize me."

She had done that, hadn't she? She had played a child's game, because she was afraid of getting caught in a woman's world. And here she was, more tangled than she'd ever thought she could be.

She thought back to the day she had arrived in town, on that unseasonably warm afternoon, with the heat shimmering off the asphalt parking lot. Then, she had thought she would melt. Now, she feared she would never be warm again. She rubbed at her arms and said, "But after that. When you started seeing me with Niffer. There must have been some part of you that knew. You must have wanted me to be Rachel, to be the woman you'd already slept with. You must have wanted us to be the family that the three of you never were."

The words ate through to the core of her heart. In all her life, she had never been jealous of Rachel. Frustrated, yes. Angry with her poor choices. Disappointed by all the times she had made promises, all the times she had lied.

But this was the first time that Kat had ever truly envied her sister. The first time she had ever wanted to change places, to *be* Rachel. Then she would have known what it was like to be the Morehouse sister Rye first made love to. To be the twin he had first chosen. To be the woman he had been drawn to from the start. If Kat had been Rachel, she never would have let Rye out of her sight.

"No," he said, and it seemed like he was damning every one of her dreams. "Kat, I never wanted you to be anyone but who you are. Don't you understand? I never loved Rachel. I'm ashamed to admit this, but I barely *knew* her. She came to me when I had just graduated from college. She'd been dating one of my fraternity brothers. She wanted to make him jealous. I was flattered and stupid and a little naive. I only knew her for a few weeks, but I think I believed that I could...save her. That I could…I don't know…make her be happy and healthy and whole."

Kat *did* know. She knew how many times she had hoped that she could reach out to her twin. How many times Rachel had manipulated Kat's own emotions, making her believe that *this* time things were different, that *this* time Rachel had changed, that *this* time she would be able to hold it all together.

Still, there was more to Rye's story than that.

"Even if I accept that," she said. "Even if I believe every word you've said about what happened six years ago, that doesn't explain now. It doesn't justify your keeping things secret for the past week. You could have called me, any night. You could have told me everything."

Rye heard the sob that cut short her anguish. And yet, that anguish gave him another faint glimmer of hope. If Kat truly hated him, if she were willing to walk away forever, she'd be speaking with more rage. With less conflict. With more of her famed commitment, holding true to the single path she had chosen.

But even as he told himself that all was not absolutely, irrevocably lost, he heard another sound—one that made his pulse quicken with fear. The train whistle keened as the Clipper neared the station. He was almost out of time.

"Kat," he said, certain she heard it, too. "You have to believe me. I never thought of Rachel when I was with you. I kissed your lips, not hers. I touched your body, not hers. In my mind, you are completely separate people. Two women so different that I can only wonder at the coincidence that you're sisters."

She shook her head, using the motion to pull her

around, to face the windows, the train tracks. The door that would carry her out of his life forever.

He knew that he could not touch her, that he could not rely on the incredible physical spark that had joined them, ever since she first returned to Eden Falls. But he could not let her walk away, either, not without making his last argument. Not without saying the words that had pounded through his head as he completed his breakneck drive from the park.

"Kat, I love you. Please. Don't get on that train."

Kat felt the change in air pressure as the locomotive blew past the station door. The train was braking; metal wheels squealed against the track as it came to a stop.

But those sounds meant nothing to her. Instead, she was trapped by the words Rye had spoken. "What did you say?" she asked, her own question almost lost in the station's dead air.

He took a step closer to her. "Kat, I love you." He glanced at the door, at the train that was almost completely stopped. "I love you, and I don't want you to go. I can't get enough of you. I want you to stay here. I *need* you to stay here. But if you can't, if you won't, then I'll get on that train with you. I'll travel to New York, or to anywhere else you go, until I know that you heard me, that you understand me, that you believe me. I love you, Kat Morehouse, and I don't want to live another day without you."

The train was ticking, temporarily settling its weight on the tracks. A conductor walked by on the short platform outside the station, calling out his bored afternoon chant: "Yankee Clipper, all aboard!"

"Kat," Rye whispered, and now he took a step closer. He held out his hand to her, as if she were a forest animal, some shy creature that he had to charm to safety.

He had hurt her. He had kept a terrible secret for days, long past the time when he should speak.

But hadn't she done the very same thing? Hadn't she kept a secret from her mother, hiding the bad news about the studio's bank account because she could not find the right words? Because it was never the right time to tell the truth?

Susan had forgiven her. Susan had told her that she understood—good motives sometimes led to bad actions. All unwitting, Susan had shown Kat the path to understanding. The way to move forward from a bad situation to one that was so much better.

The train seemed to sigh, grumbling as its engine shifted forward. The cars dragged on the track as if they were reluctant to leave Eden Falls. Kat could still run for the Clipper. With her dancer's grace, she could grab hold of the steel grip beside the stairs. She could pull herself into the vestibule, make her way down the swaying, accelerating car to an overpadded seat that would carry her all the way to New York.

But Rye's eyes were pleading with her. Those ebony eyes, darker than any she had ever seen before. No, that was a lie. Niffer's eyes were just as dark.

The train picked up speed. Its whistle blew as the engine rounded the long curve that would bring it north, to Richmond, to Washington, to New York.

The Clipper was gone.

"Thank you," Rye breathed. He was frozen, though, terrified of upsetting the balance he had somehow found, the miracle that had kept Kat in Eden Falls. His hand remained outstretched, his fingers crooked, as if they could remember the cashmere touch of her hair.

"Oh, Rye," she sighed. "I love you, too."

And then, impossibly, she was placing her hand in his. She was letting him pull her close, letting him fold his arms around her. She turned up her face, and he found the perfect offering of her lips.

He wanted to drink all that she had to give him, wanted to sweep her up in his arms and carry her over the threshold of the station, out to Noah's car, and away, far away, into a perfect sunset. He wanted to stay absolutely still, to turn to stone with this incredible woman in his arms, to spin out this moment forever. He wanted to drag her to the hard wooden bench in the center of the waiting room, to pull her down on top of him, to rip open the buttons on her spring-green blouse and lave her perfect breasts with his ever-worshipful tongue.

He wanted to lead Kat, to follow her, to be with her forever.

"Rye." She said his name again, when he finally pulled back from his chaste kiss of promise. There was so much she needed to say to him. So much she needed to hear him say. She twined her fingers in his and led him out of the waiting room, to the glinting form of his silver truck. He barely left her for long enough to walk around the cab to the driver's seat.

As he closed the door behind himself, she felt an eagerness shoot through his body, the need to confirm that she was still beside him, that she had not left him, that she never would. His fingers splayed wide across the back of her head as he pulled her close; urgency sparked from his palm like an actual electric fire. Now his lips were harsh on hers, demanding, and she might have thought that he was angry, if not for the sob that she heard at the back of his throat.

She answered his desperation with need of her own.

Her hands needed to feel the hard muscle of his back. Her arms needed to arch around his chest, to pull him close, closer than she had ever been in any pas de deux.

His clever lips found the fire banked at the base of her throat; his tongue flicked against that delicate hollow until she moaned. By then, his fingers had made their way beneath her blouse; he was doing devastating things to the single clasp of her bra.

Her own hands weren't to be outdone. She flashed through the simple mechanics of releasing his belt, loosening the leather to reach the line of worn buttons beneath. She slid the fingers of her left hand inside the waistband of his jeans as she worked, and she laughed at the feel of his flesh leaping beneath her touch.

But then, three buttons away from freedom, she paused. She flattened her palm against the taut muscles of his belly, pushing away enough that she could see his eyes.

His heartbeat pounded beneath her touch like a wild animal's, and she felt the whisper of his breath, panting as he restrained himself, as he held back for her. "What are we doing, Rye?"

"If you don't know, then I haven't been doing it right," he growled.

She smiled, but she pulled even farther away. She took advantage of his frustrated whimper to tug her blouse back into place. She ran a hand through her hair, forcing it out of her eyes. "I'm serious," she said, and she was pleased to see his hunger take a backseat to concern. "You're living in Richmond now. You've started your own business and you don't have time to do anything new. You don't need the stress of a new relationship, just as you're finally achieving all your dreams."

He caught her hand and planted a kiss in her palm before lacing his fingers between hers. "You *are* all my dreams."

She laughed softly, but she shook her head. "You can say that now, and you probably even believe it. But what are you going to say next week? Next month? Next year? What are you going to say when I keep you from landing the biggest contract you've ever tried for?"

"That's not going to happen," he vowed.

"It will. Rye, I can see a life for myself in Eden Falls. I think a part of me has seen it from the moment I walked into my parents' home. That's why I delayed getting back to New York, why I delayed signing up for the *Coppelia* audition. My body was telling me something when I broke my foot. It knew the truth before my mind did. Before my heart did. Here in Eden Falls, I can help Daddy with his physical therapy, his rehab. I can help Mama at the studio, take over more of the business side of things, teach a few of the classes. I can keep Niffer with me, help her through the pain when she realizes that Rachel is heading out again. We both know my sister will never stick around."

Rye started to tense when Kat said her sister's name. There was no rancor, though, when she spoke of her twin. Only a matter-of-fact acceptance, with just a twinge of sadness for the woman that Rachel might have been.

He used his free hand to brush back Kat's midnight hair. He wanted to make sure she could read his expression when he spoke to her. He wanted to be certain she knew he spoke the truth. "I don't need Richmond."

"But you—"

He cut her off by shaking his head. "Richmond is

just a place. It's not the magical answer to my problems. It's not the secret to the life I wanted to lead."

"Wanted? I don't understand. What was that life?"

"I wanted to be free. I wanted to be independent. I was tired of being everyone's brother, everyone's cousin, everyone's son. I wanted to make my own decisions, to grow my own business, without constantly turning aside to meet someone else's expectation."

"A-and now?" He heard the hesitation in her voice, the tendril of fear behind her question.

"And now, I *want* to be tied to someone else. To *one* someone else. To you. I want to go to work every morning, knowing I'm the best damned contractor I can be. And I want to come home every night, knowing I'm the best husband I can be." He saw her register his words, saw her amazing silver eyes widen in disbelief. "Marry me, Kat. Make me the happiest man in Eden Falls."

Marry him? Marry Rye Harmon?

Kat started to laugh, a shaky sound that mixed suspiciously with a sob in the back of her throat. "I—" she started to say, but then she gave up on that answer. "You—" She trailed off, as if she could not remember how to shape any words.

He chuckled. "I take it that means yes?"

She stared at him—at the good humor that twitched his lips into a smile. At the confidence that squared his shoulders. At the power that rippled down his arms, in the strength of his cunning fingers. At the man who had seen her heart and understood her soul, who knew who she was, and what she needed to be.

"Yes," she said. "Yes, Rye Harmon, I'll marry you."

His kiss was long and deep and satisfying. He was laughing, though, as he pulled away. "You do realize that we have to get back to the park. Everyone is going to be waiting there, worried."

She quirked a grin. There'd be time enough to follow up on the promise of that last kiss. "We can't have that, now, can we?"

She started to reach for her seat belt, but he shook his head. "Not so fast!" he taunted.

"What?"

"I drove Noah's car over here. You're going to have to drive this thing back to the park." He scooped up the keys from the floor mat and pressed them into her yielding palm. "Go ahead," he said, darting in for a quick kiss. "You lead. I'll follow."

Confident that Rye was with her—would be with her forever—she barely glanced in the rearview mirror as she pulled out of the parking lot.

Epilogue

Kat stood at the stove, flexing her ankles and testing her balance as she dropped biscuit dough into a pot of stewed chicken. The motion reminded her of the exercises she had led for the Advanced Showcase students, just that afternoon. The girls had outdone themselves at the barre. In fact, little Taylor Sutton might be ready to audition for the National come spring, if she continued to work hard under Kat's watchful eyes. And, of course, if she wanted to travel so far away from home.

A gust of wind rattled the windows, and Kat peered out at the gathering winter storm. She was glad Rye had installed the new storm windows. For that matter, it was a good thing he'd anchored all the shutters, as well.

"Niffer," Rye said in the living room. "If you don't bring your dolls in from the front yard, they'll have snow on them in the morning."

"I'll get them after dinner," the headstrong child said.

"Now." Rye's calm order made it clear he would brook no disobedience.

"Mommy wouldn't make me bring in my dolls."

"Mommy isn't here, though, is she?" Rye's voice stayed even. He was merely stating a fact. Rachel wasn't there, hadn't been for months. She hadn't even sent a postcard since…when was it? Halloween? "Niffer," Rye said, making it clear that he was through with petulant games. "Let's go. You don't want dinner to be late—Aunt Kat is making your favorite."

The child trotted over to the door, suddenly content to have lost the round. "Okay, Daddy."

Kat shivered and dropped in another dumpling. She couldn't say if her sudden shudder was a reaction to cold air wafting in the house's front door or the sudden proximity of her husband. Rye's hands closed over her belly, and he pulled her back against his chest, nuzzling her neck until she squirmed even closer.

"Good job, Mr. Harmon," she said, after she had caught her breath. "The way to a child's heart is through her stomach."

"Is *that* the secret, Mrs. Harmon?" His teasing fingers strayed to the neckline of her cobalt-blue sweater. "What do you think it would take to convince Niffer to spend the rest of the evening playing in the basement?"

She laughed and arched against him. "We don't have a basement."

"Damn." He switched his attention to the waistline of her pants, dancing around her hips with enough intensity that she had to suck in a steadying breath. "Do you think she could build herself one? Just for tonight? Even for an hour or two?"

Kat set down the wooden spoon she was using to

form the dumplings, and then she twisted in the circle of his arms. She started to fiddle with the top button of his shirt, amazed as always that he didn't need a sweater in the winter cold. "I've been meaning to talk to you about that."

"About Niffer building a basement?" He started to laugh.

"About you building onto the house," she clarified. "I've been thinking we can close in the carport. Convert it into a third bedroom."

She watched as he considered her suggestion. She saw him contemplate the work, solve the engineering problems, determine the most efficient way to add walls, to move doors. And then she saw him register the true meaning behind her suggestion. His fingers tightened deliciously on her waist.

"Really?" he asked, and there was so much love in the word, so much joy, that she found herself laughing out loud.

"Really," she said. His lips on hers were trembling, as if he were suddenly afraid of hurting her. She wasn't about to put up with that—not for eight more months. She cupped her hand on the back of his neck and tugged him closer, making sure she emphasized the demand with a sudden, quick thrust of her tongue.

"When?" he asked as he came up for air.

"Late August, I think. I haven't been to see the doctor yet."

"See the doctor for what?" Niffer's question came from the doorway, tiny and scared.

Kat whirled toward her niece, automatically kneeling to put herself at the child's eye level. "It's okay, sweetheart. No one's sick. I was just telling Daddy that we're going to have a baby join us next summer."

Niffer's eyes grew as big as pie plates. "Will it be a boy baby or a girl baby?"

"I don't know yet," Kat answered gravely. "Which do you want?"

Niffer thought for a long time, and then she said, "One of each."

Kat and Rye laughed at the same time. "Maybe we'll just take things one step at a time," Rye said, ruffling his daughter's hair. "Come on, now. Help me set the dinner table."

Kat was still grinning as Niffer hurried to grab the silverware out of its drawer. Girl or boy, it didn't matter to her—so long as everyone was healthy and happy and safe in Eden Falls.

* * * * *

“Do you still love him?”

She was pole-axed. “What?”

Noah was in front of her in three steps. “Your fiancé… do you still love him?”

“He’s dead,” she whispered.

“I know. But that wasn’t the question.” He reached for her, slid one arm around her waist and drew her against him. “The thing is,” he said, holding her firm. “If you still love him…I’ll do my best to stop…to stop wanting you.” His other hand cupped her cheek, gently, carefully. “But if you don’t love him, then I’d really like to kiss you right now.”

Her insides contracted. “No,” she said on a breath.

“No?”

“I don’t love him.”

His green eyes darkened as he traced his thumb along her jaw. “Good,” he said softly.

And then he kissed her.

Dear Reader,

I have always been a sucker for old romantic movies and corny love songs. It seemed an obvious choice then, when I decided to be a writer at the age of seven, that I would write romance. Of course, back then it was about love between a girl and her horse, but I was on the right track.

Horses have always been a big part of my life and several years ago I married a single dad, and because both those themes are a big part of this story I'm delighted that *Made for Marriage* is my first book published with Mills & Boon® Cherish™. I hope you enjoy Noah and Callie's journey and invite you to return to Crystal Point very soon.

I would love to hear from readers and can be reached via my website at www.helenlacey.com.

Warmest wishes,

Helen Lacey

MADE FOR MARRIAGE

BY

HELEN LACEY

First published in Great Britain 2012
by Mills & Boon, an imprint of Harlequin (UK) Limited,
Eton House, 18-24 Paradise Road, Richmond, Surrey TW9 1SR

2in1 ISBN: 978 0 263 89422 6

23-0412

Harlequin (UK) policy is to use papers that are natural, renewable and recyclable products and made from wood grown in sustainable forests. The logging and manufacturing processes conform to the legal environmental regulations of the country of origin.

Printed and bound in Spain
by Blackprint CPI, Barcelona

Helen Lacey grew up reading *Black Beauty, Anne of Green Gables* and *Little House on the Prairie*. These childhood classics inspired her to write her first book when she was seven years old, a story about a girl and her horse. She continued to write with the dream of one day being a published author and writing for Cherish is the realisation of that dream. She loves creating stories about strong heroes with a soft heart and heroines who get their happily ever after. For more about Helen visit her website at www.helenlacey.com.

For Robert
Emphatically, Undeniably, Categorically.

ACKNOWLEDGMENTS
To the Babes
Louise Cusack, Lesley Millar, Laura O'Connell,
CC Coburn & the amazing Helen Bianchin.
Thank you for your endless support.

To my editor Susan Litman and my agent Scott Eagan who both trusted in my storytelling.

And to Valerie Susan Hayward—for showing me how it's done.

Chapter One

Callie Jones knew trouble when she came upon it. And the thirteen-year-old who stood defiantly in front of her looked like more trouble than she wanted on a Saturday morning. For one thing, Callie liked to sleep later on the weekend, and the teenager with the impudent expression had banged on her door at an indecently early 6:00 a.m. And for another, the girl wasn't anything like she'd expected. Her long black hair was tied up in an untidy ponytail revealing at least half a dozen piercings in her ears, plus another in both her brow and nose. And the dark kohl smudged around her eyes was heavier than any acceptable trend Callie had ever seen.

"I'm Lily," the girl said, crossing her thin arms. "I'm here for my lesson."

Callie opened the front door fractionally, grateful she'd had the sense to wrap herself in an old dressing gown before she'd come to the door. It was chilly outside. "You're early," she said, spotting a bicycle at the bottom of the steps.

The teenager shrugged her shoulders. "So what? I'm here now."

Callie hung on to her patience. "I told your father eight o'clock."

Lily shrugged again, without any apology in her expression. "Then I guess he told me the wrong time." The girl looked her over, and Callie felt the burning scrutiny right down to her toes.

Callie took a deep breath and glanced over the girl's head. Dawn was just breaking on the horizon. Another hour of sleep would have been nice, but she wasn't about to send Lily home.

"Okay, Lily. Give me a few minutes to get ready." Callie pointed to the wicker love seat on the porch. "Wait here. I'll be right back."

The girl shrugged. "Whatever."

Callie locked the security mesh screen as discreetly as she could and turned quickly on her heels. She didn't want an unsupervised teenager wandering around her house while she changed her clothes. Dashing into the bathroom, she washed her face and brushed her teeth and hair before slipping into jeans and a T-shirt.

She skipped coffee, grabbed a cereal bar and shoved it into her back pocket. She really needed to do some grocery shopping. But she was too busy. Busy with her students, busy trying to ensure the utilities were paid, busy not thinking about why a recently turned thirty ex-California girl worked twelve-hour days trying to make a success of a small horse-riding school situated a few miles from the eastern edge of the Australian coastline.

Callie grabbed her sweater from the back of the kitchen chair and headed for the front door. Once she'd locked up she pulled her muddy riding boots off the shoe rack, quickly tucked her feet into them, snatched up her battered cowboy hat and placed it on her head. She turned around to find no sign of her visitor. Or the expensive-looking bicycle.

Obviously the teenager wasn't keen on following instructions.

She put the keys into her pocket and headed for the stables. The large stable complex, round yard and dressage arena were impressive. Callie had spent nearly every penny she had on Sandhills Farm to ensure it became a workable and viable business.

Okay kid—where are you?

Tessa rushed from around the back of the house. Still a pup, the Labrador/cattle dog cross bounded on lanky legs and yapped excitedly. Obviously no kid was back there, or Tessa would have hung around for attention.

So, where was she? Callie's intuition and instincts surged into overdrive. Miss Too-Many-Piercings was clearly looking for trouble. She called the girl's name. No answer.

When Callie opened the stable doors and flicked the lock mechanism into place, a few long heads immediately poked over the stalls. She looked around and found no sign of Lily.

Great—the kid had gone AWOL.

And where on earth was Joe, her farmhand? She checked her watch. Six-twenty-five. He was late and she'd have to attend to the feeding before she could start the lesson with her missing student.

First things first—find Lily…um…whatever-her-last-name-is. She clicked her fingers together. Hah—Preston. That's right. Lily Preston.

She's got the father with the sexy telephone voice, remember?

Callie shook some sense into her silly head when she heard a vehicle coming down the driveway. Joe…good. She swiveled on her heel and circumnavigated the stables, stopping abruptly, mid-stride, too stunned to move.

Indiana—her beautiful, precious and irreplaceable Hanoverian gelding—stood by the fence, wearing only an ill-fitting bridle. Lily Preston was straddled between the fence post and trough as she attempted to climb onto his back.

Think...and think quickly.

Callie willed her legs to move and raced toward the girl and horse, but it was too late. The teenager had mounted, collected the reins and clicked the gelding into a trot Callie knew she would have no hope of sustaining.

She's going to fall. And before Callie had a chance to move, Lily Preston lost control, tumbled off the horse and landed squarely on her behind.

She was gone. Ditto for her bike. Noah Preston cursed and headed back into the house. The last thing he'd told his angry daughter the night before, just as she'd slammed her bedroom door in his face, was that he'd take her to Sandhills Farm at seven-forty-five in the morning. She hadn't wanted him to take her. She wanted to go alone. Without him. He should have taken more notice. The time was now six-thirty-three and Lily had skipped. In typical Lily style.

"Daddy, I'm hungry."

Noah turned his head. His eight-year-old son, Jamie, as uncomplicated and placid a child as Lily was not, stood in the doorway.

"Okay," he said. "I'll make breakfast soon. But we have to go find Lily first."

Jamie rolled his big eyes. "Again?"

Noah smiled. "I know, mate, but I have to make sure she's safe."

"She is," Jamie assured him in a very grown-up fashion. "She's gone to see the horse lady."

"She told you that?"

His son nodded. “Yep. Told me this morning. She rode her bike. I told her not to.”

The horse lady? *Callie Jones.* Recommended as the best equestrian instructor in the district. He’d called her a week ago, inquiring about setting Lily up with some lessons. Her soft, American accent had intrigued him and he’d quickly made arrangements to bring Lily out to her riding school.

So, at least he knew where she’d gone and why. To make a point. To show him he had no control, no say, and that she could do whatever she pleased.

Noah spent the following minutes waking the twins and making sure the three kids were clothed, washed and ready to leave. Jamie grumbled a bit about being hungry, so Noah grabbed a few apples and a box of cereal bars for the trip. He found his keys, led his family outside, bundled the children into his dual-cab utility vehicle and buckled them up.

He lived just out from Crystal Point and the trip took barely ten minutes. Sandhills Farm was set back from the road and gravel crunched beneath the wheels when he turned off down the long driveway. He followed the line of white-washed fencing until he reached the house, a rundown, big, typical Queenslander with a wraparound veranda and hat-box roof. Shabby but redeemable.

So where was Lily?

He put Jamie in charge of four-year-old Hayley and Matthew, took the keys from the ignition and stepped out of the vehicle. A dog came bounding toward him, a happy-looking pup that promptly dropped to Noah’s feet and pleaded for attention. Noah patted the dog for a moment, flipped off his sunglasses and looked around. The house looked deserted. An old Ford truck lay idle near the stables and he headed for it. The keys hanging in the ignition suggested someone was around. He spotted Lily's bicycle propped against the wall of the stable. So she *was* here.

But where? And where was Callie Jones? He couldn't see a sign of anyone in the yards or the stables or in the covered sand arena to the left of the building. The stable doors were open and he took a few steps inside, instantly impressed by the setup. A couple of horses tipped their heads over the top of their stalls and watched him as he made his way through. He found the tack room and small office at the end of the row of stalls. The door was ajar and he tapped on the jamb. No one answered. But he could see inside. There were pictures on the wall—all of horses in varying competitive poses. The rider in each shot was female. Perhaps Callie Jones?

Noah lingered for another few seconds before he returned outside. The friendly dog bounded to his feet again, demanding notice. The animal stayed for just a moment before darting past him and heading off around the side of the building. Noah instructed the kids to get out of the truck and told them to follow him. As he walked with the three children in a straight line behind him, he heard the sound of voices that got louder with every step. When he turned another corner he stopped. The breath kicked from his chest.

A woman stood by the fence.

Was this Callie Jones? Not too tall, not too thin. Curves every place a woman ought to have them. Her jeans, riding low, looked molded onto her hips and legs. Long brown hair hung down her back in a ponytail and his fingers itched with the thought of threading them through it. Noah's heart suddenly knocked against his ribs. *Lightning,* he thought. *Is this what it feels like to be struck by lightning?*

Noah probably would have taken a little more time to observe her if he hadn't spotted his daughter sitting on the ground, her clothes covered in dust and a big brown horse looming over her.

* * *

"What's going on here?"

Callie jumped and turned around on her heels.

A man glared at her from about twenty feet away.

"Hey, Dad," called Lily.

Uh-oh. The father? He looked *very* unhappy. Callie switched her attention back to the girl sitting on the ground. She was sure Lily's butt would be sore for a day or so. And she was thankful Indiana had stopped once he'd realized his inexperienced rider was in trouble. Which meant all that had really happened was Lily had slipped off the side. It wasn't a serious fall. And she intended to tell him so.

Callie wiped her hands down her jeans. "Hi, I'm—"

"Lily," he barked out, interrupting her and bridging the space between them with a few strides. "What happened?"

She made a face. "I fell off."

"She's okay," Callie said quickly.

"I think I'll decide that for myself," he said and helped his daughter to her feet.

Lily dusted off her clothes and crossed her thin arms. "I'm fine, Dad."

Indiana moved toward Callie and nuzzled her elbow. "Good boy," she said softly, patting his nose.

"You're rewarding him for throwing my daughter?"

Heat prickled up her spine. "He didn't throw her."

Silence stretched like elastic between them as he looked at her with the greenest eyes Callie had ever seen. It took precisely two seconds to register he was attractive. It didn't matter that he scowled at her. She still had enough of a pulse to recognize an absolutely gorgeous man when faced with one. If she were looking. Which she wasn't.

Then she saw children behind him. A lot of children. Three. All blond.

A familiar pain pierced behind her rib cage.

"Lily, take the kids and go and wait by the truck."

"But, Dad—"

"Go," he instructed.

Callie clutched Indiana's reins tightly. Gorgeous, maybe. Friendly, not one bit.

His daughter went to say something else but stopped. She shrugged her shoulders and told the smaller children to follow her. Once Lily and the children were out of sight the man turned to her. "What exactly do you think you were doing?"

"I was—"

"My daughter gets thrown off a horse and you just left her lying in the dirt. What if she'd been seriously injured?"

Callie held her ground. She'd handled parents before. "She wasn't, though."

"Did you even check? I'll see your license revoked," he said. "You're not fit to work with children."

That got her mouth moving. "Just wait one minute," she said, planting her hands on her hips for dramatic effect. "You don't have the right—"

"I do," he said quickly. "What kind of nut are you?"

Callie's face burned. "I'm not a—"

"Of all the irresponsible things I've—"

"Would you stop interrupting me," she said, cutting him off right back. It did the trick because he clammed up instantly. He really was remarkably handsome. Callie took a deep breath. "Your daughter took my horse without permission."

"So this is Lily's fault?"

"I didn't say that."

He stepped closer and Callie was suddenly struck by how tall he was and how broad his shoulders were. "Then it's your fault?" He raised his hands. "Your property, your horse…it's not hard to figure out who's to blame."

"She took the horse without my permission," Callie said

again, firmer this time, making a point and refusing to be verbally outmaneuvered by a gorgeous man with a sexy voice.

His green eyes glittered. "So she was wandering around unsupervised, Ms. Jones?"

Annoyance weaved up her spine. *Ms. Jones? Nothing friendly about that.*

She took a deep breath and willed herself to keep her cool. "I understand how this looks and how you must feel, but I think—"

"Are you a parent?" he asked quickly.

"No."

"Then you don't know how I feel."

He was right—she didn't have a clue. She wasn't a parent. She'd never be a parent. Silence stretched. She looked at him. He looked at her. Something flickered between them. An undercurrent. Not of anger—this was something else.

He's looking at me. He's angry. He's downright furious. But he's checking me out.

Callie couldn't remember the last time she'd registered that kind of look. Or the last time she'd wanted to look back. But she knew she shouldn't. He had children. He was obviously married. She glanced at his left hand. *No wedding ring.* Her belly dipped nonsensically.

His eyes narrowed. "Have you any qualifications?"

She stared at him. "I have an instructor's ticket from the Equestrian Federation of—"

"I meant qualifications to work with kids?" he said, cutting off her ramble. "Like teaching credentials? Or a degree in child psychology? Come to think of it, do you have any qualifications other than the fact you can ride a horse?"

Outraged, Callie opened her mouth to speak but quickly stopped. She was suddenly tongue-tied, stripped of her usual ability to speak her mind. Her cheeks flamed and thankfully her silence didn't last long. "Are you always so…so rude?"

He smiled as though he found her anger amusing. "And do you always allow your students to walk around unsupervised?"

"No," she replied, burning up. "But you're not in possession of all the facts."

He watched her for a moment, every gorgeous inch of him focused on her, and she experienced a strange dip in the pit of her stomach, like she was riding a roller coaster way too fast.

"Then please…enlighten me," he said quietly.

Callie bit her temper back. "When Lily arrived early I told her to wait for me. She didn't."

"And that's when she took your horse?"

"Yes."

"Why didn't you tell her to get off?"

"I did," Callie replied. "Although I've discovered that sometimes its better practice to let people find out just how—"

"You mean the hard way?" he asked, cutting her off again.

Callie nodded. "But she wasn't in any danger. Indiana wouldn't have hurt her."

"Just for the record," he said quietly—so quietly Callie knew he was holding himself in control—"Lily knows all about hard life lessons."

She's not the only one.

Good sense thankfully prevailed and she kept her cool. "I'm sorry you had a reason to be concerned about her safety," she said quietly. "I had no idea she would do something like that."

"Did it occur to you to call me?" he asked. "I did leave you my cell number when I first phoned you. Lily arrived two hours early—didn't that set off some kind of alarm bell?"

"She said you'd told her the wrong time."

"Does that seem likely? This arrangement won't work

out," he said before she could respond. "I'll find another instructor for Lily—one who can act responsibly."

His words stung. But Callie had no illusions about Lily Preston. The girl was trouble. And she certainly didn't want to have anything more to do with the man in front of her. Despite the fact her dormant libido had suddenly resurfaced and seemed to be singing, *pick me, pick me!*

She wanted to challenge him there and then to who was the responsible one—her for taking her eyes off Lily for a matter of minutes or him for clearly having little control over his daughter. But she didn't. *Think about the business. Think about the horses.* The last run-in she had with a parent had cost her nearly a quarter of her students and she was still struggling to recoup her losses. Three months earlier Callie had caught two students breaking the rules and had quickly cancelled all lessons with the troublesome sisters. But the girls' mother had other ideas, and she'd threatened to lodge a formal complaint with the Equestrian Federation. It could have led to the suspension of her instructor's license. Of course Callie could still teach without it, but her credentials were important to her. And she didn't want that kind of trouble again.

"That's your decision."

He didn't say another word. He just turned on his heels and walked away.

Callie slumped back against a fence post. Moments later she heard the rumble of an engine and didn't take a breath until the sound of tires crunching over gravel faded into nothing.

She looked at Indiana. She'd brought the horse with her from California—just Indy and three suitcases containing her most treasured belongings. Indiana had remained quarantined for some time after her arrival. Long enough for Callie to hunt through real estate lists until she'd found the perfect place to start her riding school.

Callie loved Sandhills Farm. Indiana and the rest of her nine horses were her life…her babies. *The only babies I'll have.* It made her think of *that man* and his four children.

A strange sensation uncurled in her chest, reminding her of an old pain—of old wishes and old regrets.

She took Indy's reins and led him toward the stables. Once he was back in the stall Callie headed for the office. She liked to call it an office, even though it essentially served as a tack room. She'd added a desk, a filing cabinet and a modest computer setup.

Joe, her part-time farmhand, had arrived and began the feeding schedule. Callie looked at her appointment book and struck Lily Preston's name off her daily list. There would be no Lily in her life…and no Lily's gorgeous father.

She looked around at her ego wall and at the framed photographs she'd hung up in no particular order. Pictures from her past, pictures of herself and Indiana at some of the events they'd competed in.

But not one of Craig.

Because she didn't want the inevitable inquisition. She didn't talk about Craig Baxter. Or her past. She'd moved halfway across the world to start her new life. Crystal Point had been an easy choice. Her father had been born in the nearby town of Bellandale and Callie remembered the many happy holidays she'd spent there when she was young. It made her feel connected to her Australian roots to make her home in the place where he'd been raised and lived until he was a young man. And although she missed California, this was home now. And she wasn't about to let that life be derailed by a gorgeous man with sexy green eyes. No chance.

Callie loved yard sales. Late Sunday morning, after her last student left, she snatched a few twenty dollar bills from her desk drawer and whistled Tessa to come to heel as she headed for her truck. The dog quickly leapt into the passenger seat.

The drive into Crystal Point took exactly six minutes. The small beachside community boasted a population of just eight hundred residents and sat at the mouth of the Bellan River, one of the most pristine waterways in the state. On the third Sunday of every month the small community hosted a "trunk and treasure" sale, where anyone who had something to sell could pull up their car, open the trunk and offer their wares to the dozens of potential buyers who rolled up.

The sale was in full swing and Callie parked a hundred yards up the road outside the local grocery store. She opened a window for Tessa then headed inside to grab a soda before she trawled for bargains. The bell dinged as she stepped across the threshold. The shop was small, but crammed with everything from fishing tackle to beach towels and grocery items. There was also an ATM and a pair of ancient fuel pumps outside that clearly hadn't pumped fuel for years.

"Good morning, Callie."

"Hi, Linda," she greeted the fifty-something woman behind the counter, who was hidden from view by a tall glass cabinet housing fried food, pre-packaged sandwiches and cheese-slathered hot dogs.

She picked out a soda and headed for the counter.

Linda smiled. "I hear you had a run-in with Noah Preston yesterday."

Noah? Was that his name? He'd probably told her when he'd made arrangements for his daughter's lessons, but Callie had appalling recall for names. *Noah.* Warmth pooled low in her belly. *I don't have any interest in that awful man.* And she wasn't about to admit she'd spent the past twenty-four hours thinking about him.

"Good news travels fast," she said and passed over a twenty dollar note.

Linda took the money and cranked the register. "In this place news is news. I only heard because my daughter volunteers as a guard at the surf beach."

Callie took the bait and her change. "The surf beach?"

"Well, Cameron was there. He told her all about it."

He did? "Who's Cameron?"

Linda tutted as though Callie should know exactly who he was. "Cameron Jakowski. He and Noah are best friends."

Callie couldn't imagine anyone wanting to be friends with Noah Preston.

"Cameron volunteers there, too," she said, and Callie listened, trying to not lose track of the conversation. "Noah used to, but he's too busy with all his kids now."

"So this Cameron told your daughter what happened?"

"Yep. He said you and Noah had an all-out brawl. Something to do with that eldest terror of his."

"It wasn't exactly a brawl," Callie explained. "More like a disagreement."

"I heard he thinks you should be shut down," Linda said odiously, her voice dropping an octave.

Callie's spine stiffened. Not again. When she'd caught the Trent sisters smoking in the stables, Sonya Trent had threatened the same thing. "What?"

"Mmm," Linda said. "And it only takes one thing to go wrong to ruin a business, believe me. One whiff of you being careless around the kids and you can kiss the place goodbye."

Callie felt like throwing up. Her business meant everything to her. Her horses, her home. "I didn't do anything," she protested.

Linda made a sympathetic face. "Of course you didn't, love. But I wouldn't blame you one bit if you had because of that little hellion." Linda sighed. "That girl's been nothing but trouble since her—"

The conversation stopped abruptly when the bell pealed

and a woman, dressed in a pair of jeans and a vivid orange gauze blouse, walked into the shop. Black hair curled wildly around her face and bright green eyes regarded Callie for a brief moment.

"Hello, Linda," she said and grabbed a bottle of water from one of the fridges.

"Evie, good to see you. Are you selling at the trunk sale today?" Linda asked.

Her dancing green eyes grew wide. "For sure," she said and paid her money. "My usual stuff. But if you hear of anyone wanting a big brass bed, let me know. I'm renovating one of the upstairs rooms and it needs to go. Catch you later."

She hurried from the shop and Linda turned her attention back to Callie.

"That's Evie Dunn," Linda explained. "She runs a bed and breakfast along the waterfront. You can't miss it. It's the big A-frame place with the monstrous Norfolk pines out the front. She's an artist and sells all kinds of crafting supplies, too. You should check it out."

Callie grimaced and then smiled. "I'm not really into handicrafts."

Linda's silvery brows shot up. "Noah Preston is her brother."

Of course. No wonder those green eyes had looked so familiar. Okay, maybe now she *was* a little interested. Callie grabbed her soda and left the shop. So, he wanted her shut down, did he?

She drove the truck in the car park and leashed Tessa. There were more than thirty cars and stalls set up, and the park was teeming with browsers and buyers. It took Callie about three minutes to find Evie Dunn. The pretty brunette had a small table laid out with craft wares and costume jewelry. She wandered past once and then navigated around for another look.

"Are you interested in scrapbooking?" Evie Dunn asked on her third walk by.

Callie stalled and eased Tessa to heel. She took a step toward the table and shrugged. "Not particularly."

Black brows rose sharply. "Are you interested in a big brass bed?"

Callie shook her head. "Ah, I don't think so."

Evie planted her hands on her hips. "Then I guess you must be interested in my brother?"

Callie almost hyperventilated. "What do you—"

"You're Callie, right?" The other woman asked and thrust out her hand. "I saw the name of your riding school on the side of your truck. I'm Evie. Lily told me all about you. You made quite an impression on my niece, which is not an easy feat. From what she told me, I'm certain she still wants you as her riding instructor."

There was no chance that was going to happen. "I don't think it's up to Lily."

"Made you mad, did he?"

Callie took a step forward and shook her hand. "You could say that."

Evie, whose face was an amazing mix of vivid color—green eyes and bright cherry lips—stared at her with a thoughtful expression that said she was being thoroughly summed up. "So, about the brass bed?" she asked and smiled. "Would you like to see it?"

Brass bed? Callie shook her head. Hadn't she already said she wasn't interested? "I don't think—"

"You'll love it," Evie insisted. "I can take you to look at it now if you like. Help me pack up and we can get going."

Callie began to protest and then stopped. She was pretty sure they weren't really talking about a bed. This was Noah

Preston's sister. And because he had quickly become enemy number one, if she had a lick of sense she'd find out everything she could about him and use it to her advantage. If Noah thought she would simply sit back and allow him to ruin her reputation, he could certainly think again. Sandhills Farm was her life. If he wanted a war, she'd give him one.

Chapter Two

Noah didn't know how to reach out to his angry daughter. He hurt for her. A deep, soul-wrenching hurt that transcended right through to his bones. But what could he do? Her sullen, uncommunicative moods were impossible to read. She skulked around the house with her eyes to the floor, hiding behind her makeup, saying little, determined to disassociate herself from the family he tried so frantically to keep together.

And she pined for the mother who'd abandoned her without a backward glance.

She'd deny it, of course. But Noah knew. It had been more than four years ago. Four and a half long years and they all needed to move on.

Yeah, right...like I've moved on?

He liked to think so. Perhaps not the way his parents or sisters thought he should have. But he'd managed to pull together the fractured pieces of the life his ex-wife discarded.

He had Preston Marine, the business his grandfather created and which he now ran, his kids, his family and friends. It was enough. More than enough.

Most of the time.

Except for the past twenty-four hours.

Because as much as he tried not to, he couldn't stop thinking about the extraordinarily beautiful Callie Jones and her glittering blue eyes. And the way she'd planted her hands on her hips. And the sinful way she'd filled out her jeans. For the first time in forever he felt a spark of attraction. More than a spark. It felt like a damned raging inferno, consuming him with its heat.

Noah stacked the dishes he'd washed and dried his hands, then checked his watch. He was due at Evie's around two o'clock; he'd promised her he'd help shift some furniture. Evie loved rearranging furniture.

Within ten minutes they were on their way. Hayley and Matthew, secured in their booster seats, chatted happily to each other while Jamie sat in the front beside Noah. His one-hundred-and-forty acre farm was only minutes out of Crystal Point and was still considered part of the small town. He'd bought the place a couple of years earlier, for a song of a price, from an elderly couple wanting to retire after farming sugar cane for close to fifty years. The cane was all but gone now, and Noah leased the land to a local farmer who ran cattle.

He dropped speed along The Parade, the long road separating the houses from the shore, and pulled up outside his sister's home. There was a truck parked across the road, a beat-up blue Ford that looked familiar. He hauled Hayley into his arms, grabbed Matty's hand and allowed Jamie to seize the knapsack from the backseat and then race on ahead. The kids loved Evie's garden, with its pond and stone paved walkways, which wound in tracks to a stone wishing well. And Noah kind of liked it, too.

"Look, Daddy…it's that dog," Jamie said excitedly, running toward a happy-looking pup tied to a railing near the front veranda.

The dog looked as familiar to him as the truck parked outside. His stomach did a stupid leap.

She's here? What connection did Callie Jones have to Evie? Before he could protest, Jamie was up the steps, opening the front door and calling his aunt's name.

Noah found them in the kitchen. Evie was cutting up pineapple and *she* was sitting at the long scrubbed table, cradling a mug in her hands. She looked up when he entered the room and smiled. A killer smile. A smile with enough kick to knock the breath from his chest. He wondered if she knew she had it, if she were aware how flawless her skin looked or how red and perfectly bowed her lips were. The hat was gone and her brown hair hung over one shoulder in a long braid.

Discomfort raced through him. Noah shifted Hayley on his hip and hung on tightly to Matty's hand. She looked him over, he looked her over. Something stirred, rumbling through his blood, taunting him a little.

Evie cleared her throat and broke the silence. "Well," she said. "How about I take the kids outside and you two can… talk?"

Noah didn't want to talk with her. He also knew he wouldn't be able to drag himself away.

Callie Jones had walked into his life. And he was screwed.

Callie couldn't speak. They were twins. *Twins.* Who looked to be about…four years old?

The same age as Ryan would have been...

She smiled—she wasn't sure how—and watched him hold the twins with delightful affection. He looked like Father of the Year. And he was, according to his sister. A single dad raising four children. A good man. The best.

A heavy feeling grew in her chest, filling her blood, sharpening her breath.

The children disappeared with Evie, and once they were alone she stood and flicked her braid down her back. He watched every movement, studying her with such open regard she couldn't stop a flush from rising over her skin.

I shouldn't want him to look at me like that.

Not this man who had quickly become the enemy.

"I didn't expect to see you..." he said, then paused. "So soon."

She inhaled deeply. "I guess you didn't. Frankly, I didn't *want* to see you."

His green eyes held her captive. "And yet you're here in my sister's house?"

Callie tilted her chin. "I'm looking at a bed."

The word *bed* quickly stirred up a whole lot of awareness between them. It was bad enough she thought the man was gorgeous—her blasted body had to keep reminding her of the fact!

"A bed?"

"Yes." Callie took another breath. Longer this time because she needed it. "You know, one of those things to sleep on."

That got him thinking. "I know what a bed is," he said quietly. "And what it's used for."

I'll just bet you do!

Callie turned red from her braid to her boots. "But now that I am here, perhaps you'd like to apologize?"

"For what?" He looked stunned.

For being a gorgeous jerk. "For being rude yesterday."

"Wait just a—"

"And for telling people my school should be closed down."

"What?"

"Are you denying it? I mean, you threatened me," she said, and as soon as the words left her mouth she felt ridiculous.

"I did what?"

She didn't miss the quiet, controlled tone in his voice. Maddeningly in control, she thought. Almost too controlled, as if he was purposefully holding himself together in some calm, collected way to prove he would not, and could not, be provoked.

"You said you'd see that I lost my license," she explained herself.

He looked at her. "And because of that you think I've been saying your school needs to be closed down?"

"Yes, I do."

"And who did you hear this from?"

Callie felt foolish then. Was she being paranoid listening to small-town gossip? *Have I jumped to conclusions?* When she didn't reply he spoke again.

"Local tongues, no doubt. I haven't said a word to anyone, despite my better judgment." He cocked a brow. "Perhaps you've pissed off someone else."

Retaliation burned on the end of her tongue. The infamous Callie Jones temper rose up like bile, strangling her throat. "You're such a jerk!"

He smiled. *Smiled.* As if he found her incredibly amusing. Callie longed to wipe the grin from his handsome face, to slap her hand across his smooth skin. To touch. To feel. And then, without explanation, something altered inside her. Something altered *between them.* In an unfathomable moment, everything changed.

He sees me...

She wasn't sure why she thought it. Why she felt it through to the blood pumping in her veins. But she experienced a strange tightening in her chest, constricting her breath, her movements. Callie didn't want anyone to see her. Not this man. Especially not this man. This stranger.

But he did. She was sure of it. *He sees that I'm a fraud. I can talk a tough line. But I live alone. I work alone. I am alone.*

And Noah Preston somehow knew it.

Bells rang in her head. Warning her, telling her to leave and break the incredible eye contact that shimmered like light between them.

"You need to keep a better handle on your daughter."

"I do?" he said, still smiling.

"She broke the rules," Callie said pointedly. "And as her parent, that's your fault, not mine."

"She broke the rules because you lacked good judgment," he replied.

Callie scowled, grabbed her keys and headed for the door. "Tell your sister thank you for the coffee."

He raised an eyebrow. "Did I hit a nerve?"

She rounded her shoulders back and turned around. "I'm well aware of my faults. I may not be all wisdom regarding the behavior of teenage girls, but I certainly know plenty about men who are arrogant bullies. You can point as much blame in my direction as you like—but that doesn't change the facts."

"I *did* hit a nerve."

"I wouldn't give you the satisfaction."

As she left the house and collected Tessa, Callie wasn't sure she took a breath until she drove off down The Parade.

Noah waited until the front door clicked shut and then inhaled deeply, filling his lungs with air. A jerk? Is that what he'd sounded like? He didn't like that one bit. A protective father, yes. But a jerk? He felt like chasing after her to set her straight.

Evie returned to the kitchen in record time, minus the kids. "They're watching a DVD," she said and refilled the kettle. Evie thought caffeine was a sure cure for anything. "So, that went well, did it?"

"Like a root canal."

"Ouch." She made a face. "She called you a jerk. And a bully."

"Eavesdropping, huh?"

She shrugged. "Only a bit. So, who won that battle in this war?" she asked, smiling.

He recognized his sister's look. "It's not exactly a war."

Evie raised a brow. "But you were mad at her, right?"

"Sure." He let out an impatient breath.

"Well." Evie stopped her task of making coffee. "You don't usually get mad at people."

Noah frowned. "Of course I do."

"No, you don't," Evie said. "Not even your pesky three sisters."

He shrugged. "Does this conversation have a point?"

"I was just wondering what she did to make you so…uptight?"

"I'm sure she told you what happened," Noah said, trying to look disinterested and failing.

Evie's eyes sparkled. "Well…yes, she did. But I want to hear it from you."

"Why?"

"So I can see if you get the same look on your face that she did."

"What look?" he asked stupidly.

Evie stopped what she was doing. A tiny smile curved her lips. "*That* look."

He shook his head. "You're imagining things."

Evie chuckled. "I don't think so. Anyway, I thought she was…nice."

Yeah, like a stick of dynamite. "You like everyone."

Evie laughed out loud. "Ha—you're not fooling me. You *like* her."

"I don't know her."

Noah dismissed his sister's suspicions. If he gave an inch, if he even slightly indicated he had thoughts of Callie Jones in any kind of romantic capacity, she'd be on the telephone to their mother and two other sisters within a heartbeat.

Romance…yeah, right. With four kids, a mortgage and a business to run—women weren't exactly lining up to take part in his complicated life.

He couldn't remember the last time he'd had a date. Eight months ago, he thought, vaguely remembering a quiet spoken, divorced mother of two who'd spent the entire evening complaining about her no-good, layabout ex. One date was all they'd had. He'd barely touched her hand. *I live like a monk.* That wasn't surprising, though—the fallout from his divorce would have sent any man running to the monastery.

Besides, he didn't want a hot-tempered, irresponsible woman in his life, did he? No matter how sexy she looked in her jeans. "So, where's this furniture you want me to move?" he asked, clapping his hands together as he stood.

Evie took the hint that the subject was closed. "One of the upstairs bedrooms," she said. "I want to paint the walls. I just need the armoire taken out into the hall."

"Oh, the antique cupboard that weighs a ton? Lucky me. At least this time I'm spared the stairs. Do you remember when Gordon and I first got the thing upstairs?"

Evie smiled, clearly reminiscing, thinking of the husband she'd lost ten years earlier. "And Cameron," she said. "You were all acting like a bunch of wusses that day, huffing and puffing over one little armoire."

Noah grunted as they took the stairs. "Damn thing's made of lead."

"Wuss," she teased.

They laughed some more and spent twenty minutes shifting the heaviest piece of furniture on the planet. When he was done, Noah wanted a cold drink and a back rub.

And that idea made him think of Callie Jones and her lovely blue eyes all over again.

"Feel like staying for dinner?" Evie asked once they were back downstairs. "Trevor's at a study group tonight," she said of her fifteen-year-old son.

"On a Sunday? The kid's keen."

"The kid's smart," Evie corrected. "He wants to be an engineer like his favorite uncle."

Noah smiled. "Not tonight, but thanks. I've gotta pick Lily up from the surf club at four. And it's a school day tomorrow."

Evie groaned. "God, we're a boring lot."

Noah wasn't going to argue with that. He grabbed the kids' things and rounded up the twins and Jamie. The kids hugged Evie and she waved them off from the front step.

"And don't forget the parents are back from their trip on Wednesday," she reminded him.

"I won't," he promised.

"And don't forget I'll need your help to move the armoire back into the bedroom in a few days. I'll call to remind you."

He smiled. "I won't forget."

"And don't forget to think about why you're refusing to admit that you're hot for a certain riding instructor."

Noah shook his head. "Goodbye, Evie."

She was still laughing minutes later when he drove off.

Noah headed straight for the surf club. Lily was outside when he pulled up, talking to Cameron. She scowled when she saw him and quickly got into the backseat, squeezing between the twins' booster seats. Normally, she would have resigned Jamie to the back. But not today. She was clearly still mad with him. Mad that *he'd* made it impossible for her to go back to Sandhills Farm, at least in her mind.

Noah got out of the pickup and turned his attention to his best friend. "So, Hot Tub, what have you been up to?"

Cameron half-punched him in the shoulder. "Would you stop calling me that?"

Noah grinned at his playboy friend and the unflattering nickname he'd coined years earlier.

"I'll do my best." He changed the subject. "Did Lily say anything to you about what happened yesterday?"

Cameron nodded. "You know Lily. I hear the horse lady's real cute."

Cute? That's not how Noah would describe Callie. Cute was a bland word meant for puppies and little girls with pink ribbons in their hair. Beautiful better described Callie Jones, and even that didn't seem to do her justice. Not textbook pretty, like Margaret, his ex, had been. Callie had a warm, rich kind of beauty. She looked like…the taste of a full-bodied Bordeaux. Or the scent of jasmine on a sultry summer's evening.

Get a grip. Noah coughed. "I have to get going."

Minutes later he was back on the road and heading home. By the time they reached the house Noah knew he wanted the truth from Lily. Callie Jones had called him a jerk. If he'd misjudged her like she said, he wanted to know. Lily tried her usual tactic of skipping straight to her bedroom, but he cut her off by the front door, just after the twins and Jamie had made it inside.

"Lily," he said quietly. "I want to talk to you."

She pulled her knapsack onto her shoulder and shrugged. "Don't you mean talk *at* me?"

He took a deep breath. "Did you ride that horse without permission yesterday?"

She rolled her eyes. "I told you what happened."

"Was it the truth?"

Lily shrugged. "Sort of." Her head shot up and she stared at him with eyes outlined in dark, smudgy makeup. "Is she blaming me?"

No, she's blaming me. And probably rightly so if the look on his daughter's face was anything to go by. Noah knew instantly that he'd overreacted. *Clearly. Stupidly.*

Noah suddenly felt like he'd been slapped over the back of the head. *I never overreact.* So, why her? Evie's words came back to haunt him.

You like her.

And he did. *She's beautiful, sassy and sexy as hellfire.*

But that wasn't really Callie Jones. It was an act—Noah knew it as surely as he breathed. How he knew he wasn't sure. Instinct maybe. Something about her reached him, drew him and made him want to *know* her.

Lily's eyes grew wider and suspicious. "You've seen her again, right?"

He wondered how she'd know that and thought it might be some fledgling female intuition kicking in. "Yes, I have."

She huffed, a childish sound that reminded him she was just thirteen. "Is she going to give me lessons?"

"I said we'd find you another instructor."

Lily's expression was hollow and she flicked her black hair from her eyes. "So, she won't?"

"I don't think so."

"Couldn't you ask her?"

Good question. He could ask her. Lily wanted her. Lily never wanted anything, never asked him for anything. But she wanted Callie Jones.

"Why is it so important to you to learn from Callie? There are other instructors in town."

She cast him a scowl. "Yeah, at the big training school

in town. It's full of rich stuck-ups with their push-button ponies."

"How do you know that?"

She chewed at her bottom lip for a moment and then said, "From school. The *Pony Girls* all go there."

Pony girls? Noah felt completely out of touch. "And?"

"The Trents," Lily explained. "Lisa and *Melanieeee.* They used to go to her school. *She* kicked them out a couple of months ago."

Melanie Trent. Lily's ex-best friend. And now her nemesis. "Why?"

"They were caught smoking in the stables," Lily supplied. "Big mistake. Anyway, I know that she lost some of her other students because of it. You know what the Trents are like. They don't like *anyone* telling them what to do."

Noah did know. Sonja Trent, the girls' mother, had worked reception for him a year earlier. He'd given her the post as a favor when her husband was laid off from his job at the local sugar mill. Two weeks later she left when Noah had made it clear he wasn't interested in having an affair with her. Sonja was married and unhappy—two good reasons to steer clear of any kind of involvement.

"Did you know *she* was some big-time rider?" Lily said, bringing Noah back to the present. "Like, I mean, really big time. Like she could have gone to the Olympics or something."

He tried not to think about the way his heart skipped a beat. "No, I didn't know that."

"If *she* teaches me then I'll be good at it, too. Better than *Melanie.* Way better. And maybe then she won't be so stuck-up and mean to Maddy all the time."

Maddy Spears was Lily's new/old best friend. Friends before Melanie had arrived on the scene and broken apart because Maddy was a quiet, sweet kid and not interested in flouting her parents' wishes by covering her face in make-up or wearing inappropriate clothes.

"I could apologize," Lily suggested and shrugged her bony shoulders.

That would be a first. Noah nodded slowly. "You could," he said, although he wasn't sure it would make any difference to the situation.

"I really want Callie, Dad," Lily said desperately.

You're not the only one. He cleared his throat. "I don't know, Lily…."

Noah wasn't sure how to feel about Lily's desperation to get lessons from Callie. Other than his sisters and mother, Lily hadn't let another woman into her life since Margaret had walked out.

Neither have I.

Lily didn't trust easily.

Neither do I.

"We'll see. Go and get washed up," he told her. "And maybe later you could help me with dinner?"

She grabbed the screen door and flung it open. "Maybe."

Her feet had barely crossed the threshold when Noah called her name. She stopped and pivoted on her Doc Martens. "What now?"

"Whoever you have lessons from, you have to follow the rules, okay?"

Her lips curled in a shadow of a smile. "Sure thing, Dad."

Noah watched his daughter sprint down the hall and disappear into her room with a resounding bang of the door. *Okay...now what?* But he knew what he had to do. He had to see Callie again. More to the point, he *wanted* to see her again. And he wondered if they made bigger fools than him.

Callie unhitched the tailgate and took most of the weight as it folded down. Indiana and Titan snorted restlessly, sensing the presence of other horses being unloaded and prepared for the Bellandale Horse Club show that day. Bellandale was a regional city of more than sixty thousand people and the event attracted competitors from many of the smaller surrounding townships.

Fiona Walsh, her friend and student, led both horses off the trailer, and Callie took the geldings in turn and hitched them to the side.

"I'm nervous," Fiona admitted as she ran her hands down her ivory riding breeches.

Callie unclipped Indiana's travel rug. "You'll be fine. This is your first competition—just enjoy the day. You and Titan have worked hard for this."

Fiona's carefully secured red hair didn't budge as she nodded enthusiastically. "Thanks for the pep talk. I'll go and get our stalls sorted."

Callie organized their gear once Fiona disappeared. Both horses were already groomed, braided and ready for tack, and by the time Fiona returned Callie had saddles and bridles adjusted and set. It took thirty minutes to find their allocated stalls, shovel in a layer of fresh sawdust, turn the horses into them and change into their jackets and long riding boots.

Callie's first event was third on the agenda and once she was dressed and had her competitors number pinned to her jacket she swung into the saddle and headed for the warm-up area. The show grounds were teaming with horses and riders and more spectators than usual, which she put down to the mild October weather. She warmed Indiana up with a few laps around the ring at a slow trot and then a collected canter. She worked through her transitions and practiced simple and flying changes. When she was done she walked Indy toward the main arena and waited for her name to be called.

The dressage test was a relatively simple one, but she gave it her full concentration. This was only her third show in as many months and she wanted to perform well. Indiana, as usual, displayed the skill and proficiency in his movements that had seen him revered by followers of the show circuit when she had been competing years before.

Before it all went wrong.

Before Craig Baxter.

Handsome, charming and successful and twelve years her senior, Craig had been a gifted rider. So gifted, in fact, that Callie often overlooked his moodiness and extreme perfectionism. Because underneath the charm and success, it had always only been about the competition. About results. About being the best.

And nearly four years after his death she still hurt.

It's better to have loved and lost...

Yeah…sure it was. Callie didn't believe that for one minute.

Love hurts. And it was off her agenda. Permanently.

What about sex? Is that off the agenda, too?

She'd thought so. But…in the last week she *had* been thinking about sex. Lots of sex. And all of it with Noah Preston. The kind of sex that had somehow invaded her normally G-rated life and made her have X-rated thoughts. Well, maybe not X-rated—she was still a little too homecoming queen for that. But certainly R-rated…

The announcement of her score startled her out of her erotic thoughts. She bowed her head to acknowledge the judges and left the dressage arena. As she cornered past three other riders waiting for their turn Callie eased Indiana to a halt. Because right there, in front of her, stood the object of all her recent fantasies.

Chapter Three

Dressed in jeans, a black chambray shirt and boots Noah looked so damned sexy it literally made her gasp. He held keys in one hand and a pair of sunglasses in the other.

She stared at him, determined to hold his gaze. Finally, curiosity got the better of her and she clicked Indiana forward. "What do you want?"

He moved toward her and touched Indy's neck. "Nice-looking horse."

"Thank you," she said stiffly, hoping he couldn't see the color rising over her cheeks. Callie collected the reins and swung herself out of the saddle. "Did you want something?" she asked again once both feet were planted on the ground.

"I did."

So tell me what it is and go away so I can stop thinking about how totally gorgeous you are and how much you make me think about wanting all the things I never thought I'd want again.

"How did you know I was here?"

"Your apprentice told me where to find you."

Joe? Callie wanted to ring his neck. "So you've found me. And?"

"I'd like to talk to you."

Callie tilted her chin. "What have I done now?" she asked, clutching the reins tightly so he wouldn't notice her hands were shaking.

He half smiled and Callie's stomach did a silly leap. "I guess I deserve that," he said.

She moved Indiana forward. She wouldn't fall for any lines, no matter how nicely he said them. She wouldn't be tempted to feel again. She couldn't. It hurt too much. "Oh, I see—today you come in peace?"

"I wanted to apologize."

"You're a week too late," she said stiffly and led the horse away. Callie felt him behind her as she walked—felt his eyes looking her over as he followed her past the rows of small stables until she reached their allocated stall.

Fiona came out from the adjoining stall. "Hi, Noah," Fiona greeted with a cheek-splitting grin. Callie didn't miss how the other woman's hand fleetingly touched his arm.

Clearly, no introductions were required. Fiona saw her look and explained that she taught his son at the local primary school and took an art class with his sister, Evie.

"So you two know each other?" Fiona asked.

"Yes," he replied. "We do."

"I'd better go," Fiona said quickly and began leading Titan from his stall. "My event is up next. Wish me luck."

Callie watched her friend lead the big chestnut gelding away and then turned her attention to the man in front of her.

"Okay," she said. "You can apologize now."

He laughed and the rich, warm sound dipped her stomach

like a rolling wave. Callie felt like smiling, but she wouldn't. She *wanted* to be mad at him—it made her feel safe.

"I overreacted last week," he said. "I know Lily took your horse without permission."

Her chin came up. "Bravo. I'll bet saying that was like chewing glass," she said as she opened the stall and ushered Indiana inside. Then she clicked the bottom door in place. "So," she said, "was there something else you wanted to discuss?"

"First, that you reconsider and give Lily riding lessons."

Callie didn't try to disguise her astonishment. "I thought you were going to find her another instructor."

"Apparently you're the best around."

"Yes," she replied, fighting the rapid thump of her heart. He was close now. Too close. "I am."

"And I want the best for my daughter."

"You should have thought about that before you called me an irresponsible nutcase."

His green eyes looked her over. "Is that what I said?"

Callie unbuttoned her jacket. "Words to that effect," she said, feeling suddenly hot and sweaty in the fine-gauge wool coat she'd had tailored to fit like a glove. She longed to strip off her hat, but the idea of him seeing the very unattractive hairnet she wore to keep her thick hair secure under the helmet stopped her.

He smiled. "Then I owe you an apology for that, as well."

"Yes, you do. So, anything else?"

"That you give me another chance," he said quietly. "I might be a jerk on occasion…but I'm not such a bad guy."

She snorted and that made him smile again. God, her hormones were running riot. Did this man know how earth-shatteringly gorgeous he was? She had to pull herself together. He leaned back against the stall and Callie watched, suddenly mesmerized as the cotton shirt stretched across his chest as he moved. *One step and I could touch him. One tiny step and I could place my hands over his broad shoulders.*

"So, do we have an arrangement?"

His voice jerked her thoughts back. "No, we don't."

"Are you going to play hard to get?"

The double meaning of his words could not be denied and Callie blushed wildly. She looked at her feet, thinking that any minute she was going to plant one of her size nines into her mouth and say something she'd regret. And typically, she did exactly that.

"I'm not playing anything with you," she said hotly. "As you pointed out so clearly last weekend, I don't have the skills required to handle your daughter. What I do have is a business to run…a business that means everything to me. I work hard and I won't do anything that could tarnish my reputation."

His gaze narrowed. "And you think teaching Lily would?"

"I think…" She stopped. It wasn't about Lily. It was about him. She only hoped he didn't realize it. "I think…another teacher would be better for her. Someone she would actually listen to."

"And if I promised that she would listen to you, Callie?"

She drew in a breath. It was the first time he'd said her name. It sounded personal. Intimate almost. "You can't promise something like that."

"She'll do what I ask."

Yeah…like putty in his hands. That's how Callie felt at the moment. "Look," she said pointedly. "All I want to do is run my school and care for my horses and try to fix up my house, which is crumbling around my ears. I just don't want any drama."

It sounded lame. Callie knew it. *He* knew it.

Something passed between them. Awareness? Recognition? A look between two people who hardly knew one another...and yet, strangely, on some primal level, had a deep connection. More than merely man to woman. More...*everything.* It scared the breath out of her. Thinking about him was one thing. *Feeling* something for him was another altogether.

"And there's nothing I can offer you that might make you change your mind?"

Callie's temperature rose and launched off her usual, well-controlled sensible-gauge. It was ridiculous. She couldn't imagine everything he said to her had some kind of sexual innuendo attached to it.

"Nothing."

"Even though you say you need the cash?"

It sounded foolish put like that. But she wasn't going to give in. "Exactly."

"That doesn't make a lot of sense."

"Well, you know me—all bad judgment and recklessness." She picked up the pitch fork. "Now, if you don't mind, I have to go and watch Fiona."

He half shrugged, looked at the pitch fork as though she might consider running him through with it, then took a small card from his pocket and passed it to her. "If you change your mind—"

"I won't." Callie folded the small business card between her fingers and opened the door to Indiana's stall. She slipped inside and waited a full five minutes before emerging—and only when she was certain Noah Preston had left.

Noah usually let the kids stay up a little later on Saturday nights. But by eight-thirty the twins were falling asleep on the sofa and Jamie took himself off to bed just after Hayley and Matthew were tucked beneath the covers.

Lily, however, decided to loiter in the kitchen, flicking through cupboards as she complained about the lack of potato chips. She made do with an opened box of salted crackers.

"So," she said as she sat. "Did you ask her?"

Noah stopped packing the dishwasher and looked at his daughter. The makeup and piercings and black clothes seemed more out of place than usual in the ordinariness of the timber kitchen. He wished she'd ditch the gothic act, but he'd learned fast that barking out ultimatums only fueled her rebelliousness.

"Yes."

Lily looked hopeful and Noah's heart sank. How did he tell his kid the truth? "She's thinking about it," he said, stretching the facts.

His daughter's expression changed quickly. "She's still mad at me?" Lily dropped the box of crackers and stood. "She's the best, Dad. And learning from the best is important. It means I might get to be the best at something, too."

She looked painfully disappointed and Noah felt every ounce of her frustration. If she'd followed Callie's rules, it wouldn't have been a problem.

"Lily, whoever you get lessons from, you'll have to follow the rules."

Lily's dramatic brows rose. "I'm not the one who shouted at her."

Noah stiffened. "I didn't shout. We had a conversation."

"Yeah, and after that she said she wouldn't teach me."

He had to admit his daughter had a point. If he hadn't acted so irrationally and lost his cool with Callie, he figured Lily would have been able to stay at the school. Lily had messed up, but so had *he.*

"'Night, Dad," she said unhappily and left the room.

Noah looked at the clock. He was weary but not tired. He left the dishwasher and headed for the living room. The big sofa welcomed him as he sat and grabbed the remote.

Another long Saturday night loomed ahead. He flicked

channels absently and settled for a movie he'd seen before. It didn't hold his attention for long. He kept thinking of Callie. She was a real dynamo. All feisty and argumentative, high octane. But underneath, he saw something else…something more. He wasn't sure how he knew—but he did. Whatever was going on with her, she wore it like a suit of armor. And he was interested in knowing what lay underneath all that fire and spirit. Hell, he was more than interested. Way more. The way she'd glared at him from beneath her hat, the way she'd filled out her riding jodhpurs… His skin burned thinking about it.

He flicked channels again, but it was no use. Television wouldn't hold his attention tonight. More so than usual, he felt alone and…lonely. Absurd when he lived in a house filled with children. And when he considered how great his family was. He loved his kids. His parents were exceptional, and his sisters were the best he could ask for.

But right now he wanted more than that. He needed more than that.

But what?

Company? Someone to talk with?

Sex?

Perhaps it was more about sex than he was prepared to admit. Up until a week ago he'd been in a kind of sexual hibernation. But Callie had him thinking about it. And got him hard *just* thinking about it. And not the vague, almost indistinct inclination that usually stirred him. This was different. Way different.

Maybe I should ask her out?

That was crazy. That would be like standing in front of a bulldozer.

She can't stand you, he reminded himself. *Okay, maybe I'll just ask her to reconsider about Lily again?*

Despite his brain telling him to forget the idea, Noah

picked up the telephone and dialed the number he couldn't recall memorizing but somehow had. She answered on the fourth ring.

"Callie, it's Noah Preston."

Silence screeched like static. Finally she spoke. "Oh—hello."

"Sorry to call so late."

A pause. "That's okay—I'm not in bed yet."

His body tightened. He had a startling image in his head and shook himself. *Maybe I will ask her out.* "I was wondering if you—"

"I haven't reconsidered," she said, cutting him off.

"What?"

"About Lily," she said on a soft breath.

All he could think about was that same breath against his skin. "I was actually—"

"Janelle Evans," she said quickly, cutting him off again.

Noah paused. "What?" he asked again.

"She's an instructor just out of town. She has a good reputation. She breeds quarter horses. I have her number if you're interested."

Oh, I'm interested all right. But not in Janelle Evans.

She was talking fast and Noah knew she was eager to end the call. *Bulldozer,* he reminded himself. "Ah—sure."

He took the number she rattled off and had to ask her to repeat the last few digits because she spoke so quickly.

"Well—goodbye."

He hesitated, feeling the sting of her reluctance to engage in conversation. "Yeah, okay—goodbye."

She hung up and he dropped the telephone on the sofa. He needed a shower—as cold as he could stand. Then he'd go to bed and sleep off the idea that he wanted to make love to Callie Jones more than he'd wanted to do anything for a long time.

* * *

On Sunday morning Callie woke at seven, after spending a restless night fighting with the bedsheets.

It was all Noah Preston's fault. She didn't ask for his late-night call. She didn't want to hear his sexy voice just before she went to bed. She didn't want to spend the night thinking about him.

She dressed and made short work of a bowl of cereal topped with fruit, then grabbed her hat and headed outside. The sun was up, already warming the early October morning air. She fed Tessa then headed for the stables, where Joe waited outside Indiana's stall.

"Are you taking the big fella out this morning?"

Callie shook her head. "Not today." Indy's long head swung over the top of the door and she ran her hands down his face. "'Morning, my darling boy." She turned back to Joe. "He did well yesterday, two firsts and a third, so he gets a day off. Give him a feed, will you, and then tack up Kirra. The English saddle please."

Joe made a face. "What do I tell the kid?"

Callie frowned. "What kid?"

"The one who's here for a lesson."

Callie shook her head. "I don't have anyone booked until eleven."

"I know," Joe said. "I checked the booking sheet. But she's here." Joe pointed to the office. "I put her in there," he said, then more seriously, "and told her not to touch anything."

Callie strode the twenty meters to the office and swung the half-opened door back on its hinges. She stood in the threshold and looked at the young girl sitting at her desk.

"What are you doing here?"

Lily Preston swiveled in the chair and got to her feet. "Um…I'm here for my lesson."

Callie inhaled deeply. "You're not having a lesson."

"But I thought—"

Callie placed her hands on her hips. "You have to go home, Lily." She turned on her heels and went to walk away but stopped when the teenager spoke.

"Please."

She turned back and looked at the teenager, whose green eyes were wide open, their expression sincere. Lily *was* sorry. Callie could feel it. Something tugged at her heartstrings.

Callie took a deep breath. "Indiana is my horse, Lily. And as quiet as he is, you could have been badly hurt. And I would have been responsible."

Lily's chin lifted, half defiant. "But I can ride a bit."

"A bit isn't good enough for a horse like Indiana, especially in an ill-fitting bridle and without a saddle."

Lily looked shame-faced beneath her makeup. "I really didn't mean to cause any trouble," she said. "I just…sometimes I just *do* things. I don't know why. I do things I know are stupid, but I can't help myself."

The tug on Callie's heart grew stronger. She knew exactly what Lily meant. Kindred spirits, she thought. But, oh, God…what should she do? Say yes to this girl who looked at her with such raw intensity. A girl, she suspected, who rarely showed that side of herself to anyone. But a girl whose father she couldn't stop thinking about. Who, without even trying, was making Callie feel, imagine.

"I'll do whatever you want," Lily said quickly, almost desperately. "Please teach me."

Before Callie could reply Joe stuck his head around the door to tell her Kirra was ready. She thanked him, then returned her attention to the teenager. "I'll tell you what—you stay out of trouble while I work my horse and we'll talk after." She stood aside for Lily to pass. "No promises, just talk."

Callie led Lily from the stables and told her to stay put

near the dressage arena. She gave her an old soda crate to sit on and then took the red bay mare into the arena. She worked her for twenty minutes, trying to concentrate on the maneuvers and transitions from trot to canter. But her mind wasn't really on the job. Lily sat on the sidelines, watching her, masked behind her makeup.

Ten minutes later Noah Preston's silver utility vehicle pulled up outside the stables. Callie continued with her ride, watching as he got out and opened the back door of the truck. The children stepped out. The older boy grabbed the hands of the twins and listened as his father spoke to them. Then he headed for Lily. He had a great walk, she thought. And he looked so good in jeans and a black T-shirt. Way too good.

Callie watched as the kids followed behind him. And again it stirred something inside her. An old longing. And it gave her a snapshot of a life she'd never have.

Ryan...

The longing turned into a pain—a piercing, incredible hurt that always took root behind her ribs when she thought about the beautiful baby boy she'd lost when he was just two days old.

I miss you Ryan...I miss holding you...I miss watching you grow up and become the person you could have been.

Kirra sensed her distraction and started prancing sideways at a trot. Callie got her quickly under control and eased her to a halt in the center of the arena. And she watched as Noah began talking with his daughter. Lily nodded, he shook his head. Lily said something, he replied. The conversation lasted for some minutes and the three younger Preston children stood quietly behind their father. Finally, Lily waved her arms about and stomped off toward the truck. He said something to the three kids and they sat on the soda crate. Then he headed through the gate and into the arena.

Callie dismounted and pulled the reins over Kirra's head,

collecting them in her left hand. She fought the ridiculous impulse to take off her safety hat and smooth out her hair or rub her hands down her breeches.

He stopped about two feet in front of her. "Hello," he said.

Callie swallowed. "Hi."

He went to say something but then stopped. He patted the horse instead. He had nice hands, she noticed. Tanned and strong looking. She quickly snapped herself out of her silly female fantasy. "I was going to call you," she said. "You beat me to it."

"I knew she'd be here."

"You did? How?"

"Because you were the last thing we talked about last night. And I know Lily—when she gets her mind stuck on something, she can be impossible to deal with."

Callie raised her brows. "Looks like you're surrounded by impossible women."

My God, am I flirting? That's what it sounds like.

And he smiled. As though he liked it. "I could think of worse things."

Everything around her suddenly felt hot—the air in her lungs, the sand beneath her boots. "Anyway—she didn't do any harm while she was here."

"She's changed since her mother left."

Not what he wanted to say, Callie was sure of it. It was too familiar, too personal, too everything. And Callie wanted to clamp her hands over her ears. She didn't want to hear any more. She didn't want to know him. She didn't want to know *more* of him.

"No problem." It was a pitiful attempt at sounding indifferent.

"She used to be…sweet. A real sweet kid. And then she changed almost overnight."

Callie felt another surge of feeling for Lily. She knew all

about change. She knew what grief and hurt could do to a person. “Is that the reason for the makeup and black clothes?”

He shrugged. “Something to hide behind, I guess. She still wants riding lessons.”

Callie clicked Kirra forward and began to walk from the arena. “Well, Janelle Evans is a good instructor.”

He stepped in beside her. “She’s asked for you.”

“She can’t…you can’t…I just…”

Something happened then. Her legs stopped moving. Her lungs stopped breathing as she turned and their eyes locked. For one extraordinary moment Callie knew that whatever she was feeling, he was feeling it, too. It was crazy, heady and blindingly powerful.

He spoke first. “Lily rarely asks for anything.”

Callie continued walking. “Which means?”

“Which means I’m inclined to do whatever I can to see that she gets what she wants.”

They got to the gate. Callie tied Kirra to the railing, took a deep breath. “I’m not sure I—”

“Callie,” he said “Please, reconsider.” He placed his hand on her arm. A light touch, but the electricity coursing between their skin could not be denied. He looked at his hand but didn’t remove it. Callie stood still, held in place by his touch, by the mere wisp of space that lay between them. “Lily needs you.” He paused, watching her. “And I…and I need you.”

Chapter Four

Callie moved her arm. Away from his touch. Away from temptation. Away from the realization that she liked how his hand felt against her skin.

I need you...

There was something startlingly intimate about the way he spoke the words. She couldn't remember the last time a man had said that to her. Maybe never. Craig hadn't needed her. And Noah Preston didn't need her, either…not really. He just wanted her to teach his daughter to ride a horse.

"I can't."

He smiled. "Yes, you can."

God, he was relentless. Callie lifted her chin. "I said I can't."

"She'll be on her best behavior," he said.

Callie expelled a heavy breath. "Even if she is, I'm not—"

"Is your unwillingness actually about Lily?" he interrupted her. "Or something else?"

Her heart quickened. "Like what?"

He looked at her. Really looked. Callie felt compelled to turn her gaze away, but she didn't. *Couldn't.* She'd never felt this kind of intensity with anyone before. She'd spent years convincing herself she didn't want it.

"I thought that perhaps you and..." He stopped, hesitated and sort of half smiled. "I think we...I think *we* might have started off on the wrong foot."

He wasn't kidding. But she wasn't about to admit it. She wasn't about to admit to anything. Instead, she thought about the practical. "Why this sudden confidence in my abilities?"

"Because Lily believes in you."

Callie didn't break their eye contact. "Even though you don't?"

"And if I said I did? Would you reconsider teaching Lily? If I apologized again for being a jerk and asked you to do this for my daughter?"

Her insides quivered. *Don't be nice to me.* "You don't give up easily."

He shook his head. "Not when I want something." He looked around. "I heard you'd lost some students recently."

She stared at him. "How did you know that?"

He grinned. "Local gossip."

Callie's skin prickled. Just like the local gossip she'd listened to last weekend. "Yes, I did."

He looked around, to the house, then back to her. "So, it looks like you're not doing well financially."

More prickles. "I'm not filing for bankruptcy just yet."

A full smile this time. "I didn't mean to imply you were," he said carefully. "But I thought perhaps we could strike a deal."

Cautious, Callie's interest spiked. "What kind of deal?"

"Your usual fee—plus I'll help prevent your house from 'crumbling around your ears.'"

She stilled. "And how exactly will you do that?"

"I'll do whatever maintenance needs to be done while Lily's having her lessons."

Callie looked at him suspiciously. "Do you work construction?"

"No," he replied. "But I know my way around a toolbox."

I'll bet you do. Suddenly she was tempted. Very tempted. She *did* need the money. And as for his offer to help repair her house…that idea dangled like a juicy carrot in front of her nose. With windows that wouldn't open, doors needing repair, fence palings hanging loose and the knowledge she needed to chase the entire house with a paintbrush, the lure of his offer teased her. Refusing would be impulsive. And foolish.

And Lily…she wanted to help Lily. Helping Lily was suddenly important to her.

Oh, hell.

"Okay," she said quickly, before she had time to think about what it might mean to have him hanging around her house every Sunday morning. Him and his adorable kids.

Noah looked instantly pleased. "Good. Will you start today?"

She shook her head. "No. Next week. Sunday, nine o'clock."

He stepped back, finally, and she dipped underneath Kirra's neck, feeling safer with the horse between them. "Thank you, Callie. You won't regret it."

Too late…she already did.

He walked off without another word, collecting his kids along the way. Once his truck had disappeared down the driveway, Callie took off Kirra's tack and led her to the washing bay.

Joe appeared, his hair spotted with straw from the bales he'd been lugging off the truck and into the feed room.

"So, what's the deal with Vampira?" he asked, grimacing as he passed Callie an old towel. "Scary." He shuddered. "Do you reckon she's got tattoos, as well?"

Callie wasn't about to admit that she had one herself. "That's not nice."

He shrugged his lanky shoulders. "If my little sister went around looking like that my parents would go ballistic." He made a disagreeable face. "Was that her dad—Noah Preston?"

Callie stopped rubbing the towel over Kirra's flanks. "Do you know him?"

"I met him last weekend when he was looking for you. My Uncle Frank bought one of his boats last year."

Her interest increased tenfold. "He sells boats?"

Joe shook his head. "He designs boats," he replied. "And builds them. Top-of-the-range stuff. He's got a big factory in town. Uncle Frank reckons his boats are the best around."

Noah was a boat builder. And a single dad. And too gorgeous for her peace of mind.

As she led Kirra back to her stall, Callie couldn't stop thinking about how deeply he affected her. And how much she wished he didn't.

The Crystal Point Twilight Fair was an annual event that raised funds for the local elementary school and volunteer Rural Fire Brigade. Callie had been invited to provide horse rides for a small fee. The money collected would go directly back to the organizing committee, but it gave her an opportunity to promote her riding school. Sunshine and Peanuts, her two quietest geldings, loved the attention and happily walked around the makeshift yard she'd put together with a little help from Joe. There was also a jumping castle, a small carousel, a baby animal pen and a variety of stalls selling homemade cakes and candies and assorted handicrafts.

"So, are you staying for the dance later?" Fiona asked as she navigated Peanuts past her.

Callie checked the child clinging to Sunshine's saddle and smiled at her friend as they passed one another. "In this outfit?" she said, motioning a hand gesture to her worn jeans, thin sweater and riding boots. "I'll skip it. I have to get the horses back anyhow."

On their next passing Fiona spoke again. "I could use the company."

"Maybe another time.'

Callie didn't socialize much. Or at all. There seemed to be little time in her life for anything other than work. And she wasn't exactly in the right frame of mind to be thinking about dating.

Dating? Where did that come from?

She maneuvered the pony toward the entrance and helped the child dismount. The queue had grown and about six kids were waiting in line. She took the next one in turn.

An older woman came forward with two small children. They looked familiar and she glanced at the woman, taking in her attractive features, dark hair and deep green eyes.

Noah's children.

Callie's breath caught in her throat. The blond-haired pair were unmistakable. They were Noah's twins. And she was certain the striking-looking older woman was his mother.

"Is something wrong?" the woman asked.

Callie shook her head. "Of course not… It's just that I know your…Evie," she said quietly, suddenly self-conscious. "And Lily," she explained. "I'll be teaching Lily."

The other woman smiled. "Yes, I know. My son told me."

Callie's skin heated. She stopped herself from looking around to see if he was close by. "Let's get the kids up on the pony."

"Can they go together?"

"Yes." Callie took the little girl's hand and helped her into the saddle. She was such a pretty child and had an adorable smile. Something uncurled inside her with a sharp, ripping intensity. She'd become so adept at covering her feelings that children didn't normally do this to her...didn't make her think about Ryan. But this little girl did. With her bright eyes and rosy cheeks, Noah's daughter made her remember all she had lost.

Callie managed a smile, fought against the lump suddenly forming in her throat and helped the little boy aboard the pony. He was quieter than his sister and didn't say a word, while the little girl chatted for the entire duration of the pony ride.

She walked the perimeter of the arena a few times and learned that the girl's name was Hayley and her brother was Matthew. They were four and a half and couldn't wait to start school soon. They loved their grandma and Aunt Evie and didn't like green vegetables all that much.

By the time the ride was over Callie had a strange pain wedged behind her rib cage.

She headed for the gate, passing Fiona on another round, and was surprised to find the children's grandmother gone.

And Noah stood in her place.

"Daddy!" Hayley exclaimed. "Look at me."

He was smiling that mega-watt smile and Callie's stomach rolled over. "Hello."

She swallowed hard and tried not to think about how good he looked in jeans and a navy golf shirt. "Hi." She glanced into his eyes, saw awareness, felt that familiar jolt of attraction. "Your mother?"

He nodded. "She's gone back to trawling the craft stalls." He gestured to the kids. "Did they behave themselves?"

"They were perfect little angels."

He laughed out loud. "Angels? That doesn't sound like my kids."

Callie smiled back. "She's a natural. So is Matthew."

Both children looked pleased as could be with the praise. He hauled Hayley into his arms and then placed her onto the ground. Matthew followed soon after. The kids moved around to the front of Sunshine and began stroking his nose.

"So, can you take a break from this gig?"

"A break?" she echoed. "What for?"

He smiled. "To talk. You could let me buy you a soda."

"I really don't think—"

"I'd like to get to know you better."

There it was, right out in the open. "Why—"

"You know why, Callie."

Without anything to hide behind, Callie felt so raw, so completely exposed, she could barely draw breath. She stared at him for a moment and then looked toward the now queue of one waiting for a turn on a pony. "Um…I probably shouldn't," she said on a whisper. "There's someone still—"

"We'll wait."

We'll wait. Him and the children she wanted so desperately to avoid—but somehow couldn't.

Fiona chose that moment to come up behind her and announced she'd happily take charge of the remaining child and then volunteered Joe to help with Sunshine. Before she had a chance to protest, Joe had taken the gelding and Callie found herself leaving the arena with Noah and his children.

"That was fun, Daddy," Hayley said excitedly.

"Was it, poppet?" He looked at Callie as they walked. "Maybe the twins could have riding lessons, too."

"Maybe," Callie replied and almost jumped from her skin when Hayley grasped her hand. She stopped walking immediately and looked down. The little girl tugged her forward, giggled and acted as though holding her hand was the most natural thing in the world.

Instinct kicked in and she went to pull her hand away… but something stopped her. Maybe it was the lovely, infectious laugh coming from the little girl. Or perhaps it was that Noah was watching her with such blistering intensity she knew that if she moved, if she rejected the child's hand, he'd see it. And he'd see more than that. He'd see through her and into the parts of herself she kept so fiercely guarded.

"Anything wrong, Callie?"

Already suspicious, she thought. Already figuring her out. "Not a thing," she lied and allowed herself to be led toward a refreshments stall.

He bought drinks all round and Callie had just cranked the cap off her soda when Hayley announced she wanted her face painted.

"Can we, Daddy, please?" she pleaded and skipped toward the face-painting tent.

He nodded and they all followed. He passed the colorfully decorated painter a couple of notes from his wallet. Hayley insisted on going first while Matthew waited patiently behind his more flamboyant sister.

Callie stood to the side. "Where's your other son?" she asked. "And Lily?"

"Jamie's with Evie. And Lily doesn't do fairs."

Callie half smiled. "Too cool, huh?"

"Or stubborn."

"She's headstrong," Callie said. "And there's nothing wrong with that."

He crossed his arms and she couldn't help looking at his chest. He was remarkably fit and broad shouldered and her awareness of him spiked. It had been eons since she'd been this attracted to someone. Maybe never. She'd been with Craig for so many years, and any true desire they'd felt for one another had faded long before his death. But Noah had kickstarted her libido with a resounding thud.

"Speaking from experience?" he asked quietly while keeping a watch on his kids.

Callie got her feelings back on track. "I'm sure my parents thought me willful. I liked to do things my own way."

"And still do, I imagine."

She wasn't about to deny it. "She'll come around," Callie assured him, sensing it was true, although she had no idea why she thought so. "Raising a teenage girl wouldn't be easy—especially alone."

"Sometimes...no. But they're all pretty well behaved most of the time. Even Lily."

"Do they see their mother much?" she asked before she could stop herself. She wondered why on earth she was so interested in this man and his children. She wasn't usually so inquisitive. Who was she kidding? She was *never* inquisitive.

"No," he replied. "They don't."

Callie's tongue tingled with another question, but she held back. The more she knew about him, the more *he'd* want to know about her...and she wasn't ready for that. She wasn't sure she ever would be. But despite her reticence, she suddenly had the image of his four motherless children burned deep in her heart.

Heaven help me...I'm actually in danger of falling for this man.

Noah felt her pain. She'd done a great job of building a big wall around whatever it was that haunted the depths of her blue eyes. *But not quite good enough.*

"Will I see you tonight?" he asked, determined to keep her talking.

"For the dance?" She shook her head. "No. I have to take the horses back home."

He pressed on. "You could come later."

She stepped back. "I don't…I don't…it's just that I don't…"

"You don't what?" he asked, picking up her trailing words.

"I don't date," she said bluntly.

Noah half smiled. So they had something in common. "Neither do I," he admitted and when she looked surprised, he explained what he meant. "Four kids make dating…difficult." He raised his brows. "What's your excuse?"

She shrugged and took a deep breath. "I don't have one."

Not exactly the truth and they both knew it. "Are you nursing a broken heart?"

She crossed her arms and dangled the soda bottle between her fingertips. "Not the kind you might be imagining," she said softly.

Noah's curiosity soared. He wanted to know all about her. Everything. She'd been hurt in the past, that much was obvious. But by whom? "Want to talk about it?"

She shook her head again and stepped back fractionally, as if she was looking for an escape. "I should go." She tapped the soda bottle. "Thank you for the drink."

She said goodbye to the kids and walked away, leaving him staring after her.

Callie sat on the edge of her bed and examined the contents of her open wardrobe.

She'd arrived home an hour earlier. The horses were fed, the dog was asleep in the kitchen and she was left wondering why she was actually considering dressing up and heading back to the fair. But Fiona had called and begged her to go. So, her friend needed her. That was as good a reason as any. It wasn't because there was a band playing and that there would be dancing. It wasn't because Noah would be there.

She knew getting involved with him was out of the question.

He has four children.

He had what she would never have. Her heart felt so heavy in her chest when she thought about it. She'd kept a lid on her feelings for more than four years and had accepted she could never have another child because of complications during Ryan's birth. Ryan was her child…and he was gone. But in a matter of days, and without warning, the lid had lifted off and suddenly she was *all* feelings…*all* memory…*all* want.

Noah makes me want.

Desiring him was one thing. She hadn't expected to *like* him. She hadn't expected to like anyone ever again.

Forty minutes later she'd dressed and drove back to the fair.

It was well past eight o'clock by the time she arrived. The stalls and kiddie games had been replaced by a large dance floor and clusters of tables and chairs. The whole scene had been decorated with hundreds of tiny lights, and food and drink vendors were on hand to satisfy appetites. The turnout was impressive. People had dressed up and were clearly enjoying themselves. The band was good and the dance floor was busy. Callie spotted Fiona standing near a tent where drinks were being served and quickly headed for her friend.

"You're here!" Fiona squealed and hugged her close. "Thank goodness."

"You said you could use the company."

"I could. Great dress—aren't you glad I insisted you buy it?"

It *was* a great dress—a flimsy chiffon concoction of muted caramel shades with a halter top. The skirt fell just above her knees. "Of course."

"Fiona!"

They both turned at the sound of the pleasantly pitched female voice. A dark haired woman with the most amazing green eyes came toward them, buffering against a few people in her stride.

"M.J.," Fiona greeted. "Good to see you."

Fiona introduced them and the green-eyed beauty made a startled sound. "*You're* Callie? Lily's riding instructor?"

Callie bristled. "You know Lily?"

M.J. laughed delightfully. "She's my niece," she explained. "I'm Noah's sister."

Of course. The resemblance to Evie was unmistakable. And those eyes were all Preston. "I didn't realize he had more than one."

"There are three of us girls."

"Is Evie here?" she asked, acutely conscious that Noah would be nearby.

I'm not here for him. I'm not. I can't be.

"Nah—she's looking after the kids," M.J. said. "It's just me and Noah tonight."

And then, as if drawn by some inexplicable force, Callie turned her neck and met his gaze head-on.

Noah knew the exact moment Callie arrived. It was as if some internal radar, attuned to only her, had taken hold of him. The area seemed smaller, the air heavy, and the noise of glasses clinking and people speaking faded into a barely audible sound. She looked incredible. The dress, the hair tumbling down her back, the heels that showed off her amazing legs—he wondered if any of the half a dozen people around him heard the strangled sound that formed in his throat. She must have felt him staring at her because she turned her head and looked right at him.

A blinding and electrical visual contact hit him from his

feet to his fingertips. His best friend, Cameron Jakowski, jabbed him in the ribs with an elbow and gave a low whistle of appreciation. Noah didn't like that one bit. With three sisters and an independent working mother, he'd learned at an early age not to objectify women.

"Who is that?" Cameron asked.

"Fiona."

Cameron raised his brows. "I meant her friend with the great legs."

"Callie Jones," Noah replied quietly.

Cameron chuckled. "The horse lady? Very nice. No wonder you've been keeping her to yourself."

"That's not what I've been doing."

"Sure it is." Cameron smiled. "Shall we go over so you can introduce me?"

"No."

"I just wanna talk to her."

Noah stood perfectly still. "Hard to talk without teeth."

Cameron laughed loudly and began walking toward them. "Okay, I get the message," he said once Noah caught up. "But introduce me anyway."

He did so begrudgingly. Cameron liked women and women usually reciprocated. He was stupidly relieved when Callie seemed oblivious to his friend's brand of charm.

Once the introductions were over Fiona dragged Cameron onto the dance floor. Noah bought a round of drinks and they sat down at a table way back from the noise of the playing band. It wasn't long before M.J. went off in search of the man she'd arrived with and he and Callie were alone.

She looked nervous. And beautiful. He'd never seen her hair loose before. It was longer than he'd imagined and hung way past her bare shoulders. He felt like running his hands through it and tilting her head back so he could kiss her throat.

"You came back," he heard himself say.

She glanced at him. "Yes."

"I'm glad you did."

"It's still not a date."

Her words made him smile, and Noah's whole body thrummed with awareness. Being around her, sharing molecules of space with her, undid him on so many levels. "Of course not. *We* don't date, remember?"

Her blue eyes sparkled. "Do you have to be so agreeable?" she asked quietly.

"Do you have to keep looking for a fight?"

One brow rose sharply. "You like provoking me. It's probably because you were surrounded by women growing up. You know, the spoiled only son, indulged by his mother and adoring sisters, given license to say whatever he wants."

He laughed. "I'm sure my mother would disagree with you."

"Ha—I'd like to talk to your mother," she said and he saw her flush.

"I'm sure she'd enjoy that, too. So where's your family?"

She hesitated for a moment, like she was working out how much to reveal. "California," she replied finally. "My mom lives in Santa Barbara. My brother Scott has a place in L.A," she added. "He works for the fire department."

"And your father?"

"He died ten years ago."

Noah pushed his beer aside. "So why Crystal Point?"

"My dad was born in Bellandale and I vacationed here many times when I was young. After my—" She stopped for a moment. "After I finished professional competition I wanted to do something…else. I'd always wanted to have my own riding school and secured Sandhills Farm for a good price."

"It was a courageous move," he said. "I mean, without family support."

"I had that. I still do."

"Do you miss it?"

"California? Sometimes," she admitted. "But I needed to… to get away."

She'd said too much. He felt it with every fiber inside him. "Get away or run away?"

"Both," she admitted.

"Have you been back?"

She nodded. "I try to get back every year to see my family."

"You're close to them?" he asked.

Callie nodded. "Very."

"But you wouldn't move back to California for good, would you?"

She looked into her glass. "I'm not sure. For the moment this is home."

"That's…good news. For Lily," he clarified. "And the rest of your students." He paused, looking at her. "How many students do you have?"

"Not nearly enough," she replied. "I lost a few a while back. An unhappy client," she explained. "Or an unhappy parent, to be precise."

"Sonja Trent?"

Callie stilled. "You know her?"

"I know her." He took a drink and looked at her over the rim of his glass. "How many more students do you need?"

"To stay afloat?" He could see her doing a quick calculation in her head. "About a dozen or so. I could advertise—but of course that takes money. If I hike up my tuition fees, I risk losing the students I have to one of the bigger equestrian clubs in town who do a group rate. And with insurance costs and the price of feed sometimes I feel like I'm…"

"You feel like what?"

"Like I'm pushing a barrow of manure uphill with a faulty wheel."

He smiled, thinking how he knew that feeling. "I don't think you should dismiss the idea of raising your prices," he said after a moment. "Cheap doesn't necessarily mean value. Sure, your clients could go to the bigger establishment—but would they get what you can give them? Probably not. One-on-one lessons with someone who has your experience is what customers will pay for. Your skills and knowledge make your time valuable, Callie—you've earned the right to be rewarded for it."

Her eyes shone bright with tears, and in that moment Noah wished he knew her better. He saw vulnerability and pain and fought the instinctive urge to reach for her. Now wasn't the time. But soon, he thought. *Soon.*

The compliment went straight to Callie's heart and she fought the sting behind her eyes. Silly, but his words made her feel taller, stronger. Her defenses were down. He broke them down. No, not broke…something else. Somehow he took the barricade around her apart, piece by piece, holding each one of those pieces in his hand, showing her what he had in his palm, drawing her out, making her want and making her feel.

Making me unafraid.

She was momentarily stunned by the intensity of her feelings. What she'd first thought was just attraction suddenly seemed so much more.

She liked him…. She really liked him.

This is a good man, a tiny voice inside of her said. A good man with a dazzling smile and integrity oozing from every pore. A man who made her feel safe when she'd believed no man would ever make her feel that again.

How did she resist? She wasn't sure she could. She wasn't sure she wanted to.

But…to feel again? Where did she find the courage to do that? If she let herself care for him…she would also have to let herself care for his children. She had to allow them inside and into her heart. Into her heart that was only barely glued together these days.

"Callie?"

She realized she'd been staring at him and dropped her gaze. "Yes?"

"Would you like to dance?"

Instinct screamed no. "I can't."

"Yes, you can. It's just a dance."

It wasn't *just* anything…she knew it as surely as she breathed.

"I really—"

"Come on," he urged and took hold of her hand. Before she could protest further he'd pulled her gently from her seat and led her toward the dance floor.

She'd always liked the idea of dancing but had never been all that good at it. Craig had complained it was a precious waste of time when there were horses to train and competitions to prepare for.

The band played covers of popular tunes, and just as they reached the dance floor the beat changed to a much slower number. Callie didn't move at first. At over six feet Noah was considerably taller than her, and she tilted her head back to look at him. Everything about him drew her in. The white collared shirt he wore emphasized his broad-shouldered strength and as she curled her fingers into the soft fabric and felt the hard muscle beneath, every ounce of blood in her veins surged. She hadn't been this close to a man for so long…and never one who'd affected her so powerfully.

The music was slow and they moved well together. One

hand lay gently against her hip and he held her free hand in his. She felt the intimacy right down to her toes.

She took a deep breath. "Noah …" Saying his name set off a surge of feelings inside her. Her body tensed and she knew he felt the sudden shift.

"Yes, Callie."

"Don't expect too much."

He looked at her oddly. "Are we talking about your dancing skills or something else?"

"Something else," she admitted on a sigh and wasn't sure where the words came from. And she wasn't sure she wanted to know. She felt like the worst kind of fraud by denying the obvious and refusing to admit to the feelings running through her.

She was suddenly paralyzed by the realization. It was impossible. She had no room in her heart for anyone. Not him. Not his children. "I have to go," she said a moment later as she dropped her hand from his shoulder.

"I'll drive you home," he said quietly.

Callie stepped back, oblivious to the music, oblivious to everything other than Noah and her furiously beating heart. "I have my truck."

"Then I'll walk you to your truck."

"That's not necessary."

"Yes, it is," he said and continued to hold her hand.

By the time they'd left the dance floor their palms were pressed intimately together. Callie didn't pull away. Deep down, in that place she'd switched off and never imagined she'd switch on again, she found she liked the sensation of his fingers linked with hers. She liked it a lot.

Her truck was parked midway down the car lot and the walk took a few minutes. It was dark and there were a few couples hanging by their vehicles. Callie spotted one pair kissing madly, another simply holding each other. The entire scene screamed of the kind of intimacy she hadn't felt in a long time.

The kind of intimacy she suddenly craved.

She knew it was foolish to want it. She had nothing to offer him other than the fractured pieces of her heart. And for a man like Noah, she knew that would never be enough. He'd want the *whole* Callie. The Callie she'd been before her world had been shattered…before *she'd* been shattered.

And that woman simply didn't exist anymore.

Once they reached her truck she twisted her fingers from his. "Well, good night," she managed to say and shoved a hand into her small bag for her keys.

She found the keys, pulled them out and accidentally dropped them at her feet.

Noah quickly picked the keys up and pressed them into her palm. "Good night, Callie."

She looked at him and saw desire burning in his eyes.

He wants to kiss me...

The power of him drew Callie closer, until they were barely a foot apart. She felt her lips part, felt herself move and felt her skin come alive with anticipation. He leaned in and kissed her cheek so softly all she really felt was breath.

Not enough …

Callie instinctively reached up, grasped his shoulders and pulled him toward her with all her strength. Driven by instinct, she planted her lips on his mouth and thrust her tongue against his. He tasted good. He felt good.

No…more than that. He tasted…*divine.* And her lips, denied for so long, acted intuitively. She felt her blood heat, felt her skin come alive, felt desire uncurl way down, igniting the female part of her that had lain dormant since forever.

Callie felt his rush of breath as he started to kiss her back. She got the barest touch of his mouth, the barest taste of his tongue. She waited for more. She longed for more. But then he stopped. He pulled away, kissed her cheek again and straightened. Callie released him and stepped back on unsteady feet.

Air crashed into her lungs, making her breathless. She looked at him, felt the burning red-hot gaze. *I know he wants me...*

She knew it, felt it and tasted it in the brevity of his kiss.

"Good night, Callie," he said. "I'll see you Sunday."

Callie got into the truck and started the engine. She wasn't sure how she drove home. All she could feel was the tingle on her lips, the heat in her blood. All she could think was how she had just kissed Noah Preston.

And how her life would never be the same.

Chapter Five

Noah was thinking.

About kisses. About perfect lips and sweet breath.

"What's up with you?" Lily asked, shifting in her seat, looking incredibly young in riding breeches and a dark T-shirt.

Noah looked directly ahead. She'd become way too astute for his liking. "Nothing."

"Yeah…right." She crossed her arms. "I hope you're not gonna hang around while I have my lesson."

"I've got some work to do at the house."

Lily turned her head. "Yeah—that's right. Her place is a real dump." She huffed. "I think you just want to see *her* again. I'm not a little kid, you know. I saw exactly how you were watching her last weekend." Lily rolled her eyes wide. "And she's not bad looking, I suppose, if you go for that type. She's not like my mother."

No one was like Margaret—thank God. But he wouldn't be telling Lily that.

"Do you think you'll ever get married again?"

That was a first. He looked at his daughter. She stared straight ahead, but Noah wasn't fooled. She looked just a little afraid. And Lily never looked afraid.

Married? How could he explain his feelings to his daughter? Noah was pretty sure the younger kids would welcome a new mother into their life. And he…he truly wanted someone to share them with. He longed for a wife and a friend and a lover and all that corny stuff he knew made up a healthy marriage. He wanted what his parents had…years of trust and love. But it was a big deal, expecting a woman to take on four children. And he had no intention of bringing someone temporary into their lives. Noah didn't want temporary. If he got involved again, he wanted permanence. He wanted…forever. He wanted promises that wouldn't be broken. For the kids' sake.

And mine.

His train-wreck marriage lingered like a bad taste he couldn't get out of his mouth.

Is that why I didn't kiss her back...when all I wanted to do was haul her into my arms?

The truth rocked Noah. He'd spent thirty-six hours wondering what kind of fool didn't kiss a beautiful, desirable, passionate woman back when she'd made it so clear she wanted to be kissed. But he knew why. It wound up his spine. It filled his lungs. *Fear.* Fear that he'd want more. Oh, not sex…because he was pretty sure kissing Callie would quickly lead to making love to Callie. He wanted more of *her.* The more of her Noah suspected she wouldn't want to give. To him. To anyone. He didn't want to feel her, taste her and then have the door slammed in his face. He didn't want to be rejected…*left.*

And she'd left before, hadn't she? She'd moved across an ocean to change her life—to get away. From what, he didn't know. What if she wanted to change it back? Noah wasn't going to put his kids or himself through the risk of being wreckage in her wake.

It was best that he hadn't kissed her back. Best that he stopped thinking about kissing her at all.

"So, would you?"

Lily again. Noah got his thoughts back on track. Marriage. Right. "Maybe one day."

She scowled and *harrumphed.* "Do *we* have any say in it?" she asked, using the collective, but Noah sensed she was asking about herself. "I mean, if you're going to shack up with someone, shouldn't we at least be able to have an opinion about it?"

"Marriage is a little more than shacking up, Lily."

She shrugged, looked straight ahead and remained quiet for about twenty seconds. Lily had something on her mind. "Did you know that fifty percent of all second marriages fail?"

He almost choked. *Where the hell did she come up with this stuff?* "That's an interesting statistic, Lily. Where did you get it?"

"Social Studies," she replied. "We're studying human relationships this semester. There's a boy in my grade who's had two stepfathers—can you imagine? And Maddy told me that when her stepdad moved out last year it really sucked. She liked him a lot."

Noah got his daughter's point, delivered with all the subtlety of a sledgehammer. "I have no intention of jumping into anything, Lily," he told her.

"But if you do get married again, how do you know she won't run out like my mother did?"

I don't.

And Callie...she seemed as fragile and unpredictable as the wind.

Lily didn't say anything else, and when they arrived at Sandhills Farm she jumped out of the truck. It took him about ten seconds to find Callie. She stood near the house, in jeans and a flame-red T-shirt, one hand on her hip and the other held a cell phone to her ear.

She spun on her heels and looked at him. His heart pounded behind his ribs. That kiss…how did he forget about it? How could he not want to feel that again? Noah took a long breath and headed toward her. Lily reached her first and jumped around on impatient toes while Callie continued her telephone conversation.

She was frowning and clearly not happy with the caller. When she disconnected a few moments later he pushed aside his lingering thoughts about kissing her and immediately asked what was wrong.

"Just another irresponsible horse owner getting away with neglect," she said hotly.

He frowned. "What?"

"I volunteer with an organization that saves abused and neglected horses," she explained. "A couple of weeks ago I got word that there are three horses somewhere on the other side of town that are stuck in a bare paddock and need veterinary care. We've only had sketchy reports on their whereabouts so far. The owner moves them around to avoid impoundment."

"That's terrible. What can you do?" Lily asked in a shrill voice.

"Seize them, hopefully."

His ever-astute daughter picked up on the obvious. "Isn't that stealing?"

"Not when the owners are breaking animal protection laws."

Lily nodded. "If you need any help, I'll—"

"Leave it to the experts," Noah said. "I'm sure Callie has it under control."

"Your dad's right," Callie assured Lily. "But you can help me nurse them back to health when we finally find them. Joe's saddled Samson for you," she said as she pointed toward the sand arena.

Once Lily headed off, Callie turned to face him. Her eyes were blue and luminous. "I have a list," she said quickly. She pulled a small piece of paper from her pocket and held it toward him. "Of things for you to do." She made a dismissive gesture. "Of course, if you've changed your mind I'll—"

"We had a deal," he said, sensing she was mentally backing out from talking to him as fast as she could. She half shrugged and took a breath, trying to look causal, but Noah wasn't fooled. The tiny pulse at the base of her throat beat like a wild thing. And the promises he'd made to himself only minutes before vanished. All he wanted to do was take her in his arms and kiss her…properly.

"It's only small stuff," she said. "A couple of windows that won't lock right and the back fence—"

"No problem," he said quietly and took the list.

"I'll be about an hour with Lily," she said and pivoted on her heels.

Noah watched her walk into the arena, back rigid, arms held tight to her side. He lingered for a few minutes and observed Callie's interaction with his daughter. Lily looked unusually cheerful and he knew she was excited to finally be in the saddle. The lesson started with Callie laying down a firm set of rules and Lily agreeing to every single one.

Lily respected Callie. Somehow, Callie understood what Lily needed.

Noah experienced a strange pang in his chest, dismissed it and headed for his truck to unload the toolbox. He had a lot of work to do.

* * *

Callie was wound like a spring. She'd barely slept the night before and had struggled to concentrate during a lesson earlier that morning with Maddy Spears, her newest student.

She knew she had to concentrate on Lily…and ignore the fact that Noah was only a couple of hundred meters away.

I kissed him. And he didn't exactly kiss me back.

She wasn't sure whether she should feel relieved or insulted.

"How's this?" Lily asked Callie, interrupting her reverie.

Callie focused her attention on the teenager. She was impressed with Lily. The girl had a natural seat and good hands. Once the lesson had concluded she eased on the long reining lead and called Samson to a halt in front of her.

"That was good. Well done."

Lily raised her brows. "Do I get to ride off the lunge rein next week?"

Callie unclipped the lead. "No."

Lily dismounted and landed on her heels. "Why not?"

"Balance," Callie replied and handed the reins to her.

Lily frowned. "Huh?"

Callie began walking from the arena. "Every rider needs to start with balance. Once I know you've aced it, the lead comes off."

Lily clicked the horse forward and followed. "And what if I don't?"

"You will," Callie said. "You have a good seat and soft hands, essential for a successful rider. Take Samson to the wash-bay and Joe will help you strap him down."

Lily buried her face into the animal's neck and smiled. "I can do it by myself."

Callie raised her brows. "What was rule number five?"

Lily exhaled heavily. "Don't question the four other rules."

"Exactly. Go and get Samson sorted. I'll see you when you're done."

When Lily was out of sight Callie considered her options. Hang around the ménage or show some guts and see what *he* was up to. Her boots made their way across the yard until she reached the house. She stood at the bottom of the steps. Noah had his back to her and she watched him maneuver an old window off its track, make a few adjustments and then replace it. Her heart raced. No man should look that good in jeans. He raised his arms and she got a quick glimpse of smooth skin beneath the hem of his T-shirt. *Oh, sweet heaven.* Suddenly, he stopped what he was doing, turned and looked at her.

"How was it?" he asked.

She gulped. "Huh?"

"Lily—how'd she do?"

Callie put the image of skin out of her mind. "Very good. She's a natural."

He smiled at her and she felt the power of it through her entire body.

"Are you okay?"

It's just skin. I've seen skin before. "Yes," she replied and swallowed. "I'm fine."

He stepped away from the door. "She behaved herself?"

"She did," Callie replied. "She's quite sweet, actually."

He grinned. "Well, I'm pleased the two of you are getting along." He leaned back against the balustrade. "Seeing as that's out the way, are we going to talk about *us* now?"

Callie took a quick breath. *Here we go.* "There's nothing to talk about."

"Yeah, there is."

"It was just a kiss," she said, and the moment she'd said the word *kiss,* she regretted it immediately.

"It wasn't *just* anything, Callie."

He was right. Callie felt it down through to her bones. “Okay,” she admitted. “It wasn’t.”

“So, what shall we do about it?”

Her heart raced. *Do?* “I don’t know if we…I don’t think we should do anything.” She took a deep breath and inhaled a burst of bravado. “We just won’t kiss again.”

There’s that word again… When the word should probably be bliss. Because she suspected that’s what really being kissed by Noah would feel like.

He smiled and came down the steps. “I don’t think I can make that promise to you, Callie.”

Stupidly, she smiled back for a second. “You didn’t kiss me back.” The words popped out of her mouth. “I figured you weren’t interested.”

He took another step toward her. “Would you like me to prove to you that I am?”

Callie almost swallowed her tongue. *He is interested…he wants me.* “Right here?” she asked, wondering what kind of madness had taken hold of her.

He shrugged. “Why not?”

Callie took a step backward. He wouldn’t, would he? Kiss her out in the open, where anyone could see? Possibly in front of his daughter? She warmed from head to toe. But no…she looked at him and saw he was smiling. “Are you teasing me?”

“Just a bit.”

Callie didn’t quite know how to react. Teasing and flirting were almost an alien concept to her. Craig had never teased, never flirted. It was always business, always work, always pushing toward being better, being the best. Only now, years later, did Callie realize how little laughter there’d been in their relationship. But Noah had a relaxed sense of humor, a relaxed sense of *self.* She was sure he worked hard—but he didn’t live to work. He lived for other things. Like his kids. It would be hard alone, raising four children single-handedly.

Craig hadn't wanted one child.

In the end Craig hadn't lived to see his son born. And Callie had buried them both within days of one another—her tiny son and the man who was supposed to have loved her but instead betrayed her.

The worst week of her life. Excruciating. Soul-destroying. Heartbreaking.

"Where are the rest of your kids today?" she asked, shifting her thoughts from Ryan. And, for some reason, she wanted to know where his children were and who was caring for them.

"With Evie," he replied. "I didn't think you'd want them underfoot while you're working."

"You're right, I don't," she said quickly. Too quickly.

He'd heard the tremor in her voice because his brows slanted together for a brief second. "You don't like kids?"

You don't like my kids...that's what his question sounded like.

Callie shrugged again. *I adore kids,* she wanted to say. *If I had my way I'd have a dozen of my own and love them with every fiber inside me.*

But that was a pipe dream. Ryan was the only child she would ever have. *And I can't replace him. I won't let myself love like that again.*

"I like kids," she said softly.

"Me, too," he said, smiling again. "Can I call you sometime this week?"

Callie was startled. "For what?" she asked, her heart beating wildly.

"Don't look so suspicious," he said quietly. "Nothing sinister."

Callie felt foolish then. "Sorry," she said on a breath.

"I thought you might like to go out sometime."

Like a date? She should run as fast as she could. The idea

of going out with him was terrifying. Because she sensed it was something she could get used to. “I don’t…it’s just that I’m…I’m better with horses than I am with people.”

“And yet you became a teacher?”

She shrugged. He had a point. She could have turned her skills toward training horses for the show circuit. But teaching the kids…that’s where she found real happiness.

“Speaking of which, I have to get back to work,” she said. “I have a new student starting in fifteen minutes.”

His green eyes scanned her face. “Business looking up?”

“Yes,” she said quickly. “Much better. I had a new student start this morning, plus three calls yesterday and now four new students starting over the next two weeks.”

“That’s good news for you.”

“I know,” she said, a little breathlessly because she always felt as if she didn’t have quite enough air in her lungs when talking with him. “When I lost clients following the incident with the Trent girls I wasn’t sure I’d be able to recoup. Sonja Trent accused me of discriminating against her daughters and threatened to lodge a complaint with the equestrian federation. Nothing came of it, of course, except she managed to persuade half-a-dozen parents to pull their kids out.”

“And then some jerk says he wants to see you lose your license?”

Callie smiled fractionally. “Ah—well, that was a bit of a red flag for me.”

“Rightly so, considering the circumstances. I would never have done it, you know?”

“I know,” she said, softer this time, feeling like their worlds were moving closer. “I lost my temper. When I called you a jerk I didn’t know you.” She paused, searching for the words. “I didn’t like you. But I know you now. I…like you now.”

I more than like you…

"I like you too, Callie."

Her heart beat like a freight train and it was so loud she wondered if he could hear it.

Minutes later he took Lily and left, leaving Callie standing by the porch with a smile on her face so deep her jaw ached.

Lily arrived unexpectedly at Sandhills Farm on Wednesday afternoon, riding her bicycle. She wore her school uniform, sensible leather shoes and her black hair tied back in a ponytail. The uniform looked oddly out of place with her full makeup. "I've come to see Samson," Lily told her when Callie approached her.

"Does your father know you're here?" Callie asked.

She crossed her arms over her chest. "Sure."

Callie began her next lesson with Maddy Spears and Lily began chatting with Maddy's mother, Angela. They seemed to know one another quite well. Her suspicions were confirmed a little later, once Maddy's lesson had finished and Lily came forward with a kind of indulgent authority and steered Maddy and Sunshine toward the washing bay, flipping Callie an assurance that the gelding would be looked after.

Callie gave the girls an opportunity to do the right thing and headed over to speak with Angela Spears.

"You know Lily?" Callie asked, slipping through the fence.

"Everyone knows Lily," she replied. "Another marvelous lesson," the other woman said before Callie could open her mouth. "You are a genius," she said. "Maddy's talked of nothing else but you for days now."

"I'm flattered."

Angela Spears's perfectly bowed mouth beamed at her. Callie couldn't help noticing how immaculately groomed she was. Riding breeches and grass-stained T-shirts had become her usual garb. Too bad—she looked pretty good in a dress.

She hadn't forgotten Noah's reaction the night of the Twilight Fair dance. He'd looked at her dress, and her legs and her mouth…

"Noah was right about you."

Angela's words instantly grabbed Callie's attention. For a crazy second she wondered if she'd inadvertently said his name without realizing it. "What do you mean?"

"He told me you were an amazing instructor."

Her curiosity surged into overdrive. "He did?"

Angela nodded. "And he said I'd be foolish to let Maddy miss the opportunity to learn from you and that she couldn't be in safer hands. Of course, I completely agree now," she said. "And Maddy's so looking forward to getting her own pony." She let out an animated gasp. "Oh, you must help us select the perfect pony when the time comes—I insist. And I'll pay you a finder's fee, of course."

By the time Callie had waved Angela and her daughter goodbye, Lily had disappeared. But she wasn't hard to find. Callie headed for the paddock behind the house and found her sneaking morsels of carrot to Samson.

"So, Maddy's your friend?"

Lily nodded. "My best friend." She gave the gelding another treat.

Callie thought about the three new students she acquired that week. "And what about Jacinta and Skye Burrows and Chrissie Drew—are they friends, too?"

"Nope," Lily replied. "But I think my dad knows Mr. Burrows."

Callie's heart skipped a beat. *He's looking out for me.* It felt like forever since anyone had done that.

Normally she would have resisted the gratitude that coursed through her. On some level she should probably have resented it. Because interference meant involvement. It meant…intimacy. It meant she had cracks in her armor.

But she experienced none of those feelings. Only a deep-rooted appreciation.

And an overwhelming longing to see him again and tell him so.

Callie headed into Bellandale the following morning. She found the address for Preston Marine via the business card Noah had given her and parked outside the large building situated in the center of the town's newest industrial estate. She got out of her truck and ran her hands down her jeans.

She was impressed the moment she walked into the showroom. A long and luxurious-looking cruiser was to her left and three smaller boats, including a catamaran with full sails, sat to her right. Printed designs on easels flanked each of the boats and more designs were framed on the walls. A circular reception area greeted her as she stepped onto the tiled floor and a fifty-something man came toward her. He wore pressed trousers and a shirt with Preston Marine logo sewn onto the breast pocket.

"How can I help you?" he asked politely.

Callie hung on to her nerve. "I'd like to see Noah Preston. Is he here?"

The man, whose name badge read Len, nodded. "He's out back in the workshop."

"Oh," she shrugged. "If he's busy I can—"

"You can wait in his office," Len suggested and walked ahead, motioning her through a door on the left. "I'll call him."

Callie followed with unusual obedience, passing a small, efficient-looking woman who sat behind the reception desk, tapping on computer keys and wearing the same style shirt as Len. When she entered the office Len quickly excused himself, and Callie sat on a long black leather lounge. As far as offices went, this appeared better than most. And it was as neat as a pin.

She didn't have to wait long.

"Callie?"

Noah stood in the doorway, dressed in chinos and the same corporate shirt as his staff. He stared at her with such raw intensity she was relieved she'd been sitting. Her knees would surely have given way if she'd been standing. "Hi."

"Is everything all right?" he asked as he closed the door.

"Oh, yes. I just wanted to speak with you." Callie felt absurdly self-conscious beneath his penetrating stare. "This is a nice office," she said, desperate to fill the silence rapidly smothering the space between them.

"Do you think?" One hand moved in an arc, motioning to the chrome and glass furnishings. "I'm not sure. I've only had this place for about six months. Grace did the decorating. It's a bit too modern for me"

And just who was *that?* "Grace?" she asked as she stood.

"My other sister," he explained.

Stupidly relieved, Callie scanned the room again. "It is modern but appropriate, I think." She relaxed a bit. "You said you'd just moved here?"

He nodded. "I've kept the original workshop down by the Port, but the business needed larger premises."

"And a showroom?"

"Buyers are keen to see the finished product," he replied. "Would you like a tour?"

"Maybe after we've talked."

He closed the door and walked farther into the room. "Okay, let's talk."

Callie clutched her hands together. "I just wanted to…to thank you."

Noah tilted his head. "For what?"

"For Maddy Spears, and Jacinta and Skye Burrows and

Chrissie Drew," she said. "And as of this morning I have another two students starting next month."

He shrugged. "It was only a couple of phone calls."

Callie knew it was way more than that. "It means so much to me," she admitted. "My business…" She paused, and then shook her head. "My horses…"

"They're important to you?"

"They're everything," she breathed.

Noah saw the emotion in her eyes and his chest tightened. "Because they don't let you down?"

She took a shaky breath. "I…I…"

"Someone did," he said and figured there was no point in holding back. "Husband? Boyfriend? Lover?"

"Fiancé," she confessed on a sigh.

"What did he do?" Noah asked, preparing himself for the worst.

She hesitated for a moment. "He lied to me."

Lies and deception went hand in hand—Noah knew that from experience. The fallout from his ex-wife's infidelity had broken his world apart. "Then he wasn't worthy of you."

The emotion in her eyes shined brighter and Noah fought the impulse to reach for her. Everything about Callie affected him on some primal level. He wanted to hold her, soothe her and protect her. He'd never felt such a blinding need before.

She nodded and the gesture spoke volumes. "The horses… they make it simple, you know—uncomplicated." Her hands came together. "Anyway, I just wanted to say thank you for helping me. I guess I'll see you Sunday."

"How about Friday?"

"What?"

"Friday," he said again. "Tomorrow night. Dinner and a movie?"

Callie stilled. "I don't really think a date is—"

He smiled. "Oh, believe me, this wouldn't be a date. Just

you, me, a DVD and the kids squabbling over a bowl of spaghetti."

"Noah, I can't."

"Sure you can," he said easily. "You wanted to thank me—so, thank me." His voice faded for a moment, and then he spoke again. "Dinner, movie, simple."

Silence stretched between them. He expected another refusal and waited for it.

Instead, she nodded and said softly. "Dinner. Yes, okay."

Chapter Six

Noah picked the kids up from Evie's that afternoon. He found his sister and three youngest children in her pottery/art studio, all four of them cutting up cardboard and crepe paper. Pots of glue and an assortment of other hobby equipment lay on the big table in the middle of the room.

They all cheered a round of hellos when he walked into the room and perched on a stool near the kitchenette to the right of the door. Evie left the kids to their crafting and joined him.

"Coffee?" she asked and grabbed a couple of mugs. He nodded and she poured from the pot of filtered brew. "You're early today."

Noah glanced at his watch. "Not by much."

His sister raised her brows. "Bad day at the office?"

"Not particularly." An unusual day. A day filled with thoughts of Callie. Like most of his days lately.

"Trevor has a video-game party planned for tomorrow

night," she said of her fifteen-year-old son. "Do you feel like coming round for dinner? M.J.'s coming over, too."

"I have plans," he said and drank some coffee.

Evie's eyes widened instantly. "A date?"

Noah didn't know what to call it. "Sort of."

"Anyone I know?"

Like a dog with a bone, Noah knew his sister wouldn't let up. Besides, he had nothing to hide about his relationship with Callie. *Relationship?* Is that what it was? It felt…he didn't know what the hell it felt like. Something. Everything. Like she was the air inside his lungs and he couldn't draw in enough breath. His desire for Callie burned a hole through him. *And I haven't even really kissed her.* He'd thought about it, though. He'd imagined it. Dreamed about it. Wanted it so much he could barely think about anything else.

"Callie."

Evie didn't bat a lash. "No surprise there."

"I suppose not." He finished his coffee and stood. "I should get going."

"Sometimes you have to try people on," Evie said quietly. "To see if they fit."

Noah looked at his sister. "That's not the problem."

"So there is a problem?" she asked.

He shrugged and felt like spilling his guts, but he didn't. Because what he felt, what he knew was that beneath the sassy, quick temper and barriers she'd erected around herself was an incredibly fragile woman. A woman who'd been hurt.

I'm going to get my heart kicked in…

That's what he felt deep down. That she was all risk. Like the wildest ride at a theme park. Like parachuting without a chute. But…despite feeling that way, Noah was unbelievably drawn to her. He wanted her, even with the threat of losing himself. And knowing he was prepared to take that chance turned him inside out. Because Noah never risked himself emotionally. He couldn't afford to. The kids needed stability—they needed a parent who could be relied upon to always do the right thing by them. And if he was to bring another woman into their life, that woman had to do the right thing by them also. They needed unreserved love.

Could Callie do that? Could he trust her to love them? He just didn't know.

"There's no problem," he said to his sister. "Thanks for watching them. I'll see you soon."

As Callie zipped up her favorite sundress—the white one with sprigs of tiny blue flowers—and stepped into a pair of silver sandals, she could hear Fiona's voice calling from the kitchen. Her friend had arrived to work her horse and had stayed for a coffee and chat.

"So, you're going on a date with Noah?"

"It's not a date," Callie insisted as she headed from the bedroom. "It's just dinner."

When Callie reached the kitchen Fiona was standing by the sink. "At his home? With his kids?" Her friend raised both brows. "That's a date."

Of course it's a date. I like him. I'm attracted to him.

Just because they weren't going out dining and dancing alone didn't mean it was anything other than a real date.

I shouldn't go. I should keep to my plan and not get involved.

But Callie knew it was too late for that.

She arrived at the Preston home at exactly six o'clock. She grabbed her tote, locked the truck and headed toward the front porch. At the top of the few steps lay a sleepy-looking golden retriever who barely lifted its head at her presence. It made her smile, thinking of Tessa and her boundless energy.

"That's Harry," said a small voice. A young boy stood

behind the screen door. He opened it and stepped in front of her. "He's very lazy."

She smiled "So I see. Not much of a guard dog, then?"

Jamie giggled. "Nope. And he snores really loud." He opened the door and stood to the side. "I'm Jamie—are you coming inside?"

Callie filled her lungs with air and stepped across the threshold.

The polished timber floors, brick-faced walls and warm textures of the furnishings appealed to her immediately. She caught sight of a huge stone fireplace and headed for it, settling her sandaled feet on a thick hearth rug in the middle of the room. The two sofas were covered in a soft caramel color, and a large stone lamp was nudged between them on a round coffee table. The sideboard along one wall was dotted with an assortment of bric-a-brac, most of it obviously created by young, eager hands. The warmth radiating in the room was undeniable and she experienced a deep longing behind her ribs.

"This is the living room," Jamie informed her. "And my TV."

"*Your* TV?" she asked, noticing the huge flat screen and shelving either side showcasing a few hundred movie titles.

"Well, Dad's, really. Do you like spiders?"

"Well, I…"

The sound of feet on floorboards caught her attention, and Callie turned as Noah came down a staircase at the rear of the living room.

He stopped on the bottom step. "Hello."

She hadn't realized the home had more than one level and he must have caught her look.

"The loft," he explained. "The previous owners used it for storage but it seemed a shame not to make use of the view up there, so I had it turned into a master bedroom."

"And bathroom," Jamie supplied.

Noah's bedroom…where he slept. Callie was suddenly rooted to the spot, absorbed by the way he looked in worn jeans and a soft white T-shirt. His feet were bare and it seemed incredibly intimate somehow. His hair was damp, too, and she figured he'd just showered. Which made her think of soap and skin and water cascading over strong muscles. Before Callie could say anything the twins scrambled into the room on fast little feet and planted themselves in front of her.

The little girl touched the hem of her dress. "Callie's here!" she announced excitedly. "You look really pretty. Daddy won't let me wear nail polish."

Callie smiled, amused despite the fierce pounding of her heart. "I wasn't allowed to wear it either until I was…" She paused, looked at Noah and took a gamble. "Sixteen."

Noah smiled. "Good answer." He dropped off the step and took a few paces toward her, his eyes not leaving hers. "You do look lovely."

Eaten up with nerves, she almost told him that he looked lovely, too. But didn't. Because lovely wasn't the word. He looked…hot. And so incredibly sexy in his jeans and bare feet that she had to swallow a few times to regain her composure.

"Okay, guys—give Callie some room to breathe." He moved forward and took Matthew's hand. "I have to get these two in the bathtub. I won't be long. Make yourself at home."

"Where's Lily tonight?"

"At a sleepover at Maddy's," he replied as the trio padded off down the hall.

Callie relaxed fractionally. Until Jamie repeated his question about liking spiders. She had an awful thought he might have one in a jar for her to inspect. Within seconds he was off down the hallway. Callie dropped her tote by the sofa and moved toward the mantel. About a dozen framed photographs caught her attention. Most of them were of the children, and one was of three women. Callie recognized Evie and could see the resemblance in the striking woman beside her with dark hair and perfectly symmetrical features. The other woman, clearly younger, looked familiar, and Callie remembered M.J. from the Twilight Fair. An older couple, his parents for sure because she recognized his mother, filled another shot and then there was a picture of Noah with Cameron, both holding up a fish on a hook and both laughing in a way that only best friends could.

There were no pictures of his ex-wife and she wondered why she thought there might be. Perhaps she just wanted to get a look at the woman who had borne his children and the woman he had loved.

Callie looked at the picture of the twins again and a familiar ache filled her heart.

But she wouldn't think about Ryan tonight…she wouldn't make comparisons. And she wouldn't envy Noah his beautiful, perfect children.

Jamie returned with a heavy book and patted a spot on the sofa. Callie sat down and spent ten minutes listening to him talk about and show pictures of the most hideous-looking arachnids she felt certain would give her nightmares for weeks. But he was a charming boy, polite and very smart and quite mature for his age.

Noah came back into the room without the twins. "They're playing in their bedroom until dinner," he said. He looked at Jamie and smiled. "Hey, mate, how about you go and join Hayley and Matthew?"

"But, Callie has—"

"Seen enough crawlies for one night. Off you go."

Jamie disappeared without another protest and the air thickened between them almost instantly.

"I hope he didn't freak you out too much."

"A little." she said, shuddering. "He's a lovely child. You should be proud of him."

"I am," he replied. "Join me in the kitchen?"

Callie stood and followed him down a short hallway.

The Tasmanian oak kitchen impressed her as much as the rest of the house. She walked to the window and glanced outside. Beyond the patio there was a pool, a hot tub and a gloriously lush garden.

"Would you like a drink?" he asked and grabbed two bottles from a rack above the refrigerator. "Red or white?"

She chose the Merlot and watched as he pulled the cork and poured two glasses.

"Thanks." She took the glass and leaned against the granite countertop. She sipped her wine. "You have a lovely home."

"Thank you. We've only been here a couple of years." He drank some wine, then grabbed a pot and filled it with water. "I bought the place after my divorce."

So his ex had never lived here? She was instantly curious. "Did you have a bitter breakup?"

Surprisingly, he answered. "I guess you could call it that." He flicked on the gas.

Still curious, she asked another question. "Why doesn't she see the children?"

He pulled out a few items and dumped them on the counter. "She lives in Paris with her elderly mother. When she's not in rehab."

Callie gasped.

"Prescription meds," he explained. "Or at least that's how it started for Margaret."

She had a name. "Is that why she left?" Callie asked.

Noah stopped what he was doing and turned toward her. "She left because she didn't want to be married to me anymore." He smiled then but without humor. "Hard to imagine, eh? The addiction started afterward."

Callie allowed herself to hold his gaze.

She felt a strong surge of compassion and deep feeling. But before she could say anything he passed her a paring knife. "Can you make the salad?"

Callie took the knife. "I…I guess. But I should warn you, I'm not much of a cook."

He laughed. "It's salad, Callie—it doesn't need cooking."

"I could still mess it up," she said, trying to push back the color tinting her cheeks.

"Watch and learn."

They worked in silence for a while. Callie chopped and diced vegetables while Noah stirred the sauce simmering in a large saucepan and popped linguini into boiling water.

"That smells good," she said and sipped her wine.

He replaced the lid on the same container. "I can't take the credit, I'm afraid."

She placed a hand to her mouth in mock horror. "Store-bought? I'm devastated."

"Evie," he corrected. "She often doubles up on portions when she has guests staying at the B and B. She takes pity on my single-father status. Actually, I'm pretty sure she thinks I feed the kids macaroni and cheese five nights a week."

"And you don't?"

"Only three nights. Gotta squeeze the frozen pizzas in, too."

Callie chuckled. "Please tell me you're not serious?"

Noah put up one hand in a Boy Scout salute. "I'm not serious. They eat vegetables—even those horrible slimy green ones."

As if on cue, the children returned to the kitchen. Callie remained by the countertop, working on her salad but also watching as Jamie set the table, so serious in his task, his little tongue clicking in his mouth as he straightened cutlery and placed paper napkins beside each place setting. The twins hovered, one each side of her, stepping back and forth on small feet, as though wanting her attention.

She smiled and asked them about their daycare teachers, and Hayley immediately began to tell her everything about a usual day in the classroom. Callie listened, still chopping.

"Can I have some of that?" Hayley asked as Callie cut a carrot.

She nodded and gave them each a little piece of vegetable, which they took with eager fingers and ate just as quickly. A few moments later she did the same with a couple of snow peas. And again with a sliver of cucumber. Their infectious giggles echoed around the kitchen.

"I like having a grown-up girl here, Daddy," Hayley announced and Matthew nodded in agreement.

Callie stopped chopping and stood still. She glanced toward Noah and saw he'd stopped his task also. He was staring at her, a deeply smoldering stare that made her knees weak.

"So do I," he said quietly.

And then, without warning, Hayley hugged her, gripping Callie's leg as hard as her small arms would allow. Callie stilled her task, rooted to the spot. Her heart surged in her chest. Suddenly she was *all* feelings. All anguish. All memory. All hurt. The little girl lingered, waiting, and Callie instinctively knew what the child wanted.

She placed the knife on the counter. *I can't do this. I can't.*

But she did. She reached down and touched Hayley's head, without looking anywhere but directly at the wall in front of her. Her fingertips felt the soft, little-girl hair and her womb contracted instantly, rolling like a wave. Hayley lifted her chin and Callie's hand touched her face.

Oh, God...help me here. Help me not want this. Help me not feel this.

Her throat felt suddenly thick, burning with emotion. All her fears, all her longings bubbled to the surface. She looked at Noah again and sighed. How could she possibly explain what she felt? To explain would mean to be exposed, to be vulnerable, naked in front of him.

Hayley giggled and Callie patted her head gently a couple of times before removing her hand. Once she'd broken the connection her womb flipped again, but differently this time. She felt empty, bereft.

She looked at Noah then and saw he was watching her with such searing intensity she had to lean against the counter for support. But to have his child? An adorable child like Hayley. What a dream that would be.

Not a dream. A fantasy.

"Hayley, take your seat," Noah said quietly. "Dinner will be ready soon."

The kids all whooped and raced for their favorite spot at the table.

"This is done," Callie said and grabbed the bowl.

Meals were usually a quiet affair for Callie. She ate alone most of the time, unless Fiona was around or she offered to make lunch for Joe. But this was something else. The kind of meal she remembered from her childhood, when the kitchen had been the centerpiece of the home. Lots of laughter, lots of spillage and wipe-ups and grubby faces.

Family…

Another woman's family, she reminded herself.

But I'm here...and I feel such a part of them. Like somehow...I was made for this.

Callie's salad was a success, with Jamie kindly telling her it was the best he'd tasted—even better than his Aunt Evie's.

Afterward, she volunteered to load the dishwasher while

Noah put the twins to bed with a story. Jamie chatted to her as she worked, telling her about school and how Fiona was his favorite teacher and how he liked to make things and that he wanted to learn to play the trumpet. Then he told her he would choose a movie to watch and disappeared down the hallway. By the time Noah returned, the kitchen sparkled and the coffeemaker gurgled.

"I helped myself," she said. "Although I can't find any cups."

He opened a high cupboard, extracted a pair of matching mugs and placed them on the counter. "Milk, no sugar."

The way she liked hers, too.

Jamie reappeared, clutching Madagascar in one hand and a Harry Potter sequel in the other. They unanimously chose Madagascar. Callie took her coffee into the living room and sat down in the corner of the long sofa. She placed her coffee on the side table. Jamie said something secretly to his father then excused himself and raced down the hall.

"He likes you," Noah said quietly as he set up the DVD player.

"How do you know that?"

He turned his head and smiled. "You'll see."

Jamie returned a few minutes later. He asked her to hold out her hand and dropped something onto her palm. She stared at the thin leather strip threaded with dark, shiny stones.

"It's a bracelet," he said, pointing to the stones. "They're hematites."

Callie touched the smooth stones. "It's lovely."

"I made it," he announced proudly. "You can have it."

"You made this?" she held it up. "You're very clever. But I couldn't possibly take it."

He looked so disappointed she longed to snatch the words back. "You don't like it?"

Callie rubbed the stones again. "Of course I do. I just thought that if you made something this pretty you might want to give it to someone…like a girl."

Jamie frowned. "You're a girl."

"Smart kid," Noah said as he sat at the other end of the sofa. "My sister Mary-Jayne makes jewelry," he explained. "She lets the kids craft pieces when they stay with her." He looked at his son. "He doesn't part with them easily."

Noah watched her reaction. She looked increasingly uncomfortable. Jamie was a warm, generous child and incredibly easy to love. And although she'd interacted appropriately all evening, he sensed something else was happening to her.

His suspicions were elevated. Was it him making her nervous? Noah couldn't be sure. In the kitchen she'd been relaxed and chatty. When it was just the two of them she usually looked fired up and ready for anything. But then Hayley had hugged her, and Noah had witnessed reluctance in her response to his daughter. The realization landed on his shoulders.

The kids…it was the kids. He felt sure of it.

How can she not like my kids? They're unbelievable. Everyone likes my kids.

Finally, she spoke. "In that case, I would love to keep this. Thank you."

That settled, he flicked the play button and sank back into the sofa. With Jamie between them she seemed light years away from him. Which was probably exactly how she wanted it.

Jamie fell asleep after about twenty minutes. Noah gathered him up and carried him to his bedroom. He tucked him in bed, kissed his forehead and returned to the living room.

She hadn't moved. He flipped the DVD to a CD and

waited until the music filtered around the room before heading back to the sofa.

"Would you like some more wine?" he asked before he sat.

She shook her head. "I should probably go home."

Noah glanced at the clock on the wall. It was barely nine o'clock. He didn't want her to go. He had to say what was on his mind. "I'm not a threat to you, Callie."

She looked into her lap. "I know that."

"So why do you want to leave?"

She expelled an unsteady breath. "Because being here I feel…involved." She stopped, looked away. "I feel involved with you."

Suddenly there was something very raw about her. "Would that be so bad?"

She looked back toward him. "No," she said on a breath. "Yes…I can't—"

"I'm not your ex, Callie," he said bluntly. "And if you screwed up, and if you chose the wrong person to give your heart to, don't feel alone. Just get in line."

"Did *you* screw up?" she asked.

"With Margaret?" he nodded. "For sure. But I should never have married her in the first place." He shrugged. "She was pregnant with Lily," he explained. Not, *I loved her.* To say he'd truly loved Margaret would have been a lie. "We had a baby coming. It seemed the right thing to do."

She smiled fractionally. "It was the right thing to do."

In the beginning he'd believed so. Especially the day he'd held his newborn in his hands. But later he'd wondered if they should have considered a shared custody arrangement of their daughter instead of a marriage between two people who were never suited to one another.

She looked at him, hesitated, and then took a steadying breath. "My fiancé wasn't who I thought he was."

"Was he unfaithful?"

She shrugged. "I don't think so." She dropped her gaze for a moment, then turned back to look at him. "He was killed in a car wreck four years ago."

It wasn't what he'd been expecting and Noah saw the walls close around her as if they were made from stone. A cheating, dishonest spouse was a whole lot easier to compete with than a ghost. "And you're still grieving?"

She gave him an odd look. "Most of the time I'm simply… numb."

He reached across and took her hand. "Can you feel that?" he asked as he stroked her forefinger with his thumb.

She looked to where their hands lay linked. "Yes."

"Then you're not numb, Callie." Noah fought the impulse to drag her into his lap. He wanted her so badly he could barely breathe. "You just fell in love with the wrong man."

She closed her eyes briefly. "I know."

"So maybe we'll both get it right next time."

For a moment she looked like she wanted to be hauled into his arms. He was tempted. Very tempted. But the look lasted only a moment.

She grabbed her tote. He could see her walls closing in, could see her shutting down. "I should go."

He knew the evening was over. "I'll walk you out." Noah stood and followed her wordlessly to the front door. Even with music playing in the background, the house seemed uncommonly quiet. Harry lifted his head when Noah opened the front door, then dropped it disinterestedly.

"Well, thank you for dinner," she said, clutching her bag. "And for part of a movie."

Noah prepared himself for her hasty departure, but she stopped at the bottom step and turned. "I know what you want, Noah. And part of me wants that, too."

The air stuck in his throat. "But?"

"Right now I just…I just don't have room inside myself for any more…feelings."

The raw honesty in her voice was undeniable. He wasn't sure how the brash, argumentative woman he'd first met had morphed into this exposed, vulnerable creature he couldn't take his eyes off. His insides churned. *Don't be afraid of me. Don't be afraid of what's happening between us.* He didn't say it. He couldn't. He wanted to kiss sense into her…to make her really see him, really feel him. But she wanted to run and that annoyed him. *God, this woman's undoing me.*

"Will you ever have room?" he asked quietly.

She looked at him. Through him. "I…don't…I *can't.*"

Moments later he watched her drive away and waited on the porch until the taillights disappeared at the end of the driveway. And he knew he was falling for a woman who'd just admitted she didn't want to feel anything. For anyone. Ever.

Chapter Seven

The familiar sight of Noah's truck arrived at exactly eight fifty-five Sunday morning. Callie was coming out of the stables when she saw him retrieving his toolbox from the tray. She said hello and he said the same, but he quickly headed for the house and began repairing the screen door.

While she was left wondering if he was angry with her, she was also left facing Lily. And Lily was in a dark mood. She grunted when Callie clipped the long lead rein onto the halter secured beneath the bridle. And then again when Callie knotted the reins in the middle of the gelding's neck and instructed Lily to do arm raises.

Lily muttered a "this sucks" under her breath and began her lesson.

It became a long fifty minutes, with Callie acutely conscious of Noah's presence at the house. She wished she knew his moods better. *Was* he angry with her? He worked without breaking; he didn't even appear to look in their direction.

She hadn't heard from him since Friday night. She'd thought he might call. But he hadn't called…and as tempted as she'd been to pick up the telephone herself so she could hear his voice, she hadn't.

"What's up with *you* today?"

Lily's accusing voice vaulted her back to the present. "Nothing," she said.

"You're not paying attention to me," the teenager complained.

Callie switched her mind into instructor mode. "Of course I am. You're doing great." She grabbed a neutral subject. "How did your sleepover go at Maddy's?"

Lily's gaze snapped at her suspiciously as she trotted Samson in a circle, skillfully rising from the saddle in between beats. "How did yours go with my Dad?"

Maybe not such a neutral subject after all!

Callie's face burned. She called Samson to a halt and waited until he slowed before roping him in. Once horse and rider were in front of her she spoke. "It wasn't like that."

Lily's expression remained skeptical. "Yeah, sure."

"I stayed for dinner," she explained. "And then I went home."

Lily didn't like that, either. Her look became as black as her mood. "So you guys are friends now?"

Callie thought about how to answer. "I…suppose."

Lily dismounted. "I thought you were *my* friend?"

Uh-oh. Callie chose her words carefully. "I am, Lily. I have all different kinds of friends."

"Well, *he* doesn't look at you like he wants you to be his friend. He looks at you as if he wants you to be his *girlfriend*."

Callie grabbed the reins and tried to squash the sudden heavy thump of her heart. *He's not looking at me like anything at the moment.*

"We're *just* friends," she said firmly, unclipping the reigning lead and handing Samson to Lily. "Give him a brush down and ask Joe to get a small feed for him." She caught Lily's scowl. "Horsemanship includes ground work and is all part of learning to ride."

Lily started to move then stopped and swiveled on her boot. "I just don't want things to change, that's all. I like coming here. I like learning how to do stuff."

"Nothing's going to change," Callie assured her, sensing that it was what Lily needed to hear. "I promise."

"So you're like, not moving back to California or anything?"

California? "No."

Lily shrugged. "Because people do move. People…leave."

Like her mother. Callie took about two seconds to figure it out. "Not all people," she said gently. "Not your dad."

Lily didn't look convinced. "Yeah, I guess," she said. "It's not like I don't want him to date or anything…I mean, as long as whoever he dates is not some old witch who hates kids. But you're *my* instructor…and if you went out for a while and then stopped going out, I wouldn't be able to come here anymore. When adults break up that's what always happens."

Callie drew in a deep breath. "We're not dating. We're friends."

Lily nodded but clearly wasn't convinced. Callie remained in the arena until Lily had led the horse into the stables. She wiped her hands down her jeans, tightened the hat on her head and walked toward the house. He wasn't on the porch. The side gate was open and she headed around the back. Noah was by the fence, pulling off a couple of loose palings, while Tessa bounced around his feet.

"Lesson finished?" He spoke before she even made it twenty feet from him.

"Yes. She did a great job. A few more lessons and she'll be ready for her own horse."

He kept pulling at the palings. "I'm nearly done here."

Callie took a long breath and stepped forward. "I was talking with Lily," she said, watching as he kept working. "She knows…I mean, she thinks there's something going on between us," she blurted.

"I'm sure you set her straight."

He *was* angry.

"I said we were just friends."

He glanced at her but didn't respond. Callie took another step and called the pup to heel. But Tessa, the traitor, remained by Noah's side. He popped the palings in place with a few deft swings of the hammer.

"Sure, whatever." He started walking past her but Callie reached out and touched his shoulder to stop him. He looked at her hand and then into her eyes. "What?"

"Exactly," she said, digging her fingers into his solid flesh. "What's wrong?"

He didn't move. "Nothing."

A big fat whopping lie—and they both knew it. "Are you mad or something?"

"No." He still hadn't moved.

"So, we're…okay?"

He shrugged. "Sure."

Callie dropped her hand and felt the loss of touch immediately. He looked tense. More than that…he looked as wound up as a coil.

"Noah," she breathed his name on a sigh. "If you—"

"Just drop it, Callie," he said quietly. "I have to get going. See you later."

She stared after him and watched his tight-shouldered walk with a heavy feeling in her chest. She almost called after him. *Almost.* Tessa followed before she turned back and sat at Callie's boots. She touched the dog's head and the pup whined.

"Yeah…I know what you mean, girl," she said and waited until his truck started up and headed down the driveway.

She lingered for a moment, staring at the dust cloud from the wheels. Once the dust settled she headed back to the stables and prepared for her next student. Fiona called after lunch and made arrangements to drop over later that afternoon. Her final student left at four o'clock and once Joe took off for the day Callie grabbed her best show bridle and began cleaning the leather. Cleaning her gear had always settled her nerves, and she undid the nose band and cheek strap, set them aside and dipped an old cloth into the pot of saddle soap.

It wasn't much of a diversion, though. Because Callie had a lump in her throat so big, so constricting, she could barely swallow. For two years she'd had focus. The farm. The horses. Her students.

And now there was Noah. And Lily. And the rest of his children.

Deep down, in that place she kept for her pain and grief and thoughts of her baby son, Callie realized something that shocked her to the core. *If I reach out, I know in my heart I can make them my own.* She wasn't sure how it had happened so quickly. Feelings hadn't been on her agenda for so long. Now, faced with them, Callie could feel herself retreating.

She wondered if she should have told him about Ryan. Would he understand? He'd had his own disappointments, but he didn't appear to be weighed down with regret and grief. Maybe people *could* move on? Perhaps hearts did mend.

Right then, Callie wanted to believe that more than anything.

But to feel again? Where did she get the strength? Ryan's death had zapped all her resilience. Before that she'd been strong, unafraid, almost invincible.

She was glad when she heard Fiona's car pull up outside and called for her to join her in the tack room. Only it wasn't her friend who stood in the doorway a few moments later. It was Noah.

He was back. And he clearly had something on his mind. Callie got to her feet quickly. Her heart pumped. "Did you… did you forget something?"

He stood in the doorway, his eyes locked with hers. "Do you still love him?"

She was poleaxed. "What?"

Noah was in front of her in three steps. "Your fiancé. Do you still love him?"

"He's dead," she whispered.

"I know. But that wasn't the question." He reached for her, slid one arm around her waist and drew her against him. "The thing is," he said, holding her firm. "If you still love him, I'll do my best to stop…to stop wanting you." His other hand cupped her cheek, gently, carefully. "But if you don't love him, then I'd really like to kiss you right now."

Her insides contracted. "No," she said on a breath.

"No?"

"I don't love him."

His green eyes darkened as he traced his thumb along her jaw. "Good," he said softly.

And then he kissed her.

Callie let herself float into the warmth of his mouth against her own. It was a gentle possession, as if he knew her, as if he'd been kissing her forever. Only one other man had kissed her before this, and as she allowed Noah's lips to part hers, any recollection of that faded and then disappeared. He didn't do anything else—he just kissed her, like he couldn't get enough of her mouth, her taste, her tongue.

Instinctively, Callie's hands moved along his arms and to his shoulders. She touched his hair, felt the silky strands beneath her fingertips and slanted her mouth against his. Finally, when he lifted his head Callie felt so much a part of him she swayed toward his chest. Noah held her still, one hand on her shoulder while the other splayed on her hip and she lifted her chin higher to look into his eyes.

"Noah—I think..." Callie willed herself to move, but found such incredible comfort in his arms she simply *couldn't*.

He didn't let her go, either. "You think too much. How about you stop thinking and just feel?"

Oh, how she wanted to. But her doubts tormented her, taunting around the edges of her mind in a little dance, telling her that taking meant giving. And giving was...giving felt as far out of reach to her as the stars from some distant planet.

He leaned into her, like he knew her fears. "I'd never hurt you, Callie."

In her heart she knew that. "But...but I might hurt you."

"I'll take that risk." He kissed her again, long and slow and deliciously provocative.

Heat radiated through him, scorching her, and Callie wondered if she might melt. Kissing had never felt like this before. Nothing had ever come close to this. He was strong and safe—a haven for her shattered heart.

When the kiss was over she spoke. "But earlier today you were angry with me."

"Yes. No. Not angry...just...wanting you and not sure how to reach you." He touched her face. "Because I do want you Callie...very much."

She wanted him, too. She wanted more of his touch, more of his mouth, his breath. He gave her what her eyes asked for, kissing her passionately, cradling her against his body.

"Hey, Callie! I'm here for—"

Fiona. Noah released her instantly and she stepped back

on unsteady feet. Busted—and by the biggest blabbermouth she knew.

"Oh," Fiona said so chirpily it had to be a cover for her surprise. "Hey, Noah. So…I'll just go and make myself invisible."

Fiona Walsh invisible? Not likely. But to her credit she left the room without another word. Callie looked at Noah. He didn't look the least bit embarrassed that they'd been caught making out. "I should probably go inside," she said quietly. "Fiona is here for…"

"Don't run now."

She twisted her hands together. Her skin, her lips, the blood in her veins felt more alive than she'd believed possible. "Noah…I'm not ready for someone like you."

He stood rigid. "Like me?"

Callie exhaled heavily. "You're like this whole package—like Mr. Perfect." Suddenly the heat was back in the small room, charging the invisible atoms in the air with a heady pulse.

He laughed humorlessly. "I'm far from perfect."

Callie crossed her arms. "I mean that I don't think you're the kind of man a woman kisses and then forgets. I don't think you're the kind of man a woman simply has sex with. I think you're the kind of man a woman makes love with—and I'm not…I can't…"

His eyes glittered. "So this isn't a sex thing?"

Callie blushed wildly. "Well, of course it's a sex thing. I mean, I'm not denying that I'm attracted to you. It's obvious I am. It's not *just* a sex thing."

He didn't move. He stared at her with such burning intensity she had to look away. To the floor. To the side. Anywhere but into his eyes.

Finally, he spoke. "Within minutes of meeting you, Callie, I knew something was happening. I couldn't figure out what, but I knew it was big. I knew, on some level, that it would change my life. But I can't afford to be casual about this. I have a responsibility to my kids to keep myself in a good place and to do the right thing by them."

She took a deep breath as the sting of tears threatened. "That's just it. I know that about you…I feel that. You *have* to think about your children, Noah," she breathed. "And I…I'm not prepared to…I'm not prepared for that."

His gaze narrowed. "For what, Callie? My kids? Is that what you're saying?"

Her heart ached. *I'm saying I'm not ready to let go yet... I'm not ready to forget my baby son and move on. I'm not ready to fall for you and love another woman's children.*

Her heart contracted. "Yes." She whispered the word, knowing it would hurt him, knowing she was pushing him away because she was so afraid of all he offered her. "I don't want a ready-made family."

Silence screeched between them, like fingernails on a chalkboard.

When he spoke, his voice was quiet. "Well, I guess that's it, then. I'll see you next weekend."

Callie stepped forward. "Noah, I really—"

"There's no need to explain, Callie," he said, cutting her off. "I understand what you're saying. You don't want my kids. You don't want me. That's plain enough. I'll see you 'round."

She waited until he'd left the small room before taking a breath. And as she heard his truck pull away, she burst into tears.

Callie remained in the office for a while, but once her tears were wiped up she returned to the house. Fiona was waiting for her on the porch. Her friend sat on the love seat and held two glasses of wine.

"You look like you could use this."

She sank on the seat and took the glass. "Thanks."

Fiona's big eyes looked her over. "You've been crying. What happened? You two looked cozy when I walked in."

"I don't want to talk about it."

"You know," Fiona said, sharper than usual, "sometimes it doesn't hurt to open up a bit. That's what friends do for each other—in case you forgot."

"I'm a terrible friend," Callie said through a tiny hiccup.

"Yeah, I know."

Callie couldn't help the hint of a smile that curled her mouth. "I don't know how to feel," she admitted. "He wants… he wants…"

"Everything?" Fiona asked. "That doesn't seem like such a bad deal to me."

It didn't, no. But taking everything meant giving everything. "I can't."

Fiona took a sip of wine. "You can't live in the past forever, Callie. Believe me, I know that from experience." She leaned back in the love seat. "I know you lost a baby."

Callie gasped. "How do you—"

"I found some pictures," Fiona explained. "Remember when you first moved in and I helped you unpack? You were out with the horses and I was inside going through boxes…" Her voice trailed off.

Her memory box—given to her by the caring nursing staff at the hospital after Ryan had passed away. "Why didn't you say something sooner?"

Fiona shrugged. "I figured if you wanted to tell me, you would. The only reason I'm bringing it up now is that I like Noah. And so do you. I don't get why you'd send him away."

"It's complicated."

"Because he has kids?"

Callie wondered where her friend had gotten all this sudden intuition from. “I’m just not sure if I can do it.”

Fiona watched her over the rim of her glass. “You won’t know unless you try.”

“And if I mess up, the children will be caught in the middle.”

“I think you should cut yourself some slack. You’re smart and from what I’ve seen you’re pretty good with kids.”

“This is different,” she said quietly.

“Why? Because you’re falling in love with him? With them?” Fiona asked.

Callie gasped. Was it true? Was she falling in love with him? She liked him…really liked him. But love? Could she? Overwhelmed, Callie couldn’t find the voice to deny her friend’s suspicions.

“Have you told Noah about your son?”

“No.”

“Maybe you should,” Fiona suggested. “You know he’d understand. Or is that what you’re afraid of?”

She stared at her friend. Was that the truth? Was she so afraid of him really knowing her?

“I had a baby,” Fiona admitted. “When I was fifteen.”

Callie’s eyes almost sprang out of their sockets. “What?”

Fiona nodded. “I gave her up for adoption. There’s not a day goes by when I don’t think about her, when I don’t wonder where she is, when I don’t pray that the family she’s with are looking after her, loving her. I hope they don’t love her less because she’s adopted.”

Thunderstruck, Callie stared at her friend, saw the tears shimmering in Fiona’s eyes and pushed back the thick swell of emotion contracting her own throat. She had no idea her bubbly, eternally happy friend was holding on to such a secret. “I’m so sorry, Fee.”

Fiona managed a brittle smile. “I guess what I’m saying

is that we all have things in our past that can stop us from looking for happiness or make us blind to it when it comes along. The trick is having the courage to take the chance."

Three days after the afternoon in the tack room, Callie went for a long ride. She rode into Crystal Point and headed for the beach. It was barely ten o'clock and only a few people were about, a couple chasing sticks with their dogs and a lone jogger pounding the sand. She maneuvered Indiana past the restrooms and onto the soft sand. She spotted a couple of small children building a sand castle and urged Indiana to a halt when she heard her name being called.

It was Evie. And the two small children were Hayley and Matthew.

"Hello," Evie said as Callie dismounted.

Hayley came running up to her and hugged her so fiercely Callie was amazed by the little girl's obvious display of affection. Evie stood back and watched the interaction keenly as Hayley showed off her thumbnail painted with transparent glitter polish compliments of her Aunt Mary-Jayne.

Both kids hovered around Indiana, and he stood like an angel while the little girl patted his soft muzzle. Matthew was a little more reluctant, but after a small amount of coaxing from his aunt he stroked Indy's shoulder.

"He's such a beautiful animal," Evie said with a whistle.

Callie smiled proudly. "Yes, he is." The kids lost interest in the horse and headed back to their sand castle. "They look like they're having fun."

Evie smiled. "They love the beach. I try to bring them as much as I can."

"Do you look after them often?'

"Every Wednesday," she replied. "My mother has them on Fridays and the rest of the week they're in daycare." Evie looked at the twins affectionately. "They're off to school next year and I'm already missing them just thinking about it."

Callie stopped herself from watching the twins. "They're lucky to have you in their life."

Evie shrugged. "They're easy to love."

Yes, Callie knew that. And she could feel herself getting drawn toward them. Evie patted Indiana for a moment and then slanted Callie a look she knew instantly would be followed by a question. "So, are you and Noah seeing each other?"

"Where did that come from?"

Evie smiled. "Jamie said you make a mean salad."

Callie tipped her Akubra down on her forehead.

"I knew you were going on a date. But I was surprised when the kids told me you'd been to the house," Evie said when she didn't reply. "You're the only woman he's invited home to be with his kids since his divorce. I figured that meant something."

Callie remembered Hayley's innocent remark about *grown-up girls* and her insides contracted. She'd known it, felt it…but to hear the words, to know he'd never had another woman in the house with his children…it made her heart ache.

"He's a good guy," Evie said quietly. "He had a tough time with his ex and deserves to be treated right."

Callie managed a brittle smile. "Are you warning me off?"

Evie chuckled. "Lord, no. And Noah would strangle me if he knew I was talking with you about this. Sometimes I get into my protective-sister mode and put my foot in it. But I like you, Callie. And I love my brother. So you can tell me to back off and stop meddling if you want—but I probably won't listen."

Callie was surprised by the other woman's frankness. "I hear you."

"She didn't want her kids, you know," Evie said as she looked over toward the twins. "Imagine that. I mean, she had a lot of emotional problems, no doubt about it…but to just walk away from two new babies…it's unfathomable to me." She sighed. "And Jamie was barely more than a toddler himself. As for Lily…sometimes she acts so impulsively and I'm concerned she has abandonment issues. And you'd never really know what Noah is thinking. But I guess when your wife packs her bags and tells you she doesn't want you or your children—it must make it hard to trust someone again."

Callie's breath caught in her throat and emotion burned behind her eyes.

Abandoned, motherless children…and a good man trying to hold it all together. She suddenly felt the shame of what she'd said to him right down to the soles of her boots.

She'd said the words to hurt…said them knowing they would hit him hard.

She'd wounded him instead of doing what she should have done…which was to tell him the truth. About why she was so afraid. Fiona was right—she needed to tell him about Ryan.

"I have to go," she said as she grabbed the reins and sprung into the saddle. "Thanks, Evie," she said as she turned Indiana back toward the boat ramp and began the quick canter home.

Twenty minutes later she was back at Sandhills Farm. She untacked Indiana, turned him into one of the small paddocks behind the house and then headed inside. One telephone call and a change of clothes later and she was on the road.

She'd called Preston Marine and was told Noah was working from home that day. Within eight minutes she'd pulled her truck into his driveway. Callie turned off the ignition and got out. She heard a loud noise, like a motor running, and followed the sound around the side of the house. She saw him immediately, behind the pool fence holding a chainsaw.

In jeans and a white tank shirt, he looked hot, sweaty and gorgeous. She observed for a moment as he cut branches from an overgrown fig tree and tossed them onto a growing pile. There was something incredibly attractive about watching a man work—a kind of primitive instinct, purely female and wholly erotic. As if aware he was being watched, he stopped the task, lay the chainsaw aside and turned. He walked around the pool and came to a halt about ten feet from her.

"Hello."

She took a breath. "Hi."

He looked at his hands. "I need to wash up."

Callie followed him through one pool gate and then another until they reached the patio. She waited while he slipped through the back door and then returned a few minutes later, cleaned up and in a fresh T-shirt and carrying two cans of soda.

He pulled the ring tab and passed her one. She took it, desperate to touch his fingertips, but she didn't. "Are you playing truant today?"

"Just working off steam."

Callie suspected she was the steam he needed to work off.

He put the can down on a nearby table. "Why are you here, Callie?"

She held her breath. "I saw your sister today."

His brows came up. "Did she embarrass me?"

"No." Callie stepped back on her heels. "But she said something. She said…she said you'd never invited a woman here…to be with the kids. Before me."

"She's right."

Another breath, longer, to steady nerves stretched like elastic. "Why not?"

He pulled out a chair for her to sit on and then one for himself. Once Callie was seated he did the same. Finally, he spoke. "When you're treated badly, when the person you've committed yourself to walks out the door and says she doesn't want you, she doesn't want your children, she just wants to be free, it breaks something inside you. It broke something inside *me,*" he admitted. "I have no illusions about the kind of marriage I had. Most of the time it was a disaster. She'd left once before—the second time I told her that was it, no more. She had to make a choice. And she chose freedom." He leaned forward and rested his elbows on his knees.

Callie stood and walked across the patio. She looked at the pool and the immaculate garden and the timber cubby house she knew he would have built himself. When she'd gathered the courage to say what she come to say, she turned. He was still seated.

"I'm so sorry, Noah." Callie inhaled heavily. "About what I said the other day. I know I…I hurt you."

He didn't move.

Callie took a deep breath. "The way it came out, the way it sounded… That's not what I wanted to say. And certainly not what I meant."

He stood up and walked toward her. "So what did you want to say?"

She placed her hand on his arm and immediately felt the heat of their touch. "That your kids are amazing." She swallowed hard and kept her hand on him. "What I'm feeling, it's not about them. It's about me."

Noah covered her hand with his. "What *are* you feeling, Callie?"

Callie looked at him and her eyes glistened with moisture. She inhaled deeply, taking as much into her lungs as she could. "The reason I feel as I do…the reason I push people away…" She paused, felt the sting of tears. "The reason I push *you* away…it's because I lost someone."

Noah's grip on her hand tightened. "Your fiancé?"

She met his gaze levelly. And the tears she'd been fighting tipped down over her lashes. "No, not Craig."

"Then who? What do you—"

"My son," she whispered. "My baby."

Chapter Eight

"You had a son?" The shock in his voice was obvious.

Callie shuddered. "His name was Ryan," she said and felt the hurt right through to her bones. "He died when he was two days old."

She watched Noah think, absorb. "How long ago?"

"Three years," she said quietly and inhaled. "Ten months… one week…three days."

He swallowed hard. "How? Was he sick?"

She shrugged and turned, wrapping her arms around herself. "I was in an accident." She hesitated, took a long breath and then looked at him. "A car wreck."

Noah clearly knew what that meant. "The same one that killed your fiancé?"

"Yes."

She watched as the pieces of the puzzle came together in his head. "You lost them both?" He turned her back around and rubbed his thumb along her jawline. "Why didn't you tell me this before now?"

She looked down, taking a breath. "Because I don't talk about it. And we haven't known one another very long and I didn't…couldn't… Well, being responsible for someone's death, it isn't exactly the kind of thing I want to talk about."

Noah didn't try to hide his shock. "How were you responsible?"

"The accident," she replied. "It was my fault."

"Were you driving the car?"

She shook her head. "No, Craig was driving."

"Then how could—"

"I distracted him," she admitted. "I made him lose concentration. And I shouldn't have. I was angry because we argued." She didn't say anything for a moment. She looked up and around and then back to him. "Craig didn't want the baby."

"He didn't?"

"No. He didn't want anything other than to use me. I fell for him when I was seventeen," she explained quietly. "I moved in with him, wanted to be with him. Craig trained me, taught me everything I know. He was a gifted rider. I thought he loved me. But I found out too late that he only cared about his career. *Our career,* as he called it." Another breath. "We'd worked hard, trained hard, put in hours and used all our money. The Grand Prix Championships were at our fingertips—and after that, the big one, the Olympics, every rider's dream. But I got pregnant and everything changed. I couldn't ride, I wouldn't risk riding. Craig was furious. I'd never seen him like that. We argued about it for three days. In the end, he told me I had to make a choice."

She paused, took a long breath, gathered herself and blinked away the fresh tears in her eyes. "He wanted me to end it. The pregnancy."

Noah's mouth thinned. "What did you do?"

"Moved back in with my mom."

"And then?"

"I decided to get on with my life. When I was about five months along, Craig came back. He said he wanted to try and work things out. He said he'd changed his mind about the baby, about me. And I believed him."

She knew he heard the "but" in her voice. "What happened then?" he asked.

Callie shrugged. "For a few weeks it seemed like it would be okay. And as much as I felt betrayed by Craig, I knew my baby deserved a father. Craig even talked about setting a date for the wedding." She paused, thinking, remembering. "On the day of the accident he came around early. We talked about me moving back in with him, about turning one of the guest rooms into a nursery. He asked me to go for a drive. I was happy to do it, happy thinking everything would work out. We got in the car and drove for a while. But he seemed edgy to me, like he had something on his mind. And then… and then he said it. He said it and I knew I could never trust him again."

Noah held her tighter. "What did he say?"

"My horse," she replied. "He wanted my horse, Indiana. That was what he wanted. That was *all* he wanted. Not me, not our baby. You see, Craig was a gifted rider with a good horse, where as I was a good rider with a gifted horse. He wanted to ride Indy in the Grand Prix qualifiers. He said if I loved him, if I wanted him to be a part of my life, and the baby's life I had to do what he asked."

"And the crash?" Noah asked quietly.

"He was furious with me, called me a few names. He tried to touch me and I pushed him off." Her voice cracked, sounding hollow. "He lost control of the car. We ended up crashing into a guardrail and down an embankment."

Noah winced. He felt pain and rage rip through him. Anger toward a man he'd never met. A dead man. A man who'd hurt this woman so much, who'd broken her to a point Noah feared she'd never be whole again.

"Was he killed instantly?" he managed to ask, though he didn't know how. His heart thundered in his chest.

She nodded. "Yes."

"And you?"

"I was rushed to the hospital," she said. "I had a lot of internal injuries and the baby was in distress. I was pretty out of it. My mom was there and they told her there were no guarantees for either of us. So the doctors delivered him." Tears came again, brimming over. "He fought for two days. He was so tiny. I was so sick and only got to spend a moment holding him."

Noah swallowed, fighting the emotion in his throat. It was every parent's worst nightmare. And she'd endured it alone. He wished he could turn back the clock and be there with her, hold her through every awful moment. He took a deep breath. "I can't even imagine how you must feel."

Callie looked at him. "Ashamed that I didn't see through Craig's lack of integrity. If I had, maybe Ryan would still be alive, maybe my beautiful boy would be with me. He'd be nearly four years old now."

Four years old…

Noah drew a sharp breath. And the truth hit him with the force of a sledgehammer.

"The twins…" His words trailed and then picked up. "That's why you… Ah, of course."

Her throat convulsed. "Sometimes…it's hard to be around them."

Because they reminded her of all she lost.

"I'm so…" He stopped, searching for the words. Everything he considered seemed grossly inadequate. "Thank you for telling me," he said, and even that wasn't nearly enough.

"I needed to," she said, and Noah felt her pull against his

embrace. He let her go and she walked back to the seat and dropped into it. "I wanted you to understand that what I'm feeling is about *me.* Not them. Not you."

That didn't sound right. Her resistance, her pain was about him. And the kids. She'd lost her baby—and that loss stopped her from wanting to *feel* again. Noah could see her struggle. He could feel it. But he wasn't about to let her walk away from him.

He returned to his seat and grasped her hand. "Callie," he said gently. "What do you want to happen between us?"

She looked uncertain and he felt panic rise in his blood. He wanted her to say she wanted everything—him, the kids, the life he knew was within their reach. But her silence was suddenly deafening.

Finally, she spoke. "I've done a good job of putting my emotions on hold for the past few years. And as much as I'm drawn to you, Noah, I just don't know if I'm ready to feel again."

His fingers tenderly rubbed her knuckles as he kissed her. "I'm no expert, Callie," he said against her mouth. "But if you feel anything like I'm feeling right now, we're off to a good start."

She moaned slightly and the sound undid him. He wanted her so much. Needed her so much. He felt like saying something to her, maybe tell her exactly what she meant to him. Something uncurled in his chest, thudding loudly. *Liking* Callie, *desiring* Callie had swiftly turned into something else. And this Callie—this beautiful, fragile woman who now trembled in his arms, was suddenly the one woman he wanted for the rest of this life.

"Callie?"

She looked up. And one look did it. One look from blue eyes shimmering with tears.

I'm gone...

The feeling reached right through to every pore in his skin, every blood cell, every scrap of air that filled his lungs when he took a breath.

"Spend Saturday with me," he said quietly. He kissed her again, slanting his mouth over hers in a sweet, possessive caress and he felt her tremble. "Can you rearrange your lesson schedule?"

"Yes." She sighed. "And thank you for understanding."

He nodded. He did understand. She wasn't a woman to be rushed. And because he'd waited his entire life to feel this way, he'd do his best to give her whatever time she needed.

Wear a swimsuit.

Callie hadn't asked him why he'd insisted she make sure she had a bikini underneath her clothes for their date Saturday. However, when she spotted two long objects secured to the racks on the roof of his truck she knew why.

She frowned. "Boats?"

"Kayaks," he corrected and opened the passenger door.

"I don't really do boats."

He laughed deliciously. "It'll be fun," he said. "Trust me."

"I do," she replied. "I just don't trust boats."

He told her M.J. had arrived early that morning and was happily in charge of the kids for the day. Jamie had insisted on making Callie a matching pendant to go with the bracelet he'd gifted her and Callie was incredibly touched.

The trip to the boat ramp took about ten minutes and Callie relaxed. The nervous energy she seemed to have around him had disappeared. She felt calm and happy. And Callie sensed she was ready for the next step. Telling him about Ryan had been exactly what she needed to do. It gave her strength and, from somewhere, the courage to dare to imagine a future with the incredible man beside her.

When they reached the boat ramp he passed her something. "You'll need to wear this. There's a ladies bathroom over there."

He pointed to a concrete block building about fifty meters away. *This* turned out to be a black, stretchy, sleeveless wet suit that came to her knees and a pair of matching shoes with rubber grips on the soles. Once out of her jeans and shirt and into the wet suit, Callie ran her hands over her hips. With only a bikini beneath, she felt a little deliciously decadent. When she returned to the truck she saw he'd also changed into a similar suit.

It should be illegal for a man to look that good in black rubber.

She watched, feeling rather useless, as Noah unclipped the kayaks from the utility, prepped them for their outing and launched them into the water.

"Ready?" he asked and handed her a sun visor. It looked new, as if he'd bought it especially for her. "Can you swim?"

"Yes."

"Good," he said and passed her a life jacket. "Humor me anyway and wear this."

Callie didn't argue and slipped the jacket over her wet suit.

"We'll go up river," he said. "It's low tide at the moment. Just stick close by me."

She didn't intend to let him out of her sight.

Noah gave her quick but detailed instructions on how to use the single oar and maneuver the craft through the water. Half an hour later they were on their way.

Noah stayed at her pace and they paddled up river, splicing through the water in unison. On either side of the river the mangrove branches twisted and rose up onto the sandbank. Schools of fish crisscrossed below them and some flipped out of the water, delivering a salty spray across her face and arms.

"How are your arms holding up?" Noah asked after about an hour.

"Good. Although I think I'll be sore tomorrow."

"We'll stop for a bit," he said. "I owe you breakfast for making you get up this early."

Callie laughed. "Breakfast? Is there a café tucked along here somewhere?"

"You're sitting on it," he said, grinning. "There's a storage compartment beneath your seat. There's a cooler with food and a thermos of coffee."

Callie looked between her legs and chuckled. "So, what are you sitting on?"

He laughed. It was a rich, lovely sound. "The first-aid kit. Sunscreen. A spare life jacket. And my phone."

"You've thought of everything."

"Habit," he said, and indicated her to turn the kayak toward a smaller secluded inlet. "With kids you have to be prepared for any emergency."

Noah pointed to a tiny alcove ahead and they oared to shore. He got out first and dragged his kayak onto the sand and quickly helped Callie do the same. Once her feet hit the ground she felt the wobble in her calves and thighs. Noah grabbed her by the shoulders.

"Sea legs," he said with a smile. "It'll pass."

Callie let the warmth radiate through her. His fingers were strong and gentle against her skin. She placed her hands at his waist. That felt good, too. She wished she'd tossed off the life jacket so she could get closer to him. Then he kissed her with all the pent-up passion fuelling the long three days since they'd seen one another.

"Callie," he whispered against her mouth, before he kissed her cheek and the delicate and sensitive skin below her earlobe. "I'm starved."

She smiled. "Me, too," she admitted, not wanting to leave

his embrace but liking the idea of some food. She pushed past the nagging disappointment she felt when he released her. "What did you bring?" she asked as she slipped off the life jacket.

"Let's see."

They unpacked the kayak together. Callie grabbed the small rug he'd provided and spread it down farther up the bank in a spot shaded by a wiry native tree. She sat with her knees up, while Noah stretched out his long limbs beside her. There was fruit, soft bread rolls, cheese and smoked ham. They sat on the rug, eating and not saying much of anything for a while. Noah passed her a resin mug filled with coffee and she took it gratefully.

The weather was warm with a gentle hint of breeze and there were birds calling out from the trees above. Water lapped at the edge of the small sandy inlet and the sound was faintly hypnotic.

She put down her mug and uncurled her legs. "It's a lovely spot. Do you come here often?"

"Not much."

He wasn't looking at her, she noticed. He was looking at the sand, his feet and the drink in his hand. She said his name again and he looked up. His green eyes were vibrant and wholly aroused. Heat rode up her spine at a galloping speed.

"I didn't," he said quietly, interpreting her response, "bring you here with any motive other than to spend time with you."

"I know." Callie rested back on her elbows, felt the wet suit stretch with her movements and saw his gaze narrow. "I also know you won't rush me."

He sucked in a breath. "I'm glad you know that."

She relaxed fractionally. Dare she admit he was first man outside of her family who made her feel safe? "It's not that I'm afraid of…of…" She waved her hand between them.

"Of making love?"

"With you?" She pushed herself up and let out a long breath. "No. It's just that I've only ever been with one man in my whole life and it seems like such a long time ago."

"There's no hurry."

Noah looked so calm and controlled. But Callie wasn't fooled. He wanted her. Yet she knew he wouldn't take what she wasn't ready to give willingly. "There isn't?" she queried with a husky breath. "You're right."

His eyes glittered brilliantly. "You know, you're looking at me like that isn't helping my good intentions."

"Sorry," she said on a breath. "I guess I'm out of practice at all this."

"Don't be sorry."

The steady sincerity of his gaze raced directly to her heart. "Noah, I wish I was—"

"Come here," he directed softly. "Stop thinking. Stop talking. Just come here."

Callie resisted for a nanosecond and then she was in his arms. Noah captured her mouth in a deep, soul-wrenching kiss. She gripped his shoulders as he rolled her half on top of him. Their legs tangled and he grasped her hips, bringing her closer to the length of his body. "You're so beautiful," he whispered against her mouth.

Callie flung her head back and allowed him to trail hot kisses across her collarbone. She could feel him hard against her and her thighs parted, arching into his body. He touched her arms, her shoulders, her hands. He touched her over the wet suit, cradling her hips. Callie's hands curled over his biceps and she sighed against his mouth. Touching him became as intrinsic as breathing. They kissed and kissed, absorbing one another. Noah rolled over in one swift move, lodging a leg between hers. Callie could feel the force of his erection and it fueled her desire, driving her to kiss him more, touch him more. She sighed, a deep shuddering sound that echoed through them both. She heard him groan, felt the rising urgency in his touch, knew that he was as driven by need as she was. He kissed her as he tugged the wet suit off her shoulders. He cupped her breast through the thin fabric of her bikini top and Callie felt a flood of moisture between her thighs, a longing deep down, driving her to want more, need more. Her hips rose in anticipation, waiting, wanting and screaming with need. She reached down to touch him, felt him hard against her palm, felt the power in her hands as he grew harder still against her stroking fingers. It was as if they had been doing this forever—as if they had known one another in another time, another life.

"Callie," he muttered, like the word was ripped from his throat. "We have to stop."

She put her hands into his hair. "No, please."

"We have to stop," he said again, raggedly. "I don't have a condom. I can't protect you."

She clung to him. Some faraway voice told her he was right. But she wanted him so much. "It's okay," she breathed.

"No," he said, more groan than anything else. "It's not. I won't…I won't make you pregnant. At least, not like this. Not here. And not yet."

Callie's heart stilled, and pain filled every part of her chest. She felt herself move, retreat, pull away. She had to tell him of her pain. Her shame. "You're right, Noah," she whispered, suddenly cold. "You won't make me pregnant." A shuddering sigh came out. "I can't have children."

Noah pulled back immediately. He felt her hurt through to the blood in his bones.

She can't have children.

The pieces of the puzzle of who she was fell spectacularly into place. Of course. It made so much sense. Her son had died and she'd never have another.

Then share mine burned on the edge of his tongue. He wanted to tell her, make her see that she could have children if she wanted them. His kids, who would welcome her into their life. He knew it as surely as he breathed. Even Lily. They *needed* her. *He* needed her.

She scrambled up and took a few moments to readjust her clothing. Once she'd pushed her wetsuit back up she began collecting the leftover foodstuffs and blanket.

Noah adjusted his own wet suit and moved behind her. "Callie?"

She shook her head as she picked up the blanket and began folding. "I'd really rather not talk about it."

"I think we should," he replied, not touching her but so close he felt her nearness like a magnetic field.

"I can't have kids," she said, folding and refolding. "That's really all there is to it."

"Because of the accident?"

She turned around and faced him. "Yes." A simple response to a complicated situation. And not nearly enough. He looked at her and she continued. "I had a lot of internal injuries. The doctors told me I have about a ten-percent chance of ever carrying a baby to full term."

He stared at her. "So you can *get* pregnant?"

Obviously not the question she was expecting. "Well—yes, I suppose. I just can't stay pregnant."

"Then we did the right thing by stopping."

"I guess we did," she said stiffly.

Noah took the blanket from her. "We did, Callie. Come on," he said quietly. "The tide is coming in, we should get going."

They barely spoke on the trip back. When he dropped her home he stayed for a coffee he didn't really want. On the porch, with Tessa at his feet, Noah felt the tension of unfulfilled desire beat between them like a drum.

"You were right," she said unsteadily before she sipped her coffee. "We were sensible to stop. I don't think I could bear to get pregnant only to lose…to…well, you know what I mean. I guess that's why I tell myself I can't have children. It's easier to cope with."

"Ten percent is still ten percent," he said soothingly. "It's a chance."

She shook her head. "No. It's too big a risk. I didn't really think a lot about children before I found out I was expecting Ryan. I guess I just took it for granted." His gaze narrowed and she explained. "The feeling that a little piece of you keeps going on because of your children… It wasn't until I was told I wouldn't be a mother again that I realized just how much I really wanted it." She sighed heavily. "One of life's base instincts, I suppose."

Noah set down his mug and grasped her hand. "There are many ways to become a parent, Callie," he said and suddenly felt like spilling his guts and telling her everything about his disastrous marriage and Margaret's infidelity.

She shrugged. "I suppose."

It wasn't the response he hoped for. "You don't believe that?"

"I think…I think someone with four children wouldn't really know what I feel."

He stood up and walked to the stairs, turning around to face her with his hands on his hips. "And you once accused *me* of being arrogant," he said pointedly.

"What does that mean?"

"It means that you didn't corner the market on lousy relationships."

"I didn't say I had."

"But you imply it," he said quietly, completely frustrated. "I'm not going to pretend to fully grasp what it must have been like for you to lose your baby…or how it feels knowing you might never have another child. But despite what you might think, I do know a bit about disappointment...and loss."

Her blue eyes shone. "Because of your wife?"

"Because I married a woman I didn't love and who didn't love me," he replied. "And she spent the next ten years punishing us both for it. But I stuck with it because I'd made a commitment and I felt I owed my children a chance at a normal life with parents who stayed together." Noah dropped his arms to his sides. "It was a train wreck from the very beginning."

"But you stayed?"

"I stayed for the kids," he said honestly. "They needed me."

She stood up and reached him in a couple of steps. "You were right to stay," she said. "For Lily's sake especially. She's afraid, you know. Afraid you might leave."

Noah's chest hurt. "She said that to you?"

"She implied it. I think Lily is frightened things are changing."

"Change is inevitable, though."

Callie nodded. "I suppose. I'm not an expert on teenage girls, Noah, but I was one once. And in a way I understand what Lily is feeling. My father was sick for a long time before he died. And even though I knew my mom wasn't sick and wouldn't die, too, part of me always feared that she might. So maybe you simply need to talk to Lily and tell her you're not going anywhere."

Strange how good it felt to talk to her about Lily. The years of going it alone had been lonely ones. He could easily imagine Callie at his side, every day, every night. "Thank you for caring about Lily."

"I do care," she said quietly and looked away.

Noah stepped closer and took hold of her chin, lifting her face up. “But you’re not sure you want to, right?”

“Honestly…being around you makes me more confused than I’ve ever been in my life.” Her hands found his chest. “Would you…would you like to stay for a while?”

“Yeah,” he breathed. “But I have to pick the kids up before three.”

“Oh.” Disappointment etched on her face.

“Evie’s got guests arriving at two,” he explained. “And my folks are golfing all day.”

She moved her fingertips. “Another time, then?”

He grasped her shoulders and looked at her. “I *want* to stay with you.” He pulled her close and her hands were imprisoned between them. “Believe me.” One hand moved over her shoulder and he gently touched the back of her neck and tilted her head fractionally. “I want to make love to you so much I can barely think about anything else.” Especially after what had happened between them down by the river. “I’ll call you later,” he said, kissing her. “And of course I’ll see you tomorrow, for Lily’s lesson.”

“Of course,” she whispered.

He kissed her again and the feel and taste of her was imprinted all over his skin. And Noah knew, without a doubt, that he wanted to love her for the rest of his life.

Only, he had no idea if Callie wanted the same thing.

Chapter Nine

Callie hitched the trailer to her truck and got Fiona to check the lights. Her friend gave her the thumbs-up.

"Can I *please* come with you?" Lily asked for the third time.

"Like I said the first time, no."

Lily scowled. "But I could help. You might need me."

Rescuing the three neglected horses would be tricky, but it needed to be done. Because Animal Welfare hadn't been able to trace the horses, Callie and Fiona had found out their location through a mutual friend and horse trainer. They'd planned the rescue for late Wednesday afternoon and would inform the authorities when they had the animals loaded on the trailer. Only Callie hadn't expected Lily to turn up and insist on helping.

"Definitely not," she said. "Get your bike and head home."

"Dad will let me go if I ask him," Lily said.

Callie looked at her. "No, he won't."

She knew how Noah would react. He was a stickler for doing the right thing. And what they were doing was not exactly protocol—even if their intentions were noble. She'd considered telling him about her plans because she didn't want there to be any secrets between them. But Fiona talked her out of it, insisting the fewer people who knew the better.

"But I *want* to help," Lily insisted and then said with a pout, "I thought we were friends."

"We are," Callie said, firmer this time. "But your father is—"

"More than a friend," Lily said bluntly and pouted again. "Yeah, I get that. I'm not a little kid. I know you guys are into each other."

Callie tried to ignore the heat climbing up her neck. She suspected Lily knew about their kayaking trip. Well, not everything. But Lily was smart, she'd work it out, even if Callie was reluctant to come clean and admit she and Noah were together. "I was about to say that your father wouldn't want you mixed up in this. And neither do I," she added.

"I can take care of myself," Lily said and crossed her thin arms. "And I wish everyone would stop treating me like I'm five years old. I'm thirteen…old enough to…well, old enough to do lots of stuff. And it's not like I'm about to go and do something stupid. And the way my dad's been acting lately you'd think I was some sort of glass doll."

Callie caught Lily's resentment. "He's concerned about you."

"No need," the teenager replied. "I get that he wants a girlfriend," she said and flashed her eyes at Callie. "But who says it would work out anyway? I mean, people get together and break up all the time, right? Even married people. *Especially* married people. In fact, I don't know why adults bother to get married at all. They should just have kids and break up straight away…that way the kids don't have to get used to the idea that having parents who are together is normal."

Once she'd finished her impassioned speech, Lily bit down on her lower lip. Callie's concerns about Lily's fragile emotions increased tenfold. For all the girl's bravado, she wasn't fooled. Lily was hurting. Lily felt things deeply. And Callie knew the young girl was concerned about her relationship with her father. Noah was all she had, Lily's rock, the one constant in her life. And Callie had no intention of threatening that foundation.

"Time for you to go home," Callie said gently. "I'll see you on Sunday."

Lily begrudgingly accepted her decision and took off on her bicycle.

"Let's get going," Fiona said after they'd filled up the hay nets. "We need to get the horses back here before it gets dark."

Callie agreed. She locked Tessa in the backyard and checked the house was secure. The windows all worked now, thanks to Noah.

She maneuvered the truck and trailer around the yard and headed for the road.

"So, big date this Friday, huh?"

Callie concentrated on the driving. The trip was close to thirty kilometers west of Bellandale and would take about half an hour. But she still managed to smile at her friend. "How did you find out?"

"Evie told me," Fiona said. "She's watching the kids and asked if I wanted to drop by for a game of rummy." Her friend rolled her eyes. "I get a game of rummy and you get a dreamy date."

Dreamy? She supposed Noah was a little dreamy. *A lot dreamy.* And she was looking forward to their date more than she could have ever imagined. She had only seen him during

Lily's lesson on Sunday because the twins had come down with a slight cold. But he'd asked her to dinner on Friday night. Although after what happened by the river, Callie wasn't sure she was ready for the next step in their relationship. Oh, she wanted Noah. What surprised her was the intensity of that desire. She'd never considered herself all that sexual in the past…her life with Craig had revolved around the horses and competition and hard work. Sex and romance had come last in the list of priorities they'd set for their life together.

But with Noah…well, she thought about sex a lot. And she felt certain he thought the same. Since they'd almost made love by the river she'd been distracted and unable to think about much else.

Except now she was thinking about Lily. The young girl's obvious confusion and pain lingered in the back of Callie's mind. She needed to talk with Noah before their relationship went any further. She needed to be sure she wasn't unsettling Lily too much.

"There's the turnoff," Fiona announced.

Callie slowed down and turned into a long gravel driveway. An old farmhouse came into view behind a row of wild bamboo. The settling dusk set up an eerie mood. "Are you sure this is the right place?"

"Absolutely. Put the headlights on, will you? It's getting dark."

Callie flicked on the lights and pulled the truck to a halt. "Looks like a gate over there," she said and pointed to a break in the fence line where an old timber gate was tethered between two posts. Fiona grabbed the flashlight on the seat between them and got out. Callie followed and retrieved three halters and ropes from the back of the truck before tracing her friend's footsteps.

"I can see them," Fiona announced when she reached the fence line. "Look."

Callie saw the three horses silhouetted against the diminishing sunlight. "You get the trailer ready," she said. "I'll grab them."

"Be careful," Fiona warned and headed back to the truck.

Callie looked at the chain and padlocks on the gate and tapped the pair of bolt cutters in her back pocket. She slipped through the barbed-wire fence and headed for the trio of horses who were now watching her suspiciously. The closer she got, the more appalled she became. They were clearly neglected. Two bays and one grey, all of them in need of decent feed and veterinary attention. She haltered one of the bays and the other two automatically followed. Once the three horses were secured, Callie grabbed the snips and cut through the barbed wire. Within minutes they began angle loading them on the trailer.

Fiona suddenly shrieked. "Callie, look. A car's coming."

Sure enough, a pair of headlights turned toward the long driveway. "It could be nothing," Callie assured her friend.

Fiona didn't believe her. She didn't believe herself. "They must have seen our lights. We have to get out of here."

Callie agreed. They quickly secured the horses, closed the tailgate, then jumped into the truck. Callie turned the truck and trailer in a sharp arc and headed down the driveway.

The car kept coming. Conscious of both their own and the horse's safety, Callie accelerated fractionally and stayed on the track. With just meters to spare, the car veered to the right with a loud blast of its horn. She kept going, giving the task her full concentration. Fiona told her the car had turned and was now on their tail as they headed out of the driveway. They hit the main road and Callie increased speed. Behind, the car closed in, tailgating them, striking the horn in an attempt to intimidate. The driver didn't give up, following them down the narrow country road. In the side mirrors Callie could see that the car was in fact a truck with a menacingly heavy-duty push bar out front. And it was getting closer to the back of the trailer with each passing second. At the first contact on the push bar against the rear of the trailer, Callie was thrown forward. Fiona screamed. Callie gripped the steering wheel and held on, managing the impact by pressing the gas and surging forward. She could feel the horses moving in the trailer and straightened the rig quickly. The truck collided again, harder this time, sending them into the gravel rut on the edge of the road. Callie held her nerve and pulled the wheel with all her strength.

"Should we pull over?" Fiona asked frantically.

"No," Callie said quickly. "Cameron's a police officer, right?"

Fiona nodded. "Yeah."

"So, call and tell him where we are and what's happening."

"But he'll—"

"Just call him," she insisted. "Hurry."

Thankfully Fiona had service on her cell and hastily made the call. Cameron instructed them to keep on their route at the designated speed limit if safe and said a police car would be dispatched immediately.

They endured a frightening ten minutes until the welcome sight of blue and red flashing lights came toward them. Callie slowed the truck down and pulled over. The truck took one last ram into the back, jerking them around the cab despite their seat belts. Another police vehicle appeared and cornered the truck behind them.

The offenders were out of their truck within seconds. Two men, hurling insults about how they had stolen their horses, didn't like having to answer questions about how Callie's trailer had dents on the tailgate.

Cameron arrived in plain clothes because he'd been off duty. He was quick to check they were unharmed and asked for a detailed account of what had happened. With the men now in the back of a police car and the horses jittery but in one piece, Callie began to tell her account of the events while Fiona called Animal Welfare to come and pick up the horses. But a sharp rapping sound interrupted them, followed by a shrill voice pleading, "Let me out."

Cameron followed the sound, Callie right behind him. He rattled the handle to the storage compartment on the side of the trailer. Callie quickly gave him the key and he opened the narrow door. None of them expected Lily Preston to unfold her gangly legs from the small space.

"Damn it, Lily," Cameron demanded as he helped her out. "What are you doing in there?"

The teenager straightened, rubbed her arms and looked at Callie. "I just wanted to help."

Callie's blood ran cold. "You stowed away when I told you not to. Lily, how can—"

"Because friends should help each other."

"Does your dad know you're here?" Cameron asked.

Lily shook her head, guilt written all over her face. "Maybe we shouldn't tell him."

Good idea—but not going to happen. Callie watched as Cameron stepped away and made a quick phone call.

By the time Noah received the call from Cameron, he was about to start calling Lily's friends to see if anyone knew where she was. He'd tried Callie several times thinking she'd be there, but she hadn't picked up. Nor could he get any service on her cell. Not surprising, considering Cameron's brief account of events that led to both Lily and Callie ending up at the police station.

He dropped the kids at Evie's and headed into Bellandale. He scored a parking space outside the police station and headed inside. Cameron greeted him swiftly, minus the regulation blue issue uniform.

"Where's Lily?" he demanded.

"In the break room. She's okay," Cameron said.

Relief pitched in his chest. "And Callie?"

"She's just finished making a statement. Room three. You can go in if you like."

Noah strode away without another word. She was sitting down when he entered the room. He said her name.

She looked up, swallowed hard and let out a long, almost agonized sigh. "Noah."

He stepped closer. "Are you all right?"

"Yes, fine."

"What happened?"

She took a deep breath and placed her hands on the small table in front of her. "Fiona and I heard that the three horses we've been trying to rescue had been moved again. We found out the location and went to get them."

"To steal them?"

She raised her hands and stood, scraping the chair back. "Well, yes."

"And what?" he asked, sharper than he wanted. "You thought you'd take my kid along for the ride?"

"No…I had no idea she'd stowed away in the storage locker."

Noah stilled. "She was in the *trailer?*" Cameron hadn't mentioned that.

"Dad?"

They both stopped speaking and turned their heads toward the door. Lily stood beneath the threshold. "Don't blame Callie," his daughter insisted.

"I'm not blaming anyone," he said and tried to stop thinking about the danger his daughter had been in. "I'm trying to understand what happened."

Lily shrugged. "I wanted to help. I wanted to do something. It's not Callie's fault."

"I'm not blaming Callie," he said and tried to push back the kernel of censure rising within his chest. He knew Lily. She was headstrong and impulsive. And Callie couldn't have known his daughter would be so determined to go along for the ride.

"Good," Lily said and raised her chin. "It was *my* fault. I'm the one who should be blamed. It's always my fault. That's what I do."

There was so much pain in Lily's voice that Noah's heart constricted. "Its okay, Lily. Why don't you go and wait by the front desk. We'll go home soon."

Lily looked at them both for a moment then let out a pained breath. "So you can do what? Talk about me and work out ways to get me out of your hair so you two can get it on?"

Noah stepped toward his daughter, but she moved back. "It's not like—"

"Maybe you should send me away somewhere," she said and cut him off. "Like boarding school—that way I won't be in anyone's way. Or maybe you should send me to Paris—you could always ask my mother if she wants me." Lily's eyes glistened with tears Noah knew she wouldn't let fall. "But we know what she'd say, right? She didn't want me four years ago, so she won't want me now."

The pain in his daughter's voice pierced directly into Noah's chest. Lily had kept her feelings about her mother locked away for years. And now they were leaching out. He was staggered and anxious and partly relieved. Realizing why, Noah swallowed a hard lump in his throat. In a matter of weeks Callie had somehow become the catalyst for Lily's stirred emotions.

"You're not going to be sent away, Lily," he assured her gently. "Not ever. Go and wait by the desk. I'll be with you soon."

Before she turned Lily looked toward Callie with eyes filled with apologetic resentment. Noah knew Lily liked and respected Callie, but his daughter was also afraid of the impact Callie was having on their lives.

Once she left Callie spoke. "She's in a lot of pain, Noah."

That much was obvious. "I know."

"She's confused and frightened."

He knew that, too. What he didn't know was why Callie looked at him with such blatant despair. "I'll talk with her."

Callie let out a long sigh. "I don't…I don't think we should do this."

Suddenly Noah knew exactly what she was talking about. And he knew what was coming. She wanted out. Before they'd even begun. It cut right through to the marrow in his bones. Perhaps because part of him knew she was right. Lily's needs had to come first. And whatever his daughter was going through, Noah knew his relationship with Callie would only amplify Lily's feelings of abandonment and anger toward her mother.

But…to lose her? Sensing that it was exactly what Callie wanted made him mad. Irrational and unlike him as it was, Noah experienced a deep burst of resentment for the fact she could give up on them so easily.

"So, I guess you get what you want after all," he said, not liking the way it sounded but too stubborn to stop the words from coming.

"What does that mean?"

"No ready-made family."

Callie looked at him, all eyes, all hurt. "That's unfair. I'm only thinking of Lily. She needs—"

"What about what you need, Callie? Or maybe you don't

need anything. Needing would mean feeling, right?" He pushed past the pain that had settled behind his ribs. "It would mean giving part of yourself to me...and I don't know if you have the heart for it."

She swallowed hard. "Do you think I'm that cold?"

"I don't know," he replied, frustrated and annoyed. "Only you know what's in your heart, Callie."

"I'm trying to do what's best for Lily."

You're what's best for Lily. You're what's best for me.

But he didn't say it. He didn't push. Didn't beg her to give them a chance like he wanted to. "I have to go. I'll see you... sometime."

She lifted her shoulders. "Sure."

Noah left the room. Walking down the corridor suddenly became close to the hardest thing he'd ever done.

Callie sat on the sofa, eating ice cream covered in crushed Oreo cookies and copious amounts of chocolate sauce.

She took a mouthful, anticipating the usual buzz from the sugary sweetness, and sighed heavily when the kick didn't come.

Hopeless.

She tried again and, when disappointed with the same result, plopped the dish on the coffee table and sank back in the sofa. It was Friday night and she was alone. The same Friday night that she should have been out on a romantic date with Noah.

I should be with him right now.

Except that everything was ruined.

Even though she knew there was nothing else she could have done when she realized the extent of Lily's fears, Noah's words had hurt her deeply. She did have a heart capable of feeling. A heart that was filled with thoughts of him.

She hadn't heard from Noah all week. Nor had she seen

Lily. She only had a message on her answering machine telling her he'd decided to take his daughter to Janelle Evans for lessons from now on. Callie had replayed the message countless times, listening for something, some indication he regretted what had happened between them. And because she'd heard nothing like that in the direct, clipped tones, each day dragged out longer than the one before.

She'd tried ignoring the pain suddenly and permanently lodged inside her.

She'd tried not to think about how much she missed him.

And how much she missed Lily. And the rest of his amazing family.

And as she'd thought her heart irreparably broken and imagined she'd never feel anything deep enough to really be hurt ever again, Callie came face-to-face with the truth. And it shocked her to the core.

I love him.

She was in love with Noah.

She wasn't sure how to deal with the feelings that were new, raw and strangely precious. Her head hurt thinking about it. She looked at the melting ice cream and was just about to trade it for some aspirin when Tessa barked and moments later the doorbell rang.

Fiona stood on her doorstep and walked across the threshold holding a bottle of wine in each hand. "We thought we'd come over and cheer you up," her friend announced.

"We?"

Evie Dunn stuck her head around the open door. "She means me." Evie's wildly curling black hair bobbed around her face. "Can I come in?"

"Of course."

Within seconds the door was shut and Fiona scooted to the kitchen for glasses.

"You don't mind?" Evie asked.

Callie shook her head. "I could use the company," she admitted and suggested they take a seat.

Evie sat on the oversize love seat and curled up one foot. "It was Fee's idea."

"I'm glad you're here," Callie said, and tried not to think about how much Evie looked like her brother. And *she* was glad for the company. She had the feeling Evie could become a good friend. She pointed to the bowl on the table and smiled. "I was just about to consume a gallon of ice cream."

"As a substitute for what?" Fiona chirped as she came back into the room.

Callie fought off the embarrassment clinging to her skin and ignored her friend's teasing. "You guys have saved me from a gazillion calories."

Fiona laughed then poured wine into three glasses and passed them around.

"If it's any consolation," Evie said quietly, "he doesn't look any better than you do."

Callie tried not to think about how hearing that made her feel. It wasn't as if either of them had made any kind of declaration to one another. Their relationship had fizzled out before it had really begun. What could she say that wouldn't make her look like a silly, lovesick fool?

"Noah told me some of what happened," Evie said and took a sip of wine. "Lily's pretty broken up that you're not teaching her anymore."

"It's probably for the best."

"I'm not so sure. Sometimes you have to push past the hard times."

"Noah has to focus on Lily," Callie said and took a drink.

Evie tutted. "My brother has focused solely on his kids for the past four years. And apart from Lily's gothic rebellion and typical teenage moodiness, she's never talked about how her mother's departure made her feel. And then wham, you walk into their lives and she starts letting things slip. There's a connection, Callie. Because of you she's opening up and that's a positive thing. Talking about her mother is good for Lily."

"I agree," Callie said. "But she needs to be able to do that without being afraid her world is going to be rocked upside down."

"By you?" Evie asked. "Lily worships you."

Callie's throat tightened. "As *her* friend. Not as…something else."

"You mean Noah's girlfriend? Or a potential stepmother?"

Stepmother? Heavens. How had this happened? How had she become so deeply involved with the Preston's that Evie was suggesting marriage? Loving Noah had changed everything. Not being with him hurt so much Callie wondered how she'd get through it.

"She needs stability," Callie said. "She needs to know her father isn't about to get sidetracked."

"She has stability," Evie said a little more forcibly. "What she needs is to know relationships can work and that not all women are like her mother and will leave her."

Callie agreed. Except she wasn't sure she was the kind of role model Lily needed.

And she suspected Noah thought that, too.

Noah thrummed his fingers on the steering wheel as he waited for Lily. The twins and Jamie, buckled up in the back of the utility vehicle, chatted quietly to one another. Harry was asleep on the front porch. The morning air was warm, typical of a November day. Summer would soon be here. And summer in Crystal Point meant the little township would be buzzing with tourists and convoys of camper trailers and weekend holidaymakers searching for some relief from the unforgiving heat in the clear waters of the surf beach and river mouth. He watched as Lily shut the front door and bolted toward the vehicle. She got into the truck and put on the seat belt.

"Ready to go?" he asked.

"Sure. I hope Maddy's okay."

Maddy Spears had been in a horse-riding accident and her mother Angela had called, asking if he could bring Lily to see her at the hospital.

"I'm sure she'll be fine," Noah assured her and started the engine. "How are the lessons going?" he asked, trying to take her mind off her worrying about her best friend.

Lily rolled her eyes. "I've only had one. And like you don't know that already? I'm sure *she's* told you everything."

She. Janelle Evans. Lily's new instructor. The enemy. Noah hung on to his patience. "I thought you liked Janelle."

She huffed. "You thought wrong. She's so *old*."

He eased the vehicle into gear. "She's experienced."

Lily's eyes narrowed. "Old," she repeated.

"I think you should cut her some slack," Noah said quietly.

Another huff. "Well, you would. Seeing it was *your* idea that I go there in the first place."

"You said you wanted lessons," Noah reminded her.

"I do. But I don't want them with *her*." Lily rolled her eyes. "I don't see why I can't go back to Callie. It's not like I broke up with her or anything. I knew I'd be the one who ended up getting screwed."

"Watch the language," he warned.

"At least you're not going to start dating *this* instructor," Lily snapped back. "I mean, she's like one hundred years old or something. So I'm pretty sure you won't marry her."

"Who are you marrying, Daddy?" came a determined voice from the backseat.

Noah spotted Jamie in the rear vision mirror and smiled. "No one, mate."

"You could marry Callie," Jamie said determinedly. "We like her. You like her, too, don't you, Dad?"

"Stupid question," Lily said.

"I'm not stupid," Jamie wailed.

"Yeah, you are."

Noah called a truce. "Stop the name calling." Lily made a face and he suspected Jamie stuck his tongue out in response.

"Are you going to *marry* Callie, Dad?" Jamie asked, almost jumping out of his seat.

Marry Callie? He'd thought about. Imagined it. Wanted it. "Lily and I are only talking."

But Jamie didn't give up. "If you marry Callie she'd be our mother, right?"

"Stepmother," Lily put in.

Jamie ignored his sister. "And would she come to school sometimes and work at the canteen, Dad?"

Noah didn't miss the longing in his son's voice. Such a small thing. But for a little boy who barely remembered a mother's love, it was huge. He'd tried his best, but juggling a business and four kids often made it impossible to do the small things. His sisters pitched in, especially Evie, and his mother did what she could. But it wasn't enough. Who was he kidding? His kids needed a full-time mother.

"Would Callie be our mother, Dad?"

Jamie again, still curious and not put off by Noah's silence. He tried to maintain casualness. "I guess she would."

Lily huffed again, louder this time. "Don't get too excited. We didn't have any luck getting our real mother to hang around. I can't see how Callie would be any different."

Chapter Ten

Callie had no idea that helping Angela Spears select a new pony for her daughter Maddy would end with the teenager taking a tumble from the first horse they looked at. She was relieved that Maddy's broken arm was the worst of her injuries. She had some superficial grazes on her face but none that would scar. The hot pink cast on her arm was finally wrapped and Callie offered to grab coffee for a fraught Angela while the doctor checked the results of a few cautionary tests, including a head scan.

She headed for the cafeteria and purchased coffee for Angela and a soda for Maddy.

When she returned to Maddy's room she saw Lily sitting on the edge of the bed, then saw Jamie and the twins perched together on a single chair and Noah talking closely with Angela.

The green-eyed monster reared its ugly head and she pushed the feeling down as swiftly as she could. A blended family—wasn't that the term used now? Angela was an attractive woman. Noah would be blind not to notice. She was a single mother, he was a single father. A good solution all round—yours, mine and possibly ours one day. Lily and Maddy were best friends. It would be the perfect scenario for Noah's troubled daughter.

And if Callie had any doubts that she'd fallen in love with Noah—they scattered the moment she realized the feeling coursing across her skin was blind, burning jealousy.

She swallowed the bitter taste in her mouth.

Callie placed the coffee on the table beside the bed. The twins rushed toward her and Callie had no hesitation in accepting their warm hug. Jamie quickly did the same. Only Lily hung back. But the teenager looked at her almost hopefully. And Noah's eyes grazed over her, from her feet to the roots of her hair. She felt the energy of his stare, felt her skin heat, felt the tiny hairs on the back of her neck come alive.

Angela's beaming smile didn't help. "Oh, you're back," she said breathlessly. "I was just telling Noah how lucky we were that you were with us today. And it was my fault," Angela wailed. "But it was so hot. I had no idea the pony would spook over a little umbrella."

"It happens sometimes," Callie assured her, fighting her awareness of Noah with all her strength. "Don't feel bad."

"Can we still buy the pony?" Maddy asked, still groggy from painkillers.

Angela looked at Callie. "What do you think?"

Callie smiled and turned to the girl in the bed. "How about we wait until your arm is better and try a few more horses out before making a decision?"

Maddy nodded. "Still..." Her voice trailed. "I'd really like my own horse."

"Me, too," Lily said and looked at her father. "You promised, remember?"

"I remember," he said, still looking at Callie. "We'll see."

Lily rolled her kohl-lined eyes. "Yeah, I know what that means." She looked at her friend. "Now you've busted your arm I haven't a chance."

Angela came across the room and hugged Callie. "Thank you for everything," she said, her eyes clogged with emotion. "If you hadn't been there, I don't know what I would have done. I wouldn't have known how to splint her arm like that. And the way you knew to keep her warm in case she went into shock." She shuddered. "I wouldn't have remembered any of that."

"I'm glad I could help."

"Help?" Angela hugged her again. "You were incredible. I'm hopeless in a crisis."

"Not hopeless," Callie said gently. "And I have to know basic first aid as part of my license to teach."

"It didn't look basic to me. Anyway, I'm so grateful you were there."

"Well, I'll get going." She looked quickly around the room, focusing on Angela. "Are you sure your sister will be coming to pick you up?"

"Oh, yes," the other woman replied. "You go, please. You've done more than enough. And thank you for coming here with us. I know it helped Maddy enormously knowing you were by her side."

She said goodbye to the kids and then turned without another word, pain slicing through her with every step she took. She made it about thirty feet down the corridor when she heard Noah saying her name. *I will not look back. I will not let him see how much I miss him.*

"Callie, wait up."

That stopped her. She inhaled deeply and turned to face him. "What?"

"Are you okay?"

Can't you see that I'm not? Can't you see that I'm crazy in love with you? But I can't come between your family. I won't.

"Why wouldn't I be?"

He looked into her eyes. "You had a fairly harrowing afternoon."

"I handled it."

"So Angela said."

Angela. Perfect single mother Angela. "Is there something else you want?" she asked and couldn't believe the sound of her own voice.

"Maddy's lucky you were there."

Callie felt prickles of annoyance weave up her spine. "I guess I have my uses."

He felt the sting of her response because he expelled an almost weary breath. "I just wanted to say…that it's…it's good to see you."

"I have to go," she said quickly and pulled her keys from her pocket. "I've got a student this afternoon," she lied.

He went to say something and then stopped. "Yeah, sure."

Her heart felt like it was going to burst. *I will not fall apart in front of him.* "Goodbye, Noah."

She turned before he could say anything and walked purposefully down the corridor.

By the time she'd returned to Sandhills Farm it was nearly two o'clock. Joe was there, wheeling a barrow of soiled manure from the stables when she pulled up. He asked about Maddy and she gave him a condensed version of what had happened.

"Saddle up Indy for me, will you?" she asked. "The Western saddle please. I'm going for a long ride."

Callie rode toward Crystal Point, through the cane fields, past sweet potato farmers cultivating their crops. She rode past the local primary school, took a trail toward the river and lingered by the boat ramp for a while, eating the sandwich and water she'd packed in her saddle bag while Indy happily grazed on Rhodes grass.

I'm such a fool. For years she'd frozen herself off from feeling anything. And then along came Noah and his incredible kids and suddenly she felt like she was *all* feelings. All want. All need. But she hurt, too. And she didn't know how to stop the hurt…or how to stop loving Noah.

It was past five when she returned home, and it was an hour later when she headed for the house after strapping Indy down, returning her tack to the stables and locking the gelding into his stall. By seven o'clock, once the animals were all fed and bedded down for the night, Callie had showered, put on a pair of sweats and sat on the sofa with her laptop to check her email. One from her brother, Scott, made her smile and she was just about to hit the reply button when she heard a car pull up outside.

He's here.

She knew it somehow. Felt it deep down. Tessa barked and Callie quickly made her way to the front door and flicked on the porch light. She opened the door.

It *was* Noah.

He stood beneath the light. "Hey." He looked so good in jeans and a white golf shirt. Her heart lurched in her chest. "I probably should have called first."

Callie crossed her arms, determined to be strong. "Why didn't you?"

"I thought you might hang up." He ran his hand through his hair. "Can we talk?"

She opened the screen door and waited until he'd crossed the threshold before closing both doors. "What did you want to talk about?" she asked once they'd moved into the living room.

He cleared his throat. "I wanted to…I wanted…"

Callie didn't move as she pushed her emotions down. "What?"

He let out an exasperated breath. "I don't really know. I let Lily stay with Maddy, and after I left the hospital I dropped the kids off at my parents. For the past two hours I've been driving around, thinking, trying to get things right in my head."

"What things?" she asked quietly.

He swallowed. "Us. The kids. Why I can't stop thinking about you."

Callie's knees gave up and she sat on the edge of the sofa. "It's the same for me," she admitted.

He came forward and stood a couple of feet from her. "So, what are we going to do about it?"

Callie shrugged. "Nothing's changed, Noah."

"You're right about that."

"You'd really be better off with someone else," she heard herself say. Stupid words. Words to cover the feelings coursing through her blood.

"Someone else?"

She shrugged. "Like Angela," she said, although her voice cracked and she knew he'd heard it. "She's a single parent, she obviously loves kids—she'd make you a good match."

"I'm not interested in Angela Spears," he said quietly.

"But Lily—"

"Tell me what *you* want, Callie."

"How can it matter, Noah? Last week you—"

"Last week I said something stupid and hurtful. And I'm sorry. I told you once that I'd never hurt you. But you were about to blow me off and I got mad and screwed up." He shrugged his shoulders tightly. "Can you forgive me?"

Callie nodded. "But it doesn't change anything. Someone like Angela would fit into your life. And with Lily and Maddy being friends it makes perfect sense."

"Not to me. I'm interested in you, Callie. I *want* you. Only you."

"But Lily—"

"Will be fine with this. With *us*. I know my daughter. And I know how she feels about you."

Callie wasn't so sure. She knew the teenager was confused and at a critical point in her young life. Callie didn't want to do anything to jeopardize the young girls well-being.

"If she doesn't…" Callie's word trailed.

"She will understand."

He stood in front of her, not moving, not speaking. Just looking at her from bright-green eyes. Finally, when neither could bear the silence any longer, he dropped to his knees in front of her and wrapped his arms around her.

He shuddered in her arms. "I can hardly breathe just thinking about you."

She wanted to deny him. She wanted to refuse the clamoring needs of her body and the deep longing in her heart. But refusing him, rejecting him, would break her into tiny pieces.

I love this man…

Callie ran her hands through his hair. "Me, too."

The air suddenly filled with heat. And need. She could feel the mounting tension in him beneath her hands. His muscles tightened and she instinctively gripped him harder. Warmth spread through her body, licking over every nerve, every cell. She knew he felt it, too. It rolled like waves, creating a turbulent energy in the quiet room.

Callie's hands slid down his arms, over strong biceps. She rubbed his skin with her thumbs and heard the unsteady sound of his breathing.

"Callie," he said, drawing the words deep from his throat. "I want…I want to make love to you." He stilled, taking in a profound breath. "But if you're not ready…we'll wait. And if you want me to go I—"

She smiled. "Shhhh." She traced her hands back to his shoulders. He felt so strong. *I can have this…I can have him.* "I'm glad you're here," she whispered. "I want you here. I think I've wanted you here my whole life."

Noah immediately moved closer, fisting a handful of her hair before he tilted her head back and took her mouth in a searing, hungry kiss. She met his tongue, felt the warm slide of it against the roof her mouth, and then tangled her own around his. His arms tightened around her and slid down her back, cradling her hips and then farther, curving possessively under her bottom. Callie arched forward and wrapped her legs around his hips. She pressed into him, all need, all want. She felt him hard against her and a rush of warmth pooled between her thighs.

"Where's your bedroom?" he muttered against her lips.

"Down the hall, first door on the left."

He kissed her again and stood up, lifting her with effortless strength, and strode down the hallway, shouldering the door open. The small lamp cast shadows around the room and created a welcoming intimacy. Noah placed her on the bed as though she were a fragile doll, flipped off his shoes, shucked off his shirt and lay down beside her.

He kissed her again, her lips, her throat, her neck, and dispensed with the four buttons holding her top together. His eyes glittered when he saw the white lace bra.

"You are lovely," he said, tracing a finger up and over the generous swell of cleavage.

She moved to her knees and slowly inched down the sweat bottoms, dispensing them to the floor. He looked at her with open desire and ran one finger from the top of her neck to the base of her spine, touching the edge of her briefs.

"A tattoo?"

The winged horse looked majestic in flight and Noah moaned his approval as he reached for her and coaxed her to lie beside him. He kissed her again, long and slow, branding her with his kisses, making her his own. He cupped her breasts and gently caressed them. His tongue trailed across her skin, brushing across the edge of the lace. Her nipples ached for his touch, the feel of his mouth, his tongue.

"Take it off," she begged. "Please."

He did so with remarkable efficiency, flicking the hooks at the back with his thumb.

"You've done that before," she breathed.

He chuckled. "Not for a *very* long time," he said as he chucked the bra to the floor and his mouth closed over one straining nipple.

Callie felt the pleasure of it through to her feet. She gripped his shoulders, wanting more, needing more. It was like nothing on earth. His breath was hot against the hardened peak as he suckled. He placed his leg between hers and Callie bucked against him. Pleasure ricocheted over every nerve ending as the abrasive denim he wore rubbed against her sex. She reached down to touch him, felt him shudder as her hand slid across the hardness of his erection straining against his jeans. Her hand moved up, over the zipper, to the belt and she pulled the leather strap free and flicked the top button. Her fingers played with the silky hair arrowing downward.

He groaned and kissed her again, taking her mouth with such hot, scorching possession Callie arched her back, straining off the bed. His hand moved over her skin, her shoulders, her hip and across her belly, then dipped below the tiny triangle of fabric covering her. She felt an intense pleasure as his fingers sought access between the sweet, wet folds and found the tiny nub waiting for his touch.

"Oh, Noah."

He touched her, softly at first, finding the rhythm she liked. She was so wet and welcoming he was surprised he was able to control himself. But he took a deep breath, and another, in between kissing her beautiful mouth. He wasn't going to rush loving her, no matter how badly his body wanted release. He had lips to kiss, breasts to worship, skin to touch and taste. Things he dreamed of doing since the first time he'd met her.

And he would. All night and into the morning.

She moved beneath the pressure of his hand, spreading her thighs trustingly, saying his name over and over. Noah thought he might explode. He felt her tense, heard the change in her breathing, felt her stiffen, waiting, climbing. His aching arousal pushed against his pants. She rocked against the pressure of his hand and he cupped her, then released, then cupped her again. He felt the pulse of her orgasm through his fingertips, saw her skin flush with pleasure and heard her earthy moans of satisfaction.

Desire for her washed over him; love for her filled every cell, every ounce of his blood, and every inch of his skin. He kissed her again—wild, needy kisses that she returned.

"I've never…" she whispered. "Amazing."

Noah dragged the briefs over her thighs, suddenly impatient to see her, marveling at how beautiful she was. He licked her breasts, her rib cage, her belly and lower. He kissed her gently, exploring the soft, moist flesh with his tongue, tasting the sweet musky scent that was uniquely hers. She was incredibly responsive, moaning her pleasure. Her hands gripped his shoulders as he continued his erotic kiss. When he trailed his lips back up across her stomach she writhed beneath him.

He was so hungry for her, so desperate to lose himself inside her, his entire body shook. She held on—his shoulders, his back, his waist.

When her hands hung from his belt, she whispered. "You're wearing too many clothes."

Noah got rid of his jeans and briefs in seconds and returned to her side.

She touched him, enclosing her fingers around his erection and he almost jumped out of his skin.

It's been too long since I've done this...

He took a deep breath and filled his lungs with air. Her touch was gentle, almost uncertain. Noah covered her hand with his and whispered encouragement. She didn't need much. She caressed him from the tip to the base, slowly, building a steady rhythm, driving him crazy with need. All he could think of was Callie—of this beautiful woman who held him, touched him, kissed him back with so much passion he felt truly humbled.

He took a moment and withdrew a foil packet from his wallet. She took the condom, her hands unsteady as she sheathed him. He let her do it and when the pressure became too much, when the need to be inside her drew the breath from his throat in a ragged groan, Noah moved over her. He kissed her and she parted her thighs. He entered her slowly, kissing her more, mimicking the movement of his body as she accepted him inside her

She moved, stretching to take him in, wriggling in a deliciously sexy way. Finally, he was home, filling her, more a part of her than he'd ever been of anyone.

There would never be a moment like this again...their first time...he'd remember the feeling for the rest of his life.

Noah rested his weight on his elbows and looked into her face. She smiled. He touched her hair, remembering how it was one of the first things he'd noticed about her. Such beautiful, luscious hair fanned around the pillow. He kissed her, glorious hot kisses she returned. When he moved against her she moaned, meeting his movements, matching the steady rhythm building between them. All he could feel was Callie, her heat, her wetness surrounding him, enslaving him. He heard her soft cries of pleasure, almost felt them through to his soul as her body arched and shuddered beneath him.

And finally, when the pressure built until he couldn't hold off any longer, it claimed him with white-hot fury, taking him over the edge, ripping through him with the sheer intensity and power of release.

"I love you, Callie." He breathed the words, feeling them with every fiber inside him.

Callie waited until Noah withdrew from her and fell back against the pillow before she took a breath.

I love you...

He'd said the words. It could have been an impulse, a sex-induced moment of euphoria where anything goes. A kind of mid-orgasmic madness. But Callie doubted it. Noah wasn't the kind of man who did anything by half-measures.

He loves me.

He took her hand and kissed her knuckles. "Are you okay?"

I'm out of my mind.

"Oh, yes."

He grinned and closed his eyes. "You're so beautiful."

She felt beautiful. She felt wholly desired and so completely pleasured all she could think of was experiencing it again and again. Callie touched his chest and felt him tense as she played with one flat nipple, then the other. She leaned forward and licked the spot and smiled as the small bud peaked beneath the gentle flick of her tongue. He lay perfectly still and for a moment she thought he'd fallen asleep. But, no—he was smiling, taking long breaths, letting her explore. She kissed his shoulder, nipping at his skin with her teeth before licking the spot. She ran her hand down his stomach and lingered at his belly button, playing with the soft hair trailing downward. When her finger inched lower he quickly covered her hand with his.

"Give me a couple of hours, okay?"

Callie maneuvered her hand from his and grazed her knuckles over him. "I'll give you an hour."

As it turned out he only needed forty minutes. Then Noah made love to her again. He teased her, taunted her with his mouth and tongue and finally, when she thought she could stand no more, he flipped over and dragged her on top. He held her hips, allowing her to ease her body onto his, taking him in, sheathing him inside her. Callie felt wild and wanton as she rode above him. He linked her fingers through his and he supported her weight as she moved, slowly at first, savoring each delicious slide. Then he pulled her forward and sucked her nipples every time her breasts bounced near his mouth. She flung her head back, driving harder, feeling the pressure build and calling his name as pleasure flooded every cell. He lifted off the bed as his climax ripped through him and Callie clenched her internal muscles, taking everything, giving everything, loving him more in that moment than she'd ever imagined she could love anyone.

Spent, they lay together, legs entwined. After a while she rolled onto her stomach and he fingered the tattoo at the base of her spine.

"Do you have any idea how sexy that is?" he said, kissing her shoulder.

"Uh, no. How?"

Callie felt his breath against her skin. "Shall I show you?"

She curled her fingers through the dark smatter of hair on his chest. "Absolutely."

They lingered in bed for another half hour then took a shower together. Afterward Callie made roast beef and mustard sandwiches and they sat in front of the television and watched a rerun of David Letterman.

By midnight they were back in bed, lying on their sides, facing one another.

"So," she said, touching his face. "You're staying?"

He frowned. "Of course."

Callie closed her eyes, feeling safe, feeling loved.

Waking up beside the man who loved you really was the most wonderful way to start a new day. Especially when that man roused you with a trail of kisses along your shoulder blade.

"Good morning," he said softly, slanting his mouth over hers.

Callie smiled against his lips. "Yes, it is."

"What are your plans for today?" he asked, moving from her mouth to her jaw and then to the sensitive spot below her earlobe.

"Oh, the usual," she said on a dreamy sigh. "Well, I used to have a student at eight o'clock."

"Used to?"

"She's with someone else now."

He smiled. "Actually, that's not working out so well."

"Oh. Why not?"

"Lily wants what she wants," he replied, still kissing her. "And she wants you."

"Janelle's a good teacher."

"Not as good as you," he countered. "Then again, I don't imagine anyone is."

Callie heard the lovely compliment and sighed contentedly. "Bring her back next week."

"She'd like that," he said.

"Good. What about you?" she asked. "What are your plans?"

"I've got to pick the kids up this morning. Do you feel like doing something later?"

Callie ran her hand down his chest and lower, lingering past his belly. "What did you have in mind?"

"The beach?"

Callie's hand stilled. "You mean…all together?" A family day out, that's what he meant. *I'm not ready for that yet.*

"That was the idea."

She shifted across the bed and grabbed her gown. "We'll see what happens." She stood up and slipped efficiently into the wrap. "How about breakfast?"

Fifteen minutes later Noah emerged from the shower, dressed and sporting an incredibly sexy shadow of beard on his face. When he entered the kitchen she passed him coffee and a plate topped with some kind of charred-looking bread.

"What's that?" he asked, looking at the contents on the plate.

"Toasted bagel."

He didn't look convinced. "Okay." He sat down, grabbed the toast and took a bite. "You were right," he said easily. "You can't cook."

Callie smiled. "Told ya."

He put down the toast and looked at her. "Are you okay?"

She shrugged and turned toward the countertop. "Of course."

"No regrets?"

Callie shook her head. She had no regrets about making love with him. "No."

"You look far away."

She swallowed, wondering when he'd gotten to know her so well. "I'm right here. Promise."

He drank his coffee and then stood. "I have to get going," he said when he reached her. He turned her in his arms. "But I'll call you later."

"I'd like that."

He kissed her softly and ran his hands over her hips. "I'll let myself out."

She nodded. "Okay."

Noah kissed her again and Callie didn't let out her breath until she heard the soft click of the front screen door closing behind him.

So, what now? She didn't have a clue. He'd said he loved her and she hadn't said it back.

And pretty soon, Callie was certain, he would want to know why not.

Chapter Eleven

Something was wrong. Noah felt it, sensed it. As he drove to his parents' house to pick up the kids he couldn't get the thought out of his mind. She'd retreated. She'd pulled back into a place he couldn't reach. The passionate woman he'd made love with had been absorbed by the woman he remembered from weeks earlier. The woman who didn't want to get involved.

Did she regret it? Was that it? She'd said no. But how could he be sure?

Noah certainly wasn't about to regret the most incredible sex he'd ever had. Because it was more than that. More than sex. Just…more. More everything. More in a way he'd never imagined possible. Touching Callie, loving her, waking up beside her had filled the empty place he'd had inside him for so long.

But the niggling thought stayed with him.

I said I love you. And she didn't say it back.

He'd felt it. In her touch, her sighs, the tears shining in her blue eyes. But, as much as he tried to convince himself it didn't matter, he knew he wanted the words.

He *needed* the words.

When he pulled into the driveway of his parents' home he saw Evie's car outside. His sister was in the kitchen, baking alongside their mother, while the twins and Jamie were in the backyard tormenting his father with a game of Twister.

His mother and sister smiled when he entered the room and then looked at each other.

"Hi. The kids are out the back," Evie said, elbow deep in a large bowl of dough. "Poor Dad," she said with a laugh.

When M.J. trounced into the room moments later, Noah felt the full scrutiny of three sets of curious female eyes.

"Is that a hickey on your neck?" M.J. asked with straight-faced innocence.

Noah's hand instinctively went to his throat.

"Gotcha," M.J. laughed.

"You should never have been taught how to speak," he said quietly, removing his hand and trying not to look self-conscious.

"So, are there wedding bells in the air?" M.J. asked with a big grin.

He scowled. "Watch yourself, kid."

"We have it on good authority."

Noah looked at M.J. and then his mother and Evie.

"Jamie said something this morning," Evie explained. "He's quite excited about the idea."

Noah remembered the conversation he'd had in the truck with the kids. He turned to his mother. "Thanks for watching them."

"How's Maddy?" Evie asked, still digging into dough.

"Broken arm."

"She's lucky Callie was there," Evie said. "Lily called and told us what happened."

He nodded. "Quite the hotline you girls have going."

"Well you never tell us anything," M.J. complained.

Nor did he intend to. "With good reason," he quipped. "Thanks again," he said to his mother, Barbara, who patted his shoulder affectionately.

It took ten minutes to finish saying goodbye and load the kids in the truck. Noah collected Lily on the way home, declining Angela's offer for coffee. When he got home he called Callie, amused by his own eagerness. She answered her cell on the seventh ring and he wondered if she'd considered not picking up. She sounded friendly enough and they talked for a while. She told him she had a new student that afternoon and would have to take a rain check on his idea for the beach.

Noah didn't push the idea. He ended the call with an invitation to his parents' home for the coming Saturday. But instinct told him something was wrong.

Callie knew Noah felt her pull back. And she knew she was acting like a first-rate coward. One mention of his kids and she'd panicked. It wasn't remotely rational. But since when was fear ever rational?

The kids were part of him. His blood. His life.

If she wanted Noah—and she did—then she had to learn how to deal with the reality of his children. She had to love them with her whole heart.

And without really understanding why, her heart simply didn't feel big enough for all that love. It was something she needed to talk to him about. He was smart. If he hadn't figured it out already, he would soon enough. He'd sensed something was wrong, and Callie knew if they had any chance of a future together they needed complete honesty between them.

But she put it off.

On Saturday night they were going to his parents' home for an anniversary party.

She waited on the porch for him to collect her while counting bugs brave enough to aim flight at the mosquito zapper hung from the ceiling. She was nervous about meeting his family. Foolish, she supposed. She already knew Evie, and M.J. and Cameron and she suspected his parents were good people—they would have to be to have raised such a son.

He arrived on time and her stomach did a silly roll when he got out of the truck. He looked great in dark cargo pants and a polo shirt. Her heart crunched up. The kids were in the backseat, she noticed, minus Lily, and she wondered if that was why he didn't kiss her.

"You look beautiful," he said as she got into his vehicle.

Callie smiled and looked in the back, and the three younger children greeted her with a chorus of hellos. They were clearly excited to see her. Shame licked along her spine. They were great kids. And they genuinely cared for her.

I just have to let myself love them without guilt. Without feeling like I'm letting go of Ryan.

Because *that* was what she was afraid of. Losing Ryan. Forgetting Ryan. Replacing Ryan.

"Where's Lily?" she asked, pushing the idea aside for the moment. She'd concentrate on the present and enjoy the moment. There was time for thoughts later.

"With Evie," he replied. "They're meeting us there."

He drove into Crystal Point and pulled up outside a large, two-story home one street back from The Parade in a quiet cul-de-sac. The gardens were immaculate; the home looked like it was made for a large family. A couple of cars were parked in the driveway and he pulled up off the curb.

The moment she walked into their home, Barbara and Bill Preston greeted her with smiles and a warm welcome. Barbara hugged her son closely and Callie didn't miss the gentle way she ruffled his hair and smiled at him, like they had a lovely secret between them. The twins and Jamie clearly adored their grandparents and were rustled away with their grandfather to play a game of Wii bowling before the guests began to arrive.

"The girls are in the kitchen," Barbara said. "Join us after you've shown Callie the house."

Callie followed when Noah led her upstairs.

"So," she said, standing in the middle of a room at the top of the stairway. "This was your bedroom when you were growing up?"

He smiled. "Yep."

It appeared to be as typical a teenage boy's room as you'd get. Blue quilt and accessories, shelves filled with trophies, faded posters of rock bands on the walls. She took a closer look at the trophies—some for sports, some for academics.

"So you were a jock?" she asked, picking up a medal awarded for a code of football she'd vaguely heard of. She fingered another one granted for rowing. "Looks like you were good at it." She placed the medal down. "How old were you when you moved out?"

"Eighteen," he said. "I moved to Brisbane to study engineering."

"Is that where you met your wife?"

He took a step toward her. "Ex-wife," he corrected. "And no. I always knew I'd take the business over from my father, but I wanted to experience life a bit before I came back to Crystal Point." He picked an old volleyball off the floor and tossed it onto the narrow bed. "I finished my degree in three years, then took off. I backpacked in Europe for about a year, until my money ran out. Then I worked at a pub in London trying to save enough for my fare back home, which is where I met Margaret. She was there on a dancing scholarship. We hooked up and I stayed for another year or so. But I always intended to come back." He shrugged. "A couple of months after I got home she called to say she was pregnant."

"And then you married her?" She hoped he didn't hear the tinge of jealousy in her tone.

He reached for her. "Let's not talk about that, okay?" His arms tightened around her. "I'd much rather kiss you."

And he did. So thoroughly Callie thought she might pass out.

When they returned downstairs the kitchen was a hive of activity. Mary-Jayne was there decorating a cheesecake, and Evie was wrapping potatoes in aluminum foil.

Both sisters' eyes popped wide when they saw them, but to their credit they didn't say anything. Lily was there, glaring at Callie with confused eyes. The teenager headed to the living room and mumbled something about how it was "typical" and no one cared what she wanted.

"Should I go and talk with her?" Callie asked.

Noah shook his head. "She'll be fine."

"He's right," Evie said. "She's just reacting. Lily doesn't know how she's feeling."

"All teenagers are obnoxious," Mary-Jayne announced. "Remember how I was?"

Noah smiled. "Was?"

Everyone laughed and Callie was struck by the deep affection they shared for one another. It made her miss her own family.

Within half an hour the celebration had taken itself outside. The outdoor entertainment area was huge and had been transformed with a long buffet table and chairs for those inclined to sit. Music filtered through strategically placed speakers. People started arriving, including Cameron Jakowski and Fiona, who were both well acquainted with the Prestons. He shook Noah's hand, kissed Barbara on the cheek while stealing a piece of cheese off a plate and teased M.J. about her Don't Blame Me…I Voted For The Other Guy apron.

Fiona gave Callie an unexpected hug. "I'm glad you're here," she whispered. She grabbed Callie's arm and pulled her aside. "So you're really dating now?" Fiona asked in a ludicrously excited voice.

Dating? They were lovers—did that count as dating? "We're…something."

She looked across the deck to where Noah stood with Cameron—and also the most beautiful woman Callie had ever seen, decked out in what was clearly a high-end designer dress of deep red and incredible four-inch heels. "Who's that?" she asked.

Fiona looked up and her pretty face turned into a grimace. "Princess Grace."

"Huh?'

"Noah's sister," she explained. "She's some hot-shot businesswoman in New York. A real cold fish. You can freeze ice on her—"

"I get the picture." Callie smiled. "She's stunning."

Fiona made a face. "Yeah, yeah. Beautiful and about as pleasant as global warming."

Callie's eyes widened. "Would your opinion have anything to do with the fact she's talking to Cameron right now?"

Fiona blushed. "No point," she admitted. "We're destined to be *just friends*."

Callie sensed the disappointment in her friend's voice. "There's someone out there for you."

Fiona raised both her brows. "Spoken like a woman who's fallen in love."

Callie froze when she felt a strong arm unexpectedly moved around her waist. She looked at Fiona and her friend's eyes popped wide open.

Had he heard Fiona's teasing?

She felt his breath in her ear. "Dance with me?"

She pulled back. "Dance where?"

"By the pool," he said.

Callie looked toward the pool area. Strategically placed candles created a soft, romantic mood and she couldn't resist joining the few couples already swaying to the music. "Okay."

Moments later she was in his arms. His parents were there, she noticed, dancing cheek to cheek and clearly still in love after many years of marriage.

"What are you thinking?" he asked.

"That your parents look happy together."

Noah smiled. "They make it look easy."

She looked at him, conscious of how close they were as he kissed her forehead gently. She could feel his thighs against her own every time they moved and a jolt of need arrowed low in her belly.

She knew what he read in her eyes, knew he could feel it in the vibration coming off her skin. "Ah, Callie," he said, so close to her ear his mouth was against the lobe. He kissed the sensitive spot. "I want to take you home and make love to you."

"I want that, too," she breathed.

"In my bed?" he queried.

His bed? Somewhere they hadn't ventured. "I'm not…"

"Not ready for that?"

Callie sighed. "I want us to be close, Noah. Really, I do."

"As what? Lovers?"

They were lovers. And she wanted to make love with him again. But she knew that for Noah that wouldn't be enough. "Yes…for now."

"We're going to have to talk about the future at some—"

"I know," she said quickly and pressed closer. *But later,* she thought cowardly.

For the moment she wanted to enjoy the dance, the moment, the knowledge that she was safe in his arms. She rested her head against his shoulder.

"Callie?"

"Mmm," she murmured, inhaling the scent of him, the mixtures of some citrusy shampoo and masculine soap.

"What Fiona said…is it true?"

So he had heard?

Callie's gaze dropped. "I…feel it."

"But you can't say it?" If he was frustrated by her response, he didn't show it. He rubbed her cheek with his thumb. "One day, maybe?"

She nodded, her head and heart pounding.

"One day," she said on a breath. "I promise."

Becoming lovers changed everything. With complete intimacy came vulnerability. Noah was an incredible lover—caring, unselfish and delightfully energetic. But despite all that, Callie felt the wedge growing between them, gaining momentum. *It's of my own making.* And she was positive Noah could feel it, too.

He didn't say a word. But he was on edge. Like he was waiting, anticipating.

He's waiting for me to say something. He's waiting for me to say "I love you…" or "I can't be with you…"

Four days later she still felt it, even as she rolled over, caught up in a tangle of limbs and sighed with a mix of pleasure and utter exhaustion.

It was light inside her bedroom, despite the thick curtains being drawn. The sun peeked through, teasing her, making her feel just that little bit wicked. Speaking of wicked, she thought, running lazy fingers through the hair on Noah's chest, which was still rising and falling as he took in deep breaths. He had such a wickedly good body…

"You know," he said between breaths. "I really can't keep taking time off during the day." He smiled. "Not that this isn't a great way to spend the afternoon."

She fingered one flat nipple. "Mmm…great."

"I've got a business to run."

The nipple pebbled. "Mmm…I know."

"My staff will start wondering why I'm leaving every afternoon."

She trailed her fingertips downward. "You could tell them it's a long lunch."

He smiled. "Speaking of lunch, we should probably eat something."

"Food for energy, hey?" Callie wriggled and rolled toward him. "Am I working you too hard?" she asked, smiling and kissing his rib cage.

Noah reached for her chin and tilted her face upward. "I'm not one of your horses you have to exercise to keep in shape."

Callie pulled herself up and lay on top of him. "No, you're not. I mean, I do love my horses…" She trailed kisses across his jaw. "But you're…I mean I'm…" The words got lost.

Noah cupped her cheek and made her look at him. "Don't backpedal now."

For the past three days they'd spent each afternoon in bed together. Callie couldn't get enough of him. She couldn't feel him enough, kiss him enough and love him enough. But she knew it was a fantasy. A fabulous fantasy—but still a fantasy. Being lovers, uninterrupted by the realities of life, wasn't sustainable.

They *had* to talk. About their future. About his children. About Lily.

About Ryan.

"Are you free Friday night?" he asked instead. "I thought you could come over and let me cook for you. What do you say?"

"I have a competition on Saturday," she replied. "And Fiona's staying over Friday night so we can get an early start."

"Right. What about Saturday night?"

She moved, shifting off him. "I'll probably be quite tired. Can I see how I feel after the comp?"

He sat up and draped the sheet over his legs. "Sure. And Sunday?"

"Lily's having a lesson Sunday."

Callie averted her eyes, trying not to get distracted by his chest as she slipped out of bed. She felt completely comfortable walking naked around the room and liked the way he admired her as she retrieved her clothes from the floor. She looked at the clock on the bedside table. It was three-thirty. "We should get moving. I have a student at four o'clock. And Lily—"

"Usually comes here Wednesdays," he said when she hesitated. "Yes, I know."

"Well I wouldn't want her to see you…see us…"

Noah frowned and pushed back the bedclothes. "She knows about us, Callie. I took you to meet my parents…she also knows I wouldn't do that unless we were serious."

"I just—"

"At least, *I'm* serious," he said, cutting her off. "You—I'm not so sure."

Callie inhaled a shaky breath. "Of course I'm serious. I just don't want to upset Lily."

Noah reached for his clothes, which were still on the floor. "Lily will have to get used to it." He pulled on his briefs and chinos and started adjusting his belt but then stopped. He looked at her. "You know, Callie, Lily is precious to me… but she doesn't get to decide who I fall in love with."

Callie's blood stilled. Her eyes never left his face. "Can't we just keep a low profile for a while?" she asked quietly and grabbed an elastic band off the dresser to tie up her hair.

He shrugged. "I won't hide our relationship from my kids."

Callie took a deep breath. "I'm only asking for a little time."

"It sounds like you're asking me to lie to my children."

She didn't like the accusation and quickly gave him a look that said so. "That's not what I want. But please just respect my wishes."

"As you respect mine?"

"That's not fair."

Noah pulled his shirt over his shoulders. "Neither is making me feel as though you're not in this for the long haul."

"Because I want to take things slowly?"

He grabbed his keys from the bedside table. "Slowly? Ripping one another's clothes off every time we're together isn't exactly slow, Callie." Noah grabbed his shoes and sat on the edge of the bed to put them on. When he was done he stood, turned and faced her. "It's pretty clear you don't want to spend time with the kids," he said quietly.

She shook her head, wanting to deny it because it sounded so incredibly callous.

"I can see in your eyes that you want to negotiate," he said. "And if I loved you less, Callie…maybe I could."

"Noah, I—"

"I've been hammered in the past," he said quietly and came around the bed. "And honestly, I didn't think I'd ever want to take a chance at feeling this way. I didn't think I'd ever want to share my life with someone again…or trust someone…or maybe get married again. But if I learned anything from those years with my ex-wife, it was that I intend on living the rest of my life true to myself. That's what I'm trying to do here." He took a deep breath. "And I can't be your lover if that's all it's ever going to be."

Callie couldn't move. "I don't know what to say to you."

He stood barely feet in front of her. "Well, when you figure it out, maybe you can let me know."

"Don't leave like this," she said shakily. "Not after we've..." She looked at the bed and the rumpled bedclothes.

"Sex isn't enough for me," he said. "Not even incredible sex." He rattled his keys impatiently. "I told you I couldn't and wouldn't enter into something casual. My kids deserve better...and frankly, so do I." He headed for the door and once there, turned back to face her. "And, Callie, so do you."

It took about thirty seconds for her feet to work. By then she'd already heard the front door close.

I'm losing him.

So do something.

Callie pushed determination into her legs and followed him. When she swung the front screen door wide she saw two things—Lily's bicycle left haphazardly at the bottom of the stairs and Lily standing by the bottom step, glaring up at her father who stood on the porch.

She looked like thunder. "Great," she said when she saw Callie. "This is just great."

"It's nothing to do with you, Lily," Noah said quietly.

"Ha." She rolled her green eyes. "It will be when it turns to crap. Adults can't get anything right." She crossed her arms. "It always turns to crap. Always. Look at Maddy's stepfather. And my mother." She made a pained, huffing sound. "She didn't hang around." She gave Callie a searing, accusing look. "And this will be the same."

Callie wanted to assure the teenager that it wouldn't. But the words got stranded on the end of her tongue.

"How about you move your bike to the truck and I'll take you home?" Noah said.

Lily's mouth pursed. "I came to see Samson," she said hotly. "See—it's starting already. You guys had a fight and now I have to do what you want."

"We haven't fought," Callie heard herself deny.

Lily's brows snapped up. "Yeah, right." She pointed to her father. "He comes out and slams the door and you come out after. That's a fight. I'm not a little kid, you know. So go ahead and fight—see if I care."

She turned around and raced toward the stables. Noah took the steps to go after her but Callie called him back.

"Let me go," Callie offered. "I'll talk with her. You know, girl to woman." She pulled on her boots near the door and headed toward the stables.

Callie found Lily by the fence in the yard behind the stables. Samson was with her, butting his whiskery chin against Lily's hand as he searched for morsels of carrot. As she watched them together she saw the bond forming between the teenager and the lovable gelding. It made her remember the early days of her relationship with Indiana and how sixteen years later they were still together.

"He's very attached to you," she said to Lily as she approached.

Lily shrugged. "He's a good horse." She stroked his neck. "Maybe I'll get to have a horse of my own one day."

Callie reached the fence and laid one boot on the bottom rung. "I'm sure you will. Lily, about your dad and me. I want to explain—"

"I think my dad loves you," Lily said unexpectedly.

Callie blinked away the heat in her eyes. "I know he does."

Lily took a deep breath. "So…do you love him?"

Callie felt the weight of admission grasp her shoulders with two hands. She wasn't about to deny it. She wouldn't dishonor what she had shared with Noah by doing that. "Yes… very much."

Lily's jaw clenched with emotion. "But what if it doesn't work out?"

Callie put her arms around Lily's thin shoulders and experienced a fierce burst of protectiveness inside her chest. "What if it does?"

Lily swallowed hard and flashed defiant eyes at her as she pulled away. "You don't know that. People leave all the time."

"Not all people," Callie assured her.

Lily shrugged but Callie wasn't fooled. She was in tremendous pain.

"Yeah, well, I know Dad said I could come back here for lessons, but I think I'll stick with Janelle." Lily lifted her chin, patted Samson one more time and pushed herself away from the fence. "She's a pretty good teacher after all. And she's got way better horses than you."

She took off and Callie gave her a lead of fifty feet before following. When she reached Noah, Lily was already tucked inside the truck with her bicycle in the back.

Another car had turned into the driveway. Her four o'clock appointment.

"I'll call you," he said quietly.

"Sure. Noah…" Her words trailed and she waited for him to respond.

He did. "I'm trying to give you space, Callie. I'm trying to understand everything you've been through and how hard it is for you to trust me, to trust *us*. But at some point you're going to have to meet me halfway. When you're ready for that, give me a call."

He walked off. There was no touch. No kiss. Only the sound of his truck disappearing over the gravel as he drove off.

Halfway. She was still thinking about his words the following afternoon. And trust. It didn't take a genius to figure the two things went hand in hand. Callie left Joe in charge of bedding the horses down for the night and headed into Bellandale. She stopped at a popular Mexican restaurant and ordered takeout, then drove back toward Crystal Point. By the time she pulled up outside Noah's house it was past five o'clock. An unfamiliar flashy-looking blue car was out front, parked next to Noah's truck.

Harry came off his usual spot on the porch and ambled toward her as she unloaded the plastic carry bags containing the food. She was a few steps from the porch when the front opened and Officer Cameron Jakowski stepped outside.

He flashed a too-brilliant smile when he saw her. "Hey, Callie."

"Hi. Is Noah—"

"On the phone," he supplied, rattling his keys. "Hey, I was going to call you."

He was? For what? "Really?"

"I have some news about your recent entanglement with the law." He was smiling and she relaxed.

Apparently the men who'd rammed her trailer had pleaded guilty and were due for a hearing in front of the local magistrate. Cameron suspected they'd get a suspended sentence, but Callie hoped it would at least be enough to stop them from doing anything that stupid again. She told him her insurance had covered the repairs to her trailer.

She said goodbye to Cameron and waited until he'd driven off before she headed inside the house. She could hear Noah's voice and followed the sound until she reached the kitchen. He stood by the counter and had his back to her, the telephone cradled against his ear. He still wore his work clothes and the perfectly tailored chinos did little to disguise the body beneath. Callie's heart hammered behind her ribs just thinking about it.

He turned immediately and looked surprised to find her in his kitchen. He quickly ended the call. "I didn't expect to see you tonight."

She held the bags in front of her. “I brought dinner,” she said and placed the bags and her tote on the granite top.

“Don’t you have a competition tomorrow?”

Callie nodded. “I do. But I thought dinner might be a good idea.” She tried to sound cheerful. “Where are the kids?”

“With my mother.”

Callie looked at the large quantity of food she’d bought. “Oh.”

“They’ll be home in an hour.”

“And Lily?”

He didn’t move. He didn’t break eye contact. “At Maddy’s, as usual.”

Callie was concerned for his daughter. “Is she okay?”

“She’s quiet,” he replied. “But Lily gets like that.”

Callie took a couple of steps toward him. “She was upset the other day. I tried to talk with her…but I don’t know if I got through. She said she didn’t want to come back to Sandhills.”

“Lily doesn’t know what she wants.” He pushed himself away from the counter. “She likes you but doesn’t want to admit it.”

The irony in his words weren’t missed. Hadn’t he said the same thing about their relationship only yesterday? She’d come to his house to talk, to explain. It was time to open up.

She pulled out a chair and sat down at the table. “Halfway.”

“What?”

“That’s why I’m here. Yesterday you said I needed to meet you halfway. So, I’m here.” She drew in a breath. “Halfway.”

“Callie, I—”

“You know, all my life I’ve pretty much done what I wanted,” she said quietly. “I left school at seventeen—I didn’t even finish senior year. I wanted to ride. I wanted to be with Craig. And nothing could have stopped me from realizing my dream. Looking back, I was quite self-indulgent. But then I got pregnant and my life changed. Suddenly it wasn't just about me."

"Kids do change your priorities."

Callie nodded. "And I wanted the baby. Having Ryan was the most incredible gift. Even though he only lived for two days I will treasure those moments forever."

"You should, Callie," he said, with such gentleness. "You *should* celebrate his life."

"And get on with my own, is that what you mean?" She sighed heavily. "I want to. And I am trying. Despite how it might seem, I *have* accepted the fact I'll probably never have children. I know people can live full and meaningful lives without having kids."

"But?"

Moisture sprang into her eyes. "But I met you. And you have these incredible children who look at me with such… hope." Tears hovered on her lashes. "I know what they want. I know what they need. And I certainly know what they deserve. But because of Ryan…because I feel so much hurt…I don't know if I could ever give it to them. I don't know if I could ever feel what they would need me to feel."

He looked at her in that way no one else ever had. "Because you didn't carry them? Because you didn't give birth to them?"

She nodded, ashamed of her feelings but unable to deny the truth of them. "Partly, yes."

He stepped closer, bridging the gap. "Do you really think genetics make a parent, Callie?"

She shrugged, without words, without voice.

"What about all the adopted kids out there, the fostered kids, the babies born to a surrogate—do you think their parents love them less because they carry different blood?" His eyes never left hers. "Blood doesn't make you a parent."

"I know it sounds…selfish. It sounds self-absorbed and I'm ashamed to have these kinds of feelings. But, Noah, you have four children who—"

"One," he said quietly, silencing her immediately. "I have one child."

Chapter Twelve

Noah saw her shock and felt the heaviness of his admittance crush right down between his shoulder blades.

"What?"

"I have one *biological* child," he said with emphasis. "I have two who I know definitely aren't mine, another who might not be."

"But Lily—"

"Is mine," he said. "The twins, no…Jamie, I'm not sure."

She looked staggered by his admission and he couldn't blame her. "But you love them so much," she whispered incredulously.

He nodded and fought the lump of emotion that suddenly formed in his throat. "Of course I do. They are *mine,* Callie, despite how they were conceived. That's what I'm trying to say to you—it doesn't matter how they came into the world. What matters is how they are raised, nurtured, loved."

She nodded and he hoped she believed him. He loved her

so much and wanted to share his life with her and marry her as soon as she was ready. He wanted to ask her now. He wanted to drop to his knees and worship her and beg her to become his wife. But he knew they could only have that if she was prepared to accept his children as her own.

"And you're sure the twins aren't yours?"

"Yeah. Margaret took off to Paris to visit her mother and when she came back announced she was pregnant with twins. I knew straight away they weren't mine."

"You did?"

"I'd stopped sleeping with her a long time before. When I suspected she was cheating," he admitted, "I stuck it out for as long as I could for the kids. But I knew the day would come when we'd split. Margaret's moods were unpredictable. Looking back I'm certain she suffered from some kind of depression."

"What did you do?"

"I said I wanted a divorce. I was prepared to let her have the house, but I demanded joint custody." He moved to the table and pulled out a chair. "But instead she walked out after the twins were born. I think she knew, on some level, that leaving them was the best thing she could do for them. She just didn't want them."

"And Jamie?"

He sat down. "She told me the morning she left. That she wasn't sure if he was my son."

"You must have been devastated." Callie grabbed his hand and held on tight.

He nodded, remembering the shock and disbelief he'd experienced. "For about ten seconds I thought I'd been robbed of my son. But that feeling didn't last. He's my child in every way that counts. Just as the twins are."

"Does anyone know?"

"Cameron knows. My parents. Evie. And you."

"Do you think you'll ever tell them?"

He shrugged. "I'm not sure. Perhaps when they're older and can comprehend what it means."

He'd thought about it. Wondered how he would ever broach the subject with them.

"They'll understand," she said softly. "They love you."

"And that's really all it takes, Callie."

Callie knew he was right. And when the kids returned home a little while later and raced toward her with hugs full of unbridled excitement she couldn't control the urge to hug them back. Noah's parents stayed for dinner of reheated fajitas, enchiladas and refried beans, and it was such a delightfully animated and loving evening Callie was tempted to ask Noah to go and collect Lily so she could be part of it.

He was an amazing man. He cherished children that weren't his own. But Craig hadn't wanted his own child.

How could I have loved two men who were so very different?

Callie knew she had to let go of her hurt over Craig. And strangely, as though she'd willed it from sheer thought, her anger, the bitterness she'd clung onto, drifted off.

I don't hate Craig anymore.

It felt good to release all the bad feelings that had been weighing her down. And to know she could love again…to know she *did* love again…filled her with an extraordinary sense of peace. But Callie knew she had one more thing to do. One more hurdle to take. The hardest thing of all was ahead of her. It was something she had to do before she could completely let herself love and be loved.

I have to say goodbye to Ryan.

And the only place she could do that was in California.

The following day Callie called her mother, booked her flight for Wednesday evening, and arranged for Joe to stay at the farm for the time she would be away.

She hadn't stayed at Noah's the previous night. Instead, she'd gone home and stared at the ceiling. She hadn't told him of her plans. She was going to his home on Monday night and she would explain it to him. And she prayed he would understand.

On Monday afternoon Angela Spears arrived with Maddy. The young girl flew from the Lexus with lightning speed and showed Callie her cast. There was no lesson for Maddy, but she wanted to pet Sunshine and spend time with the horses.

Both women were surprised to see Noah's truck pull into the driveway and park beside Angela's Lexus.

The kids jumped out, headed straight for Callie and hugged her tightly. Hayley grabbed her hand and Angela didn't miss a thing.

"Goodness, you're popular," she said good-humoredly and looked toward Noah. "With everyone."

Callie blushed and turned her attention to the man who stood smiling. "I didn't expect you this afternoon. Are we still on for tonight?"

He nodded. "Of course. I'm here to pick up Lily," he said. "Is she with that horse?"

Callie shook her head. "Lily's not here."

He frowned. "What do you mean, she's not here?" His gaze snapped toward Angela. "She told me this morning that you'd bring her here this afternoon so I could pick her up."

Angela's face prickled with concern. "I haven't seen Lily since yesterday."

Callie looked at Noah. She saw the alarm in his eyes. "I'm sure she's somewhere close," Callie said quickly. "Perhaps she's with Evie."

"We just left Evie's."

"Well, your parents? Or Mary-Jayne?" she suggested, trying to sound hopeful. "Call them."

He did that while Callie questioned Jamie, but he said he

had no idea where she was. However, he did say he'd noticed her big backpack was missing and her iPod.

"No luck," he said after a few minutes. "I'll try her cell."

It was switched off. Angela called for Maddy and the teenager came toward them swiftly. She stood in front of her mother, wide-eyed, as if sensing the adults around her were on high alert.

"Madison," Angela said quietly. "Do you know where Lily is?"

"I—um…"

"Maddy?" Noah's voice, calm, deep. "Please…where is she?"

Maddy's eyes filled with tears. "I told her not to," she said. "I said she shouldn't do it. But she wouldn't listen to me."

"What do you mean, Madison?" Angela again, in formidable mother mode.

"When she didn't come to school today I knew she had really done it." Maddy took a huge gulp of air. "She's gone."

Gone. Callie's stomach sank. She clutched Noah's arm instinctively.

Noah took a heavy breath. "Where's she gone, Maddy?"

Maddy swallowed, looked to the ground, then back at her mother and clearly knew she had little choice but to tell the truth. "Paris."

Callie was certain their hearts stopped beating. Angela looked like she would hyperventilate. Noah paled when the reality of it hit him.

"How's she getting there?" he asked evenly, but Callie wasn't fooled. He was out of his mind with worry.

Tears flowed down Maddy's check. "She caught the train to Brisbane this morning. She said she was going to buy a ticket at the airport."

"Surely she wouldn't be able to do that," Angela said, all wide-eyed. "Oh, this is bad, this is—"

"Does she have a passport?" Callie asked, cutting off Angela.

Noah nodded. "Yeah. I took the kids to Hawaii last year."

"Why Paris?" Angela asked.

Callie looked at Noah. She knew why, as he did. But it was Maddy Spears who spoke.

"She wants to see her mother."

Callie got Noah into the house so they could make the appropriate telephone calls. She settled the kids in the kitchen with a snack and returned to the living room. Angela left with Maddy, but insisted she'd do whatever was needed to help.

Noah was on the phone, obviously to Cameron by the cryptic conversation. When he hung up he called Evie and instructed her to fill their parents in on the details. "Cameron's going to get her picture to the airport security," he said when he'd hung up.

"That should help," she said. "Is there anything I can do?"

He nodded. "Watch the kids. I have to get to the city as fast as I can," he said. He unclipped his keys and left one by the telephone. "House key," he said. "They'd probably prefer to sleep in their own beds."

Callie didn't hesitate to agree. "I'll take them home soon. You just…go…and call me when you know anything."

"Thanks." He ran a hand across his face. "This is my fault," he said. "I should have paid more attention. She's been quiet since…"

"Since she saw you here last week?"

He nodded and Callie saw the concern in his eyes. She knew what he was thinking, fearing. There were dangers in the big city, people who did bad things, predators waiting to pounce on a naïve young girl from a small town. She rallied instead. "She'll be fine. And she'll be found before you know it." She took a few steps toward him and placed her hands on his chest. "You have to believe that, Noah. For your own peace of mind."

She hugged him close and then watched as he drove off, waiting until she saw the taillights fade before she closed the door. The kids were relaxed enough in her company that they barely questioned their father's quick departure. Jamie talked to her about Lily, though, and because he was such a sensitive child she tried to put his fears at ease the best she could.

She left Joe to bed the horses down for the night, packed a small overnight bag, collected the children and Tessa and took them home.

Noah drove faster than he should have. A flight would have been sensible, but none would have gotten him to Brisbane airport in better time. Thankful that he had a full tank of gas, he drove straight through the four-and-a-half-hour trip without stopping. It was nine-thirty when he raced into the international terminal. He headed directly for airport security and, despite his impatience, was appreciative of their assistance.

"We have her picture here," a female officer told him. "But so far no one matching this description has shown up."

"Her train got in hours ago," Noah told them. "She has to be here somewhere."

"She can't pass this point unless she has a ticket," she assured him.

"Is there any chance she might get one?" he asked, his heart pumping.

"No," the officer said confidently. "The airlines are not in the habit of allowing minors to purchase tickets. You could try the domestic terminal," she said. "If she's resourceful enough, she could think it easier to try for a ticket to Sydney and then perhaps catch a connecting flight."

Noah's head felt like it was about to burst. "I'll go and check." He handed her a business card. "If she turns up here, please call me."

He jumped into a taxi to get to the domestic terminal and once there was scanned by a handheld metal detection device before a uniformed officer led him through. There were plenty of travelers about, browsing the shops; some were sitting in the departure lounges. Noah couldn't see Lily. Panic rose like bile in his throat. What if she wasn't here? What if something had already happened to her? Perhaps she never made it off the train.

He continued his search, checking cafés and a few of the stores that might appeal to a thirteen-year-old girl. He checked every one, showed her picture to as many sales assistants as he could and found some relief when one told him she looked a little familiar.

Fifteen minutes later he was almost out of his mind. He stopped by the escalators and looked up and down the long terminal while the security officer left to check the washrooms. Then just when his hope faded, he noticed a girl, standing alone, looking out of the observation window at the farthest end of the terminal. She had her back to him, and her hair was brown… *Not Lily.*

Noah turned to walk back to the main departure lounge but stopped. He had another look, longer this time. And suddenly his feet were moving toward her. Something about the way she held her shoulders, the angle of her head as she gazed out toward the runway and watched the departing aircraft niggled at him. The departure gates at this end of the terminal were all shut down for the night and she seemed oddly out of place in her solitude.

He kept walking, faster until he was almost at a jog. He halted about thirty feet from her. He noticed details within seconds. She wore a denim skirt and white top. Lily only wore black. And the hair—wrong color completely. And the shoes—not her trademark Doc Martens, but bright pink flip-flops with sequins sewn on them.

But there was a backpack at her feet. Lily's backpack. "Lily?"

She turned and Noah's jaw nearly dropped to his feet. No dark makeup, no piercings, just his daughter's beautiful face staring at him.

"Dad!"

Noah wasn't sure what to expect from her. He didn't have to wait long. She ran toward him and threw herself against him with a sturdy thump. *I have my kid. She's safe.*

"I'm sorry, Dad," she choked the words into his shoulder.

"It's okay." Noah touched her hair. "You scared me to death, Lily."

"I know…I'm so sorry."

"Come and sit down," he said to Lily.

She sat in one of the chairs and Noah retrieved her backpack.

"You travel light," he said, dropping it at her feet. He sat down beside her. "What are you doing here?"

She shrugged and inhaled a shaky breath. "I'm not sure."

"Maddy said you were going to find your mother," he said, gently because he sensed that was all she could cope with. "Is that true?"

Another shrug, this time accompanied by tears. "No. Yes."

Noah felt her pain right through to his bones. "Why now?"

"I wanted to ask her something."

Noah held his breath for a moment. "Do you know where she lives?"

Lily shook her head.

"How did you plan to find her once you got to Paris?" he asked.

She dropped her gaze. "I've got Grandma's address."

Noah could only imagine what seventy-four-year-old Leila would think about having Lily turn up at her door. "So what did you want to ask your mother?"

She shrugged again. "What we did. What *I* did."

"What you did?"

"To make her not want us."

Noah sighed and chose his words carefully. "You didn't do anything, Lily. Your mother was unhappy. And she didn't want to be married to me. But *you,*" he took her hand and squeezed. "You didn't do anything. I promise."

"It feels like she left because of me. I mean, it couldn't have been the others—they were little. And everyone loves little kids."

"It wasn't you," he said again, firmer this time. "Lily, is this really about your mother, or is it Callie?"

Lily looked at him. Her bottom lip quivered and her gaze fell to the floor.

"Are you afraid she'll try to replace your mother?" he asked gently.

Lily turned her face into his shoulder and sobbed against him. "That's just it, Dad," she said brokenly. "I really want her to be replaced. Sometimes I forget what she'd looked like. Jamie doesn't even remember her—it's like she never existed."

"She did exist," Noah said, holding her. "You're proof of that."

Lily hiccupped. "But she left. We weren't enough for her. None of us. If she didn't love us enough to stay…why would someone else? She had to love us, and even that wasn't enough. And Callie, well, she wouldn't *have* to love us, would she? So I thought if I just asked her what made her leave, I could make sure it didn't happen again so that Callie…so that Callie wouldn't leave us, too."

Noah felt pain rip through his chest. Pain for the child

he held in his arms. And he understood, finally. Lily's fears weren't that another woman would come into their life and try to replace the mother she knew. She was afraid another woman might leave them in the same painful fashion.

He pulled back and made her look at him. "You know, Lily, there are no guarantees in any relationship. But if you trust me—you'll trust that I'll always do what's right by you and your sister and brothers."

"I do trust you, Dad," she said, hugging him. "I love you."

"I love you too, kid."

"I'm sorry I ran off," she said, smiling now, even though tears remained in her eyes. "I know you were worried. But I don't think I would have gotten on the plane. I was standing here before, thinking about you and Jamie and the twins and Aunt Evie and everyone else, and thought I'd miss everyone so much if I left. And I'd miss Maddy and Callie and Samson."

Emotion closed his throat. "And I'd miss you, Lily."

"Besides," she said with a sniff, "it's my birthday next week."

Enough said. "Okay. How about we get out of here?"

She reached for her backpack. "So, Dad, you haven't said what a dork I look like."

He ruffled her hair. "I think you look pretty."

She laughed. "Well, the hair's pretty cool…but these shoes have gotta go."

Callie spent the night in Noah's bed, wrapped up in the sheets, secure and safe. It was a lovely room. The huge bed was covered in a quilt in neutral beige and moss green, and the timber walls and silky oak furnishings were rich and warm.

He called her just before ten o'clock and told her that he'd found Lily and they were on their way home. He told her not to wait up and she hung up the telephone, missing him, craving him and feeling relieved he'd found his daughter.

Her heart went out to Lily. To all the kids. And to Noah. Being in his house, sleeping in his bed…it made their relationship seem very *real.* Perhaps for the first time since they'd met. And the responsibility of what that meant weighed heavily. Accepting the children into her heart was only a part of it. First her heart, then her life. Saying goodbye to Ryan was the first step.

But then what?

She'd return to Sandhills and everything would still be there, waiting for her.

Including Noah.

Only, a niggling thought lingered in the back of her mind. What if she couldn't say goodbye to her son? What if it was too much, too hard, too…everything. What then? Could she come back and face Noah and the kids, knowing she'd break their hearts into tiny pieces? Bathing the kids, dressing them in their pajamas, laughing over a botched dinner of grilled cheese and cookies had been wonderful. And she enjoyed their company so much. But there was doubt, too. And fear that she wouldn't measure up. They would expect all of her. An expectation they deserved. Did she have enough left inside herself for all that love?

Later that night, with the kids all tucked into their beds, Tessa locked in the laundry room and Harry guarding the front porch, Callie drifted into sleep.

She was quickly dreaming. Dreaming about Noah, about strong arms and warm lips and gentle hands. She could feel his touch; feel the love in his fingertips as he caressed her back and hips. Callie stretched her limbs, feeling him, wanting him.

And then the dream suddenly wasn't a dream. It was

real. She was in his arms, pressed against his chest. "You're here," she murmured into his throat. "You're home. I'm glad. Lily—"

"Shhhh," he said against her hair. "Lily's fine. Go back to sleep."

When Callie awoke a couple of hours later she could hear the rhythmic sound of the bedside clock and Noah's steady breathing. He lay on his stomach, his face turned away from her. She touched his back, rested her hand on him for a few moments and then slipped out of bed as quietly as she could.

When she padded downstairs a few minutes later she heard young voices whispering. The twins were awake, still in their beds but chatting to each other. Jamie emerged as though he had some kind of adult radar and quickly said he was hungry. Lily's door was still closed and Callie knew she'd still be sleeping. Breakfast was as hit-and-miss as dinner the night before, but the kids didn't complain. She gave them cereal and put on a pot of coffee and when they were done Callie herded them back to their rooms with instructions to stay quiet for at least another hour.

When she returned to the upstairs bedroom Noah was lying on his side with his eyes open. She closed the door softly and sat on the bed. "Sorry, did I wake you?"

He sighed wearily. "It was a long night."

"You should have stayed over and driven back this morning."

"I needed to get back."

"The kids were fine. Another few hours wouldn't have made any difference."

He looked at her. "Okay, I *wanted* to get back. As for them being fine," he said quietly and reached for her hand, "I knew they would be." He kissed her wrist and turned her hand over and kissed her knuckles. "In fact, I can't remember the last time the house was so quiet in the morning."

She smiled. "They're under strict instructions to be as quiet as mice for the next hour."

"What about you—don't you have to get back to your horses?"

"Joe will see to them this morning." She touched his face with her free hand. "How's Lily?"

"She's okay. She slept most of the drive home. We had a good talk about things. I think she'll be fine."

Callie had to ask what she feared. "Did she do this because of me? Because of us?"

"Not in the way you might think." He held her hand firm and told her how Lily was feeling. "You know, she's more like you than you realize."

Callie's breath caught in her throat. "In what way?"

Noah smiled lightly. "Impulsive. Sometimes hardheaded. But…extraordinary." He kissed her hand again. "I thought that the first time I met you. Those beautiful eyes of yours were glaring at me from under that big hat." He sighed. "It blew me away."

He shifted and raised himself up. Callie looked at his bare chest and then lower to where the sheet slipped past his hips and flat stomach. Her fingers suddenly itched with the need to touch, to feel, to taste.

"Keep looking at me like that and I'll forget how tired I am."

She colored hotly. What was she thinking? He'd just driven practically ten hours straight and she was leering at him. "You're right," she said and hopped off the bed. "You should hit the shower and have some breakfast when you've had enough sleep. I'll make sure the twins get to daycare and Jamie gets to school."

Callie sucked in a breath. She had to tell him now. Before she lost her nerve. Before they were any more involved. His name escaped from her lips.

He smiled again and kept his eyes closed. “Hmm.”

She took a steadying breath, pushed out some courage and told him of her plans.

“You’re going where?” he asked and pulled himself up.

“Los Angeles.”

His eyes glittered, narrowing as he took in her words. “Why?” he asked. “Why now?”

Callie saw the confusion on his face. She knew he’d feel this way, knew he’d think her leaving was her way of running, of putting space between them.

Isn’t it?

The truth pierced through her. Wasn’t she running away? She took another breath.

“Please, Noah, try to understand…” She took his hands. “Please,” she said again. “I know it might look like I’m—”

“What?” he said, cutting her off. “Running away? Running out? You forget I know what it feels like to be left, Callie.”

She turned her hands in his and held them against his chest. “It’s not like that.”

He looked at her, deep, way down, like he was trying to absorb her with his eyes. Callie felt his frustration, his confusion, the sense he wanted to believe her but didn’t quite know how. “Are you coming back?”

She hesitated and knew Noah felt it deep inside. “I’m… I’m…”

He grabbed her left hand and gently rubbed the ring finger with his thumb. “You know what I want, Callie. You know that I love you and want to be with you—as your friend and lover and husband.”

Tears filled her eyes. “I know,” she whispered and wrapped her arms around his waist.

“But that’s not enough?”

She wanted to rest her head against his chest. “I just… don’t know.”

Noah pulled back. “Then I guess there’s nothing left to say.”

Chapter Thirteen

"You don't look so great."

Noah faked a smile. "Thanks."

Evie was never one to hold back her thoughts. "When's Callie due back?"

"I'm not sure." He felt like he had glass in his mouth. Because he had no idea when she was coming back. Or if.

His sister spun around in his kitchen and continued to chop watermelon with a big knife. "The kids are missing her."

So am I...

Noah tensed. He was in no mood for his sister's counsel. He wasn't in a mood for socializing, either. But it was Lily's birthday and the whole family had arrived to celebrate her day. "She'll be back when she's back." *If she comes back...*

"Have you spoken with her?"

"Is there a point to these questions?"

"Just trying to get you to talk," Evie said, raising both brows. "That's not an easy feat these days."

Noah didn't want to talk. He didn't want fake conversation with well-meaning relatives about how he was feeling. His mother had tried, now Evie. He just wanted to lick his wounds in private. He didn't want to talk about Callie. He didn't want to *think* about Callie.

But he remembered her look the night before she'd left. She'd made love with him, so deeply and with such an acute response to his touch it had felt like…it felt like…*goodbye.*

"So have you?"

Evie's voice shuttled Noah quickly back to the present. "Have I what?"

"Talked with her?"

He nodded. "Of course." Not exactly the truth. She'd called him when she'd landed in Los Angeles and he'd heard nothing since.

"Can I ask you something?"

Noah frowned. "Would it make any difference if I said no?"

Evie shrugged. "Probably not."

Noah grabbed the barbecue tongs and fork. "Go ahead."

"Why didn't you go with her?"

He stilled. Evie always knew the wrong question to ask. "Impossible."

"I could have watched the kids," she said. "So, what's your excuse?"

Because she didn't ask me to.

Part of him had longed to go with her, to meet her family, to see where she'd been raised, to be with her. He'd hated the idea of Callie traveling alone. Some base male instinct had kicked in and he wanted to protect her, to keep her safe. He should have insisted. He should have proposed marriage to her like he'd planned to do and taken the trip as an opportunity to meet her mother and brother.

"What's his excuse for what?"

Lily came into the kitchen. Without the gothic makeup and sporting only earrings—no other piercings—and jeans and a T-shirt, she looked so pretty, like a young version of his sister Grace. He smiled as she stole a piece of melon and took a bite.

"Were you guys talking about me?" she asked, suspicious but grinning.

"Of course," Evie said. "What else. How's the head cold?"

"Better," Lily replied. "I'm still sneezing."

Evie passed Lily the plate of fruit. "Well, if you're better, go and take this outside. Your Poppy loves watermelon." She looked at Noah. "You might want to light up the barbecue."

Lily was just about out of the room when Jamie raced into the kitchen. "Callie's here! Callie's here!" he said excitedly. "It's her truck coming."

Noah's stomach did a wild leap. He looked at his sister. "It's not possible."

"Go on," Evie said, shooing him out of the kitchen.

Noah headed for the front door, with Jamie and Lily barely feet behind him. Sure enough, Callie's truck was barreling down the long driveway. And it was hitching a horse trailer.

He opened the screen door. Lily was beside him instantly. So was Evie.

But it wasn't Callie behind the wheel. It was Joe. The skinny youth got out of the truck as Noah took the steps. He could feel Lily in his wake.

"Hi, there," Joe said. "Got a delivery."

Lily gripped Noah's arm. "Dad?"

He shrugged. "I don't know."

By now Evie and Mary-Jayne and his parents were standing by the front steps, with the twins squeezing between them, while Jamie jumped up and down excitedly.

Joe disappeared to the rear of the trailer and lowered the

tailgate. Lily's grip tightened when they saw the solid chestnut gelding step down from the trailer.

"Samson," she whispered. "Dad…look."

"I see him."

Joe led the horse around the truck and held the rope out to an astonished Lily. His daughter took the lead and buried her face in the animal's neck.

Joe pulled an envelope from his pocket and handed it to Lily. "Callie said to give this to you." He shook Noah's hand. "Well, I'll be seeing ya."

They waited until the truck pulled out from the driveway before Lily looked at the card inside. She read it out loud. *Dear Lily, I wish I was there with you. Happy birthday! Love, Callie.*

Tears welled in his daughter's eyes and tipped over her cheeks. "Oh, Dad." She hugged the horse. "I can't believe Callie did this."

Noah couldn't believe it, either. The woman he loved had given his daughter the one thing she longed for. It was an incredible gesture toward Lily. He ached inside thinking about it.

Lily didn't stop crying. "He's mine, he's really mine?"

"It looks that way."

Evie looked at Noah and raised her brows. "Some gift," she said.

Within minutes Lily had led the horse into the small pasture behind the house.

"That's one happy kid," his father said.

His parents had returned to the pool area with the kids and Evie pushed Noah to start up the barbecue. He was just flicking up the heat when Lily rushed through the back door and let it bang with a resounding thud.

"Dad!"

Her stricken look alarmed him and he set the utensils aside. "What is it?"

Lily shook her head frantically. "I want to call Callie."

Noah checked his watch. "Later tonight."

"I want to call her now," Lily insisted. "I want to call her and say thank you. And I want to tell her we miss her and want her to come home."

"You can't do that."

Lily tugged on his arm. "Why not?"

"Because you just can't."

Lily rolled her eyes. "No offense, Dad, but that sounds really dumb."

He shrugged, although he wasn't sure how he moved.

"So, you're not going to do anything?"

His back stiffened. "What exactly do you want me to do?"

Lily's eyes grew huge. "If you don't want me to call her—then you do it. You call her up and tell her we miss her. Tell her *you* miss her. She said in the card that she wished she was here—so call her up and tell her to come back."

Everyone stared at him. Evie raised her eyes questioningly.

He took a deep breath. "I can't tell Callie how to live her life." Another breath. "She's gone to see her family."

Tears filled Lily's eyes again. "I thought…I thought *we* were her family. So if she wants to be with her family she should be here, because *we* live here, *you* live here."

Noah wished he could stop his daughter's relentless logic. "She'll be back when she's ready."

Lily scowled. "Are you sure? What if she changes her mind? What if she stays there?"

Noah had spent the past week thinking of little else. He'd thought about it every night when he laid in his bed, twisting in sheets that still held the scent of her perfume in them. He missed her so much, wanted her so much he hurt all over.

"It's not up to me," he said quietly.

Lily hopped on her feet. "That doesn't make much sense. You love her, right?"

Eight sets of eyes zoomed in on him and he felt their scrutiny. "Well…I—"

"And she loves you," Lily said quickly. "She told me."

Noah rocked back on his heels. "She told you that?"

Lily looked at him like he needed a brain transplant. "I just don't get adults. You give all these lectures about being honest and then you can't even be honest with yourself." She puffed out a breath. "Why don't you just call her up and ask her to marry you?"

Noah's jaw almost fell to his feet. "What happened to your fifty percent of second marriages end in divorce speech?"

Lily swung her arm around. "Who listens to me? What do I know?" Lily blurted. "You guys are the grown-ups—work it out."

He saw Evie nodding. "Don't start," he warned his sister.

"She's got a point."

"Of course I've got a point," Lily said through her tears. "Callie loves you. You love Callie. We all love Callie."

"Yeah, Daddy, we love Callie," Jamie piped in, suddenly next to his sister. The twins weren't far away, either. And his parents hovered nearby.

She really does love me... She told my kid she loves me.

But she left.

And then, with a jolt, he realized he'd been so angry, so hurt, he hadn't really listened when she'd tried to explain. He'd cut her off, his ego dented, his heart smashed.

If he'd really listened he might have heard something other than his own lingering bitterness chanting inside his head. He might have heard that she needed to go home to lay her ghosts to rest.

Suddenly Noah understood. The past—Callie needed to

face her past, come full circle and deal with the grief of losing her fiancé and her son.

He felt the kick of truth knock against his ribs.

She loves me. He looked at his kids, all watching him, their little faces filled with hope. *She loves them.*

"Then I guess we'd better come up with a plan," he said and smiled when he saw everyone around him nodding.

Callie had been back in her old room for a week. It seemed so small now. And it didn't give her the comfort it once used to. But it was good to be home with her mother, especially since Scott had arrived two days after she had.

Her mother's stucco house was small compared to most in this part of Santa Barbara, but it was neat and her gardens were the envy of the neighborhood. She walked into the kitchen for a late breakfast and discovered her brother burning sourdough toast.

"Don't say anything," he cautioned. "I can still cook better than you."

Callie tapped him on the arm. "Ha, so you say."

She took the strawberry cream cheese from the refrigerator and waited while he scraped the burnt offering with a knife. Once he was done he passed it to her. Callie smeared it with spread and sat down.

"So, Mom said you're thinking of taking some time off?"

He shrugged. "Maybe."

"Because of what happened?"

Scott didn't like to discuss the tragic death of a friend and colleague a few months earlier. But she suspected the event had taken its toll on her brother.

"I don't know what I'm doing just yet."

"But you're not thinking of leaving the fire department, right?"

He shrugged. "Like I said, I haven't decided."

"You've wanted to be a fireman since you were four years old."

Scott grinned. "And you wanted to be a vet."

Callie shrugged and bit her bagel. "Nah—not smart enough."

"You could go back to school," he suggested. "Mom said you always got good grades. Not that I remember, being so much younger than you."

Callie held up three fingers. "That's how many years. Hardly worth mentioning."

He grinned again. "So would you?"

"I like my job. And I'm happy."

"Are you? You don't seem so happy to me."

Callie rolled her eyes. "Look who's talking."

"Well I never said I was happy," he replied. "So, what gives?" He smiled and ruffled her hair. "Why this sudden trip home?"

"I wanted to see you and Mom."

"And?"

And I'm in love...and I miss him so much I can hardly breathe. All I want is to go home and run into Noah's arms and stay there for the rest of my life.

"Stop badgering your sister."

Their mother came into the kitchen, a striking, willowy figure in a multicolored silk caftan, who looked much younger than her fifty-five years.

"Just asking," Scott said and grabbed another piece of bread. "You have to admit she showed up out of the blue. It makes me wonder what she's up to."

Callie placed her hands on her hips. "I am in the room, you know."

Scott chuckled. "So, spill."

She held her shoulders stiff. "I have nothing to say."

He bit into a bagel. "She's definitely hiding something."

Eleanor scolded her son and told him to take the dog for a walk. Still grinning, he grabbed his toast and left.

"Is he right?" her mother asked once the back door banged shut.

Callie nodded.

"A man?" Eleanor guessed correctly.

She nodded again.

Her mother sat down and swooshed the swirl of fabric around her legs. "I thought you might have changed," Eleanor said gently.

"Changed how?"

"I thought your time away might have loosened the tight control you've always had on what's inside you."

Callie knew what her mother meant. "I'm not good at talking about this stuff."

But she was with Noah. Callie had shared more with him than she had with anyone. Her heart, her body…all of herself.

"That's why things hurt you so much, Calliope. Even when you were a little girl you never talked about how you were feeling. You were always so happy on the outside. But I worried about you, keeping your feelings in. Your dad was like that, too." Eleanor pushed her bangs from her face. "After his accident, when he was really sick and knew he was dying, he didn't let me know how bad it was until the end."

"I remember."

"That hurt me for a long time," Eleanor admitted. "I thought he didn't trust me."

"He loved you, though. And you loved him."

"Of course," her mother said. "But when someone loves you, you should give them your whole heart."

"Like I did with Craig? That didn't turn out so great."

Eleanor raised her brows questioningly. "Craig was self-absorbed. And you were very young when you met. Had you met him now, as a woman, you probably would have seen right through his lack of integrity. He never deserved you, Callie…but if you've met someone who does, what are you doing here in my kitchen?" Her mother didn't wait for a reply and didn't hold back. "Do you love this man?"

Callie nodded. "I…yes."

Eleanor smiled. "Good. Because he called me yesterday."

"Noah called *you?*" Callie couldn't hide the shock in her voice.

"Mmm. We had a nice long talk about you."

Callie almost spluttered the coffee she'd just sipped. "What?"

"I liked him very much."

Callie was aghast. Why on earth would Noah want to talk with her mother? "Why didn't he call *me?*"

Eleanor widened her bright blue eyes. "Did you give him reason to?"

Did she? "Well, I didn't say he *couldn't* call me." She put down her coffee. Curiosity burned through her. "What did he say?"

Eleanor lifted her shoulders dramatically. "Oh, this and that. He asked how you were doing."

Callie's skin heated. "And what did you tell him?"

"Oh, this and that."

"Mom…please?"

Her mother stood up. "Come for a walk with me in the garden."

Callie followed her mother out the back door and across the lawn toward the small wooden bench in the far corner. They sat in front of a tiny rose garden her mother tended to daily.

"This is my favorite spot," her mother said as she arranged her housecoat on the bench.

Callie sat beside her and looked at the beautiful deep burgundy rosebush just about to bloom. "Dad's flower."

Eleanor smiled. "Not just that." She pointed to a small miniature rose shrub with tiny yellow buds on it. "That one is for my grandson."

Ryan's rose. Of course her mother would do that. Callie grasped her mother's hand. "Thank you, Mom." Callie sighed. "You know, I never thought I'd feel whole again. After Ryan died I shut myself off from everything." She looked at her mother. "And everyone."

She took a long, shuddering breath. "And then one morning Lily Preston knocked on my door and my life changed."

"Kids do that," her mother said fondly. "So does love."

He mother was so right and Callie didn't know whether she should laugh or cry. "The children are incredible. And they…they need me."

"So why are you here?"

Callie looked at the rose planted in her son's memory and said a silent prayer and thank you to the precious baby she'd never forget. And slowly the pain began to ease. She thought about Craig, and there was no anger, no lingering resentment for a man she now realized was never who she'd believed him to be. She felt sad for him. Sad for the time lost. But that was all, and it made her feel incredibly free. She thought about Noah loving children who weren't biologically his and knew he was right—blood and genetics were merely words. And Fiona—forced to give up her baby and living with the belief and hope that her child was being loved and cherished. And she knew, as her heart filled with a heady joy at what the future promised, that loving Noah was the greatest gift she could give his children.

"Why am I here?" Callie echoed her mother's words. "I'm letting go of the past."

"Are you about done?"

Callie nodded. "I'm done. I need to go home now." She

squeezed her mother's hand. "Will you come with me, Mom? I'd like you to meet Noah…and the…and my…"

"Your kids?"

Callie's heart contracted. "Yes."

Eleanor reached across and hugged Callie close. "We're booked to leave tomorrow. That young man of yours can be very persuasive."

Callie laughed with delight. "Oh, Mom, don't I know it."

Bellandale airport only accepted small aircraft, so Callie and her mother caught a connecting flight with a small domestic airline and because of the time difference arrived late Tuesday afternoon.

The airplane hit the runway and took a few minutes to come to a complete stop. Stairs were placed near the door and Callie felt the warm morning air hit her the moment she stepped out into the sunshine.

It was good to be back. And she couldn't wait to see Noah and the children. Fiona was picking them up and Callie intended to go directly to his house to surprise him. She clutched her cabin bag and followed her mother down the steps behind a line of other passengers. The walk across the tarmac took no time at all and when they reached the terminal and walked through the automatic doors the strong rush of the air conditioner was a welcome relief.

People disbursed in front of them, some greeting waiting relatives, some linking up with rental cars or taxis. Callie looked around for the familiar face of her friend and then stopped dead in her tracks as the throng of people in front of her disappeared.

For a moment she couldn't move. Couldn't speak. Couldn't think. She dropped her bag to her feet. Then, through the blur of tears she knew it was true.

Callie saw Lily first, then Jamie, then the twins. Lily held up a sign, as did Jamie, and the little ones had a hand each on a wide piece of cardboard. It spelled three words.

Please... Marry... Us...

The kids all looked hopeful. And Lily—looking so naturally beautiful with her newly colored hair and clean face, stared at her with luminous green eyes that shone brightly with tears. Jamie was smiling the widest smile she'd ever seen and the twins chuckled with such enchanting mischief she just wanted to hug them close.

I love these kids. I want to love them for the rest of my life. I want to be their mother.

She smiled through her tears and Lily came forward and hugged her so tight Callie thought she might break something. "Thank you for my birthday present," Lily said breathlessly. "Please say yes to my dad."

Callie hugged her back as emotion welled inside her. "Where is he?"

"Callie?"

She heard his voice, felt his presence vibrating though her entire body. He was behind her. Callie turned. Her breath caught in her throat. He looked so good. Sounds disappeared, people faded, until there was just him. Only this man she loved so much.

"You're here?" she whispered.

He nodded. "I'm here."

Callie saw Evie and Fiona from the corner of her eye, and watched as they ushered the children toward them and took Eleanor into their inner circle and headed for the exit doors. Noah stepped forward and took her hand. She felt his touch through to every part of her body.

"I can't stand being away from you," he admitted, drawing her closer. "It's killing me."

And right there, in the middle of the airport, with people moving around them, Noah kissed her.

"I'm sorry I left you," she managed to say, when the kiss-ng stopped and she could draw a breath. "I know my reasons lidn't make a lot of sense to you. But I had something I had o do before I could give you…all of my heart."

Noah held her in the circle of his arms. "What did you nave to do?"

"I had to say goodbye to Ryan."

He swallowed hard and Callie saw the emotion glittering n his green eyes. "I understand."

"I'll always cherish him," she said, holding on to Noah, vaguely aware that people around them were dwindling to ust a few. "But I knew I had to let go of all my anger toward Craig and my grief over losing Ryan. I guess it came down to his fear I had of messing up…of not being able to feel what knew your children deserved me to feel."

"And did you let it go?"

Callie nodded. "Yes—once I realized that I *wanted* to love he kids and that I wanted to be part of their life."

Noah held her hands in front of his chest. "You know what t means, Callie? The whole deal—forever."

"I know what it means," she said on a rush of breath. "I vant forever. I want the kids. I want you." She looked into nis eyes. *"I love you."*

"It's about time," he breathed into her hair. He kissed her, he sweetest kiss she'd ever known.

"Thank you for not giving up on me," she whispered be-ween kisses.

He held her in his arms. "I never will. Marry me, Callie? need you. We need you."

She nodded. "Yes," she said, her gaze filled with love. Yes, I will. I love you," she whispered. "I love you."

"Marry me soon."

"Mmm," she agreed through kisses. "Soon. How about Christmas Eve?"

He smiled against her mouth. "That soon? Good." He reached into his pocket and pulled out a small box. "Because I've been carrying this around with me for days."

Callie stared at the box as he flipped the lid. Inside lay the most beautiful ring she'd ever seen—a gorgeous champagne diamond surrounded by a cluster of pure white stones. She looked at the ring, then Noah. "It's beautiful."

He slipped the ring on her finger and it fit perfectly.

"The kids helped me pick it out." He kissed her forehead gently. "I love you, Callie." He lifted her chin and tilted her head. "And if you ever want to explore that ten-percent chance and look at trying to have a baby—then that's what we'll do. Whatever you decide, I'll be beside you."

Callie felt fresh tears behind her eyes. "Thank you for that. We'll see what happens. For the moment…I just want to learn how to be the best mother I can be to your children."

"Our children now," he said softly. "Maybe we should head outside and break the news?" he suggested and pointed toward the long glass windows and the sea of eager and clearly happy faces watching them.

She nodded and he linked their hands and they walked outside together. As soon as they hit the pavement Lily raced forward and hugged her close and Jamie and the twins followed her lead. With her mother, Evie and Fiona smiling, the kids laughing and hugging and Noah holding her hand so tightly she felt the connection through to her soul, any doubts disappeared. This was what she was made for. This man. This family. Her family.

* * * * *

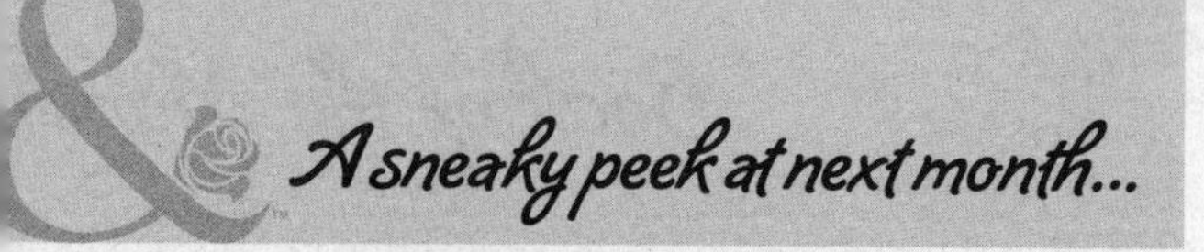
A sneaky peek at next month...

Cherish™

ROMANCE TO MELT THE HEART EVERY TIME

My wish list for next month's titles...

In stores from 20th April 2012:

- ❑ The Cop, the Puppy and Me – Cara Colter
- & Courtney's Baby Plan – Allison Leigh
- ❑ Daddy on Her Doorstep – Lilian Darcy
- & Courting His Favourite Nurse – Lynne Marshall

In stores from 4th May 2012:

- ❑ The Cattle King's Bride – Margaret Way
- & The Last Real Cowboy – Donna Alward
- ❑ Taming the Lost Prince – Raye Morgan
- & Inherited: Expectant Cinderella – Myrna Mackenzie

Available at WHSmith, Tesco, Asda, Eason, Amazon and Apple

Just can't wait?

Visit us Online

You can buy our books online a month before they hit the shops! **www.millsandboon.co.uk**

0412/23

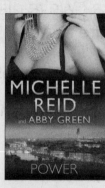